ALL AT SEA

Tony Houghton

MINERVA PRESS
LONDON
ATLANTA MONTREUX SYDNEY

ALL AT SEA
Copyright © Tony Houghton 1998

All Rights Reserved

No part of this book may be reproduced in any form
by photocopying or by any electronic or mechanical means,
including information storage or retrieval systems,
without permission in writing from both the copyright owner
and the publisher of this book.

ISBN 1 86106 815 8

First Published 1998 by
MINERVA PRESS
195 Knightsbridge
London SW7 1RE

Printed in Great Britain for Minerva Press

ALL AT SEA

By the Same Author

Memoirs of a Cross-eyed Cat

Chapter One

So fascinated was he, their Uncle Arthur, with ships and the sea, and so apparently knowledgeable about all aspects of navigation, that his nephews were at a loss to understand why he'd never sailed, but spent his life, rather, in oak-panelled offices – with, to be sure, wide views of the oily river, and handsome, gilt-framed paintings of the company's ships, depicted cresting mountainous waves bolt-upright. And downstairs, in the marbled hallway of the Red Funnel Line Building, there were extraordinary scale models of ships, six feet long and correct to the last rivet, in glass cases. But this was going to sea vicariously, and couldn't be anywhere near as satisfying. Worse, this not going to sea had become, it seemed, a recent and regrettable principle in their family, on both sides; the boys' own father, Walter Darwin Miller, leaving school, like Uncle Arthur, at the age of fourteen, had signed on with the Elder Dempster Line as a galley boy but jumped ship the day before the *Accra* sailed for West Africa, though his father, and his, and his, and his as far back as anyone knew, had all sailed out of the port of Liverpool, as engineers and pursers, third mates and carpenters. The older boy, Alan Townsend Miller, felt the sea in his blood, was convinced of it, stared squint-eyed at the samson-posts, the derricks, mastheads, funnels, and superstructures of vessels glimpsed exasperatingly between warehouse buildings and cranes from the grimy windows of Liverpool Overhead Railway trains. There were grand views, fortunately, of some of the docks; the Cunard dock, where the *Media* and the *Parthia* berthed, the *Scythia*, *Samaria*, and *Franconia*, sailing to marvellous places: sky-scrapered New York, Boston, Baltimore, Halifax, snowy Montreal. The Cunard dock was in sight, as the train rocked by, for several exciting seconds, the great ships with their proud red funnels, black-banded, in unobstructed view: so was the Huskisson Dock where the graceful, admired Blue Funnel liners lay, with their handsome, upright, black-topped stacks, sparkling white superstructures, and bewitching mythological names. The Blue Funnel Line sailed to other marvellous places, indeed to anywhere in the world which had deep enough water, a wharf, a crane and a man to work it. But all ships' destinations were marvellous.

Uncle Arthur didn't need to read the name and hail-port on a stern, he recognised a ship from the merest glimpse of a raked mast, a house flag – well, he was Deputy Chairman of the Red Funnel Line. He had special favourites too, favourite lines and favourite steamers; considered the Anchor Line vessels, for instance, 'very handsome', and the Booth Line ships also, and the graceful four-masters of the Bibby Line, steamships almost as beautiful as sailing ships, and named, quaintly, after quiet inland shires.

'I would love to have gone to sea, boys,' Uncle Arthur told them. 'But your grandfather never worked, so I had to look after your mother, and your Uncle George who was just a little boy. You see, I was the oldest. Your grandmother took in laundry, and I was fortunate enough to land a job as an office boy with the Red Funnel Line.'

Uncle Arthur spoke very precisely, pronounced each syllable perfectly. He made up sentences as if each word had a capital letter, with the faint suggestion of a glottal stop in between. He was fifty years old when the boys were eleven and nine; a tall, punctilious, handsome man with thinning black hair brushed well back, rimless spectacles, a well-shaped, almost Roman nose. He would lower those spectacles sometimes to dab with a clean linen handkerchief at his eyes, which seemed to water. He wore perfectly pressed trousers with a shirt and tie, as if he was going to the office, except that for Sunday trips like this, on the Overhead, he'd put on a light showerproof windcheater, zipped down the front, instead of a jacket. And ah, how the boys adored him.

They'd take the number 73 bus, the three of them, from Childwall, where Uncle Arthur lived with his mother (very modestly for a man in his position with a fine shipping company) in a grey pebbledashed semi-detached, and board the Overhead at Pier Head. With round-trip tickets they'd travel north first, sway along rusty iron girders as far as the Gladstone Dock at Seaforth, where the magnificent thirty-five thousand ton Cunard liner *Mauritania* had finished her post-war refit, then south, past Pier Head again, to Dingle, where the Overhead Railway plunged into a short, dark, tunnel terminating at Dingle station, a cavernous, echoing place that smelled of sulphur, soot and pee. No one ever seemed to get out of the train there, or board it. Small wonder: it was difficult to imagine what creatures of eternal twilight would frequent such a dismal cave, except perhaps human bats or talking rats. On the return journey to Pier Head the train passed some of the older docks, including the Brunswick Dock where the Harrison Line ships loaded, steamers named after manly careers, with tall yellow funnels; and the Queen's Dock, where Uncle Arthur's own Red Funnel Line vessels berthed, named after bays – *Chesapeake Bay*, *Bantry Bay*, *Jamaica Bay*, and so forth – and appropriately handsome, with their single, oversized red funnels, black-topped, their castellated superstructures dipped, you'd say, in Jersey cream; and the Elder Dempster boats which traded along palm-girt African coasts, anchored in tepid lagoons, moored to noisy wharves miles up confusing rivers. Confusing, but oh, marvellous places.

And Pier Head too, Pier Head, Liverpool, was a marvellous place. All the seagulls in the world soared and cried and fought at Pier Head, and half the world's pigeons hobbled underfoot, and a hundred tall green buses lined up, and the high Cunard building stared down, and the twin-towered Liver Building with its great stone birds anchored by cables. All this, when it wasn't raining, in that leaden Liverpool light, the clouds parting to allow, reluctantly, only a few brave shafts of sunshine. Uncle Arthur would lead the boys down the ornate covered gangways to the Landing Stage, which rose and fell on the Mersey tides, and the brown water splashed and echoed underneath, so it was almost like being at sea. Here the ferries came and went, belching black smoke, ringing with a thousand footsteps: the Woodside Ferry which went to Birkenhead, the Seacombe Ferry which went to Wallasey, and best of all the New Brighton Ferry, which sailed all the way to the estuary of the Mersey in half an hour. The New Brighton ferries

Royal Daffodil and *Royal Iris* had sailed to Dunkirk, evacuated hundreds of men from the beaches, boasted stirring paintings and plaques to prove it. Then came the Welsh boats; the *St Tudno*, a notorious roller, which sailed every morning at eight o'clock for Llandudno and the Menai Straits, returning at dusk, crowded with seasick excursionists all summer, and the safer, good-looking *St Seriol* which sailed at two o'clock for Llandudno. Next in line came the Manx boats, the *Manxman*, or the *Manx Maid*, the *King Orry*, or the *Ben-ma-Crae*; they made morning, afternoon, and midnight voyages to Douglas, Isle of Man; then the Irish boats, first the Belfast boat, *Ulster Prince*, or *Ulster Monarch*, then the Dublin boat, *St Patrick*, or *St Columba*; they sailed at night, echoed all day to the shouts and squeals of maids laundering sheets and pillowcases, remaking narrow beds. After the Irish boats came the liners. Today, the handsome Anchor liner *Circassia*, with its huge, single black funnel and its all-white upperworks, rows of lifeboats, sweeping bridge, Blue Peter fluttering at her starboard yardarm promising imminent departure for Rio de Janeiro, Montevideo, Buenos Aires: marvellous places.

But Uncle Arthur, Alan Townsend Miller, and Toby Walker Miller, were not bound, just yet, for Rio de Janeiro, Montevideo or Buenos Aires, not bound for Africa or New York, nor even for Belfast or New Brighton. Instead they clambered aboard the number 73 bus for Childwall, and grabbed the front seats on the top. Uncle Arthur would point out the huge, soot-encrusted, Corinthian becolumned mass of St George's Hall and the impressive white maw of the Mersey Tunnel; Lewis's and the Bon Marché (known as the Bon March by the boys' grandmother, and her cranky sisters); Lord Street, all one side of it demolished by German bombs and not yet rebuilt: basements, seen from the top of the bus, still gaped open, scraps of wallpaper fluttered from shattered walls like flags of surrender. Then came the once impeccable Georgian terraces of Upper Parliament Street, where respectable people couldn't walk now, and the sad, rundown, still graceful, Victorian houses along Croxteth Road, their gingerbread barge-boards tucked under high, peaked gables; and, eventually, after Wavertree, rows of stucco-fronted or pebbledashed, bay-windowed, semi-detached villas, with the number 4 tram whispering along between clipped box hedges, and hawthorn, till the three friends got off at the Shopping Parade in Childwall, and trudged along Taggart Avenue to number 118, for lunch.

Number 118 was not quite like number 120, its neighbour, being the same, only inside out. It was exactly like number 122, and exactly like number 119, across the road; and, for sure, it could have been in Manchester, or Sheffield, or London, could have been in all kinds of places, but for the boys, this was the only number 118 in the world, and it was magic. It had a small front garden behind a thick privet hedge where the boys discovered hawk-moths; the garden had grey roses, sprinkled with sooty rain. Inside, a narrow entrance hall, with a hatstand but no hats – Uncle Arthur went bareheaded to work; a carpeted front room with a fireplace never used, in spite of the formidable brass andirons, coal tongs, and scuttle; a bookcase with the volumes won as prizes at school by Uncle Arthur and Uncle George. A dining room, formal, with a thin-legged table, mock Sheraton, mock something. A brightly-lit kitchen with a square table where the women drank tea, and a door to the back garden where Uncle Arthur grew useful things: lettuce and tomato for salads, leek and potatoes for soup. Upstairs, Uncle Arthur's neat small bedroom, smelling slightly of cologne, over the front hall; a master bedroom nearly filled by an enormous bed covered with green eiderdowns the boys loved to bounce on: here their mother and father slept, when they visited; their grandmother's bedroom, which smelled of their grandmother, at the back; and of course a small bathroom, with a bath that had loofahs and sponges, and a lavatory, which you tugged at a long chain to flush, and boys had to jump to reach the chain.

When Uncle Arthur and the boys got home, Pat McMahon was visiting, so was her mother, and their little dog, a wiry, worried, elderly terrier. They had been walking; had called by. How glad they were not to have missed Uncle Arthur and the boys!

'My, aren't you boys growing up?' Mrs McMahon said, Pat's silvery-coiffed parent: oh, Alan and Toby hated that kind of question: what were you supposed to answer? Pat herself caught the boys' eyes; she raised her own slightly, in apology; Alan was old enough to blush.

'What ships were in?' Pat asked, to make amends.

'Oh, the Anchor liner *Circassia* was at the Landing Stage. I think she must be sailing on the afternoon tide. She was flying the Blue Peter,' Alan said, proud to display the knowledge his Uncle Arthur had imparted.

'Don't you wish you were sailing on her?'

'Oh, rather!'

'It would be nice, wouldn't it?' Pat agreed; and Alan, who liked Pat, was sorry for her, because it was doubtful she would ever sail to Montevideo or Buenos Aires, whereas he most certainly would.

Pat McMahon and her mother came to play bridge with Uncle Arthur and Granny, every Monday: Irish Catholic ladies from the capital of Ireland – Liverpool. They both spoke in soft, low, cooing voices, like doves; Mrs McMahon very briskly, Pat's phrases better measured. The mother wore a grey, buttoned-up cardigan over a blouse with a frilled collar, and a grey tweed skirt; the daughter was in black, except for a dark little fox draped about her white neck. She had a short jacket with black net sleeves that showed how thin her arms were, and a long pleated skirt, and black stockings. She smelled very faintly of perfume, and her fox as faintly of talcum powder. She had lovely brown hair which she wore long, and a finely modelled face with a thin nose, and very soft, slightly downcast eyes with heavy eyebrows. It was a patient, perhaps a beautiful face, accustomed to pain. She was thirty-five years old and had never been well; she was said to wear a steel corset but the boys weren't sure if that wasn't mere malicious talk on their grandmother's part. She walked, though not all the time, with the help of a black cane which had a handle carved in the shape of a duck's head. She had never married – too delicate, the boys supposed – and seemed to have no prospects; not much of a life, either, except for walks with her mother, and bridge on Mondays with Arthur and his.

Mrs McMahon and Pat, Pat twisting the dog's lead about her thin wrist, departed because the family was obviously waiting to have lunch. Alan felt sad that Pat had gone: the faint smell of her perfume and the talc on her fox seemed to linger, though, and he thought he wouldn't forget it.

'Pat looks terrible,' said the boys' grandmother.

'She doesn't seem well,' their Uncle Arthur admitted, with more sympathy.

These observations greatly discouraged the boys. Their mother, Enid Evelyn Miller, née Carruth, lowering her voice so that her brother, gone to the kitchen to bring in a plate of tongue, couldn't hear, said, 'You know, Mum, I'm not sure it's wise to have Mrs McMahon and Pat here for bridge every week.'

'Why ever not?' the old lady snapped.

'Because I think Pat has her eye on Uncle Arthur.'

'Oh, nonsense,' said the old lady, Mrs Carruth.

They took their places around the thin-legged dining room table, the boys' father, Walter Darwin Miller, finally putting out his cigarette and joining them. He had fine red hair, that one, and freckles he'd never grown out of, tired eyes and a huge nose. He smoked incessantly so all his clothes stank of cigarettes, as did his car and the whole house in Cheshire, stank, stank, stank. His long fingers – what a fine pianist he was, could sight-read a concerto, and perform it flawlessly, straight off – were stained brown with nicotine beyond ever scrubbing clean. He wore, today, a reddish-brown suit and a dark red tie. The boys' mother, who had sensed that Pat McMahon had her eyes on Uncle Arthur, got her sometimes outspoken candour from her virago of a mother, but was otherwise an attractive woman with a mop of black curls; she dressed in cotton blouses and pretty skirts, or billowy, summery frocks; there was something nice and girl-like about her, something fresh and hopeful, which Walter loved.

Uncle Arthur carved slices of canned tongue with the grace of a fine chef carving game. Each helping came with a half tomato, from the garden, and an offer of Colman's Mustard or HP Sauce. Walter waved his plate away.

'I'm sorry, Arthur. I can't eat that.'

'I'll poach you an egg,' said his wife, jumping up. 'I was going to, but Pat and her mother were here.'

What a fussy eater he was, Walter Miller; no trencherman, for sure; would have won no prizes at a pie-eating competition. As a boy he'd survived on a penny bun nibbled occasionally, made to last; now the only things he'd eat were eggs, good fillet steaks and breaded Dover sole – all too dear to share: Enid spoiled him. The boys ate canned spaghetti: she drank tea.

'Some nice tongue, boys?' enquired Uncle Arthur.

'Oh, rather,' Alan said; he didn't much like tongue but was very polite, at that age, and keen to please.

'Yes, please,' said Toby, who didn't care.

Of the boys, Alan, the older, was decidedly the more exuberant. What interested him interested him very much. Ships, most obviously: at home he had drawers full of nautical paraphernalia; he'd write letters to shipping lines begging for publicity material and they'd mail him elaborate brochures, sailing schedules, calendars with pictures of ships, postcards of their more famous liners. He also collected stamps and had three albums, two for stamps of the British Empire and one for all others. At school he aggressively swapped stamps or bought them with marbles, seashells collected at New Brighton, pressed leaves, and other small treasures of inferior value. Cricket was another passion; cricket and cricket memorabilia: he had a good eye, could hit Mr Andrews' fast bowling, his history teacher's, and he pored over *Wisden's Cricketing Almanac*, knew the batting averages of nearly every player in the county championship. At the age of eleven he had an egg-shaped head, a very oval face, long, rather feminine eyelashes, and shorts that reached to below his knees.

His younger brother was thoughtful and quiet by comparison, with his mother's curly locks, in his case golden. He shared in Alan's enthusiasms only in so far as he didn't have much option; was dragged off on Overhead Railways, ferries, and the upper decks of buses, but his enjoyment of these jaunts was passive. He soon got bored, though he was not a complainer. He took music lessons from his father, unlike Alan who showed absolutely no interest, but he quickly tired of practising. Fortunately for his brother, he was a useful bowler, who never pitched wides or full tosses, so at home the two of them played endless cricket in the back garden.

'You may say it's nonsense, Mum,' Enid Miller said, returning to the subject of Pat McMahon, with a slight flash of her eyes and a sideways jerk of her mop of hair, 'but I'm always right about these things.'

She hadn't bothered to lower her voice, because only her mother would know what she was talking about. But the old lady gave her away.

'Arthur, Enid thinks Pat McMahon's interested in you. I'm sure you're not interested in her. She's completely unsuitable. She's horribly delicate. She could never have children. She wears a steel corset. And she's a Roman Catholic.'

This vicious attack on a person he found not only nice but who talked to him like an adult outraged young Alan. But his Uncle Arthur didn't seem to mind a bit. It was as if his stupid old mother had said nothing at all, just sat there munching canned tongue. In fact Arthur treated his mother with unfailing respect. That's how he treated everyone; that's how he'd risen from the mail room to the Boardroom. Well, that's partly how. Whatever his feelings were, at the time, for Pat McMahon, it would have been absolutely impossible for anyone at the table to guess them, for the simple reason that Uncle Arthur, unlike his mother and unlike his sister, did not think it polite to talk about feelings.

In the afternoon the Millers left for Cheshire, where they lived, an hour and a half's drive away, in that car of Walter's that stank of cigarette smoke: he worked for The Imperial Tobacco Company, who sent him three cartons of Richmond Gems each week, for his personal consumption. Walter was always sleepy after lunch, as if he'd eaten a grand repast, followed by brandy and liqueurs, in a gentleman's club, not just a poached egg in Childwall: he had to pull over for a nap; it always amazed Enid how much the man slept, he was like some hibernating badger, or bear, not to be woken till spring. Alan, in the back with Toby, amused himself by noting in a book the license plates of passing cars, and it annoyed him that his younger brother wasn't interested in anything.

'Next weekend, can we go to New Brighton on the ferry?' Alan asked, when his father had shaken himself awake and they were once more on the move, driving through leafy Cheshire lanes towards home. Soft fields flashed by, and brooding woods; ponds twinkled in the afternoon sun, cows munched, a jay swooped over, out of a wood, a train roared under a bridge.

'Next weekend I thought we'd stay at home and have a roast,' said his mother.

'Oh, Mum!' cried the boy, in protest. 'It's fun going to Liverpool!'

'It's fun for you because you're interested in ships and your Uncle Arthur takes you for rides on the Overhead.'

'Well, why don't you come with us, Mum?'

'I won't come with you on the Overhead, it's a dirty, noisy, thing. But I'll come if we go to New Brighton.'

'Oh, Mum! Do you think we can? I just love going to New Brighton.'

'Well, we'll see.'

In fact, the Millers were at number 118 Taggart Avenue nearly every weekend that summer, which shows the kind of pressure Alan was able to exert, without realising it. Anyway, Walter and Enid were both very fond of Uncle Arthur – 'There goes the nicest man I know,' Walter had once said – and they felt badly that he should be stuck on his own with the old lady. They knew what it was like living with her, didn't they just, and it was Uncle Arthur, after the war, who'd insisted that it was his turn to shoulder the burden, buying the little house on Taggart Avenue and moving in with her. So the least they could do was visit, and give poor old Arthur some time off. The truth is, too, that the Millers didn't really have any close friends at home;

they were a very self-sufficient family; knew the neighbours only to nod at in the street.

They were both from Liverpool, Walter and Enid. Walter's old mother, a frail little lady, lived in Waterloo with a difficult cousin of Walter's, known to the boys as Aunt Beatrice. Some weekends, to the boys' distress, there would be afternoons spent in a dark little house with a tiny brick backyard and no views, no views of anything, and a front room where the curtains were kept permanently drawn, as if there was somebody dead in there, and the air was thick and unbreathable. And on Enid's side there was a whole gaggle of aunts and uncles whom the boys were not often subjected to, though a sneak afternoon visit couldn't be ruled out: Auntie Edie was an especial trial. 'We'll have such fun!' she'd tell the boys. 'What shall we play? What shall we play?'

Walter and Enid Miller had moved away from Liverpool, even if it hadn't been very far, just to Cheshire, though it was worlds away in every respect. The firm could have sent him to the Outer Hebrides, but it was Mr E.C. Jewitt who retired, and his territory was Cheshire and North Staffordshire, so that's where young Mr Miller went. Uncle George, the brilliant one, who came between Arthur and Enid, had also moved. After four years looking for a job he'd landed one as a chemist in London, where he worked for a company that made shoe polish, and where he'd now been miserable for twenty-seven years. And, finally, Walter's younger brother, Greg, a widower like Uncle Arthur, had moved to West Bromwich, where he'd courted Kathleen, and he still lived there, he had a job as a clerk with a tooling company, with his two girls, straight-haired Sally and ravishing Anita, the boys' cousins. But the boys had never been either to London or West Brom, and they hardly knew their cousins, only met them on stiff, horrible occasions in Waterloo, which was fine by the boys because they became absolutely speechless in the presence of girls.

Next Saturday, alas, it rained, so the New Brighton trip was postponed until Sunday. Uncle Arthur sat on the floor of the front room with the boys, which wasn't easy for him because his legs were so long, and turned the pages of one of Alan's favourite books: the subject was Greek mythology, and the book was one of Uncle Arthur's school prizes. In fact it was one of the comparatively few he'd won: Uncle George, his younger brother, had won far more – but then Uncle George had stayed at school much longer and, as everyone said, was brilliant. Toby was soon bored with the peculiar adventures of Greek gods and heroes, but there was nowhere else to go and nothing else to do so he sat there and studied the pictures, which were coloured reproductions of paintings by Pre-Raphaelites and showed limpid females clad in knee-length red hair and nothing else. These females seemed to be out of doors, but didn't look at all cold.

'Achilles!' exclaimed Alan, who didn't seem to share Toby's interest in nude women. 'We saw the *Achilles* in dock last weekend, didn't we, Uncle Arthur? The Blue Funnel Line.'

'Yes, and as I recall we also saw the *Agamemnon* and the *Castor*. Handsome ships.'

'Let's look up Agamemnon and Castor in the book and see what they did.'

But another coloured plate caught Toby's eye and he held the page open.

'Jocasta,' said Uncle Arthur. 'The mother of Oedipus.'

'Don't you think she'd be cold? She has nothing on, and she's standing by the sea with a knife.'

'I think Greece has a very warm climate.'

'Is there a Blue Funnel liner called *Oedipus*?' Alan asked.

'I believe not,' Uncle Arthur told him.

The wet afternoon passed this way. Walter drifted about the house, at a loose end without his piano or his darkroom; drank tea in the kitchen with his wife and his mother-in-law, watched the boys reading with Uncle Arthur, and eventually flopped in a chair to smoke. He was not a great reader himself, except of the works of Winston Churchill, which he read as fast as Mr Churchill could write them. Walter had been a Flight Lieutenant in the Royal Air Force during the war, and had been called upon by Mr Churchill to risk his life on numerous occasions, in the dark skies over the Ruhr, which he had been very willing to do. Failing a volume by Churchill, Walter was content to smoke, and watch the rain stream down the windows; he was a bit awkward with the boys, quite unlike their Uncle Arthur, he couldn't just chat with them like his brother-in-law did; had been absent on Mr Churchill's business when they were small, and hadn't played much with them as they grew. But he loved to hold them tight each night before they went to bed, saying nothing, just burying his face in the soft down on the back of their necks, which he called 'having a snog'; and which they didn't like.

Enid Miller spent the afternoon with her mother, in the kitchen, talking. Her mother, Mrs Annie Sadie Carruth, now eighty-one years old, wore a baggy black jumper and an ankle length black flannel skirt. Or perhaps two jumpers, and two skirts; or even three of each; and all her skirts smelled strongly of pee. Her mouth hung open a good inch, revealing her yellow false teeth, which she took out every night and kept in a tumbler of water at the side of her bed. The boys found out about this and had endless fun inventing conversations between their Granny and her teeth ('What are you grinning at?' 'You, of course, you toothless old hag.') With all her jumpers and skirts, Granny couldn't see her shoes. When her glasses fell off she trod on them. She was always treading on things. She trod on her friend Mrs McMahon's little dog, which was nervous enough already. The boys feared for their toys when she was about. Her upper denture fell out once and she trod on that too. It cracked in two, but she refused to have it fixed by the dentist; she just glued the two pieces together, which seemed to work, so she'd been right to save the money.

'Well, I suppose you played bridge with Pat and her mother again, last Monday, did you?' her daughter said, in the kitchen, as she drank tea; she was a great tea-drinker, was Enid – maybe it was all that tea that put the sparkle in her eyes.

'Oh yes. There's nothing in what you said, you know. Our Arthur doesn't care at all for Pat McMahon. You can tell. Of course he's very gracious and nice to her, but then he's gracious and nice to everyone, isn't he? He's just as gracious and nice to her mother.'

'I wouldn't trust her, Mum.'

'I trust Arthur not to be a fool.'

'Maybe you don't understand men.'

'What do you mean by that? I was married to one, wasn't I?'

'She appeals to his niceness. She is the poor, lonely, weak female. Her only company is her mother. He could save her from all that. Take her to Paris on honeymoon. Buy a nice house for her in Formby. Or Ainsdale Beach.'

'Arthur's much too sensible.'

'He's a man.'

'But he's not a fool, Enid. If Arthur marries again, it'll be to have children. He loves children. See the way he plays with your two. It's a tragedy Arthur's never had children. Grace was too delicate, with her heart. Arthur's not going to marry another delicate woman. I don't think Pat is much longer for this world, if you must know. The things her mother tells me. It's doctors, doctors, doctors. She's had three operations. She swallows medicine like it was gin. And pills. Pills. She wears a steel corset, you know. She'd fall apart if she didn't.'

'I wouldn't mind a honeymoon in Paris myself,' Enid mused. 'Or a house in Formby or Ainsdale Beach.'

'In that case, you should have married Harry, like we all hoped you would.'

'Who was Harry?'

'That nice young man you brought home, from the tennis club.'

'That was Walt. We got married.'

'No, no. Before Walter.'

'Oh. You mean Jeffrey.' Enid tossed her black mop.

'Jeffrey, Harry, I don't know who I mean. But he's a bigwig at the Royal Insurance Company now, a very successful man, like Uncle Arthur. Why didn't you marry him?'

'He didn't ask me.'

'Well, he would have done, if you'd given him any encouragement.'

'What do you mean by that?'

'You know perfectly well what I mean by that. Harry would have taken you to Paris on honeymoon. Bought you a nice house at Formby too, I'm sure.'

'You mean, Jeffrey would have.'

'I'm sure of it. But you only had eyes for Walter. And he's a nobody. A failure. Let's call a spade a spade, Enid.'

'How dare you say that about Walt?'

'Because it's the truth. A travelling salesman all his life.'

'He loves his job. He does what he does best.'

'Well, you deserve better. Are you going to peel the potatoes for me, or not?'

'Peel your own potatoes.'

Enid put down her cup. Elbows on the little kitchen table, she rubbed her eyes, in case there was a tear. She was stuck in a dangerous no-man's-land between anger and amusement; always was when she discussed things with her mother. She stood up, took the potato peeler off her, and began peeling, while the old lady fastened the meat grinder to the table and pushed in stewing beef. Leaning over the grinder, her lower denture fell out and into the machine, but she caught it in time to avert disaster, and her daughter didn't notice.

'You must be very disappointed with us all, mustn't you, Mum,' Enid observed, after a few minutes. 'Uncle George and I have both married beneath us, in your opinion, and Uncle Arthur's wife died on him.'

'If you're happy, why should I be disappointed? I just know you're missing out on things. Things another man could have given you.'

'No one else could have given me Alan and Toby. I have two lovely sons.'

'Yes, who'd have a better chance in life if their father had a bit more push in him.'

'We'll give the boys the best chance we can. They'll go to a public school.'

'What they need, Enid, is ambition. They haven't got any, as far as I can see. They take after their father.'

'Mum, they're still children.'

'When our Arthur was Anthony's age—'

'You mean, Alan's age. Why can't you get people's names right?'

'When our Arthur was Alan's age he knew exactly what he wanted to do. Get to the top. He left school when he was fourteen, he never went to a fancy boarding school because I couldn't afford it. He started in the mail room, Arthur did, but he knew what he wanted, and he worked for it. Nobody's ever worked harder than our Arthur. And look at him now: Deputy Chairman of the Red Funnel Line. A successful man, Enid, a successful man. Give me a handkerchief.'

'It's the onions.'

'It isn't the onions.'

She dabbed her eyes, returned the handkerchief.

'Well, you have a right to be proud of Uncle Arthur,' said Enid. 'He's a lovely man. And we all know how hard he worked. But I don't think he got to be Deputy Chairman just because he worked hard. He got where he is because he's very clever, and never had an enemy in his life. Never a cruel word for anyone. Which is more than we can say for some people.'

'Your brother George is every bit as nice. And brilliant with it, much cleverer than Uncle Arthur, if I do say so. It was George who won all the prizes at school. George was top scholar in Liverpool. But with his dreadful stammer, nobody would give him the time of day.'

'George doesn't have Uncle Arthur's way with people.'

'That's because of his stammer.'

'Not really. George was terribly popular when he was young, at the tennis club. Nobody else is bothered by his stammer. It's all in his head. That's why he's a failure.'

'George is not a failure, he's a brilliant man.'

'He's a failure. Like Walt.'

After dinner (Enid poached Walter an egg) it stopped raining, so Uncle Arthur proposed a walk.

'Coming, boys?'

'Oh, rather, Uncle Arthur!' Alan cried, leaping up. Toby obediently followed, but the others stayed home. Walter hated walking, the old lady was too slow, and Enid stayed to keep her company.

They walked, in the dripping dusk, as far as Menlove Avenue, where the number 8 tram swished by; how cosy and inviting it looked inside, yellow lights shining on the advertisements; then they crossed the road to Calderstones Park.

'Are we going into the park, Uncle Arthur? It's getting awfully dark,' Alan said nervously.

The park stood like a dark forest against an evening sky washed clean by the rain; it seemed a place where frightening things might happen; things reach out and trip a person; the boys had been in there before, by day, and even by day Alan didn't like it. It might have been all right if the park hadn't been surrounded by such a high stone wall, so that if anything came after you, you wouldn't be able to get out.

'We'll take a tramp through the park, boys. Though it's a pity you don't have good walking shoes. You need good shoes, to go walking.'

'We only have our school shoes,' Toby said.

How particular he was, Uncle Arthur, about the importance of proper outfitting and equipment; had learned to be particular when he was Head of Purchasing, years ago, at the Line. Alan felt justified in making a counter-proposal.

'Couldn't we go for a ride on the number 8 tram, Uncle Arthur?'

'Not tonight, Alan. Perhaps in the summer. The number 8 tram goes to Garston; we could take a look at Garston Dock.'

Calderstones Park, planted with massive, threatening firs, was gloomy at the best of times, to be quite honest. They tramped through the damp twilight, Toby, unafraid, ranging ahead, Alan sticking close to his uncle.

Uncle Arthur stopped. 'Listen – do you hear that?' he said.

'Somebody clapping,' said Toby.

'Wood doves,' Uncle Arthur explained. 'When the dove takes off from a branch, he claps his wings.'

'You know everything, Uncle Arthur,' said Alan, because it was true, as far as he could see; Uncle Arthur was always telling them interesting things, like that purple foxgloves were used to make digitalis, which was a drug given to people with heart problems, and that the bats which scared them by swooping in front of their faces were blind, and navigated by radar.'

'I know about half,' said Uncle Arthur.

They came out of the dark trees, and there was the house. Calderstones Hall had been empty for years; its tall, narrow windows were boarded up, fallen slates and crumbling bricks lay in the thick wet grass. Whoever had lived there must, surely, have managed to escape from it, and very thankfully, because only unhappy or sick people could ever have lived in such a place. At the front was a paved terrace with stone balustrades, reached by steps made slippery by moss. Uncle Arthur and the boys paced the terrace, staring up at the blind windows.

'Do you believe in ghosts, Uncle Arthur?' Alan said.

'Ghosts? No.'

'Of course he doesn't,' said Toby. 'Only superstitious people believe in ghosts.'

'Who owns Calderstones Hall, Uncle Arthur?' asked Alan.

'Liverpool Corporation. They plan to knock it down, which is a pity. The Hall would make a wonderful youth hostel, or perhaps a hospital. A rehabilitation centre. Something useful.'

Early Sunday morning the boys raided Uncle Arthur's bedroom, leaping on top of him in their pyjamas. They'd been waking him up on Sundays like this since they were both very small.

'Boys, boys! You'll wake up the others.'

They climbed into bed with him, one on either side.

'Uncle Arthur! Be the big bad Tiddlypod!'

Uncle Arthur clenched his fists and pretended to bore holes in them as if his fists were the augurs of drills. They squealed with glee.

'Ow! Ow! Ow!'

'Ssssh!' begged Uncle Arthur.

'Then stop boring us!'

'Too late!'

'Ow! Ouch! Ow!'

He left off boring holes in them and they lay there with him, giggling, getting their breath back. Sunlight came in through the little window, filtered by the net curtain, promising well for their trip on the ferry to New Brighton. Uncle Arthur's bed had an embroidered coverlet made by some forgotten aunt; and on the polished mahogany dressing table, besides Uncle Arthur's simple toiletries, was a framed photograph of Auntie Grace: a round face, a frank smile, brown curls. A wedding photograph hung on the wall – Auntie Grace, with a huge bouquet, laughing at the groom's side, a younger Uncle Arthur, with more hair, looking jolly.

'Uncle Arthur,' Alan said, snuggling under the sheets against his uncle's long, pyjama-clad body, 'did we ever know Auntie Grace?'

'Oh, you were very young, Alan, but yes, she knew you. She died before Toby was born.'

'Was she nice?' said Toby.

'Yes, Toby. She was nice.'
'What did she die of?'
'She had a weak heart.'
'Were you sad?'
'Of course I was sad. I was very sad.'
'I'm sorry we didn't know Auntie Grace,' Alan said.
'We could have cheered you up when she died,' said Toby.
'You've been cheering me up ever since.'
'Mum thinks you'll marry Pat McMahon. I hope you do, Uncle Arthur.'
'Maybe she wouldn't have me.'
'She's awfully pretty.'
'She's also very nice to us,' added Toby. 'She talks to us like we were grown-ups.'
'I love that little fox she wears. Do you think it used to be a real fox? I like the way it smells.'
'Mum doesn't like Pat.'
'Nor does Granny,' Alan said. 'But then, she doesn't like Dad either. She thinks he's a failure. I've heard her talk.'
'You shouldn't listen in to people's conversations,' Uncle Arthur said.
'I wasn't trying to. Mum says he isn't a failure at all, he's happy doing what he does. They both say you are a terrific success, Uncle Arthur.'
'I don't know about that,' their uncle smiled.
'I wonder if I'll be a success. I don't expect so. I've thought about it a lot. But I don't know how much money you make if you're the captain of the New Brighton ferry, which is what I want to be. It may not be enough.'

Success, failure. Failure, success. Might there not be a middle ground? A half-way station? Alan pondered this a great deal. He was a bright boy, always top of his class at school: the headmaster thought he had a chance at a scholarship. He hoped he'd win one, because he hated the idea of failing anything. But perhaps he might fail only partly.

Chapter Two

It was the women, it seemed, who lived to a ripe old age in this family, on both sides of it: because here was Mrs Annie Sadie Carruth, who wore layers of skirts that smelled of pee, and kept her false teeth in a tumbler, the boys' Granny, aged eighty-one; and here was Mrs Eliza Miller, fragile but alive – Little Gran, the boys called her – their father's mother, aged eighty-three, a diminutive person with bad breath and fine, wispy red hair, who always wore an apron, took it off only twice, for weddings. Both were widows, Arthur Simon Carruth having died at the age of seventy-five, of a chill caught on a rare outing to the shops, to buy a newspaper, in order to confirm, three months after the event, the end of World War Two; and Walt's father, Clarence Wilberforce Miller, dead at sea aged forty-eight. A brown photograph of Clarence Wilberforce, heavily bearded, in the uniform of a Chief Engineer of the Cunard Line, hung on the wall in Walter's darkroom, to which the boys were admitted only after knocking, so as not to spoil the prints their father, cigarette dangling from his lips, pushed about with metal tweezers in a dish of chemicals. The room glowed with an eerie red light, so it was difficult to make out the features of the bearded engineer; and their father never spoke of him, because he'd known him only slightly himself; he was said, though, to have died of a tumour on the brain, and to have been haunted to the last by imaginary clocks, chiming out of control.

The boys' maternal grandparents had lived with the Millers, in Cheshire, during the war. Alan and Toby remembered their grandfather as a lean, yellow man with a prickly white beard; they hated having to kiss him because his beard gave them a rash on their cheeks; and he stalked the house silently in a dark navy three-piece suit which hung loosely about his bones: he was all bony, his face was bony; why didn't he rattle? From the pockets of his waistcoat hung a fine gold watch on a long chain; it was always understood that Alan, as his elder grandson, would one day inherit this watch, which Grandfather was forever consulting, taking it from his fob and inspecting it: he was obsessed with the passage of time, God knows why because he'd never had a real job. When asked to perform the slightest task, such as carry a tea tray back to the kitchen, or perhaps take the boys for a little walk, he would shake his head apologetically and mutter 'I haven't got time'. Mutter was all he did, he didn't say anything, he muttered. He wore slippers about the house, with his three-piece suit, and rarely ventured outdoors. He also wore a funny little smoking cap, of purple velvet, with a small black tassel, which made him look like an absent-minded Turkish bey. On one of the few occasions when he was prevailed upon to walk to the shops and fetch groceries, the boys, who'd gone with him, saw that he'd forgotten to remove his smoking cap and that people were giving him queer looks, but they roguishly decided not to tell him. He was angry when he found out, but their mother thought it was funny and wasn't cross.

He was an artist, the old man. That is to say, a painter, of exceptionally detailed pictures, done in oils. Three hung in the Millers' house: the most uninteresting, in the boys' opinion, showed a stony beach, with the sea in the distance and, across the sea, mountains. But it was painted as seen by a whelk, or other small crustacean, so that the first row of stones was enormous, and of very variegated colour; and also he'd painted every stone on the beach, which must have taken him months. Another painting, the concept more conventional, showed a cosy, half-timbered farmhouse beneath a huge tree: showing the same preoccupation with detail, Arthur Simon Carruth had not only painted every brick of the farm house, but every leaf of the tree. The composition, however, was pleasing; the clouds finely done. And the third painting in the possession of the Millers was of Conway Castle in North Wales; this was also an admirable composition, well captured the blue and grey Welsh light, with the gloomy fortress reflected in the muddy waves of the Conway River, and the imposing mass of the mountains of Snowdonia behind it, wreathed in threatening cloud. And as you can imagine, the painter had found it necessary to depict every wavelet on the river as well as every stone of the castle.

Grandfather had been unable to sell any of his paintings; perhaps buyers were deterred by all that detail. He attempted commercial art unsuccessfully, was briefly employed, quickly dismissed. Then he washed his hands of the whole thing, refused to take another job, stalked about looking at his watch. His stout-hearted spouse set out to rescue the family: she took in laundry. She washed and scrubbed other people's sheets and pillowcases, their dirty petticoats and underpants, their smelly socks. Starched and ironed other men's shirts and collars. She worked fifteen hours a day. Her business prospered; she took on help; in the end she rented separate premises for her laundry, and made enough money to send all three of her children to the Merchant Tailors' School in Crosby, best in the neighbourhood, with a clock tower and a cricket field. This bankrupted her after a couple of years so Arthur had to leave, at the age of fourteen, landing his job in the mail room at the Red Funnel Line, but his mother went on working, and Arthur contributed more and more, and in the end George went on to Liverpool University.

Clearly there was an artistic gene trapped in the family chemistry. The surprise was that it didn't wreak more havoc. It missed Arthur, and it missed George, reappearing in little Enid. She had been, if photographs were anything to go by, an enchanting child, with jet black curls, twinkling eyes, dimpled cheeks, and a huge sense of fun. She was forever dancing, or skipping about; she skipped with her mother all the way to the shops, and all the way back. She was never still from the time she woke up to the time she fell asleep, exhausted and happy. Her brothers were extraordinarily protective of her, especially Arthur. Arthur enjoyed walking, and would take his small sister for long walks on the sands, clutching her hand, the little girl skipping delightedly beside him. He helped her take her sandals off, and carried them for her. Tearing herself free, she'd gallop after shore birds: plovers, sandpipers, gulls. The birds joined in the fun, first running across the sand, then taking off in flocks, wheeling, landing. The incoming tide would create sandy streams that widened into shallow lakes; the ribbed sand felt good to bare feet; the girl's shouts, the gulls' cries, surely enchanted the wind itself. Arthur would end up chasing his errant sister, heading her off when she made for the sea, worried that she'd find herself trapped on sand banks that became long islands as the tide came in, or caught in quicksands; he'd chase her up into the dunes, where it was hard to run, and when he caught her they'd flop down, panting and laughing, and he'd point out the low brown line of the revetment where the Crosby Channel was, and talk of the *Lusitania*, and the old *Mauritania*, and the other great transatlantic liners that he'd seen steam out there, their four huge, raked, funnels silhouetted, unmistakably, against the western sky over the storm-wracked Irish Sea, four gigantic smoke plumes merging with low clouds. Already Arthur knew the names of all the great ships that sailed out of Liverpool, just as he knew the names of all the scurrying, wheeling, soaring birds his sister loved to run at. He tried to teach young Enid the names of the birds, but she forgot them, she was interested in the birds only as dance partners in the lonely ballets she choreographed on the empty sands, watched by her anxious brother.

He was a very precocious young man, was Arthur. You can see it in photographs: he comes across as remarkably self-possessed, eyes the camera with a stern and rather dark regard, aware of how important it is to make a good impression.

When Enid was eleven, her teacher at school asked to speak seriously to her parents, who had recently moved into a yellowbrick Victorian home in Crosby, off the Southport Road. The house occupied a corner lot and there were apple trees in the garden. Mrs Carruth had made Arthur string clothes lines from tree to tree, so that she could hang laundry out to dry. When the wind blew round the corner of the house, the laundry billowed and flapped like sails, so the yellow house looked like a galleon hard aground. Enid's teacher was shown into a dark front room – every room in the house was dark – with so much furniture it was difficult to navigate. There was an enormous sofa, finished in a shiny black brocade; and voluminous armchairs, upholstered in deep red. Two heavy dressers crammed with china, and a gigantic, glass-fronted bookcase that reached almost to the ceiling, the shelves being full of neatly-folded sheets, trousseaus for a dozen daughters. If you avoided, in the gloom, bumping into any of this intimidating furniture, you were bound to trip over a footstool, or the huge brass fender that encompassed the empty hearth. There was no evidence of a fire ever having been kindled in that black grate, which was more like the entrance to a coalmine, or perhaps to a tunnel that came up on the other side of the Mersey. The room was cold, although heavy velvet drapes hung in front of the door, to keep out draughts. They failed to do so, and the whole house was as cold as this ornate front room, cold even in July.

The visitor sat herself on the edge of a red armchair, with her knees hunched up and her legs pressed together, as if concerned that, should she sit back, she would somehow be swallowed up. She was a willowy maiden lady of thirty-six called Miss Tuttle; her first name was Bridget and it saddened her that nobody knew. She was given a cup of tea and she refused a piece of fruit cake. Mrs Carruth lowered herself into another chair, where she ate cake with noisy enjoyment, as if determined to ignore whatever this young person might have to say. Enid's father lurked in the doorway, with his watch; he'd said he didn't have time to speak with Miss Tuttle. But he appeared when his spouse let out a shriek, spitting currants all over the carpet.

'No! I will not let Enid take ballet lessons!' Mrs Carruth had protested.

Poor Miss Tuttle was embarrassed and shocked. 'Taking lessons does not commit Enid to a career as a dancer,' she protested, pressing her knees even more tightly together. 'But the child has such a gift. She is not just talented; other children are talented. Enid has a gift. I firmly believe she should take lessons.'

'No daughter of mine is going on the stage,' said Enid's father.

'We're not talking about her going on the stage, Mr Carruth. We are talking about her taking lessons. Lessons would not only make her a dancer. They would teach her self-discipline. Give her self-confidence. An awareness of herself. Teach her poise. By not letting her take lessons, you are denying the child more than you understand.'

'Don't be impertinent,' said Mrs Carruth.

'I am sorry if you think me impertinent. I can assure you, I have only the child's best interests at heart.'

The child's father said, 'If she takes lessons, she'll want to go on the stage.'

Miss Tuttle looked up at him; he had not sat down. 'Is that so terrible?' she asked.

'Yes, it is. It would be a disgrace to the family.'

A disgrace to the family! And here was an old fraud who didn't earn a penny, lived off the labour of his wife, muttered and scolded his way through life, lost his temper with his children, made even the tradesmen miserable, wore a loose suit, and had no curiosity but to know the time!

'I, myself, when I was younger,' said Miss Tuttle, with fragile dignity, 'wished to be a dancer. I believe I could possibly have gone on to – be a dancer. Instead, I am a teacher.'

'That's nothing to be ashamed of,' said Enid's mother. 'I wouldn't mind if Enid became a teacher. That's a perfectly respectable job. But she's not going to be a dancer, and she's not going to have lessons. I couldn't afford lessons, anyway.'

'Mrs Carruth,' said Miss Tuttle, 'if cost were the only obstacle, I'm sure ways could be found to circumvent it.'

'What do you mean?'

'I believe the Board of Governors would be prepared to consider a grant of some kind. In the case of exceptionally gifted children—'

Might the girl's mother be swayed by the suggestion of financial relief? Miss Tuttle had wondered, not that the Board of Governors had ever considered underwriting the cost of extracurricular activities: ah, Miss Tuttle was speaking out of turn, she was inspired only by enthusiasm; if necessary she was prepared to help herself with the cost of ballet lessons for little Enid Carruth, which shows how strongly she felt. But the child's father would have none of it.

'You're wasting our time, Miss,' he interrupted. 'There's no point Enid taking lessons if she's not going to be a dancer, and she is not going to be a dancer.'

'I believe you are an artist, Mr Carruth.'

'I paint.'

Miss Tuttle looked around at the paintings, in their heavy gilt frames, like dim lanterns in the gloom.

'You paint very well. I am not really a judge, but the stones on that beach seem to be exceptionally well done, and the glint of sun on a distant sea.'

'What are you driving at, Miss?'

'Did you ever have lessons, Mr Carruth?'

'Lessons? Me? Of course not! Waste of time. Waste of money.'

'Perhaps if you'd had lessons…'

This was too much for Enid's father, who became very angry. When he was angry, he jerked his head up and down; his beard became a blur of white bristle. Miss Tuttle thought he was about to have some kind of a seizure, and she stood up. Mrs Carruth hustled her to the front door.

'Could we talk again, Mrs Carruth? You might find it more convenient to come down to the school—'

'I'm sorry, Miss Tuttle. Enid is not going to have lessons. Don't waste your time any further.'

Enid, it turned out, had known about Miss Tuttle's visit, and how upset she was at the outcome, though she can't have been greatly surprised. She knew better than to confront her outraged parents, but when they were alone together she cried in her brother Arthur's arms, up in the little attic room she had all to herself.

'It's not fair! It's not fair! They won't let me take lessons! And I would so love to be a dancer!'

'Do you want me to talk to them?'

'Oh, yes! Please! Would you?'

'I shall. I have an idea that may make them change their minds.'

'What is it? What is it?'

'I'll tell you if it works, how's that?'

'Oh, Arthur! I love you! I love you!'

Arthur was already, at the age of eighteen, a shrewd diplomat: you have to admire him. Old beyond his years: always was; difficult to think of Arthur as a boy, with a boy's hopes, a boy's fears. Now he asked his sister only to be patient. One night a week his mother's friend, Mrs McMahon, whom she'd been to school with in Seaforth, came over to play bridge with the Carruths, and Arthur was dragged in: he had no gift for cards but he was a good sport. Mrs McMahon of course brought her daughter, Pat, that lean, sickly little girl who walked with the aid of a stick. Arthur who was very charming to her. She would sit and read on her own while the others played bridge, but Arthur would find opportunities to jump up and fetch her sweets or help her understand a difficult passage, or suggest a new volume.

Arthur's idea was to broach the subject of Enid's dancing lessons when his mother was in one of her more amenable moods, such as when she had just won handsomely at cards, and he also counted on the potential support of an innocent third party, Mrs McMahon.

As the game broke up, therefore, some three weeks after Miss Tuttle's unfortunate visit, and as Mrs Carruth added up her winning score, Arthur said, 'I understand there's some talk of Enid's having ballet lessons.'

'There is no talk at all,' snapped his mother.

'No daughter of mine is going on the stage,' said his father, with a single jerk of his beard.

'They say at school that she's awfully good.'

'Good she may be, but she's not having lessons.'

'Mrs McMahon,' tried Arthur, 'would you object to your daughter Pat's going on the stage?'

Mrs McMahon smiled sadly. 'I'm afraid – I don't know – Pat is a little delicate for that kind of thing,' she said.

'But suppose she – I mean, if she gets well – I mean, *when* she gets well – would you have an objection?'

'Well, no, I don't think so.'

'Enid has set her heart on having lessons,' Arthur said boldly. 'If it'll help, mother, I will pay for them.'

'Pay for them? You? How can you pay for them? You're already working hard enough so that your brother George can go to university.'

'I think dancing is as important to Enid as university is to George. What I have in mind is taking a second job.'

'That's ridiculous!' his mother exploded. 'I won't have it! I won't have it, Arthur, I won't have it!'

'Mr Clay, the grocer, is prepared to take me on as a delivery boy on Saturdays, and the bank on the Parade needs a night watchman.'

'Arthur, this is madness! I will not allow you to ruin your health so that your sister can have her dancing lessons! The reason your father and I will not allow her to take dancing lessons is nothing to do with money! It is a matter of principle!'

'Principle? What principle?' Arthur was interested to know. He never raised his voice; that wasn't his style at all. Oh no. Not Arthur Carruth. And if anything, this infuriated his parents all the more.

'I think we'd better leave,' said Mrs McMahon. 'Come on, Pat, dear. We're off.'

'The principle is, that my daughter does not go on the stage!' thundered Mr Carruth, the artist.

'I will pay for the lessons,' offered Arthur again, after a moment.

'There are not going to be any lessons!'

Poor Arthur was obliged to confess total failure to his little sister, which he hated doing.

'I'll run away!' she cried.

'I don't think I would, if I were you,' Arthur advised. The defeated diplomat already had a new plan: Arthur would never concede defeat, only an occasional setback. He believed that in the end he'd win, that time healed all wounds, and that invariably, given time, people would come round to his way of thinking. He never lost this optimistic view of things, or his faith in his own ability to change peoples' minds. 'Running away won't get you dancing lessons. I think what we should do is wait a little. I will continue to work on Mother. Father seems quite determined, for now, but if Mother decides that lessons are a good idea, you will have lessons.'

'I'll be dead by the time they let me have lessons,' sniffed Enid.

'I think in another year we'll be able to talk them into it.'

'Another year? That's forever, Arthur!'

Before another year was out, Private Arthur Carruth was at the front, near Armentières, with the 1st Battalion of the Black Watch; another year was, indeed, forever.

Arthur's letters home were censored, but the censorship, in his case, was needless; his letters were cheerful and reassuring, for his family's sake; to read them, you'd be amazed that Jerry hadn't yet thrown in the towel.

He wrote his little sister her own letter.

Dear Enid,

Guess what, I'm learning French! Here is a song we sing when we march:

Mademoiselle from Armentières,
Parlez-vous?
Mademoiselle from Armentières,
Parlez-vous?
Mademoiselle from Armentières,
Mademoiselle from Armentières,
Inky, pinky, parlez-vous?

What do you think? It's nonsense really, of course. Another thing we do, when we're marching, is somebody will sing out, 'Some say, Good old Sergeant-Major!' and everybody laughs, because the obvious rejoinder is 'Others tell the truth!' Here's another song we sing:

Here's to the good old whiskey,
Drink it down, drink it down!
Here's to the good old whiskey,

> *It makes you feel so frisky!*
> *Here's to the good old whiskey,*
> *Drink it down!*
>
> *Here's to the good old beer,*
> *Drink it down, drink it down!*
> *Here's to the good old beer,*
> *It makes you feel so queer!*
> *Here's to the good old beer,*
> *Drink it down!*
>
> *Silly, but it passes the time! Can't wait to get home on leave, then we'll go walking on the sands again, and chase birds! And perhaps I'll have another go at mother about those dancing lessons.*

Enid was immensely proud to receive this letter from her brother at the front; she took it to school and showed it to all her friends. She also went about singing the two marching songs Arthur had written down for her, but as she had no idea what the tunes were she made up tunes of her own.

To his parents Arthur wrote:

> *Dear Mother and Father,*
>
> *All goes pretty well here. The grub is surprisingly good, as long as you don't mind eating custard out of the same mess tin as your gravy.*
>
> *Our lieutenant says I should apply for a commission, presumably because I speak the King's English, unlike most of the men, who come from very poor parts of Glasgow and speak an almost*

> *incomprehensible patois. But I have no particular ambition to be an officer. The men in my unit are first-rate sorts, in so far as I can understand what they're saying, and I have some good chums. If I went for a commission I would feel bad about it, because it would make me different from them, and I'm not.*
>
> *We gave Jerry a bit of a fright last night, I can tell you! They tried a night attack, but our patrols got wind of it and we were ready for 'em! None of them got near our lines. We sent them scurrying back for safety as fast as their legs could carry them. I don't think Kaiser Bill will be pinning any medals on 'em for that attempt!*

Arthur's reason for not pursuing a commission was in fact a simple one: he was not prepared to order other men to their death, and that was that. What a very high-principled young man he must have been, because he was, himself, quite devoid of fear, would volunteer for patrols and other dangerous jobs, like forays into No Man's Land to bring back bodies, and he performed these tasks with a jaunty air, as if it was all a bit of a rag. He actually whistled; yes, it's true: loading a bloodied corpse on to a makeshift stretcher, he'd find himself whistling, and tell himself to stop. Another remarkable thing about him was that he never used foul language. This certainly distinguished him, in an army where every second word was an obscenity; but nobody thought to deride him for this apparent fastidiousness because nobody thought him fastidious.

His mother was certain he'd be killed; her attitude was completely fatalistic, she didn't believe his cheerful letters, she'd written him off. She only prayed that the war would be over before the brilliant George became eligible to join up. Might as well admit it, George had always been her favourite; Arthur was too clever, too suave. And too much her match!

Arthur's section was ordered to take up a fresh position on the flank of a low hill spiked with the skeletons of burned trees. Detecting movement, German snipers opened fire as the men crawled across duckboards laid on thick mud in hastily-dug communicating trenches. The man in front of Arthur was hit; a terrible wound to the face, he died at once. Arthur heaved the body aside with his shoulder, keeping as low as he could, inching forward to safety. The man behind him was hit in the side. Arthur crawled back for him and managed to tug him to a more protected position before discovering that he'd tugged a corpse.

> *Dear Mother and Father,*
>
> *We're all feeling good about things here. The general feeling is that Old Jerry has taken a bit of a hammering. He seems to have lost enthusiasm for the fight! As a result things are quiet. No attacks, no shelling. We'd even be able to get a decent night's sleep if it wasn't for the Sergeant-Major bawling us out and insisting we mount patrols!*
>
> *Even going out on patrol isn't bad though, these days. At least it gets a fellow out of the trenches! And Jerry leaves us alone. It's weird, in a way, this inactivity, because things were quite hot when we first arrived at the front.*

One night when Arthur was on patrol in No Man's Land – the task was to try and detect any sign of activity on the enemy's part, such as mine-laying, or tunnelling – a green flare, from over the German lines, burst almost directly overhead, the light drifting downwards on the wind, suddenly silhouetting the men of Arthur's patrol. There was a burst of machine-gun fire, then another, from further away; Arthur actually stood there, for a moment, quite interested, as his patrol dove for cover. One man was hit: he let out a curious shout, as if of surprise, then spun slowly round, and fell. When the machine-guns started again Arthur remembered he should probably take cover; he threw himself forward, and landed, fortuitously, in the bottom of a deep and muddy foxhole, but had the impression he'd twisted his ankle in falling. He found to his dismay that he could hardly move, but as his position seemed relatively safe he settled down to wait for the pain to ease. Groping with his hands, he discovered that he was not the only occupant of the foxhole: a man lay on his back, face to the sky. Not sure whether the fellow was dead or severely wounded, Arthur could only wait for another flare; didn't have to wait long, either. A starshell burst: this time the world turned red. The man was a German. He wasn't dead, his eyes rolled, he focused on Arthur.

'Don't shoot me, Tommy,' he gasped.

The red flare was spent. The thought of shooting this wounded man would never have occurred to Arthur, unless perhaps to put the poor blighter out of his misery. 'I won't shoot you,' he said.

'Please. Thank you.'

Arthur wriggled, painfully, to the man's side and lay companionably beside him, looking up at the sky from their bed of mud.

'Are you hurt badly?'

'I think, very badly,' breathed the German soldier.

In the mud, in the dark, Arthur reached his hand across and began feeling, gingerly, the man's body, trying to ascertain where the wound was; not that he had any medical skill, but with the thought of perhaps being able to make a bandage out of his shirt and stop the bleeding. His exploration didn't take long: as far as he could tell, the man's stomach had been shot away.

'Are you in great pain?' asked Arthur.

'No. Very little pain.'

'That's good,' Arthur said, though he thought the man must be in atrocious pain; and was lying; because his voice seemed to come from the other side of the world.

After a few moments the man whispered, 'Speak to me, Tommy.'

'How long have you been here?'

'I don't know. Some time.'

'When our burial squad comes, they'll look after you.'

Arthur knew quite well, having several times been part of one, that burial squads did not bring back wounded enemy, but in this case he would wait and make sure they did, at gunpoint if necessary.

'I hope they come.'

'Well, they'll come,' Arthur assured him.

But it was unlikely a burial party would be sent out tonight, after the flares and the bursts of enemy fire. There didn't seem, to Arthur, to be much he could do to make this horribly wounded man more comfortable, but he got himself out of his battle-jacket, which he rolled into a pillow so that he could prop the man's head up. Another flare went up from the German lines, a green one; Arthur leaned over the man's face. It was, for a few seconds, the colour of green cheese. The man's eyes opened as the flare died.

'Speak to me, Tommy,' the German said again.
'Well – where are you from, old chap?'
'From Hanover.'
'Ah. "Hamelin Town's in Brunswick, by famous Hanover City." That's the first line of a famous English poem called The Pied Piper, by Robert Browning.'
'It sounds like a very beautiful poem, Tommy.'
'It's a very long poem. I had to learn all of it, one school holiday.'
'Where are you from, Tommy?'
'Liverpool.'
'Ah. I have heard of Liverpool. Liverpool is a big city, ja?'
'Ja. Yes. I'm afraid I speak no German. You speak English very well.'
'Are there any poems about Liverpool?'
Arthur thought for a moment. 'I don't think so.'
About an hour later, the man said, very faintly, 'Photograph.'
'Photograph?'
The German seemed to struggle with his hand, indicated a pocket; Arthur drew from the pocket a crumpled photograph but it was still too dark to make out.
'Please send to my wife,' murmured the dying man.

'I will need an address.'

'You will find the address.'

When it grew light enough Arthur went through the man's other pockets, discovered his identity papers, and hid them in his boot. He then spent a whole day in that foxhole, with the body of the dead German, out in No Man's Land. It was a quiet day, there were no attacks. He wondered how long it would be before he was posted missing; and in fact this was his only real concern: he wanted no regretful telegrams wired to Crosby. In the afternoon the sun shone; it was warm and really quite pleasant, Arthur thought. He took back his battle-jacket and used it as his own pillow, and lay there whistling quietly to himself in that immense lunar landscape. He was hungry, so he ate a small piece of chocolate which he'd found in the dead German's pocket. It was good chocolate, and he wondered whether it was standard German Army issue, which seemed unlikely, or whether it had been sent in a food parcel by the widow who didn't know she was a widow, in Hanover. By the time it was dark again Arthur's ankle felt easier, and he began the long crawl back to his own lines. The only password he knew was a day out of date, but when he was challenged somebody recognised him. On his next leave, Arthur mailed the German's photograph (it showed a woman with very short hair holding a baby; they stood in front of a corner building with ornate windows) to the neutral Swiss consulate in Liverpool, with a request they forward it. He thought maybe after the war he'd go to Hanover and find out if the widow ever received the photograph.

Arthur, on leave, had walked jauntily into the house in Crosby, without telling anyone he was coming, in full dress uniform. His mother treated him like a ghost who somehow had no right to be there. His father paraded up and down, demanding to know what progress the Allied armies were really making in France. He had become extremely sceptical about the war, had decided that all the British and French generals were ninnies.

'On the contrary,' Arthur assured him, 'as far as I can tell the war is going mighty well.'

'Well, what's your rate of advance?'

'I'm not sure we've advanced very far. But we certainly haven't retreated.'

'Why won't you go for a commission?' his mother badgered.

'That is a personal decision, mother.'

He left it at that and they did not pursue it. They were beginning to have the uncomfortable feeling that Arthur, once described by the headmaster of Merchant Taylors' as 'average', was too smart for them.

His brother, George, who was sixteen, had joined a tennis club. He invited Arthur along to a Saturday night dance, and what a jolly affair it was, the pavilion of the tennis club decorated with fresh flowers. White-painted walls, glass cases full of silver cups, photos of people who'd won tournaments. At one end of the room a small orchestra played dance music, the musicians in white dinner jackets with black bow ties and sprays of flowering cherry in their buttonholes. Many of the male club members were, like Arthur, in uniform: the women seemed astonishingly pretty, their faces flushed with dancing. They'd pinned flowers in their hair. Everybody seemed to be drinking rather a lot, though Arthur abstained. George introduced his brother to friends: he seemed to have many, in spite of his youth: it turned out he was an excellent tennis player, much in demand as a partner in men's doubles. Mixed doubles too. If Arthur was a strikingly handsome young man, with his black hair combed neatly back, his straight, Roman, nose, his kindly but assured regard, his immaculately pressed uniform, George, though also tall, as tall already as Arthur, was an angel. He had a shock of hair, and a very grave face, the eyes extraordinarily trusting, the lips always slightly parted.

'Arthur, I'd l-l-l-like you to meet Grace F-f-f-fairweather, this is her b-b-b-brother, C-c-c-claud, this is David Eaton, and this is Angela D-d-d-dunbar.'

Arthur shook hands all round; invited Grace Fairweather, as the orchestra had struck up, to dance. He was not a good dancer, but he gave the impression of enjoying it so much it didn't matter. Grace was charmed by him; he thought her delightful.

'You should join our club,' she told him. 'I mean, after the war.'

'Perhaps I shall. Does one have to play tennis?'

Grace laughed, and Arthur didn't think he'd heard a laugh so lovely. 'Well – no, I suppose not, if you don't want to. But this is a tennis club.'

'I'm hopeless at games. I can't hit a ball to save my life.'

'I'll teach you to play,' laughed Grace. 'As it happens, I'm a good teacher.'

'You'll need to be.'

'I teach at Merchant Taylors'.'

'You're not old enough to be a teacher.'

Grace had a charming, round face, and wispy brown hair which she wore in tight little curls; she had on a white dress with black polka dots and puffed sleeves that left her arms bare from the elbows; they were covered with a fair down that glistened with her perspiration.

'Certainly I am. I'm twenty-one. As a matter of fact I teach your brother.'

'I thought he knew everything already.'

She laughed again. 'Not quite. Though he's certainly very brilliant, and a superb tennis player, with it. You should see his forehand. And his volley – wow. What about you though? I can't believe George has all the brains.'

'Oh, he does. I'm quite ordinary.'

'I don't believe that.'

'That's because you don't know me.'

'My bad luck.'

'Luck can change.'

'Oh, I'm sure there's some nice little French mademoiselle who's quite stolen your heart.'

'I don't know what you think life is like at the front, but I certainly haven't had the opportunity to meet any nice mademoiselles.'

'Well, how about a tennis lesson tomorrow morning? When do you – I mean, when do you have to go back?'

'Tomorrow night. In the morning I promised to take my sister for a walk on the beach. We could play in the afternoon, if you like.'

'All right. That's very nice of you, to take your sister for a walk.'

'I like walking.'

'Then perhaps one day we can go walking.'

'Certainly. My next leave.'

The brothers walked home, through the silent streets. The flowering cherries were in full bloom, extravagant pink petals floated down in a mild breeze off the sea, with its smell of bladderwrack and kelp, sand and salt. Arthur's boots rang on the pavement. His head was full of music; he wanted to dance forever.

'I say, you m-m-m-made quite a h-h-h-hit at the club,' George said, when they'd crossed a couple of streets.

'Apparently so have you. Your forehand is widely admired. Your volley too.'

'Christ, Arthur. I wish I could j-j-j-join up, like you.'

His brother let out a laugh. 'Why on earth would you want to volunteer to get killed?'

'I feel so useless here. It's very aggravating s-s-s-seeing all the ch-ch-ch-chaps in uniform and I'm still at school. I don't think I'm d-d-d-doing my bit. Besides, it's so unfair.'

'What's so unfair, George?'

'It's so unfair that you had to leave school. To help pay for me. How do you think that m-m-m-akes me feel Arthur? It makes me f-f-f-feel like a worm. And now to m-m-m-make matters worse now you're at the front, getting sh-sh-sh-shot at by a bunch of Jerries, and I'm here perfecting my v-v-v-volleys.'

'There's nothing to feel bad about. You're the brains of the family, George. I want you to go on to university. It's important to me. It's important to all of us.'

George stopped still. Arthur walked on a few paces, then turned round. They were at the corner of the Southport Road, and the wind whipped up from the sea.

'You are the sweetest man, Arthur. But it d-d-d-doesn't help. You are every bit as smart as I am. You will g-g-g-go much further in life, I'm sure. One day I will probably ask you for m-m-m-money, and when I do, I won't feel bad. But just for n-n-n-now, I feel like a sh-sh-sh-shit.'

Arthur took his brother's elbow; they walked on, along the deserted Parade, the shops shuttered up, flowering cherry petals racing them, making funny scratching noises on the pavement, like mice, frail little mice made of pink wrapping paper.

'What's it l-l-l-like, Arthur? You must have seen d-d-d-dreadful things, I mean, d-d-d-dead people and h-h-h-horrible wounds. But it seems to have had absolutely no effect on you at all.'

'What does that make me, George?'

'It probably m-m-m-makes you the m-m-m-most admirable man in the world.'

'Or the most unfeeling bastard?' suggested Arthur.

'Oh no, I don't think so,' George said.

Arthur walked with Enid for miles along the sands. It was a fine Sunday morning; high clouds flew inland. The wind blew sand like grit into their faces; the girl clasped her brother's hand tightly, seemed to have no desire to run at the birds or gallop through water. Ships with tall thin funnels crawled down the Crosby Channel, trailing straight lines of black smoke, their hulls in camouflage paint; two lean destroyers steamed with them.

'You'll be very careful, won't you, when you go back to the front,' Enid said.

'I promise.'

In March of the following year, after a few days of north-easterly gales, the Germans exploded canisters of mustard gas which drifted down on to the British trenches along the Armentières front. Stretcher-bearers carried Private Arthur Carruth, kicking and blinded, away from the screaming.

Chapter Three

Grace's doctor said, 'You have a slight heart murmur.'
She cocked her head to one side and looked at him.
'What does that mean?'
'The beat is a little irregular. For each beat there is a faint half-beat. Listen to it.'
He took the stethoscope from around his neck, and hung it about hers; held the rubber disc just below her left breast.
'Can you hear it?'
'I'm not sure. Yes, I think so.'
She listened, as best she could, to the sound of her own heart, but wasn't sure if she detected the little half-beats Dr McKenzie described, so he took back the stethoscope. He had a heavy face, with red cheeks and broken veins, silvery hair.
'You can get dressed now.'
'Is it serious? Should I be worried?'
'Not unduly, I think. There is no history of heart trouble in your family.'
'But what about – I mean – I play tennis, I – go walking, I dance—'
'I would avoid any prolonged strain on the heart. I'm sure a couple of sets of tennis is all right.'
'I'm – getting married, I—'

'Good. There's no reason you shouldn't have a perfectly normal life.'

'Should I see a specialist?'

'Oh, if you like. For your peace of mind. I can give you a couple of telephone numbers.'

She saw a frightening man with a pince-nez called Dr Lawrence, who had offices with a brass bell-push on Lower Parliament Street, and who took a more serious view of Grace's heart condition than cheery Dr McKenzie had: no, he did not think she should play tennis, not a couple of sets, not any; what he prescribed was regular walks.

Grace Fairweather was twenty-eight now. She was engaged to marry handsome Arthur Carruth, and he was described, these days, in shipping circles, as a rising young star at the Red Funnel Line; Grace and Arthur had been engaged for two years; which everybody agreed was the right length of time, young people should not rush to get married; they should wait until they could afford to.

Though he was only twenty-five, three years younger than Grace, Arthur had certainly drawn attention to himself at the Line, not so much because he worked long hours, which he did, but because he had rare instinct. So they'd put him in charge of the Purchasing Department, where he took over from an old greybeard of sixty-three who'd had a stroke while he was ordering new crockery for the fussy captain of the *Bantry Bay* after a knockabout homeward passage from Belo Horizonte. Now Arthur was responsible for the purchase of just about anything that went into a Red Funnel Line ship, from the grand piano in the first-class lounge of the *Chesapeake Bay* to the red blankets on the bunks in steerage, from the crystal in the captain's cocktail cabinet to the tin mugs in the stokers' mess. Lots of things he wasn't nearly greybearded enough to know much about, though his knowledge was surprising. This was because, having left school at fourteen, he'd educated himself out of encyclopaedias, spent hours poring through the *Britannica* in the Crosby Public Library after long days at the office. Not only encyclopaedias, either: he'd also ploughed through weighty lexicons and memorised anthologies. Now he charmed ship-chandlers and compared catalogues, talked his way into wholesalers' warehouses. Realising that the more he ordered, the less it cost, which incidentally nobody had bothered to tell him, he bought a whole warehouse full of linen and sold the surplus to the Cunard Line, at a profit, then he took to visiting the mills and buying direct from mill-owners, spent hours on smoky trains that trundled across industrial Lancashire, struck bargains with hard men in Rochdale and Oldham who chewed on pipes and smelled of beer.

Ah yes, he was doing well, and with his new promotion had come a giddy raise; Arthur now earned two hundred and twenty-five pounds a year. He and Grace would be married in August, when the summer term ended at Merchant Taylors', and she would give up teaching: of course she would give up teaching: when you were married, you stopped work if you were a woman.

At a tennis club dance – they held dances every Saturday – Grace danced the Charleston all night in a short green dress and a loose necklace of brown beads; she was a blur of green crepe and silk stockings, her necklace twirling – she had to keep grabbing it, with a laugh at her partner – her brown curls plastered to her forehead. She exhausted the band: implored them to strike up again whenever they took a breather between numbers, mopping their brows with purple handkerchiefs from the breast pockets of their white dinner jackets. No one had ever seen her so jolly. But then, why shouldn't she be jolly? In a month's time she would be married to Arthur Carruth, whom everybody liked, who was probably the most popular man in the club, even if he was a rotten tennis player. Only that afternoon Grace had played ten straight sets of tennis, three sets of singles, two of mixed doubles, in which she played with Arthur – they lost – and five sets of ladies' doubles.

They were married at St Stephen's Church, in Crosby; the reception was at the club. And what a delicacy: cantaloupe melon, shipped on the Red Funnel steamer *Marigot Bay*, by courtesy of the Line's directors. That was recognition. The couple boarded the Isle of Man Steam Packet Company's elegant new ship *Manx Maid*, two thousand five hundred tons, sailing at two thirty p.m. for Douglas.

The day was fine; the sea a rare sapphire blue, and calm; the waves, cleft by the fine sharp bow of the *Manx Maid*, hissed by; astern, the churning maelstrom of her wake tumbled white and green. Seagulls followed her, mewing and crying, catching potato peels thrown from her galley and sandwich crusts chucked by her passengers, dodging the black smoke from her single raked funnel, red with a black top like a dwarf Cunarder, but with two black bands instead of the Cunard Line's three.

For all his wide knowledge of the sea and ships, this was the first time Arthur had been any further on a ship than

New Brighton, on the Cheshire side of the estuary, reached in half an hour by *Royal Daffodil* or *Royal Iris* from the Liverpool Landing Stage. Travelling first class, he stood with Grace on the open observation deck below the bridge, and felt the throb of the ship's powerful engines beneath their feet, as the buoys of the Crosby Channel jogged by, leaning to the tide. It was curious to be alone with Grace; almost, Arthur realised, for the first time; she seemed a bit shy, which she never had before. She'd entrusted herself to him, and he'd make her very glad she had. He found himself whistling; stopped; didn't know whether she'd noticed. In the distance, beyond the revetment, stretched the low Lancashire shore, the Crosby sands where he'd walked with his little sister, and she'd danced and scampered, chasing birds. Now came the Crosby light-ship, painted red with the name CROSBY in huge white letters, wallowing in a trough between waves, moored at the entrance to the Channel. After the light-ship the shore-line receded, became indistinguishable from the sky. Grace gave Arthur's elbow a little squeeze; they walked side by side along the promenade deck, then up a flight of stairs to the boat deck, below the huge red funnel, which vomited black smoke. It was warm near the funnel, with the smell of fresh oil and smooth machinery blasting from the ventilators that flanked it. A small sign prohibited entry to the bridge, where unseen hands steered the ship on a course for the gull-girt cliffs of the Isle of Man.

She must have seen his glance. 'You could tell them you're Head of Purchasing at the Red Funnel Line,' Grace suggested. 'I'm sure they'd let you steer.'

'They'd be crazy. I'm as blind as a bat,' laughed Arthur.

They took tea in the first-class lounge. Arthur believed her tired: not shy now, but thoughtful. Her going-away outfit was a pleated white skirt and a loose-fitting navy-blue jacket with long sleeves, so nautical-looking, and she wore a small navy-blue hat atop her trim brown curls. They ate tiny cucumber sandwiches with the crusts neatly removed, and thin slabs of sponge cake.

Arthur, his normally well-combed hair blown about by the wind on the boat deck, in a well-cut pale grey suit with wide lapels, and a small pink rose in his buttonhole, felt as if something deep inside him, warm and fulsome, like blood, had brimmed over. And how he admired this lovely creature sitting opposite him at the little table with its crisp white napery and the tea cups printed with the monogram of the Line. His to look after now, his to mind. He loved her calm round face, her dainty curls. He loved the white of her neck, the outfit she'd chosen so tastefully, the navy-blue jacket, the white skirt. She belonged to him, this person; she would live in the same house, eat at the same dining table, sit in the same sitting room, sleep in the same bedroom; garden, perhaps, in the same garden. And the prospect was delightful. He looked around him. Right now, Arthur loved everything: he loved this handsome ship, which was taking them on honeymoon; he loved its quiet first-class lounge, with the hidden hum of the engines; he even loved the smooth folds of the tablecloth and the elegant IOMSP tea cups.

At Douglas, when they left the ship, Arthur commandeered a taxi for the fifteen-mile ride to Port Erin, rather than take the sooty little train. This was extravagant, even for a man who earned two hundred and twenty-five pounds a year, but he felt that Grace was exhausted. They sat in the back of the taxi, which smelled of leather and disinfectant, a little apart from each other, Arthur whistling quietly to himself, Grace with her knees tucked together, looking out of the windows.

'It's pretty,' she said; it was the first time she'd spoken for a while.

'Yes. I believe the Isle of Man is very charming.'

They drove through narrow lanes made golden by the evening sunlight, past small white houses with climbing roses and grey slate roofs. At Castletown, the herring drifters lay rafted alongside narrow quays, beneath the tough old castle, still in such good shape it would hold out, surely, for weeks against a siege; at Port St Mary, more boats, at anchor in the wide bay; and another castle, larger, with blasted walls and broken turrets: no, Port St Mary would not hold out.

They were both enchanted with their hotel at Port Erin, which had grey stone walls with mock battlements at the top, and a battlemented tower at the corner, over its main entrance; what a land of castles this was! It was called The Hydro, spelt out in iron letters painted gold; and it was on the sea, overlooked a deep bay with a pair of heathery headlands. Herring boats were anchored here too, and seagulls wheeled and screamed, driven mad by the stink of fish. The honeymoon couple were ushered to their table in the dining room, in a corner close to the front window, which was hung with huge white curtains that stirred slightly in a soft breeze off the bay, while a three-piece band played dance music.

'Shall we dance?' Arthur said, when they'd ordered their dinner. 'Or do you still feel tired?'

'I do feel rather tired. Perhaps tomorrow.'

'Of course. And the next day. And the next day, for two weeks.' How wonderful it would all be.

She took his hands, across the table. 'I have a weak heart, you know,' she said.

Arthur tried to understand what she'd said, wasn't sure if he'd heard her right.

'A weak heart?'

'Yes, I – I mean I – don't think I'm going to drop down dead on you but – I have a weak heart.'

He thought she'd never looked more lovely. He tried to digest the information she'd given him, but it was difficult.

'For someone with a weak heart, you have a tremendous serve,' he said, trying to smile.

'Well yes, that's just it, I probably shouldn't play any more tennis.'

Arthur felt as if the smile had been hammered into his face; but he wouldn't show it, stayed chipper.

'Well in that case I won't either. That will come as good news to most of our friends at the club.'

'And I'm not sure about – the Charleston and – that kind of thing.'

Arthur considered. 'How long have you known about this?'

'I found out a few weeks ago. I'm sorry. I thought I'd better tell you. I mean I should perhaps have told you before.'

'Before we were married? Why? Do you think I'd have broken off our engagement?'

He looked at her very tenderly.

'No,' she said. She looked down. 'I don't know. Maybe. I wouldn't have blamed you.'

A waiter brought mock turtle soup. Arthur picked up his spoon, and put it down again.

'You're forgetting something, Grace.'

'What's that?'

'I love you. I love you totally. There is nothing about you I don't love.'

'Well. Thank you. You are very generous.'

'When we get back to Liverpool, I'll take you to see a specialist.' He had got over his initial shock very quickly, was immediately making plans: everything, surely, could be set right.

Grace shook her head. 'I've seen a specialist.'

'Then we'll see one in London, we—'

'No. I don't want you to treat me like an invalid, Arthur. I just have to – well, I just have to – take care, that's all. I've been advised to take long walks. You like walking, so we'll be able to take long walks together.'

They took a long walk next day, they trudged for miles through heather and gorse, broom and bracken, along Bradda Head, to the stubby round tower at the end, its crumbling stone walls overgrown with yellow lichen, lovers' initials carved into them with penknives (are lovers always armed with penknives?). It was another clear day and in the distance, to the west, the Mountains of Mourne, in Ireland, fifty miles away, loomed blue on the horizon. Grace stood there, in the wind, filled her lungs with the raw sea air, bent to pick a bunch of red valerian and sea-pink.

'You are a very understanding man, Arthur,' she smiled at him.

'I love you.'

'I know. You told me.'

'I will always love you.'

'Always is a long time.'

He kissed her, felt the softness of her body, knew that something precious and fragile had been made over to him, more precious and more fragile than he'd known, and he loved her all the more, now that he knew.

'Silly Grace. Why didn't you tell me, before?'

'I told you before why I didn't tell you before. I was afraid.'

'You underestimate me. People don't underestimate me at the office. Why should you?'

'I never will again.'

'From now on, you must tell me everything. I mean, as soon as it happens.'

'All right. And will you tell me everything, too, as soon as it happens?'

'Of course.'

But hadn't there been the slightest of pauses, though, before he agreed? There had, for Arthur didn't necessarily believe in telling people things he didn't think it helped if they knew. A hundred feet below them, the cobalt-blue Irish Sea surged and thundered.

'If I'm going to tell you everything,' he said that night, at dinner, 'perhaps I'd better begin.'

'Where will you begin?' she smiled.

'Where would you like me to begin?'

'With you.'

'I'm not sure that will be very interesting.'

'On the contrary, you're a very interesting man. Already a success story. I love that – I mean, success. I want us to be a success, Arthur. Success means so much to you.'

Arthur smiled. He dabbed his eyes with his handkerchief. 'Not of itself. But it's important to my family. My father has always believed that the world owes him a living, but for some reason the world has never seen it that way. If it wasn't for Mother's determination to make the most of a bad job, we'd have finished in the poorhouse. But Mother's not so young as she used to be. She can't go on working like she's worked. And then there's George. George can't get a job. A brilliant man, but he can't get a job.'

'That's because of his stammer.'

'It's because his stammer makes him peevish and aggressive. Besides, after the war, most of the jobs that were going went to ex-servicemen. Now the poor fellow has got fatalistic about the whole thing, which doesn't help. It can't be much fun, trying to get a job for four years, and not getting one.'

'Can no one do anything for his stammer? I know he's seen people, and taken courses, but – surely now – surely now that we have some money—'

'If it was a question of money – of course. But I think he's tried everything. Nothing seems to work.'

'All right. What about your sister? Is she going to be a success, as a teacher?'

'I'm sure Enid will be a fine teacher, when she finishes teachers' training college. The tragedy in her case is that she might have been a successful dancer, but Father wouldn't let her take ballet lessons, which she'd set her heart on when she was very young. I have to say I encouraged her, to my regret, but you can imagine what it was like, talking to those two.'

'You pay for her to go to teachers' training college, don't you?'

'Yes, as a matter of fact.'

'My poor sweet Arthur.'

'Try the roast chicken, it's very good. And the chipolata sausages—'

'You're funny. You're so kind, and funny too. But I'm not sure I accept your explanation.'

'What explanation?'

'About not caring for success.'

'But I don't.'

Grace was wrong, that's the truth. Success wasn't important to Arthur, not at all. Responsibility was. People depended on him, that was the thing. He'd taken his responsibilities very seriously, from the age of fourteen. He believed that he could be relied upon.

On a long walk she asked Arthur about the war, which he never talked about. They'd followed, this time, the coast road towards the southern headland, and, when the road ended, tramped across windy heath to a spectacular overview, from soaring cliffs, of the Calf of Man, an off-lying island said to be farmed by a madman who raised sheep, his only company the gulls, and guillemots, and puffins that cried around the place day and night.

'I know what your worst experience was,' Grace said. 'At least, I suppose it was your worst experience – when you were gassed. But did you have any good experiences? I've talked to people who fought in the trenches and seem to remember them with a kind of fondness. I mean, fondness for the comradeship, and all that sort of thing.'

'I had one good experience,' Arthur said, after a few moments. 'We were on patrol. Things had been rather quiet for the last little while, and I suppose we'd got careless. Anyway, the Germans sent up a green flare, and saw us. I remember staring at the flare, as it fell, quite slowly, it wasn't in much of a hurry, towards the trenches; and then of course the guns started up. I threw myself down, landed in a deep foxhole. There was a German in it. He was dying. Before he died he gave me a photograph of his wife and children and asked me to try and send it back to Hanover, where he came from.'

'And did you?'

'I sent it to the Swiss consulate. But I also thought that after the war I'd try and find the widow.'

'And you did?'

'Yes, as a matter of fact I did. I tracked her down. It wasn't easy, because she'd moved in with her parents after her husband was killed, and they lived in Cologne, but yes, I tracked her down. It wasn't easy talking to her, either, because my German wasn't up to much and nor was her English. I tried to explain, though, that her husband had died bravely – and that he wasn't alone, when he did.'

'And you explained.'

'Yes. I believe so.'

She looked at him, and he thought she was going to sob. The wind snatched at her hair, tore at her skirt. She felt it was blowing right through her, fresh and strong off the Irish Sea, whipping up white-caps. Gulls hung over the foaming channel between the mainland of Man and the madman's island.

It had taken Arthur two years to convalesce, for the first three months at a hospital near Compiègne, in France, blinded, spitting; then at a military convalescent home outside Dorking, Surrey. It was here that, taken for his usual afternoon's outing in a wheelchair pushed by a male nurse, he was first aware of rhododendrons. Midnight-red, shocking purple. He'd been looking at them for a while, marvelling at the density of their colour, before he realised he could see them; they were not being described, he could see them. From then on, he started getting better; he was moved to another floor of the airy, cream-painted hospital. In the next bed to his, on one side, was a man, still heavily bandaged, whose face had been burned off by the premature ignition of a flare; the skin was being replaced by grafts, little by little. Arthur did not tell Grace about this man; nor did he tell her about the man in the bed on his other side, who had lost both legs in a burning tank. Arthur's worst experiences in the war were not at all of the trenches, but of this Surrey hospital, where it had been almost impossible to whistle.

One day he and Grace took a charabanc tour to Snaefell, highest mountain on the island. They rode the rack-and-pinion train that inched its clanking way to the summit. It had rained in the morning, but a watery sun now broke through; there was no wind; and the short turf scrunched underfoot. They followed a sheep-track into heather, which led to a small lake where the mist hung like smoke. Two coots poked about on the flat surface of the lake, dipping their bills into the shiny water. Arthur clasped his Grace, her face wet with mist, her hair damp like cobwebs on a cold morning.

'I haven't told you everything,' he said.

'You've told me more than everything.'

When they turned to make their way back to the mountain railway station the mist had thickened, so they had to walk carefully, Arthur ahead, she grasping his fingers. The train had left; there wasn't another.

'Walking is good,' she said, and what a valiant smile.

'The easiest way down is to follow the railway track, I suppose,' said Arthur; which is what they did: it took them two hours, and they were wet through by the time they reached the bottom, and the charabanc had left, but they found a telephone kiosk, summoned a taxi. When they arrived back at the hotel Arthur wanted to wrap her in warm blankets, but Grace laughed.

'I'm not consumptive or anything,' she said. 'I have a weak heart. I told you, you don't have to treat me like an invalid.'

Her face was flushed, though, at dinner. But she was in fine spirits, she laughed a lot, and when the three-piece band struck up, she reached a hand across the table and clutched his.

'Let's dance!'

'Of course.'

The band played a foxtrot, and then a waltz.

'I wonder if they know the Charleston!' she said.

'I understood the Charleston was rather specifically forbidden!'

'Oh, come on! I'll ask them.'

When the waltz was over she went and spoke to the band leader. Arthur had hoped the man had no knowledge of the Charleston, with any luck had never heard of it; so he was dismayed to see the chubby face break into a wide smile. Grace came floating back to him, holding out both hands, laughing merrily.

'I am the world's worst Charleston dancer,' Arthur protested.

'It doesn't matter!'

The music began; they danced, and Grace was wonderful. To Arthur's dismay none of their timid fellow-guests at The Hydro would dare the Charleston. Grace kicked up her heels, slapped her legs above the knees, a lovely smile on her happy face. Oh, it was virtually a solo performance, to which her partner contributed some inept steps, and when it was over the other diners clapped, and quite right too. Arthur led his bride back to their table.

'Just once in a while!' she said, recovering her breath. 'I am sometimes – a little disobedient. You will have to tolerate it,' she smiled.

He felt he could never be close enough to her. At night, in their room, standing at the window, with the riding lights of the drifter fleet sparkling on the bay, he said 'We will be very happy, you know.'

'I do know.'

'Always.'

'I think so.'

'You told me that always was a long time.'

'It will be long enough.'

'I believe it will.'

'Do you know what, Arthur? You're very romantic. I didn't realise how romantic you'd turn out to be.'

'Not a problem, I hope.'

'Oh, no! It's lovely.'

On the last night of their honeymoon he ordered champagne, at dinner.

'Champagne! I've never seen you drink,' Grace laughed, brushing the curls off her forehead.

'I'm not a teetotaller.'

'Good! Nor am I.'

'To us,' said Arthur, raising his glass.

'To us.'

'That's excellent champagne.'

'Are you an authority?'

'I know Moet et Chandon. Red Funnel Line ships are traditionally christened with a bottle of Moet et Chandon.'

'I'd like to propose another toast,' she said.

'That's allowed.'

'To success.'

He raised an eyebrow. 'I told you, success is of no importance to me.'

'I think it's important to us.'

'All right. To success, then.'

'Thank you for a wonderful honeymoon,' Grace said, suddenly whispering, across the little table. 'It was the most beautiful honeymoon a girl could have.'

'Even getting lost in the fog and having to walk down a mountain?' smiled Arthur.

'That especially. I'm sorry – I'm sorry there were some surprises.'

'You are all the more precious to me, Mrs Carruth.'

'You've never called me that before.'

'You'll have to get used to it.'

Later, in their big double bed, before they fell asleep, she said, 'Do you want to listen to it?'

'Listen?'

'Listen to my famous heartbeat. Lay your head there. Press your ear to my – breast. There. Do you hear it?'

'I'm not sure. I don't know.'

'Dr McKenzie gave me the stethoscope but I couldn't really hear.'

They moved into a furnished flat in Seaforth, a couple of stations down the line from Crosby. How happy they seemed, thought everyone.

The other Mrs Carruth, Arthur's mother, was not happy. She actually came to see Arthur in town, which she'd never done, but she needed to talk to him and he never went anywhere without Grace, except to the office. They met at the Kardomah Café on Bold Street, an old-established place where a lot of shipping people took their lunch. It was dark and noisy, with framed photographs of ships and worried-looking waitresses who wore brown dresses with white aprons, and pencils stuck into their hair. Its coffee was famous and probably the freshest in England because they had a contract with the Blue Star Line, which sailed to Brazil. The Kardomah was also well-known for its uniquely stodgy potato croquettes, which accompanied most of its luncheon dishes: mixed grill with potato croquettes, pork pie with potato croquettes, mushrooms on toast with potato croquettes. Scorning these dishes, Mrs Carruth ordered a cup of tea and a currant bun. Arthur selected the mixed grill, he loved potato croquettes, and the stodgier the better.

'She married you under false pretences,' his mother told him, when the waitress went away. She did not believe in beating around the bush.

'Whatever do you mean, Mother?'

'She never told you she has a weak heart.'

Arthur looked at his mother. He frowned. 'How do you know about that?'

'Everybody knows, at the club. She's given up tennis, doctor's orders.'

Arthur's mother was already buxom, but she hadn't taken to wearing multiple skirts yet. She still had her teeth. She didn't shut her mouth much. She wore a black coat with an imitation fur collar, and three strings of shiny beads. And she had a mind like a rat in a treadmill, it never stopped. She'd worked her fingers to the bone, and had no idea what rest was.

'Grace has a slightly irregular heartbeat, Mother. That's all. Her condition is not serious.'

'Have you spoken to the specialist?'

'I, personally? No.'

'Why not? She's your wife, isn't she?'

'Yes, she is my wife.'

'She has no right to be. She trapped you into marriage, Arthur. She knew she was sick, but she didn't tell you. She kept it from you, because if she'd told you, you'd have broken off the engagement.'

'I most certainly would not.'

'Then you'd have been a fool. As it is, you've been duped.'

'Mother,' said Arthur with his usual courtesy, 'you have absolutely no right to impute such motives to Grace.'

'Arthur, you may not like it, but you have to face up to the truth. Did she tell you before you were married?'

'No.'

'Then, when did she tell you?'

'On the first night of our honeymoon.'

His mother sipped her tea. She considered her point had been made, didn't she. 'You probably won't be able to have children,' she said.

'Whyever not?'

'Because the woman is an invalid, Arthur!'

'She is not an invalid.'

'The next thing we know, you'll be pushing her around in a bathchair. You don't need a wife like that, Arthur. She'll hold you back. You'll be looking after her, when you should be at work. You have great promise. That's what everybody says. You've done yourself proud. You've done the family proud, you've done us all proud. There's your poor brother, George, who's brilliant, and he can't get a job for love nor money. And you, who we all thought just an average scholar, Arthur – don't be offended again, it's the truth, and you know it – you are considered a rising star. You could get to the top, Arthur. You could get right to the top. You could finish up as Chairman of the Red Funnel Line. Chairman of the Cunard Line, if you set your mind to it. But not if you let that woman hold you back.'

Arthur drank his tea, but he pushed aside his mixed grill. It would be fair to say that he felt miserable.

'Grace will not hold me back, Mother,' he said.

'You say that. And you mean it. I know you have great ambition, Arthur. But all the same, she will hold you back. She'll need you to be with her. She'll make more and more demands on you. If you tell her you need to be at work late, she'll resent it. And that'll upset you. You're a very nice man, Arthur – too nice. Too nice for your own good.'

'What are you suggesting I do? Divorce her? You know I'd never do that.'

'No. I'm not suggesting you divorce her. I'm just warning you, Arthur. I'm warning you of the dangers.'

On a Sunday afternoon, Arthur and Grace had George over to their flat in Seaforth for tea. To their surprise, he positively bounced in, kissed Grace, and flung himself into an armchair.

'I believe you have to c-c-c-congratulate me, chaps,' he said. He wore an open-necked shirt, white sweater, and slacks. 'I've been offered a j-j-j-job, f-f-f-finally.'

'George, that's wonderful!' Grace exclaimed; she sat herself on the arm of George's chair and gave him a kiss.

'Good show, George,' said Arthur. 'Tell us.'

The job was as a laboratory technician for a company that made shoe polish. 'It may not be a w-w-w-wonderful job but at least it's a j-j-j-job, and quite honestly any job is b-b-b-better than k-k-k-kicking my heels around and g-g-g-going to interviews.'

'You'll probably be able to use the experience to land something better, when you've been there a year or so,' Arthur said.

'Well yes. Rather. That's the idea. The j-j-j-job means I'll have to move to L-l-l- london.'

'London?' cried Grace, both shocked and pleased.

'Yes, they want me to m-m-m-move to London.'

'Well – why not?'

'We'll come and see you in London. Won't we, Arthur?'

'Certainly we will. Just as soon as George has found his feet, we'll come down.'

'I've never been to London,' said Grace. 'I've always wanted to.'

'Anyway, I'm s-s-s-sorry to g-g-g-go on about myself,' George said. 'B-b-b-but I wanted you b-b-b-both to know.'

'Does Mother know?'

'No.'

'She won't like the idea of your moving to London,' Arthur said.

George lit a cigarette. 'She can g-g-g-go to blazes as far as I'm concerned. The prospect of living t-t-t-two hundred miles away from M-m-m-mother is very appealing.'

'Mother cares about you very much,' said Arthur.

'It's a b-b-b-bit scary, though, going to London. I mean, all my f-f-f-friends are here.'

'Join a tennis club,' suggested Arthur.

'Yes, I s-s-s-suppose I'll do that.'

'How are you going to break it to Mother?'

'C-c-c-arefully,' said George, with a sudden laugh.

Grace brought in a tray with tea and some little sandwiches, which George gobbled up; then he sat back and looked at them.

'You are the luckiest m-m-m-man in the world, Arthur,' was what he said.

'I think so too.'

'I always thought Grace was the prettiest g-g-g-girl in the c-c-c-club. When I introduced you two I n-n-n-never thought you'd get married. Otherwise I wouldn't have introduced you.'

George didn't often smile; what he did was tilt his head, like a bird, and challenge you to laugh.

'A great mistake, George,' his brother smiled.

'I didn't see it that way at the time. I always thought Grace would marry D-d-d-david Eaton.'

'Oh no!' laughed Grace. 'As soon as I met Arthur, Arthur was the only man for me.'

'Now Arthur has everything a m-m-m-man could wish for. A lovely wife, a g-g-g-great job. The c-c-c-curse of it is, I should have s-s-s-stayed on at university. I c-c-c-could have taken a Ph.D. Got a f-f-f-fellowship somewhere. Perhaps gone to Oxford, or C-c-c-cambridge, and become a d-d-d-don. You two could have come to s-s-s-see me at my rooms, I'd have g-g-g-given you sherry. I could have been Doctor G-g-g-eorge Carruth. Or even P-p-p-professor George Carruth. But Mother wouldn't hear of it. I had to get a j-j-j-job. Well, now I've g-g-g-got a b-b-b-bloody job. And I hope she's happy.'

After a few moments Arthur said, 'Well, I think the important thing now, George, however unsuitable you think the job is, is to make a success of it.'

'Well yes, that's all v-v-v-very well, but the truth is, it's a d-d-d-dead end job.'

Grace carried the tea out, George followed her with his eyes.

'She did the same for poor Enid,' George continued, while Grace was out of the room. 'Enid wanted to take d-d-d-dancing lessons, but oh no, she had to be a teacher, so she's at a bloody t-t-t-teachers' training college, and you're p-p-p-paying for it.'

'I'd have paid for her dancing lessons too.'

'Oh, I know.'

Arthur walked with George to the railway station. It wasn't the end of August yet, but leaves were coming down, and a mist crept off the sea, like phantom strangers climbing off the beach. Out on the Crosby Channel, the bell buoys clanged their mournful warnings as the tide tugged at them; autumn was on the way. The two brothers waited on the platform for the electric train. The station lights came on, all at once, a row of feeble bulbs; moths materialised to bombard them.

'The only g-g-g-good thing, is g-g-g-going to London. Do you think you and Grace will really c-c-c-come to see me?'

'Yes, George, of course we will.'

'They're not paying me much m-m-m-money, you know.'

'They know a bargain when they see one, I'm sure.'

'I envy you, Arthur.'

'You probably shouldn't,' said his brother, after a second.

'Why on earth not, you've g-g-g-got everything a m-m-m-man could wish for. You're going home to Grace, and I'm g-g-g-going home to M-m-m-mother.'

'Mother does not approve of our marriage, since she found out about Grace's heart condition.'

'I know about that. Worry about G-g-g-grace, but don't worry about Mother.'

The train was coming; electric sparks flew from its shoes as they brushed the live rail.

'I try not to. You know me, the infernal optimist.'

The train swept to a halt, the doors slid open. George stepped in.

'I still envy you!' he mouthed, again, with a wave.

Chapter Four

By the end of 1930 Arthur Carruth was earning four hundred and thirty-two pounds a year. And he'd been promoted again. Now he had an airy office with an oak desk, and a swivelling chair, upholstered in red with brass studs, and a window that looked across, should he need inspiration, at the Cunard building, which resembled, as well it might, a Gothic cathedral, all towers and gargoyles; you'd expect to see the Hunchback of Notre Dame making faces from the roof. Arthur's grand new office was on a floor with panelled walls, on which hung masterly oil paintings of the Red Funnel Line's early steamers, now long gone to the breakers, alas, or foundered on stormy reefs, or in two famous cases sent to the bottom by German torpedoes: hundreds of men, unrescued, had drowned in frigid waters.

And a brass plate on the outside of Arthur's door read 'Mr A. Carruth. Insurance Manager.'

What an interesting discovery the new manager made, too: every cargo carried by the Line was insured, of course, but as far as Arthur could make out, no claims seemed to have been filed since before the war, or if they had, there was no record. And it was unlikely, he thought, that no loss or damage had been sustained; very unlikely indeed, in fact, because pilferage was common at the docks, so common it was taken for granted, and cargoes were dropped from cranes, got wet at sea in rough weather. Did the fact no claims had been filed mean that the Red Funnel Line was miraculously immune to maritime disaster? Well, hardly. The *Admiralty Bay* had been severely damaged by fire alongside a wharf at Pernambuco, Brazil, loading copra, in 1926; and only one year later the *Hudson Bay*, a pretty ship, was in a collision, in fog, on the Clyde. Lloyd's of London had paid full compensation, in both cases. And as part of wartime reparations the Government had compensated the Line for the loss of its two fine ships torpedoed in the Western Approaches. But that was it. No record of any claim filed for loss or damage to cargo, not since 1914. So Arthur Carruth embarked on a massive task, he had to sift through sixteen years' worth of cargo manifests. Again and again, he found, the Line had reimbursed its customers for loss, as was right and proper, but filed no claims. Arthur went to the insurers. By combining charm with hard talk about future business, he was surprisingly successful at getting them to settle, even in cases where the insurers' own records had long ago been consigned to the archives. He strolled back from these meetings, hands in his pockets, whistling, enjoying the sun, and the Red Funnel Line found itself three and a half million pounds to the good.

Before long, Arthur realised he had influence. At a time when everyone else was reneging on building contracts, it was Arthur who talked the Board of the Red Funnel Line out of cancelling their order for a grand new ship, the twenty-five thousand ton *English Bay*, which was to be the flagship of the Line. The keel of this beauty had already been laid, at Cammell Laird's in Birkenhead; but Liverpool was in the throes of the Great Depression, ah, what a bad time it was, with many city businesses failing, fine buildings boarded up, hundreds of grey-faced unemployed workers lining up at soup kitchens. Arthur believed that in the circumstances Cammell Laird's might be willing to talk turkey. And the fact was that the Red Funnel Line had money in the bank, because it did business all over the world, and though some of its routes were hit, others were still doing well. Arthur reckoned that it would be at least two years before business as a whole started picking up, and when it did the Line, if it played its cards right now, would have a shiny new flagship, perhaps at a very good price. The Board listened to him, because Arthur made sense; he was young, but he made sense. There was a nodding of heads, though Poindexter, Alfred Poindexter, the Company Treasurer, made a brief speech stressing the wisdom of cancellation – 'given the current economic uncertainty.' Sir William Crashaw, Chairman of the Line, a short, wiry man with silvery hair and intensely blue eyes, leaned back in his chair. He thought for a few moments, then glared up at the crystal chandelier that overhung the Boardroom table.

'As I understand, Mr Carruth, you are suggesting we renegotiate our contract with the builders,' Sir William said to the chandelier.

'Yes, Sir William, for the reasons I have explained.'

'The Red Funnel Line, young man, has never sought to renegotiate a contract.'

'Never is too long,' said Arthur, after a moment.

Sir William lowered his gaze, looked around the table, looked at Arthur. 'I think you've changed our minds, Mr Carruth,' he said. 'Mr Poindexter has argued the advantages of cancellation. He's done his job. Thank you, Alfred, for being the conscience of the company. That's what we pay you for. We will renegotiate. Gentlemen, wish me luck.'

And a few days later Arthur received, through Sir William's timid secretary, an invitation to dinner at the Chairman's house, in Formby; 'Bring your wife,' Miss Gray whispered. Alfred Poindexter, who was a bachelor, had been invited also, and he very kindly offered to take them, in his car. Well, both Sir William and Lady Crashaw found Grace utterly charming; utterly, utterly; and Lady Crashaw was enormously impressed by Arthur, whom she described to her husband later as a 'delightful boy', although Arthur was now thirty-three years old and at least six inches taller than Sir William. That said, his hair was becoming disappointingly thin on top, and he wore rimless spectacles; his eyes were weak and tended to water. But he had an impressive presence, did Arthur; calm radiated out from him like ripples from a stone cast into the flat water of a woodland pool; he spoke quietly, and very precisely, still pronounced each word as if it was stolen from the Crown Jewels; he never needed to repeat himself. Yes, he was certainly going far; and his wife, Grace, in spite of her sour old mother-in-law's dire warnings, did not appear to be 'holding him back'; quite the contrary: she delighted in the limelight, success certainly mattered to her and she was out to charm, make no mistake.

Lady Crashaw was very interested in Grace's work for the unemployed.

'William,' she said to her husband, 'are we doing enough, these days?'

'We are going ahead with building the *English Bay*. I should have thought that was enough,' said Sir William, whose wife had always amused him.

Grace said, 'When you see the despair in their faces, Sir William, you realise that nothing is enough.'

'She's right, William,' said Lady Crashaw. 'Whatever my husband decides, Mrs Carruth, I will write you a personal cheque for a hundred pounds to enable your work of feeding the needy to continue.'

As the evening broke up Poindexter took Arthur's elbow. 'My congratulations, Arthur,' he said. 'You've made a big hit with the old man. I wouldn't want you to think I harbour any ill feelings, even if I did argue the other course. The decision has my complete support.'

'That is very handsome of you, Alfred,' Arthur acknowledged.

Though Arthur was a shrewd businessman, and though his fight to save the *English Bay* was based on sound business instinct, he knew he'd saved hundreds of jobs. He was distressed at the sight of hungry men lounging at the dock gates with no work: these men had fought in the war, and he'd fought with them; and sometimes he'd scrutinise their faces, as if in the hope of recognising a former comrade, though he never did. As for Grace, after a year, she'd gone back to teaching, again at Merchant Taylors' in Crosby; but during school holidays she helped in the soup kitchen set up near the Gladstone Dock, where she ladled soup to thousands of grim-eyed out-of-work dockers, and their families, twice a day.

Grace and Arthur had moved, a year before, out of their furnished flat in Seaforth to much larger, unfurnished, accommodation; the top two floors of a handsome house on Laburnum Avenue in Blundellsands. No longer would they live with someone else's furniture, or sleep in an absentee's bed; they would buy their own, which Arthur found a very intimate adventure.

'You're whistling!' Grace said, squeezing his hand. 'I like it when you whistle, because I know you're feeling cheerful.'

He'd been whistling unconsciously as they browsed the bedding department at Waring and Gillow's on Lord Street, where they eventually chose a bed with a polished cherry headboard, in the modern style: Grace wanted everything to be modern, she had a passion for modernity. The sales assistant tried to sell them matching bedside tables, but Grace said 'We never read in bed,' and laughed, and Arthur took his spectacles off, and dabbed his eyes.

And they'd gone back to Port Erin, on the Isle of Man, each year for a two-week holiday; stayed at The Hydro with its battlements and towers; taken long walks, and tramped through heather – he told her the difference between bell heather and ling – pummelled by the wind, they were, and gulls screamed at them. In the evening, at dinner, they danced a little to the three-piece band. The Charleston, to Arthur's relief, was no longer in favour; it had been superseded by the samba and the rumba, much less frenetic, and decidedly modern: Grace, of course, mastered both at once; Arthur never.

He admired her so. She now wore lovely crepe dresses, the hems just above her ankles, with a little fur stole to walk out. She laughed as readily as ever; she gave him sensible advice. He never left her out of his business life; her success was not only social, she was his mentor in many ways.

They fulfilled their promise to visit brother George in London. George had been laid off, but then, against the odds, rehired; all the same, he was out of work for seven weeks, and Arthur, at Grace's suggestion, paid the rent. But George had a wretched job, even if, on re-engaging him, they'd called him 'Product Development Consultant,' because they never took his advice; he couldn't persuade them to sell a liquid shoe polish he'd invented, and for which the world had to wait another thirty years. His spirits, when his brother and sister-in-law came to see him, were not high.

He met them, though, at Euston. They'd travelled down on The Merseyside Express, and eaten lunch off fine London Midland and Scottish Railway china, at a little table with a small Tiffany-style lamp, as the train sped across flat Cheshire, howled through the sandy tunnels of Staffordshire, pounded across the Midlands, hissed to a stop in the steamy caverns of Euston Station.

'Hello, ch-ch-ch-chaps.'

George insisted on carrying both their suitcases, and guided them down the escalators to the underground, and pushed them on to a Piccadilly Line train, and generally bossed them about. He lived in a depressing flat in Muswell Hill, the top floor of a grey-brick terraced house, reached on a trolley bus from the underground station, but only a short bus ride from the dreary laboratory where he worked; of course he gave them the room at the front, and slept, himself, on a settee in the room at the back, which had no other furniture but an empty cage, designed for some guinea pig or hamster, and left behind by a previous tenant.

Grace seemed dreadfully tired by the journey and asked if they'd excuse her while she lay down. 'I'm sorry, George,' she said. 'But in the morning, I'll be fun.'

The brothers sat across from each other at a formica-topped table in the miserable little kitchen (two gas-rings, greasy tiles). It was October, the sun was low, the small room full of shadows, half-human ones, as if the previous tenant had gassed himself, maybe after the guinea pig died.

'How is she, Arthur? Is she all r-r-r-right? I think of you two all the time, you know.'

'She seems to be fine. Of course, I look after her, in so far as she'll let me. As a matter of fact, we have an appointment with a specialist in Harley Street, in a couple of days.'

'I l-l-l-love her, Arthur. I've always loved her. I was m-m-m-mad as hell when you two started g-g-g-going out, but rather you than that idiot D-d-d-david Eaton, who was f-f-f-frightfully keen on her. It's kind of s-s-s-stupid, isn't it, two b-b-brothers being in l-l-l-love with the same g-g-g-girl, but I can't help myself, Arthur. I thought I'd g-g-g-got over it because it's been two years s-s-s-since I saw her, but as s-s-s-soon as I met you at Euston I realised that n-n-n-nothing's changed.'

'I know, George. I know, old chap.'

'You always knew?'

'I always knew.'

'Oh Christ. D-d-d-didn't realise it was s-s-s-so obvious. Don't worry, I won't make a f-f-f-fool of myself. I have my p-p-p-pride.'

'George, have you joined a tennis club, like we agreed you would?'

'Oh yes, I have, and it's n-n-n-not bad. In f-f-f-fact I thought we'd g-g-g-go there and you could m-m-m-meet some of the people. There are some decent sorts. Would you c-c-c-care for a game, whilst you're d-d-d-down here? I know Grace doesn't play anymore, but I thought, perhaps the two of us c-c-c-could take on the opposition.'

'With pleasure, but you seem to have forgotten what a lousy player I am,' Arthur smiled.

'Well you seem to have forgotten what a b-b-b-brilliant player I am,' said George. 'We can still b-b-b-beat them, even with you as my partner. Just don't get between m-m-m-me and the ball.'

'What about the job? It's still no better?'

'N-n-n-no, it's bloody awful, quite honestly.'

Arthur said, 'George, why don't you come back to Liverpool? I could get you a job with the Red Funnel Line.'

'N-n-n-no thanks, Arthur. It's awfully d-d-d-decent of you, and I know you would. But it wouldn't l-l-l-look good and I'd f-f-f-fluff the opportunity anyway.'

'The offer stands, George. I don't believe you would fluff the opportunity.'

'I would. And I could not be s-s-s-so beholden to you. No, I have to m-m-m-make it on my own, dear chap. I'm supposed to be the brilliant one, remember. Sooner or later I have to prove it, that's all. I have my pride – as I seem to keep s-s-s-saying.'

Grace and Arthur rode the Piccadilly Line, stood on the long escalators at Leicester Square. It was a fine, late autumn day; golden leaves hung gamely from the trees, the sky was a pale, silvery blue. They sauntered along Piccadilly; she clung to his hand, her face rosy with the crisp air, her brown curls blown about; they ambled through the Burlington Arcade, glancing at jewels; then they crossed Green Park towards the Mall, and in the park grey squirrels, to Grace's delight, scampered across the grass, begged and capered, spiralled up trees.

'It would be nice to walk on the grass, but I don't have the right shoes,' Grace said.

'Take them off,' smiled Arthur.

She looked at him, and saw that he meant it. He carried her shoes and she walked on the short sweet grass in stockinged feet. God! He'd carried women's shoes from an early age, had carried little Enid's on Crosby sands.

'It's cold!' she laughed. 'It's wet! But it's nice!'

She put her shoes on again when they reached the Mall; Arthur propped her up as she stood on one leg. A troop of the Royal Horse Guards clattered by on black horses, the autumn sun glinting on their polished breast-plates; and the Royal Standard fluttered over Buckingham Palace; His Majesty King George the Fifth was in residence. In St James's Park they watched Muscovy ducks cruise the lake, under the weeping willows. Foreigners in berets and plastic raincoats took photographs, and nannies in starched uniforms pushed wealthy babies in prams.

'If we had a baby, would we have a nanny, to push him in his pram?' Grace wondered.

She looked up at him. He touched the tip of her nose with his finger, kissed her lips.

They squinted up at Big Ben as it boomed twelve o'clock. A silent crowd of unemployed waited outside the

Houses of Parliament; policemen with their hands clasped firmly behind their backs strolled up and down, in case of a scuffle, but there was no sign of any: a few of the demonstrators held up banners; pleas for work. Grace watched the crowds for a few minutes.

'How terrible.'

'One's heart goes out,' said Arthur.

'Can we sit down somewhere?'

They went into a café but it was noisy and crowded, trays clattered, waitresses pushed their way between tables, and everybody looked as if they were about to cry; they backed out and crossed Parliament Square, skirting sullen agitators; and entered Westminster Abbey, where they sat on little cane seats with prayer books and hymnals in wooden pockets. Grace laid her head on Arthur's shoulder; her face, so rosy earlier on, was pale. He breathed the faint perfume she'd dabbed on her neck.

'I'm sorry I seem to get so tired so quickly,' she smiled.

'I expect it's London,' said Arthur. 'In the Isle of Man we walk for miles, don't we?'

'We did. I'm not sure I could again.'

'Then we'll stay in bed, and listen to the seagulls, and pretend.'

'What shall we pretend?' she said, after a moment.

'We shall pretend to be seagulls. Or puffins. Wouldn't you like to be a puffin? Or an albatross. Or a sailing ship.'

'All right. Perhaps a puffin. Puffins seem to have a good time, and they don't take too much strenuous exercise.'

The next day, Grace and Arthur arrived for their appointment with the Harley Street specialist. It was a very quiet, handsome, Georgian house, and they were shown into a charming room with deep armchairs and glass-fronted bookcases, where a fine grandfather clock, its face inscribed with the name of a Scottish maker, and hand-painted with the sun and moon and two angels holding roses, tick-tocked very slowly, as if it had the capacity of slowing down time, and perhaps prolonging the lives of the specialist's patients.

After Sir Geoffrey had examined Grace he escorted her back to his beautiful waiting room, where Arthur stood with his hands thrust deep into his pockets, inspecting Sir Geoffrey's books; he'd actually caught himself whistling, for a moment, had Arthur, and been shocked at himself.

The distinguished doctor was a very tall man, with a deeply lined face and the complexion of a chestnut, as if he'd spent years in the sun; and he wore a beautifully-cut suit of pale grey. Arthur looked at Grace, who met his eyes.

'Mr Carruth,' said Sir Geoffrey, whose voice was very soft for such a large man, 'I have explained to your wife that she has a quite unusual heart condition; from a medical point of view, a not uninteresting one. Unfortunately, there isn't really a whole lot we can do. I have prescribed medication, which she is to take every night before retiring, but I must stress that the important thing is to ensure she has as much rest as possible. Gallivanting around London, for instance, is not what I would recommend. Nor is working in soup kitchens. I think she can continue teaching. The main thing is to avoid any kind of undue stress, or excitement. I don't think this means your life has to be boring but – no excitement. I stress this because I believe your wife has a wilful streak. But if she behaves herself, I think she will live for a good few years.'

He took them to his front door.

'I'm sorry I don't have better news, but it's not all bad. Oh, and Mr Carruth, take a cab home.'

Grace burst into tears in the street, and hung on Arthur's neck.

'Oh, Arthur! I want to be a puffin! I want to be a – what else did you say? An albatross. A sailing ship… I don't want to be an invalid.'

'I won't let you be an invalid, Grace,' he promised her. 'I'll look after you better. We'll go for walks. Just not too long ones. We won't ever be bored. You, and I, bored? Impossible! I'll tell you things. I'll tell you the names of everything. I'll tell you the names of all the birds. I know most of them. I'll tell you the names of all the trees, and all the wild flowers. All the butterflies, and all the different kinds of moss, and mushrooms. The names I don't know, I'll find out. I'll tell you the names of all the ships that go out to sea.'

'Yes. And tell me the names of all the dances. All the dances I can't dance. Tell me the names of all the games. All the games I can't play.'

He clutched her against him, between the streetlights that had come on, as if his heart could beat for the two of them. 'I'll tell you,' he promised.

'Don't let me die, Arthur,' she whispered.

'I won't let you die.'

'It's so dark, where dead people go. I want it to be light, wherever I am.'

He hailed a cab.

Grace was a brave woman, thank goodness: she got over the fright Sir Geoffrey had given her, and the next day she was laughing about it.

'Let's go to a show!' she said. 'We can't be in London and not go to the theatre! But nothing exciting, remember! Find something boring, Arthur!'

'How about *The Importance of Being Earnest,* by Oscar Wilde? It's supposed to be an excellent production.'

'I thought it was supposed to be funny. Am I allowed to laugh?'

'Of course you're allowed to laugh!'

'Am I allowed to cry? Maybe there's something tragic we could see.'

'*Romeo and Juliet?*'

'Much too exciting. Swordfights. Duels to the death. Poison.'

They couldn't decide, so in the end, instead of going to a show, they took George to the Trocadero, at Piccadilly Circus – poor old George couldn't afford even the occasional trip to the West End – and the Trocadero was where everybody went to dance, to the latest dances, played by the latest bands. The Troc, which was what the in-crowd called it, was a huge pink and golden palace, with lots of small tables, each one with a dainty pink-shaded lamp, and pink padded chairs, and it had a stage, with a proscenium lit by chaser lights, and gold lamé curtains that hung in puckered folds. At ten o'clock, the curtains would be raised, and showgirls in top hats and stockings with frilly garters would dance the Parisian can-can, but until showtime, everybody danced, and waitresses balanced

Singapore Slings and Tom Collinses and Angostura Fizzes on tiny round trays.

George had put on his best suit, which didn't fit him: for some reason, nothing fitted George, but it didn't matter, he looked angelic as ever, with his tousled hair, and his long, serious, face.

The band struck up a samba; Grace leaned across and grabbed Arthur's hand.

'I want to dance!' she said, her eyes sparkling.

'Sir Geoffrey wouldn't approve,' smiled Arthur.

'Well, damn Sir Geoffrey! He won't find out!'

He danced with her. She looked ravishing, too, in a long, lavender dress with a flimsy little scarf; she'd had her hair done for the occasion, she'd found a small salon in Muswell Hill; her brown curls flopped about her forehead. When he led her back to their table George stood up and requested the honour; Grace whisked him off to the dance floor. George was a superb dancer: they danced three numbers together, swayed and jitterbugged, and she came back laughing happily.

'Dance with me again, Arthur!' she begged.

'We should probably go home.'

'Does that mean you're looking after me?'

'It means you're being wilful, as Sir Geoffrey warned.'

'All right. We'll sit this one out.'

But she looked so forlorn, sitting there, tapping her toes to the music, staring wistfully at the dancers, that he stood up and escorted her back to the floor, where she leaned lazily against him; their bodies swayed to the beat of the rumba; their lips met.

'Sir Geoffrey's an awful old quack,' she said. 'I feel terrific.'

'You're not at all tired?'

'I don't feel tired a bit!'

He took her back to Liverpool, on Sunday, on the night train, which had sleeping cars, because he thought it would exhaust her less. They boarded the train at eleven, after saying good-bye to George. An attendant brought them tea; they declined a brandy. Arthur held her very tightly all night; they woke up once, she kissed him.

'I am doomed,' she whispered. 'You are much too exciting for me.'

'Then I'll make myself boring.'

The train rushed quietly through the night, clattering over points, leaning through curves, thundering past stations, the locomotive whistling like a lost owl.

'Do you know where this train is going?' she smiled.

'Liverpool, unless we got on the wrong one. Perhaps we'll wake up in Scotland.'

'Our destination is tomorrow.'

'What do you mean?'

'That's where it's taking us. We got on board yesterday. We'll get off tomorrow. Where we go is incidental. The important thing is, it'll be tomorrow. And I'll have lived another day.'

Mrs Annie Sadie Carruth, after her earlier warnings, now approved of Grace, though her approval was qualified: Arthur, true, was doing very well, though it still pained her that George languished in that dead-end job of his in London, for all his brains, whilst Arthur shone. However, there were two problems with Grace, as far as the older

Mrs Carruth was concerned: she and Arthur had no children, and the woman couldn't cook for toffee. Grace made no pretence, she bought things ready-made. On most Sundays, she and Arthur ate at the big house in Crosby, but sometimes they took the electric train to Southport and had lunch there, then strolled along the lengthy pier. The sea, for some reason, had receded at Southport since the pier was built, and only at the very end of it could you look down at waves. Also, because the coast trended northwards after Crosby, Liverpool shipping was rarely visible; you might, with good binoculars, detect a smudge of smoke on the horizon, and Arthur did in fact bring binoculars, and he could sometimes name the ship from its smudge of smoke; if there'd been any prizes for this remarkable skill, he'd have won hands down.

There was snow on the ground in December 1931. Grace and Arthur always took a short morning walk before Arthur caught the train to Liverpool, and Grace made snowballs and threw them at him. Ducking to avoid them, Arthur scooped up snow and shied snowballs back at her. Being, God knows, a gentleman, he took care to miss, but, being Arthur, a duffer at games, he hit her; with her hands on her knees she rocked with laughter. Then she hit him with one snowball after the other.

'I'll miss my train!' Arthur protested.
'Are you bored already?' she laughed.
'I am never bored!'

They ran at each other through the snow, and a light breeze shook snow down on them from the trees overhead, like confetti, as if they were newly-weds. When Arthur got home that night he found that Grace had built a snowman in their front garden on Laburnum Avenue, and propped a pair of his spectacles on its empty face.

'You should have seen Grace's snowman,' he said, as the family all arrived for Christmas dinner, in Crosby. 'He was a very fine snowman. He was nearly as tall as me, and he was wearing my glasses.'

'He was supposed to be you,' laughed Grace.

'I wish I'd seen him,' said Enid. 'If it snows again, will you help me make another one, Grace?'

'Certainly. Shall we make him look like Walter?'

Enid glanced at her fiancé and blushed. 'No. Let's make him look like Mother.'

'We'll pinch one of her big black hats, he'll be the living image,' Grace promised.

The older Mrs Carruth bustled in, carrying steaming dishes. 'I thought Grace was not supposed to do things like that,' she said, putting mashed potatoes on the table, and soggy sprouts.

'Oh, no one's said anything about not making snowmen,' Grace said, with pretended innocence. 'Did you have snow in London, George? Did you make a snowman?'

'We had a l-l-l-little s-s-s-snow, but I d-d-d-didn't make a s-s-s-snowman.' George had arrived home the day before; Arthur had sent him money for his railway ticket, then met him at Lime Street Station. George was not in a jolly mood.

'I g-g-g-got out at Crewe,' he said. 'I had a c-c-c-cup of tea in the buffet and d-d-d-decided to go back to London, but I'd left my suitcase on the train and by the t-t-t-time I f-f-f-found it the train was moving.'

They'd stopped off at the house in Blundellsands and Grace had poured George a sherry.

'The silly old fool nearly didn't come,' Arthur said.

Grace put her arms round George and kissed him. 'Poor dear George,' she said, because she thought there was a tear in his eye. 'Promise to be good tomorrow and not upset your mother.'

'Oh, I'll be g-g-g-good.'

Enid's fiancé, Walter Miller, had wavy chestnut hair, very tired-looking pale blue eyes, a huge nose, and a brown woollen suit. He didn't say much, and was ill at ease in the company of so many Carruths; smoked incessantly, too, in fact Enid had to nudge him to put out his cigarette before they all sat down around the table. Her mother brought in the turkey and her father, who was beginning to look bony, and shook a bit, carved it.

'Don't give Walter too much,' Enid said. 'Just a little white meat, and no potatoes or sausages or sprouts or anything. He doesn't eat a lot.'

'That's because he smokes too much,' said the older Mrs Carruth.

There was still snow on the ground, like soap flakes on washing day, but Christmas Day was bright and sunny; and sunlight streamed through the tall windows of the yellow-brick house and made people squint. It was a jolly occasion, in spite of George's low spirits and Walter's apparent preoccupation with distant subterranean objects.

Enid had met Walter Miller at the tennis club. His father, a Chief Engineer with the Cunard Line, having died at sea, Walter's diminutive wisp of a mother had somehow reared Walter and his brother, Greg, on the scant pension she was entitled to. They must have eaten very little; Walter remained sparrow-chested; you were aware, whatever he wore, of his ribs and shoulder blades. Walter was the older brother, and as soon as he could he left school and signed on as a galley hand with the Elder Dempster Line. He was miserable as soon as he stepped on board. He was given a rough time, because he was timid and ashamed of his poor build. The day before the ship sailed, for Lagos, Nigeria, and other lagoons, other rivers, Walter remembered that he was scared to death of drowning. The reason he was scared to death of drowning was that he'd been pushed into the deep end of a public swimming pool by some lout, at the age of nine. He couldn't swim, and had come up for the third time when an attendant fished him out. He retained a wariness of water all his life, and although he was later to become a fine photographer who loved to take pictures of breaking waves and flying spray, he preferred it to be from land. He jumped ship. He was too scared to tell anyone, so he just walked down a gangway and out of the dock, terrified that somebody would come running after him and make him go back on board. He walked around Liverpool for three days, starving because he had no money and didn't dare go home penniless and jobless; he thought it would break his tiny mother's heart. He walked into every non-maritime business he saw, until they gave him a job as an office boy at Ogden's Tobacco on Binns Road. On his second day he fainted because he'd had nothing to eat since he left the ship. They gave him a small advance. One shilling. It was plenty.

He was now aged twenty-seven and a clerk in the sales department, but he'd been offered a place on the next training course. If he did well, he'd become a sales representative, with a territory of his own, which could be anywhere in England and Wales, or Scotland, or Northern Ireland.

He'd joined the tennis club a year ago, at the instigation of a chum from the office; his little old mother was tickled pink: a tennis club! Walter was not a particularly good player, though much better than Arthur, but he loved dancing, and was useful enough on the dance floor to dare ask the woman he considered the prettiest in the club, Enid Carruth, to dance with him.

And what an attractive woman she had indeed grown up to be, our Enid, with thick black curls and a very pale, very pure complexion, and a beautiful figure; though she wasn't slight enough to have made a ballerina. She was a kindergarten teacher; and she absolutely adored children; at school she always seemed to be covered with them. She'd sit on the floor, with toys and books, teaching them to count and spell, and there'd be tots balancing on her shoulders, and sitting on her lap, and lying on their backs between her legs. Enid had also inherited something of her mother's boldness, not to say her cheek, and her impatience. There was a sparkle in her eye; she had a temper, but most of the time she kept it tightly bottled up.

In fact, she was the only one of the three children who seemed at all like a Carruth. There was something basic about her that her two brothers didn't share at all. Arthur and George had a polish that was, to say the least, lacking in their parents; no doubt it was a reaction, because they couldn't have been more unlike their cantankerous mother or their idle father if they'd tried.

Neither Annie Sadie nor Arthur Simon Carruth particularly approved of Enid's choice of fiancé. They had much preferred Jeffrey Talbot, a young man she'd brought home before. With a jutting jaw and a keen eye, he seemed to them to have the ambition and the self-confidence that mousy, self-absorbed, altogether too quiet Walter Miller didn't. But Enid was a dangerous young woman to cross. They would live with her choice, but they clung to the hope that somebody better would turn up before she actually married. At least they'd managed to prevail upon Enid to defer the date until Walter was more firmly established.

Grace handled her not easy mother-in-law adroitly. Sometimes she even made her laugh, which no one else did. Mrs Carruth had already chuckled over the idea of a snowman in the likeness of Arthur, whom she thought increasingly pompous.

'George has a wonderful new idea for a liquid shoe polish,' Grace announced. 'But his company won't listen. Their heads are buried in the sand. Ostrich Brand Shoe Polish, that's what they should call it.'

Mrs Carruth Senior laughed out loud.

'Maybe the idea wouldn't work.' Everyone looked at Mr Carruth Senior. Because of some digestive weakness he would cut his food into very small pieces, then chew each piece for ages, with his mouth open.

'Of course it would work,' Grace said loyally.

'Well, I think it's a shame my son George is fiddling around inventing shoe polish when he could be a top chemist,' said his mother.

'What does a top chemist do?' asked Enid.

'He invents new kinds of shoe polish,' said Grace.

'George only needs time,' said his brother Arthur.

'Your son George is a marvellous dancer,' said Grace, changing the subject. 'He could be a ballroom dancing champion. He could be in the movies, and wear a top hat and tails. He could dance with Enid. I've never danced with Enid myself, but Walter says she's terrific. Why is it I end up with the only Carruth who can't dance?' she laughed.

Mrs Carruth laughed again.

'George,' said his mother, 'you're eating like a pig. Don't you ever eat, in London? You need a woman to look after you. You need to get married, George. Here's Arthur married to Grace, and Enid's engaged to marry Walter, so what are you doing? Find yourself a good wife. Am I ever going to have grandchildren?'

'I'm sure you'll have lots of grandchildren, Mrs Carruth,' said her daughter-in-law. 'George will marry, one of these days, and Walter and Enid will have children.'

Walter stared into space, completely baffled by this family, who talked of things that would never be mentioned by his meek and beloved little mother.

'Yes, we will,' said Enid, not abashed at all.

When the turkey had been taken out Mrs Carruth brought in a Christmas pudding, holding the basin with oven-mitts. Grace clapped her hands.

'We should pour brandy on it and light it!' she said.

'We don't have brandy,' said her mother-in-law.

'Do you disapprove?'

'No. But we don't have it.'

'Next Christmas, Arthur and I will bring a bottle of brandy,' Grace promised.

'Indeed we will,' said Arthur. 'And perhaps a bottle of claret.'

'My, oh my,' said his mother. 'You two are getting highfalutin'. The next thing we know, you'll have us all drinking champagne.'

'I hope so,' said Arthur, taking out a handkerchief to dab his eyes.

'Moet et Chandon!' said Grace. 'We must all acquire a taste for Moet et Chandon.'

It was a family custom at the Carruths to exchange Christmas presents after the meal. After much to and froing between the front room and the dining room, and some giggling and excuse-me's, a small pile of gaily-wrapped boxes stood in front of everyone's place at table. The men traditionally received ties, boxed sets of handkerchiefs, and socks, but Grace gave Arthur a pair of expensive cufflinks, which were admired by everybody, and he gave her a small necklace with minute green stones, which she adored and put on immediately. Arthur gave his sister Enid a pair of earrings, which she exclaimed over happily. Walter was mortified because he hadn't bought anyone anything, though he received tartan socks and a handsome silk tie.

Later in the afternoon the McMahons came by for tea. Mrs McMahon had prematurely silver hair, but lots of it, in tight curls; she had a ready smile and spoke in a low voice very quickly. Pat had inherited the dove-like voice. She was now seventeen. She had long brown hair tied loosely at the back with a black ribbon, and very fine features, with dark eyebrows, a thin nose, and high cheekbones, her cheeks slightly sunken, already, from pain. She had no make-up but a drop or two of perfume. She wore a black blouse with a shawl, presumably her mother's, and a long black skirt.

'How are you feeling, Pat?' Arthur enquired kindly.

'Much better,' she said, after a second, in that slightly breathless low voice of hers.

'Two operations,' said her mother. 'Two operations already, at her age. Can you imagine what the poor girl has been through? But she has the courage of a lion.'

It was difficult to think of such a fragile being in leonine terms, but she was certainly courageous, Pat was.

'We have a present for you, Pat,' Arthur said. 'It's from Grace and myself.'

It was a silk scarf, very flimsy, and dark green; so Pat took off her shawl and wrapped the scarf around her thin white neck.

'Thank you so much.' She kissed both Arthur and Grace lightly on their cheeks.

'We were just going out for a short walk, to work off our huge Christmas dinner,' Grace said. 'Pat, would you like to come?'

Pat glanced at her mother, who had drawn a chair up close to Mrs Carruth; the two were chatting happily.

'Well yes, I think I could manage that,' Pat said. 'As long as it's not too far.'

'I'm not allowed to go far,' Grace smiled.

Arthur walked the two of them, one on each arm, as far as the Southport Road. The short day was coming to an end, and the low sun made the snow look blue under the trees. Grace laid her head on Arthur's shoulder as they walked. From the Crosby Channel came the low boom of foghorns.

Chapter Five

She was two years building, was the Red Funnel Line's new flagship, *English Bay*. For two years the yards at Cammell Laird's had echoed to the pounding of steel hammers; and towering cranes had circled overhead like prehistoric birds; and the welders' torches roared, splashing bright showers of yellow sparks; and in the machine shops, huge presses forced curves into three-quarter inch steel. From the decks of the Birkenhead ferries, ploughing their tireless furrows through the brown, sloppy waters of the Mersey, passengers on their way to work in Liverpool watched the great ship grow, saw it slowly emerge from its cocoon of iron scaffolding. Then, for a day and a night, like the thunder of a distant cannonade, came a crash, and a crash, and a crash, as men swung enormous mallets, knocking away the stout oak chocks which supported the hull; till it stood poised on the greased slipway which it would slide down, come morning. And this was when men were killed in shipyards, crushed like beetles if an obstruction had to be hammered clear; which was why, after the speech-making, when the champagne bottle swung across, a thousand wives and mothers held their breaths, and a thousand men in cloth caps shut their eyes until they heard the sound of cheering, and then they flung their caps high, high in the air, and wondered when they'd be next employed.

A soft grey rain fell on the morning of May 28th, so the crowds who had gathered to watch the launch wore mackintoshes and carried umbrellas, and rain ran down their necks, and members of the Salvation Army Brass Band, the men in dark raincoats, the women with black ribbons in their hats, kept having to tip water out of their instruments. A wooden platform had been put up, with a striped canvas awning, and microphones, and it was so decked out with flags and pennants you'd think it would fly away, with all the grandees and bigwigs aboard waving down. The hull glistened with new paint, coal-black above the waterline, fire-red below; and the Red Funnel Line's proud house flag hung from the jackstaff, while the red ensign, flag of the British merchant marine, drooped at her stern; and a hundred miles of coloured ribbon stretched up to her bulwarks; and there on her bow her name was emblazoned, each letter cast in bronze, *ENGLISH BAY*.

The rain slackened off during the speeches, and an aeroplane droned overhead, appearing out of low clouds, then swallowed back up in them. On the brown river tugs flocked, smoke blasting from their tall yellow funnels; and the busy Birkenhead ferries trundled to and fro; and this, surely, was the centre of the known universe.

In spite of the microphones, no one among the sopping crowds could hear the speeches, or probably cared to, because they were here to watch the awful drama of a twenty-five thousand ton hull sent stern first into the river. Sir William Crashaw, though, had said, at one point, 'Two years ago, when most of us couldn't see our way out of the Depression, we were faced with a choice: cancel our order for the *English Bay*, or proceed. The wisdom of the time said 'cancel'. Our highly-paid financial advisors said 'cancel'. Our competitors at the Cunard Line said 'cancel'.

Derogatory cheering, by the few who heard him, at the expense of Cunard; who had, only a month ago, finally decided to go ahead and start work on the *Mauritania*, whose keel was now being laid in the next slip. Oh, Cunard had bided their time, but there was a strong rumour now that orders for two vast Cunarders, which would be the biggest ships in the world, had been awarded to John Brown's of Clydebank, because the Mersey wasn't deep enough to float an eighty-thousand ton vessel.

'One man offered different advice,' Sir William continued. 'He was a young fellow whose first job in the company was in the mail room. He exhibited, from early on in his career, a rare diligence, as a result of which he was promoted, and continued to be promoted. But he possessed something more than diligence. He possessed a shrewd instinct. It was this instinct which led him to advise us against cancellation. One voice against many. One voice. To our credit – I like to think – we listened to that one voice. Ladies and gentlemen, our newest Board member, Mr Arthur Carruth.'

Arthur took the microphone, but whatever he had to say was drowned by the noise of the circling aeroplane, which emerged from the clouds again to make a low pass over the yard; Arthur resumed his place at the back of the platform to sporadic applause, and Lady Crashaw came forward; there was, finally, a hush. Flags stirred in a sudden breeze; under the leaden sky, whitecaps whipped across the Mersey.

'My pleasant task,' Lady Crashaw said, and hundreds of sodden spectators tried to hear what she said, 'is to introduce to you all Mrs Grace Carruth, who will launch this splendid ship. Mrs Grace Carruth is not only the wife of Arthur Carruth, who as you've just heard was instrumental in having construction of the Line's new flagship continue at a time when hoarier heads, my husband's included, were saying 'no'. Mrs Grace Carruth is also a woman who worked for two and a half years in the soup kitchens at the Gladstone Dock, helping to feed the needy. She laboured unstintingly at this task, in spite of warnings from her doctors that she should stop. She ignored their advice, putting her own health at risk, so that others, less fortunate, could have at least a bowl of soup each day. Ladies and gentlemen, Mrs Grace Carruth.'

The aeroplane had vanished. A ship's siren boomed, from out on the river. Mrs Grace Carruth, in a long white dress with a grey fur wrap, stepped forward. But she didn't make a speech, she just said, as was traditional, 'I name this ship *English Bay*, and I wish her, and all who sail in her, Godspeed, and good fortune.'

She raised the magnum of Moet et Chandon and the bottle was whisked away from her on its wire, to shatter against the bow of the ship. In the sudden silence, the tinkle of broken glass must have been audible across the Mersey. The great hulk remained motionless, for a few agonising seconds, then it moved, at first very slowly, then faster, and as it moved faster, the lines of ribbons snapped, one after the other; coloured ribbons were fluttering down over the crowd, as they lowered their umbrellas. The stern reached the river; setting up a huge wave, then another, then another; the afterbirth of the grand ship reached the Landing Stage, at Liverpool, rocked the ferries as they strained at their mooring lines. The *English Bay* was afloat, nuzzled by a dozen tugboats; later in the morning, she would be moved to the fitting-out basin, where her engines would be installed, her superstructure built. It was raining again. On the forgotten launching platform, hands were shaken, beams exchanged. Hero for a few brief moments, Arthur took his wife's hand. 'I wasn't excited a bit,' she gasped.

'A beautiful launch, a beautiful launch,' Sir William enthused. 'And a proud day for you, Mr Carruth. My hearty congratulations.'

'Nicely done, my dear,' Lady Crashaw whispered to Grace.

'My congratulations too, Arthur,' said Alfred Poindexter. 'As Sir William said, I don't think we'll regret this thing.'

'I sincerely hope not,' Arthur smiled.

'It's nice to see our friends at Cunard following our lead for once,' said Sir William, meaning the *Mauritania* order, though he would also have heard about the two eighty-thousand ton monsters. 'They obviously share our confidence in the future. We've been through bad times, but we've survived them, and the Line is in as good a shape as it's ever been. Now Arthur, we expect to see you and your lovely wife aboard for the speed trials. Ten months from now: because we're holding Cammell Laird's to their schedule. The *English Bay* will be earning revenue by the end of next year.'

At night, after a great dinner at the Adelphi Hotel, hosted by Sir William Crashaw, Arthur stroked Grace's cold cheek.

'Was this the face that launched a thousand ships, And burned the topless towers of Ilium?' he smiled.

'One ship is enough,' she said.

'Sir Geoffrey said nothing about launching ships.'

'I launched her for you. She's your ship.'

'Oh – in a way, I suppose you could say so.'

'To success!' Grace smiled.

'But think of the responsibility!' said Arthur, with a rueful laugh.

Arthur's mother was upset that she hadn't been invited to join the launching party on the platform, and she did not accept Arthur's explanation that only directors of the company, with their spouses, and representatives of the builders, and of course the Mayors of Birkenhead and Liverpool, would be there. However, it wasn't long before Annie Sadie Carruth's wide circle of acquaintances, including all the customers of her laundry, knew that her son was a director of the Red Funnel Line, and that her daughter-in-law Grace had launched the *English Bay*, and they were reminded of both facts constantly, in case they forgot.

Arthur's father, Arthur Simon Carruth, who hadn't lifted a brush in years, announced that he might try a painting of the new ship as she was fitting out, if he had the time, and Arthur did his best to hold him to that decision; rode with him on the Birkenhead ferry and took him to the fitting-out basin. This was one of the bony old gentleman's increasingly rare outings; he walked with a stick, and held on to Arthur's arm, for comfort as well as support: he didn't like the world very much. It was a fine day in July though, an easy to day to like, surely; seagulls mewed and hung on a fresh wind coming off the sea. The *English Bay's* triple expansion steam engines, which were expected to give her a cruising speed of twenty knots, had already been lifted into her; and work had begun on her superstructure; giant cranes lowered prefabricated sections; the oxyacetylene torches of the welders roared. The artist took out his sketch pad, and worked for an hour on some preliminary ideas; no doubt the finished work would show every rivet.

Then he said, 'I'm tired now,' and shut up his sketchbook and dropped his pencils into a black canvas bag. 'I want to go home.'

Arthur received a letter of congratulation on his appointment to the Board from his brother George. How odd it was to read George's letters, which were fluent, even racy: it was like listening to George himself, miraculously cured of his stammer. In his reply, Arthur repeated his standing offer of a job, but George did not write back, so Grace suggested Arthur make the offer official, using the company's stationery, naming the position and exact salary, but Arthur wasn't keen, he thought this would only irritate George, hurt his pride.

George's unhappiness upset Grace. 'If only poor old George would marry somebody,' she said. 'I hate to think of him down there all on his own in that horrible flat.'

'Let's hope he meets somebody nice at the tennis club.'

'I wouldn't mind marrying somebody with a stammer. Would you mind it if I stammered?'

'Not a bit.'

'And I wouldn't mind if you did.'

'Well, George didn't stammer when he was a child. He began when he was eight. The doctors say it was all his mother's doing. She had such high expectations. Fortunately, she never had high expectations for me, otherwise you might indeed be married to a stammerer.'

'No. Your mother would never have upset you. Nobody ever does, nobody and nothing. Don't you realise, that's what your mother resents. It ticks her off, that she can't rattle you. You are unannoyable.'

Arthur may have been unannoyable, but he'd also lost more hair, and he wore thicker glasses. But he was still by any standards a handsome man, dressed soberly in well-cut suits. They made a handsome couple, without a doubt.

Grace needed lights on all the time; she was really obsessive, now, about light; hated dark corners, didn't even like to see cupboard doors kept closed, light had to be everywhere, their flat would have been no place for a mouse, or an insomniac. She wore more make-up than she used to, and felt betrayed by the laugh lines that spread from her eyes. 'I shouldn't have laughed so much,' she lamented sometimes.

As a director of the Line, Arthur was expected to entertain, and as the wife of a director of the Line, Grace was expected to entertain with him. They became excellent entertainers, they held receptions at the flat in Blundellsands, hosted cocktail parties at the Adelphi Hotel, took important people to the theatre – to the Playhouse, in Williamson Square, or the Liverpool Empire – and to concerts at the Liverpool Philharmonic. Though he took his social responsibilities seriously, Arthur often wished he was tramping the moors of the Isle of Man instead, and sometimes his mind wandered there, and he found himself whistling. This amused Grace, who was in her element, she loved it all, the parties, the plays, the music, the attention. And they were very popular, Arthur and Grace were.

One night, when they got home from the Phil (Arthur had no ear for music, but Grace had become enamoured of it, and especially of passionate romantic music) Grace said, 'There's one thing we must never forget.'

'Which is?' smiled Arthur, taking off his bow tie – before the concert, they had hosted a small dinner party at the Adelphi, their guests including the Chairman of the Mersey Docks and Harbour Board, and his wife, together with the Vice Consul for Chile.

'That we are more important than anyone we meet.'

'We are indeed.'

'We give so much of our time to – others. Perhaps we should reserve some special time for you and me.'

'You're right. I'll reserve some tomorrow.'

So that weekend they took the train to Chester, where they stayed at the Blossoms Hotel, and walked, arm in arm, along the beautiful Rows, those unique, arcaded, elevated promenades, and squinted up at towering gables, lofty pinnacles, mullioned windows, and soaring roofs: a walk they might have made four centuries earlier, she in a wimple, he in doublet and hose, and good they'd have looked. Down to earth, they browsed in shops, and in the end Grace tried on jewellery, and Arthur bought her a charming necklace, with tiny diamonds.

Afterwards they rode in a chunky motor launch on the River Dee, along with a bus-load of excited children in school uniform, grey skirts and pants, and little black blazers with thin yellow stripes, and Grace wanted to buy them all ice creams, so Arthur did, over the teachers' objections. They cruised past the rose-grey walls of the city, where strolling tourists stared down, the river a wet carpet of fallen leaves.

'This is like being on honeymoon again,' she said. 'What were those birds you said we could pretend to be, when we get too old?'

'Puffins,' smiled Arthur, after a second, dabbing with a handkerchief at his weak eyes.

Enid was to be married to Walter Darwin Miller at the end of September: to the disappointment of her mother, nobody 'better' had turned up. Walter, though, had performed very well on the training course, so he'd been recommended for promotion to sales representative as soon as a territory became available, which gave his self-confidence a boost, and he lost that habit of staring, with a perplexed look, into space below the table. Once he'd learned to talk to people there was no stopping him; within minutes he'd often be telling total strangers about his precarious start in life; about his father's early death, at sea, of cancer; about his frail little mother's struggle to raise two boys on a pittance from the Cunard Line; about signing on as a galley hand with the Elder Dempster Line and then realising that he hated the sea; about joining the tennis club at Crosby and dancing with Enid Carruth of the sparkling eyes and thick black curls. His lack of pretence, his readiness to seek advice – advice about the best way to go about his job, advice about how to deal with difficult customers, advice about cheap places for lunch, advice about wedding etiquette, what would be expected of him and so forth, and about honeymoon etiquette – this candour of his, was very endearing. In return he found himself the recipient of equal confidences, listened attentively to many a tale of triumph or woe, became unpaid father confessor to the proprietors of a hundred small businesses, and sometimes to their wives and families. The territory they gave him, upon the retirement of Mr E.C. Jewitt, stretched from the southern suburbs of Manchester through most of East Cheshire into North Staffordshire – the smoky Pottery towns of Stoke, Hanley, Burslem, Alsager, and drab, immortal Etruria. He inherited his predecessor's small Vauxhall car.

Walter was to work this territory, hobnobbing with newsagents and tobacconists, and with their customers – machinists, mechanics, men in cloth caps and scarves, farm labourers, cottagers, shepherds, shop assistants, the occasional doctor, or works manager, or council school teacher – for the rest of his career. Head Office fiddled with it from time to time, adding a town, taking one away, but essentially, this land was Walter's. His wife would teach kindergarten in it. His two sons would grow up in it. He would go off to the war from it, and come back. Eventually, he would die in it.

In search of somewhere to live, because this would be their first home and, as it happened, their last, Walt and Enid took off in the Vauxhall to explore, and what an adventure this promised to be. After grey, flat, urban Lancashire they found themselves in a foreign land, a land of hayfields, green woods, slow-moving brooks lined with willow trees. When they got out of the car they breathed sweet, sleepy, Cheshire air. For Liverpool kids, brought up on the smell of the sea and the river, on the smoke of a hundred ships, on the pungent, fire-streaked clouds that wafted from the refineries and chemical works at Bromborough, driving through Cheshire was like turning the pages of a child's picture book; Enid half-expected to see little animals in clothes picnicking under the trees.

'Are we in your territory yet?' she asked more than once.

'No. I don't think so. Not yet.'

Walt had been hoping his first territory would be somewhere much further away from Liverpool, some place he'd never been and couldn't imagine: the West Country, perhaps, Devon or Cornwall; or London; or perhaps the Highlands of Scotland; so he'd been a bit disappointed when they gave him East Cheshire and North Staffordshire, though Enid was pleased they'd be living not more than a couple of hours' drive from Crosby. But this country they found themselves in, one Saturday in late July, was wonderful.

'I would think we're in my territory now,' Walter said, gazing on parkland planted with enormous trees, on a herd of black and white cows waiting to be milked outside a tin-roofed barn, on drowsy woods where jays and magpies flew – as if he owned all this.

'We do own it,' Enid said, reading his thoughts. 'It's ours.'

In a brick village, not far from a railway station, close to shops that sold fresh pies, rounds of cheese, rabbits and grouse by the brace, they found a pleasant semi-detached house for rent, with an arched front porch and a climbing rose over it: they sniffed the fragrance of those roses as their estate agent searched for his key. Inside, the house was airy and light – and empty: like Grace and Arthur, they'd have to buy furniture. But the rent was so low, they thought they could afford it: the rent was low because the house had been inherited by a widow who lived in Bournemouth and had no idea what she owned; it was an example of what Walter recognised as his luck. They walked through the house, listening to the echoes of their own voices.

'We'll live here,' Enid said. 'It's ours.'

Throwing open the upstairs windows they could see, in the distance, the Derbyshire hills, where one day they'd drive for picnics, with the boys, and the boys would scramble up rocks and swim in cold streams. They looked at each other, Walt and Enid. Below was their garden, hidden by thick privet hedges from the road, well-stocked with flowers: phlox, lupins, peonies, delphiniums; and flowering shrubs: hydrangeas, azaleas.

'Do you think you'll like gardening?' Enid said.

'I don't know. In Waterloo we only had a small brick yard. A ginger tom cat used to sit on the wall. My mother hated it. I don't know why my poor old mother hated that cat so much, but she hated it.'

'We'll get a cat,' said Enid. 'This would be a wonderful place for a cat.'

'This will be a wonderful place for us all,' said Walter.

For Walter Darwin Miller, what a long, long way this was from that small brick yard, and the ginger tom; the narrow, dark rowhouse where'd spent his hard-up boyhood, doing without his lunchtime bun so that he could give a few pennies back to his mother on Fridays, which he said he'd won playing marbles.

Walter couldn't believe this luck of his. He couldn't believe his luck that he was going to live in this lovely house, that it would be filled one day with the laughter of his boys, that its garden would echo to the thwack of bat on ball when they played cricket here. He couldn't believe his luck in landing this job, and driving this car that went with it. Above all, he couldn't believe his luck in meeting Enid Carruth, and that she'd agreed to marry him. No wonder that he treated her, all his life, with such deep respect that he never once saw her naked. He never really thought he was worthy of her. With his large nose, uncontrollable red hair like a boy's, and freckles, he was no heart-throb, in fact he thought himself downright peculiar-looking and didn't like seeing photographs of himself, whereas Enid, with her unquestioned beauty, her rich black curls, her dancing eyes, her fine-cut, ballet dancer's features, could surely have married anyone at the tennis club she wanted to, but instead, astonishingly, she'd picked Walter.

And there were people at the back of the church, when Walter and Enid were married, passers-by, people who couldn't resist a wedding, who said 'Such a pretty girl. What on earth does she see in him?'

What she saw in Walter was spunk and struggle. He was unlike any of the other young men she'd partnered in mixed doubles, or danced with at night. They had the brash self-confidence that came from not worrying too much about money. They were not rich men; but they had been raised in homes where there was always food on the table, on streets lined with double-flowering cherry trees. They had junior executive jobs in offices. They took the electric train into Liverpool every morning, ate meat pie with potato croquettes at the Kardomah Café for lunch, swallowed a pint of Walker's Warrington Ale after work, then they caught the train home to Crosby, or Hall Road, or Formby. Admirable, ordinary, young men. Even Enid's brother, George, with his dreadful stammer, fitted in, he was liked, and listened to patiently, and laughed with; but Walter did not fit in, and the truth was that nobody really knew what to make of him. Oh, it wasn't that they were unfriendly, no, quite the reverse, Walter was always being asked to make up a foursome, for tennis or for bridge. But he laughed at different things. When everyone else was serious, he laughed; when they laughed, he was glum. And then they'd catch him staring down, the way he did, or frowning slightly at some thought he couldn't share.

He was small when he was a boy, and was bullied, shoved around, cuffed. He was never actually beaten up, just made to feel miserable. His particular tormentor one year was a lad named Bradley, who was six inches taller than Walter and a year older. Bradley went about with a permanent sneer, and whenever he saw Walter he'd whisper threats of torture and mutilation, which Walter believed.

One day Walter'd had enough. He challenged Bradley to a fight. The news spread quickly around the school, and a big crowd gathered in the playground, after classes, to see Walter slaughtered. Bradley hovered around him for a few minutes, that sneer on his face, throwing occasional punches, most of which landed, until Walter's face was bruised and his mouth was bleeding. Was he going to fight back, or what? It didn't look like it. Some of the more responsible older boys wondered if they shouldn't break up the fight, call a halt before the kid was really hurt. But somehow it didn't turn out that way. Perhaps Bradley got careless. Because there he was, suddenly, on the ground, on his back, and Walter was sitting on his stomach, hammering his fists into Bradley's face. Bradley seemed unable to defend himself, which was because Walter had winded him with a sudden, vicious blow to his private parts. In the end it was Walter who had to be pulled away, and Bradley couldn't come to school for a week.

Enid liked Walter because he had guts. He knew exactly how things stood. He came from a very poor home, and he'd never be quite accepted by the Carruths. But the thing was, he understood himself much better than most people do. He wouldn't push his luck. He did not contemplate further promotion; did not aspire to become, one day, an Area Sales Manager, or to be offered a position at Head Office. To get on well with his customers, to enjoy his own territory, to be his own boss, to work his own hours – that was what Walter wanted to do, and that's what he was happy doing: he knew what he was capable of. Which did not mean he wasn't capable of surprising people: just as he'd challenged Bradley to fight, so he'd asked Enid Carruth to marry him. At the age of twenty-nine, Walter had already achieved his life's ambition. All he had to do now was get through the next fifty years.

They were married at St Stephen's, Crosby, where Grace and Arthur had been married nine years before, and it was a nice September day, with a trace of mist from off the river. It was also the first time in her life that Walter's little mother had ridden in a car: what a stir its arrival must have caused in Oakdale Road, Waterloo, how many net curtains were gingerly pulled aside as the uniformed driver pressed the doorbell at number 37! At the church, which was all of ten minutes' drive away, tiny Mrs Miller had emerged, blinking, from the shiny black Daimler; and stood there, not quite knowing what happened next, until Walter came round from the other side of the car and took her arm. It struck Walter, who wore a rented suit, with tails, and carried a top hat, that just as he'd never seen his little mother get out of a car before, this was also the first time he'd seen her not wearing an apron. She had on a thin black coat, which was the only coat she owned, and under it a dark blue dress, with white dots, and a black cardigan, and Walter knew that this was the proudest moment of her life.

Greg, Walter's brother, the best man, arrived a few moments later in a second black Daimler, with their cousin, Beatrice. Greg put his top hat on. He had the same large nose that Walter had, but his face survived it better, there was a twinkle in Greg's eye and a nice smile on his face, he even slept smiling, as if his dreams were amusing. He was a man of a very affable disposition, was Greg; found the world a funny place, and was full of wry observations.

Cousin Beatrice was the opposite, oh my, wasn't she just. Nothing pleased her, nothing at all. She radiated discontent. She was a few years older than Walter, and unmarried, which was hardly surprising, because there wasn't a man alive who could live up to her expectations. She worked as a typist in a lawyer's office in Liverpool, where she made herself disagreeable to all, and spent an undue part of her salary on hair-dos; she'd taken to having her silvery hair tinted blue, and for Walter's wedding she wore a blue silk dress that matched her coiffure.

As the groom's party walked towards the church they were met by Arthur and George Carruth, also in top hats and tails, and Arthur pinned white carnations in their buttonholes: he was, generous fellow, footing the bill, and had paid for the Daimlers. Grace, who looked beautiful but rather pale, in a rose-coloured suit with a skirt that reached almost to her ankles, after shaking everybody's hand – she wore expensive grey gloves – bent down and gave Walter's mother a kiss. The little lady was very surprised to be kissed by this gorgeous, and presumably rich, person, and Grace sensed her terror.

'This is going to be fun!' she assured her.

Mrs Miller was also surprised to hear that the wedding was going to be fun.

'Do you think so?' she said.

'Believe me, it will be fun,' said Grace. 'And afterwards, we'll have a wonderful party, which will be even more fun.'

'A party?'

'Yes. I mean, the reception. I'll tell you what, I'll sit next to you. Do you mind if I sit next to you? Then, just in case the speeches are boring, we can have a quiet chat together, you and I.'

'I'd like to sit next to you, very much.'

The photographer appeared, and took all the usual group pictures. Walter had brought his own camera, he'd bought it two years before, so everything was held up while he took his own pictures, lots of them too; in fact, all the best photographs of his own wedding were the ones he took himself. Naturally, he wasn't in any of them. Years later, his boys thought that this was very funny.

'Good job the ugly fellow isn't in any of these,' they ribbed him.

'That was the intent,' smiled their father.

'And who's that absolutely gorgeous woman in pink? Is that Auntie Grace?'

'Yes, that's Grace.'

'She's stunning. I didn't realise she was so stunning.'

'She was lovely. Very charming, too.'

'Old Uncle Arthur had good taste.'

'He certainly did. What about me, though? Didn't I?'

'Of course you did, Dad. Mum looks smashing too.'

And indeed she did, Enid Carruth, shortly to be Enid Miller, as she came up the aisle of the church on her father's arm, in a lovely white dress with a long train held up by two little bridesmaids, two small Carruths from a Birkenhead branch of the family. The bride's side of the church was filled with Carruths, several rows of them; Carruths of various shapes and ages, elderly aunts and uncles, strapping boys and black-haired girls; Carruths from Birkenhead and Wallasey, Carruths from Maghull and Sefton Park, Carruths from Fazakerley and Everton, Carruths from all over Liverpool, who didn't all know each other too well, but exchanged Christmas cards and came to weddings.

The Carruth pews also included friends, neighbours, and intimates of the Carruths, for instance Mrs McMahon, with her dutiful daughter – and Pat looked really good, there was more colour in her thin cheeks than there usually was; she held her head high. She was in black, as per usual, but her dress was all net and muslin; it must have taken her months to stitch, and men noticed. She walked without her stick and her step was firm.

The groom's side was empty, except for the four figures in the front row: Walter, with his brother Greg next to him, then their mother, who had wanted to sit on the other side, next to Grace, but wasn't allowed to, then Beatrice, who stared about with a disapproving frown, and let out a loud sniff from time to time. She watched with especial displeasure as the bride took her place at the altar next to the man about to be her husband.

However, when the Vicar of St Stephen's asked if anyone in the congregation knew of any let or hindrance, Beatrice only sniffed. So Walter and Enid were married.

The official photographer took all the expected pictures outside the church, after the ceremony. The mists had disappeared, and it was actually warm in the sun. Walter again took himself out of the groups being photographed as soon as he could, to concentrate on his own pictures: mostly of Enid, dancing with her bouquet, feigning grande jetées, having fun.

The reception was at the Crosby Lawn Tennis Club, which Arthur had put Grace in charge of decorating. She'd organised white streamers and white flowers. There was Moet et Chandon champagne. Arthur's little mother had never tasted champagne, and didn't want to, but Grace, who sat next to her as she'd promised, made her sip. She puckered.

'I don't like it,' she said.

'That's all right. Don't drink it.'

'Oh, I'll drink it,' said the old lady. 'It would be a shame to waste it. It's champagne.'

Greg, as best man, got to his feet and proposed the appropriate toasts.

'I've finished my champagne,' Arthur's mother whispered to Grace, so Grace emptied half of her own glass into the old lady's.

Greg went on to make a number of observations, rocking gently back and forth on his heels as he spoke. It was clear that his observations were supposed to be funny because the speaker himself kept laughing.

'I see Grace, looking lovely. She launched the *English Bay*, you know, a few weeks ago, at Cammell Laird's. Made quite a splash... I see my brother took more photos than the official photographer. When people look at photos of this wedding, they'll wonder where the groom was. It would be like going to watch Everton at Goodison Park and the goalie was taking the photographs.'

'I want to go to the toilet,' Arthur's mother said, in Grace's ear. 'Will you take me?'

'Yes, of course I'll take you.'

When Greg sat down, Arthur made a short, gracious speech, welcoming Walter to the family, and wishing the couple every happiness, which Greg had forgotten to do.

George drank a lot of champagne, and he was still drinking when the bridal pair left; in fact he missed their departure because he was wandering up and down the courts, holding a champagne bottle by the neck. He'd dropped three glasses and found it easier to drink straight out of the bottle. Arthur came to find him; George silently handed him the bottle, and Arthur took a swig.

'You should quit that job of yours, George,' Arthur said.

'Oh, don't s-s-s-start on that.'

'You're getting nowhere. You're making yourself miserable.'

'I'm n-n-n-not coming back here to work for you.'

They stood looking at each other, Arthur still immaculate in his grey tails and striped trousers, George already dishevelled; he'd loosened his grey tie and stuck his white carnation into the top of his pants.

'It's n-n-n-not that I'm ungrateful—'

Arthur cut him short. 'I'm not talking about your coming back to Liverpool, George. I'm talking about your quitting your dead-end job in London.'

George swayed back and forth on his toes. 'Then what?' he said.

'Times are better. We're coming out of the Depression. There are openings for chemists. I read about them in the newspaper every day.'

'I do too.'

'Then why don't you apply?'

George made an effort to focus on his brother, gave up and put the bottle to his mouth. It was empty. He dropped it and it broke; George kicked broken glass under a hedge.

'I can't go through all that again. Applying. Interviewing. Being t-t-t-turned d-d-d-down.'

'Old chap,' said Arthur, after a second. 'I know people. I am not without connections. They need a senior research chemist at ICI, in Runcorn. I've met a number of the people there—'

'Arthur, no. I don't want you to find me a job. Please stop trying to c-c-c-control my life.'

'I'm not trying to control your life. But you're not enjoying it and—'

'I will not be controlled by you. I am the only one of us you can't control.'

'What do you mean, George? What do you mean, 'control'? I don't control anyone. Maybe a few of my clerks.'

'One of these d-d-d-days everyone's g-g-g-going to turn against you, Arthur. You f-f-f-find that impossible to b-b-b-believe, but one day, it will happen.'

'What are you talking about? Why should anyone turn against me?'

Grace appeared and insisted they both come back inside, because the floor had been cleared for dancing. The white flowers were starting to wilt and the younger Carruths were throwing them about; the air was full of flying petals; Grace wanted to dance.

Tiny Mrs Miller appeared. 'I want to go home,' she said to Grace.

'You want to go home? But the fun's just starting. We're about to have dancing. Wouldn't you like to dance? Would you like to dance with me?'

'No, thank you. I want to go home.'

'I understand. That's fine. Let's find you your nice shiny car.'

'I can take the bus.'

'No, we'll find you your nice shiny car.'

Beatrice went home with the old lady. She didn't want to dance either. She found everything about the wedding, and especially the reception, quite tasteless.

Walter and Enid drove to Chester, where they were booked into the Blossoms Hotel, at Arthur's suggestion, for the first night of their honeymoon.

'If you'll give me the keys, sir, I'll park the car,' said the doorman.

'It's all right, thank you, I can park it,' said Walter.

'Let the man park it!' Enid told him.

Walter had never been inside such a beautiful hotel. There was a vast urn of flowers in the middle of the pink and gold lobby; Walter stared at it. There were orchids and lilies, clusters of purple lilac.

'Aren't the flowers marvellous?' said Enid. Her eyes shone; she felt light-headed, she wanted to laugh. Walter took a huge spray of lilac out of the flower arrangement and gave it to her. The couple were taken to their room, which was not a large one. Enid flung herself on her back on the bed and kicked her legs in the air.

'That was a wonderful wedding!' she said.

Dinner wasn't until seven o'clock so Walter suggested they take a walk around Chester.

One night in November of that year Arthur woke up and found that Grace wasn't in bed with him. He discovered her sitting at their dining room table, in her nightdress; she seemed to be trying to get her breath back, her fists were tightly clenched in front of her, on the table.

He rushed for the telephone, called the doctor, didn't know what to do to help her. He sat down beside her, covered her pounding fists with his own big hands.

'I'm sorry!' she gasped. 'It was bound to happen sooner or later.'

'The doctor's on the way.'

'It's exciting really.'

'What is exciting?'

'Having a heart attack. It's exciting.'

He put his arms around her, and held her very tight. She pressed her mouth into his neck, bit on to him, out of some instinct, like an animal. At first he didn't even hear the ring at the door, then he didn't want to leave her to answer it.

'Go,' she said, taking some deep breaths, gently pushing him away.

Dr McKenzie gave her digitalis, supported her back to bed. 'It was a mild attack,' he told Arthur. 'I think she'll be all right.'

'I thought I was going to die,' Grace sighed, with an exhausted smile.

'No,' promised the doctor. He took his leave. Arthur sat at the bedside. She seemed calm now.

'You gave me an awful fright, puffin,' Arthur said.

'What did you call me?'

'Puffin. Remember?'

'Yes, darling. I remember.'

After a moment Arthur said, 'What did you call me?'

But she was asleep.

Chapter Six

In May of 1938 Grace and Arthur sailed to New York on the *English Bay*.

They took the Owners' Suite. The *English Bay*, like all Red Funnel Line ships, carried mostly cargo, but she had twelve nicely fitted cabins for passengers, the woodwork cherry, the floors holly, the furnishings from a mill in Rochdale visited years ago by Arthur Carruth, Purchasing Manager, at the end of a smoky train journey; the Owners' Suite was on A deck, just below the boat deck and behind the Captain's cabin; Captain Burling, as Commodore of the Line, had a grand suite too, very spacious, with a Persian carpet, his most treasured possession, inherited from an aunt.

Grace had suffered one more heart attack, fortunately also mild, a year before, so she'd given up teaching, for the second time, but she'd got herself involved with a bunch of women's charities, and for them she organised lunches, charity balls, suchlike fund-raising events; her connections helped. She and Arthur entertained at least twice a week; ah, they knew everybody now, everybody important, that is, including the Lord Lieutenant of Lancashire, the Lord Mayor of Liverpool, several Members of Parliament, the Chairman of the Mersey Docks and Harbour Board, and the Chairmen and senior Directors of Cunard, the Blue

Star Line, Elder Dempster, the Anchor Line, Lamport and Holt, the Booth Line, and the Harrison Line. What a charming hostess Grace was, too; she found time to talk to everybody and no one ever felt left out: the receptions she and her husband hosted in their own flat in Blundellsands were lovely affairs. The house was always bursting with flowers, even in the dead of winter: gorgeous blooms imported from Costa Rica on Red Funnel Line ships. Grace could probably have started her own flower import business, if Arthur had let her. Her parties were very tastefully managed; elegant waitresses in black dresses and starched white aprons circulated with silver trays piled with canapés, shrimps on tooth-picks, miniature sausage rolls; handsome young men wearing black ties and white monkey-jackets served cocktails. The Carruths' parties – receptions, cocktails, soirées, dinners at the Adelphi, evenings at the theatre or at the Phil – cost the company money, a lot of money; but Sir William Crashaw considered it money well spent, and he was right. Besides, the Line was doing well. Even the *English Bay* had just about paid for herself.

One of the few people in England who believed that the world would soon be at war was Arthur Carruth.

'I have long admired your instincts, Arthur,' Sir William had said, helping himself to another snifter of Napoleon cognac from a cut glass decanter: the two men faced each other across Sir William's dining room table; Grace and Lady Crashaw had taken themselves off to finalise arrangements for the forthcoming Annual Ball of the Crosby Cancer Society, which was to be a very grand affair, at the Adelphi Hotel. 'But supposing you're right, is there all that much we can do about it? The Government will requisition our entire fleet, just as they did in the last war. We'll probably lose half our ships to submarine attack, which is a gloomy thought. Half our ships, and half our men. But if we win the war in the end, as you also seem to think we will, no doubt we'll receive compensation. Do you have any other ideas?'

'Well yes, Sir William, I have one or two.'

Sir William Crashaw, holding his snifter in two hands, to warm the precious liquid, smiled at Arthur over its rim.

'I might have known.'

Arthur lowered his glasses, dabbed at his eyes with his white handkerchief. He'd put on a little weight – not surprising, with all the entertaining he had to do, though Grace had managed not to, because she hardly ate anything, just floated about being friendly – and his black hair was very thin on top, but he was still a handsome man. His voice had acquired a slight huskiness, which worried him: he'd seen doctors, fearing a growth, but the x-rays showed nothing. He still pronounced each syllable with great care, as if it had been entrusted to him for safe keeping.

'The *Montego Bay*', he said, 'the *Stanley Bay*, and the *Cadiz Bay* are old ships. They survived the last war. It's unlikely they'll survive this one, they're too slow. None of them can make more than eight knots. I think we should sell all three to breakers, immediately.'

'Who'd buy them? None of the breakers here—'

'Breakers in the Far East. I have had a few preliminary conversations. There are people who are interested... if we are interested.'

'Hm. Well, I suppose we might be interested.'

'Yes. These gentlemen's interest may wane though, unless we act quickly.'

'Where are the ships now? Do you know? Do we have to send them out East in ballast? That's an expensive proposition.'

'As a matter of fact, Sir William, the *Montego Bay* and the *Stanley Bay* both happen to be on their way from Valparaiso to Pusan, Korea, with Chilean nitrate.'

'Good God, Arthur! Did you connive that?'

'I wouldn't say 'connive', Sir William. Both vessels had loaded; I merely re-routed them.'

'Hmm. What about the other ship? The *Cadiz Bay*?'

'The *Cadiz Bay* is currently unloading copra, in Hong Kong.'

Sir William held his peace. He looked at the ceiling. 'We'll have to put it to the Board,' he said in the end.

'I have drafted the motion,' said Arthur.

'Good. Good, good, good. You said you had other ideas.'

'Some of our newer, and faster, ships – I'm thinking of the *Biscaine Bay*, the *Thunder Bay*, the *James Bay*, perhaps the *Chesapeake Bay* – I'd put guns on them.'

'What?' Sir William slammed down his brandy glass.

'An eight-millimetre gun turret, mounted aft. And – ah – concealed, of course, for the time being.'

'You're suggesting we arm our ships?'

'Not all of them – only the fastest.'

'We're not the bloody Royal Navy, you know.'

'I realise that.'

'I very much doubt if it's legal.'

'I believe the work would have to be done at a foreign port, Sir William.'

'I trust you haven't had any 'preliminary conversations' about this one, Arthur?'

'No, I haven't.'

'Good. Well, I'm against it. If we put guns on our ships they'll be sitting ducks for German submarines. The Nazis will be absolutely justified in sending them to the bottom.'

'German submariners have shown few scruples about sinking unarmed merchantmen, Sir William. Neither of the ships we lost in the last war was armed. Nor was the *Lusitania*. If I was going to sea on a sitting duck, I think I'd prefer it to be one with an eight-millimetre gun turret. You can inflict a lot of damage to a surfaced submarine, with an eight-millimetre gun.'

'Why should the Jerry surface? Why not just fire a torpedo?'

'A submarine would do that if the vessel were in convoy, with escort ships, because of the risk of pursuit. But if our ships sailed without escort – and because of their speed they might be allowed to – it's likely that a submarine would surface and try to sink her by gunfire, rather than waste torpedoes. At which point we have a little surprise for Jerry.'

'Hah!' roared Sir William; obviously the thought appealed to him. 'At which point, we blow him out of the water!'

'Yes.'

Sir William was tickled, in spite of himself. 'We could never get the Board to agree to this, Arthur,' he said, after rubbing his hands together for a while.

'I'm not sure we'd go to the Board.'

'We'd have to.'

'I don't think so. In time of war, or threat of war, this would come under the Military Secrets Act.'

'Hmm. Poindexter would have to know, of course.'

'Yes. I have spoken to Alfred. It was he who remembered the Military Secrets Act.'

'Arthur... you might just be a genius. Christ!' he suddenly exploded, pounding his fist on the table. 'Let's do it! Let's do it!'

'At least let me make some preliminary enquiries—'

'The hell with preliminary enquiries! Let's do it! Let's blow the bastards out of the water!'

He stood up and walked excitedly up and down. He had a tremendous urge to fling open the drawing room door and tell Lady Crashaw that he planned to put guns on Red Funnel Line ships, but realised he couldn't; nobody should know, not even Lady Crashaw. He stopped.

'Do you have another idea?' he said.

'Yes. I have one other idea. The *English Bay*.'

'What about her? I suppose you want to convert her into a battleship?'

'Quite the opposite. A hospital ship.'

'A hospital ship?'

'Not even the Germans will sink a hospital ship.'

Sir William gaped at him. 'It's a brilliant idea. But the Government won't want the *English Bay*, she's not big enough. They'll requisition the *Mauritania*, and the *Queen Mary*. The *Queen Elizabeth*, too, if she's built in time. They'll want the big Canadian Pacific ships, the *Empress of Canada*, the *Empress of Japan*. And the good old *Reina del Pacifico*, and the *Orion*, the *Orontes*—'

'They will,' Arthur interrupted – not many men interrupted Sir William – 'but they'll want them as troop ships.'

'Troop ships? Troop ships! By God! You're right! They'll want the biggest ships they can lay their hands on as troop ships.'

'We could put hospital decks in the holds of the *English Bay*. She could take six hundred beds.'

'Six hundred? How do you know? No, don't tell me, you've had some "preliminary conversations", haven't you?'

'No. I went around with a measuring tape, when she was last in port.'

It was Sir William Crashaw who insisted that Arthur take his wife for a voyage on the *English Bay*, because in spite of two heart attacks, Grace found it impossible to sit and do nothing. She was now forty-three years old, but most people thought she looked as lovely as she ever had. Apart from the laugh-lines that spread from the corners of her eyes, nature was treating her with especial favour. Arthur would look at her sometimes, and shudder: in return for the early death Sir Geoffrey predicted, Grace would never be old, never know grey hair, never have to wear false teeth, or a hearing aid, or spectacles, never lose her memory, or control of her bowels, never hobble on a stick; she would die as beautiful as she lived; she'd be buried with shining eyes and soft brown curls.

'Take Grace on a sea voyage,' Sir William had said. 'How about the *English Bay*? That would seem to me appropriate. For about three weeks the woman won't be able to do anything. Enforced rest. Sea air. Good food. What do you think? Or would it drive her nuts?'

'I think it's a good idea. I think she'd enjoy it.'

'Now he's taken her on a sea voyage,' Mrs Annie Sadie Carruth complained to her old friend, Mrs McMahon. 'It's all very well for some people. What with theatres, and concerts. And charities. She wouldn't be able to go gallivanting about like she does, if she'd had children.'

'That's true, of course,' agreed Mrs McMahon. 'It's a great shame they have no children. And Arthur would make a wonderful father.'

Whether or not Grace would make a wonderful mother was not discussed. Mrs McMahon looked forlornly at her own daughter, Pat, who also, presumably, would have no children. Pat, reconciled to childlessness, merely agreed that Arthur would have made a good father. She'd been sick all her life, was on familiar terms with pain, so there wasn't much Pat McMahon didn't know about deprivation. And she'd had little company, only her mother's; the two of them didn't go out: they lived on the old lady's modest pension. But Pat had no self-pity, none at all; and if her life was empty, her mother seemed to worry about it a lot more than Pat did.

'What's going to happen to you when I pass on?' Mrs McMahon would sometimes say.

'Oh, Mother, don't worry about that. I'll be all right. I'll manage perfectly well, if I have to. But the chances are you'll live to be a hundred.'

Grace had been thrilled to bits at the prospect of a voyage on the *English Bay*. She and Arthur had spent three days aboard already, during her speed trials on the Clyde: three days of nonstop cocktails, boat deck lunches, and black tie dinners, because Red Funnel Line directors were official guests of Cammell Laird's, the builders, and Cammell Laird's knew how to entertain. And although Sir William Crashaw had negotiated, over dinner at the Adelphi, a very satisfactory price, Cammell Laird's had not skimped when it came to fitting out the *English Bay*. She'd been luxuriously appointed. She had a dining saloon with a Steinway grand piano; and an airy lounge with wicker furniture and a large oil painting, by Norman Wilkinson, of the first *English Bay*, built on the Tyne in 1888. Working from early photographs, Mr Wilkinson, foremost marine artist of the day, had depicted the ship at New York following her maiden transatlantic voyage: dressed overall, flags and bunting stretched from bow to stern across her three tall masts; sails neatly stowed; black smoke pouring from her single funnel; fire-boats saluted her with graceful jets of water; tugs scurried about her like eager bridesmaids.

The new *English Bay* had the crisp lines of all Red Funnel vessels; fine bow, low, Jersey-cream superstructure, graceful counter-stern. Her single funnel, red with a black top, raked in the old-fashioned way, seemed almost too big for her, but the general effect was pleasing: Arthur, not easy to please, God knows, in the matter of naval architecture, believed her handsome.

The broad white furrow of her wake stretched to a blue horizon. Grace and Arthur lay in comfortable reclining chairs on the open boat deck, out of the wind, facing aft, both covered with tartan blankets; Grace had made hers into a hood. Four days of Atlantic breezes had brought the colour to her cheeks, and to Arthur's.

'I've decided to live for ever,' she announced; they'd been silent for a while, and Arthur had thought she was asleep.

'That sounds like an excellent decision. What changed your mind?' smiled Arthur.

'I have too much fun. Dead people have no fun.'

'Perhaps they do.'

Grace shook her head. 'I don't think so.'

'I can imagine the two of us dead,' mused Arthur. 'We'd dance. We'd dance indefinitely, I not very well, you wonderfully.'

'That would be nice. But where?'

'Oh… at the tennis club, I suppose. Or The Hydro, in Port Erin.'

Grace turned her head to look at him, from under her hood. She smiled. A tear went down her cheek.

'There is not much theological foundation… for what you propose,' she said, after a few moments.

'I'm sure you know better than I,' said Arthur. 'I never had much time for theology.'

'We were married in church,' Grace reminded him.

'That's the only time I've been. Well, perhaps the second. I suppose I was baptised.'

'Perhaps we should become religious.'

'I think I would need a little more evidence.'

Did Arthur remember this conversation, years later, when he converted and became a Roman Catholic? Well, almost certainly. He remembered so much. It took him many years to bury Grace. It took him another war. It took him disaster and success. It took him his two nephews, Enid's sons, the boys he never had himself. It took him long walks with them, the boys scampering ahead, kicking up autumn leaves, collecting acorns, and pine cones, field mushrooms, broken birds' eggs. It took him ferry boat rides with them, and excursions on the Overhead Railway. It took him mornings on the floor with them, going through books and explaining stories. It took him weekends in Cheshire and hikes in the Lakes. It took him green fells, brown mountains, and sparkling water; it took him Helvellyn and Skiddaw and Blencathra, Coniston Water and Ambleside, the places he loved. It took him all that.

Grace thought New York magnificent. They were shown the town by the company's agent, Mr Carey. Ernest Carey was an ambitious young man; he fell in love with Grace Carruth. He took them to the top of the Empire State Building, and for carriage rides in Central Park. He bought them champagne in The Rainbow Room, pointed out the glittering nightscape of the city. He esquired them to the theatre; they saw the latest Broadway musical, *I Married an Angel*, with dances arranged by the struggling George Balanchine; he explored night clubs with them, heard Fats Waller play in a little basement on 48th Street. He never left them alone. Finally they had to give him the slip; pleading exhaustion they retired to their hotel, then hailed a taxi and went to Harlem, where they listened to jazz. And, of course, Grace wanted to dance.

'This is Heaven!' she whispered, as he held her tightly, eyes closed, and saxophones wailed.

'This is Liverpool!' Arthur said, next day, as they stood on the Staten Island ferry, and breathed the familiar smell of salt water and smoke, wharves and cargoes. The *Queen Mary* was at the Cunard pier; the German liner *Bremen*, of the Hamburg-Amerika Line, outward bound, a fine sight, the Swastika snapping at her stern, steamed slowly past the Statue of Liberty, heading for the sea.

After three days in New York, from the Red Funnel Line's pier at the foot of West 35th Street, the *English Bay* sailed for Savannah, Georgia, to load cotton for the return voyage. She came up the Savannah river on the tide, with the last of the light; for the first time the ship's distinguished passengers, Grace and Arthur Carruth, breathed the seductive fragrance of mangrove and pine barren, mud and live oak, cobbles baked in the sun. Grace was enchanted, next day, by the gracious old town, with its shady squares and handsome fountains, its avenues planted with massive trees draped with Spanish moss, its dappled sunlight. They sauntered along the cobbled quays that lined the brown river, climbed steep little streets between old brick warehouses, The line's agent, Mr Clarence Sawyer, drove them, in his fine Packard automobile, into the shimmering green country. They peered from bridges that spanned deep creeks and sparkling rivers, hoping to see alligators. They lunched with a valued customer of the Line, Mr Jefferson Fouquet, and his wife Sabrina, at the Fouquets' colonnaded mansion, on the family plantation, with a view of ancient parkland from the oak-floored, high-ceilinged dining room.

'Your house is ravishing!' Grace said. 'I've never been in such an old house. You must have ghosts! Don't you have ghosts, of famous belles in crinoline, and fine Southern gentlemen with moustaches?'

'I thought all you Britons lived in houses much older than this,' smiled their host, 'which you share with legions of phantoms.'

'No, we live in a modern flat, which is quite ghostless; though we leave the lights on just the same.'

They strolled, after lunch, with the Fouquets and Mr Clarence Sawyer, under the fine old trees of the park. They heard children shouting, playing; came upon a bunch of black girls and boys who stopped to gape at them.

That night, on the ship, Arthur pointed out a white heron who stood motionless on the mud. They watched him as the light faded. Finally he flapped lazily away, his great wings almost touching the water. The smell of mud in hot countries came off the tidal flats.

'I love it here!' Grace said.

'Old slave town,' said Arthur. 'Old slave town, like Liverpool.'

'The Red Funnel Line never carried slaves,' Grace said, finding his hand.

'No. But it probably would have, if it had been founded fifty years earlier. Liverpool ships sailed in ballast to West Africa. They bought slaves off local kings and shipped them to the Americas, to Charleston and Savannah. They sailed home with cotton.'

'Mr Carruth would never have condoned that trade,' Grace said.

'I hope not,' sighed Arthur. 'My goodness, I hope not.'

Enid Miller's first son, Alan Townsend Miller, was born as his Uncle Arthur and his Auntie Grace sailed back to England.

He was born at home, Enid attended by the doctor, by a midwife, and by her mother. And Walter stood at the open window in what would one day be the boys' room; and smoked; he'd smoked since Enid went into labour, at eleven o'clock at night. No, he didn't pace; he just stood there, watched dawn lighten the distant Derbyshire hills; saw the last owls flop home to roost, in the beech trees across the road. He heard dogs bark somewhere, perhaps at Potts' farm as Mr Potts went out with his lantern to milk. He heard trains rumble. Walter was not anxious; he thought his luck would hold, didn't imagine there'd be a problem with the delivery. When the midwife came in, smiling, and told him he was the father of a lovely healthy boy, he put out his cigarette and went to join his wife. And he was a little shocked to see the baby nibbling her breasts.

'Don't you want to hold him?' said the midwife.

'Well, perhaps later,' Walter said.

He thought Enid had never looked so beautiful, and he was very proud of her. It had been an easy birth, too; Enid had seemed to enjoy it. Alan's brother, Toby, three years later, was to give her a worse time. By then, bombs were falling on Liverpool.

Alan Townsend Miller was christened at St Philip's Church, stoutly built of Cheshire sandstone, rosy-grey, with a high spire of grey slate. Uncle Arthur was Alan's godfather; Walter's cousin Beatrice his godmother. To everybody's relief Beatrice did not sniff, as she had throughout the wedding; Walter's photographs of his cousin holding the baby, wrapped, apparently, in several yards of white blanket, showed her positively smiling, a rare feat. The baby slept.

George had come up from London, and Walter's brother Greg from West Bromwich. Greg had married the previous year; his wife, Kathleen, six months pregnant now, had stayed behind in the small semi-detached house they rented. Walter, as you can imagine, took many photographs of what was probably the largest family gathering of Carruths and Millers ever to happen, and certainly the last such family gathering that would include Grace; Grace who made everyone laugh. How tanned and fit they looked, she and Arthur, after that three-week voyage of theirs on the *English Bay*. But George had lost his angelic looks as well as his mop of hair. He was balder now than his older brother, and his lips had grown flabby; he wore a grey moustache; remained a bachelor. Enid, who already had her figure back, looked delightful, shook her black curls, her eyes danced. Walter's tiny mother seemed tinier every year; she wore a black skirt that finished well above her ankles, and very shiny black shoes; had left off her usual apron for the christening, at church, but had put it on again as soon as the party arrived back at the house, where Walter took more pictures, first in the garden, a riot of flowers, and later in the living room. Here they prevailed upon him to play the piano: which he'd bought soon after the move to Cheshire. He'd never had lessons, so he couldn't sight-read, though he was teaching himself; but he had a wonderful ear, was naturally gifted; played Cole Porter and Jerome Kern, Ivor Novello and Noel Coward. Grace couldn't resist; she laid her hands on Arthur's shoulders, and the two of them moved, very slowly, to the music. Enid clapped; then took her baby off its smaller grandmother, danced with it in flowing circles, holding the child and its yards of blanket high above her head. Then, at Grace's request, Walter flung himself into Rachmaninoff's passionate *Prelude in C Sharp Minor*, which he'd heard on the radio. Arthur, beaming fondly, clasped his wife tight around the waist to hold her still.

Greg felt called upon to make some of his witty observations. A sherry glass in one hand, he described vague motions in thin air with the other. He hadn't lost the nice half-smile which seemed to belong to his face, or the tentative, softly spoken, Liverpool accent.

'I see Grace, looking lovely as usual, and Arthur, both returned from their luxury cruise on the *English Bay*. They obviously visited sunnier shores than the Mersey's, as we can see from their complexions. I'm told they both had trouble with His Majesty's customs and immigration authorities when the ship docked at Liverpool. There seemed to be a discrepancy between their Jamaican appearance and their passport photographs. Sir William Crashaw himself had to vouch for their identity.'

It didn't matter at all to Greg that nobody laughed; he was never especially conscious of his audience; like as not he'd have rambled on happily to himself in an empty room.

'I see George has managed to tear himself away from his laboratory to be here. He was halfway through inventing a new kind of shoe-polish which works by swallowing a spoonful with a tumbler of water.'

Arthur thought this was funny, and laughed out loud; Grace, who loved to see her husband laugh, squeezed his hand.

'I'm glad to see that Cousin Beatrice has taken her duties as godmother very seriously.' Beatrice was holding the baby, which she'd taken from its mother; was rocking it gently. 'Wait till it wee-wees.'

Annie Sadie Carruth told her daughter, 'You'll have to get rid of that cat.'

'Get rid of The Woo? We couldn't do that! Whyever would we want to do that?'

'The cat will lie on the baby's face in its pram, and smother it.'

Enid protested, but her mother's dire prophesies worried her; within three weeks she found the kitten a new home. Later, as the boys grew older, there would be other cats.

Arthur and Grace gave the baby its only christening present, a silver napkin ring with Master Alan Townsend Miller's initials engraved on it. Grace had made no fuss of the baby, but when she eventually took it in her arms it smiled and gurgled at her. She wandered outside into the still sunny garden, holding the child; sat with it on an old kitchen chair, under the big weeping wych-elm, a vast umbrella of a tree, which, years later, it would be the boys' ambition to climb, an ambition not realised until Alan was twelve years old and made it up the straight fifteen-foot trunk, hanging off the bole on top to haul young Toby up by the wrists.

Grace smelled the child's small breath. She carefully kissed its little mouth. 'I have the feeling I will die soon,' she told the baby. 'When I'm gone, be nice to your Uncle Arthur. Your Uncle Arthur always wanted to have his own children, but you are the nearest he'll get. I'm sure he'll take you for long, lovely walks, just like he took me for long, lovely walks. He'll show you all the things he showed me, and he'll tell you their names. Because he knows all their names. He believes it important to know the names of things. Unfortunately, I could never remember the names, which considering all the names he told me is perhaps not surprising; but what I do remember... what I will not forget, not ever, is why he told me: he told me because he loved me; and that's why he'll tell you the names of everything, too.'

She kissed the child again, very softly; it giggled at her happily. She smiled down at it. Wandering out of the house to smoke a cigarette, Walter Miller stole back for his camera, and took several pictures, without her realising it, of his sister-in-law chatting with the child. Years later, when Arthur died, Alan found these photographs in an album which his uncle left to him, but had never shown a soul.

'You probably won't remember me,' Grace told the baby. 'But I expect they'll talk about me, and I hope not unkindly. They'll say, "It's a pity you didn't know your Auntie Grace." Or something like that. But you can tell them, "Well, as a matter of fact, I did. My Auntie Grace and I used to talk. We had a very long talk, under that tree, in the garden. Uncle Arthur told me what kind of a tree it is, but I've forgotten. Anyway, Auntie Grace and I, we talked under that tree."'

Walter brought Enid out into the garden. Grace stood up and handed the child to its mother. Enid would not forget how happy Grace looked, or the peaceful smile on her lovely round face, the afternoon sun burnishing her brown curls.

Three months later, at the end of September, Neville Chamberlain flew back from Munich. Outside Number 10 Downing Street a large crowd, cheering themselves hoarse with relief, sang 'For he's a jolly good fellow'. Chamberlain held up the document a grateful Adolf Hitler had just signed. He had reason to be grateful: Britain and France had given him permission to take over Czechoslovakia. The Czechs had thirty-five well-armed divisions, behind fortifications stronger than the Maginot Line: in mountainous country, they would have been brutally difficult to dislodge. Now Hitler didn't even have to try. 'My good friends,' Chamberlain told the crowd, 'I bring you peace with honour. I believe it is peace in our time.' There were shouts of 'Good old Neville!'

Mrs Annie Sadie Carruth did not share Mr Chamberlain's optimism. 'Chamberlain's soft,' she told anyone who would listen. 'You can't give in to dictators. What this country needs is Churchill.'

Churchill said, 'We have sustained a total and unmitigated defeat. We are in the midst of a disaster of the first magnitude. Do not suppose that this is the end. It is only the beginning.'

Mrs Annie Sadie said, 'There's only one thing dictators understand, and that's force. I'd like to get that Adolph Hitler over my knee. I'd give him a thrashing he wouldn't forget.'

Thanks to Arthur's foresight, the Red Funnel Line had sold half a dozen of its older ships to breakers – 'minimising our exposure', as he put it to the Board. And, though the Board didn't know it, four of the fastest vessels had been secretly fitted with eight-millimetre gun turrets, the work being contracted to yards in the United States; the turrets were hidden by temporary afterworks. For several years Arthur had believed war inevitable. He was the most peaceable of men, but he was no fool: and after Munich, he knew that war would come soon. He wanted Grace to go to Canada.

'We have relatives,' he explained. 'Through mother's side of the family. She was one of sixteen children; as a matter of fact two of the sons emigrated. Of course, I never knew them, but we have corresponded. One lives in Calgary, but the other is in Montreal. You could travel on the *Chesapeake Bay* or her sister ship the *James Bay*; one or other of them sails from Liverpool every Thursday night, and calls at Halifax and Quebec City. I could arrange passage for you very easily, and Uncle Jack would meet you off the ship in Montreal.'

Grace heard him out. She smiled and touched the tip of his nose with a finger. They sat on the settee in the flat at Blundellsands; it was a pleasant, early autumn evening, unusually warm; the windows were open; the smell of burning leaves from garden bonfires drifted into the house. For once, Grace and Arthur were alone, though tomorrow they'd be taking the Vice Chairman of Cammell Laird's and the Member of Parliament for Birkenhead to the theatre. Grace wore a loose peignoir of dark blue silk.

'Do you think I'd go to Canada and leave you here?' she said.

'Probably not,' sighed Arthur. 'But I would be greatly relieved if you agreed to.'

'My job is with you.'

'Obviously, I have to stay here.'

'Then I stay.'

'We will be at war with Germany within a year,' said Arthur, standing up. 'Hitler will not stop at Czechoslovakia. Next he will want Poland; and after that he'll want Rumania. Sooner or later Britain and France will run out of countries to give him. Then it'll be our turn. I don't want you to be here. Liverpool will be a major target for the German air force. The docks, shipping in the river, Cammell Laird's, the refineries at Ellesmere Port. Go to Canada, my puffin. You'll be safe there. You'll be able to go for sledge rides in the snow.'

'And leave you to fight the war single-handed? No, Arthur. I won't go.'

'We can write. You can send me photographs of yourself wrapped up in furs.'

'No, Arthur. If Mr Hitler's going to bomb us, he'll have to bomb us both.'

'It's not much fun being bombed. There's not an awful lot you can do.'

'You can be together.'

Having failed to persuade Grace to take refuge in Canada, Arthur wrote to his brother-in-law, Walter, about Walter's little mother in Waterloo.

'I think you should seriously consider having your mother to live with you, in Cheshire,' he wrote. 'The old lady's only a quarter of a mile from the docks. There is bound to be fearful damage. Whole streets will be destroyed.'

Walter, like many others, did not share Arthur's fatalism, but he did go and see his mother, and he put it to her that if war broke out, he and Enid would feel better if she was living with them.

She refused. 'No, I'm not leaving,' she said.

'We'll come and take you away,' threatened Walter.

'No, you won't. I've lived here all my life. I'm much too old to leave.'

A month later, this tiny, stubborn lady's second grandchild, Greg's first daughter, was born: Kathleen Sally Miller, to be known as Sally, which was already decided for her. Her christening, compared to that of her cousin Alan Townsend Miller, was a subdued affair. Cousin Beatrice, for the second time in less than a year, found herself a godmother; she seemed to disapprove of Greg's choice of a wife much less than she'd disapproved of Walter's, probably because Kathleen wouldn't say boo to a goose. Walter was the godfather; and Enid was the only Carruth to attend: and Kathleen was so weak she could hardly stand, because the birth had been very difficult; in fact for a few days nobody thought she'd live. She was, besides, shy, with long hair that she wore in plaits like a little girl's; company terrified her, and especially the company of Aunt Beatrice, who was actually quite nice to her and kept offering to stay and help.

The little old lady was sorry that Grace wasn't there, her lovely friend from Walter's wedding, who'd given her half of her glass of champagne and taken her to the toilet during somebody's speech. Greg made some witty observations.

At a Board meeting of the Red Funnel Line in early November, Arthur found himself under unaccustomed fire.

'Whether or not there is war with Germany,' said Cuthbert Tilson, a young Board member with a bit of a reputation as a firebrand, 'we have to look beyond. We've scrapped six perfectly serviceable ships. They weren't fast, but they could have been earning us revenue for another five to ten years. Thanks to Mr Carruth's policy of "minimising our exposure", as he calls it, we have built no new tonnage since the *English Bay*, which I don't need to remind you was launched in 1933. I find it ironic that it was this same Mr Carruth who argued so strongly for building the *English Bay* at a time when every other shipping line in Europe was cancelling orders. Everybody must have thought us crazy. Yet what we have now is a problem of dwindling tonnage. Mr Carruth fears that our fleet will be decimated in the coming war, assuming of course that war does come. But the way we're headed, we're not going to have much of a fleet left to decimate. Nazi U-boats will have a hard time finding it.'

There was some laughter. Mr Tilson took a short drink of water. Sir William Crashaw looked amused.

'Gentlemen,' Tilson went on, 'we have four ships on the drawing boards, each of twenty-three thousand tons. They would be amongst the most modern vessels in the British Merchant Marine. They will be oil-fired, with thirty-four thousand horse-power Vosper Thorneycroft diesel engines. Yet we have dithered for nearly a year. Mr Carruth believes it pointless to build ships that will be torpedoed as soon as they're launched. But in the meantime we're losing valuable revenues. What if we don't declare war on Germany? We run the risk of going out of business! I believe we should invite tenders, and I have an idea which – which I know will be controversial.'

'We have made controversial decisions before,' said Sir William.

'My idea is – we go to a German yard.'

Tilson looked around him. He saw only long faces. Sir William leaned back in his chair at the head of the Boardroom table and stared at the chandelier.

After at least a minute he said, 'I suppose if war breaks out we'll have to move that chandelier to the basement for storage.'

'I suggest a German yard,' said Tilson, who thought perhaps he'd gone too far, 'in order to "minimise our exposure".'

'Perhaps you could explain.'

'In the event of war, I would assume the contract cancellable.'

Sir William looked down from the chandelier, focused on Arthur Carruth, who removed his spectacles to dab his eyes with a white handkerchief.

'Arthur, what do you think of all this?'

'I do not believe we should place an order with a German shipyard. I would consider such a move highly unethical.'

'Well, I agree with you,' said Sir William. 'But what about inviting tenders from British yards, right now? Wouldn't that be a shot in the arm for morale? Wouldn't that show we – believe in victory?'

'Certainly it would. And don't misunderstand me – I believe we will win a war with Germany. But it will take us time to win it. In the meantime, British yards will be heavily bombed by Hitler. Mr Tilson is right in lamenting our dwindling fleet. But I believe the steps we have taken will put us in a very strong position after the war. I believe the Red Funnel Line will recover more quickly than our competitors. The new ships should, certainly, be built. It's simply a question of when. And where. Let's agree the time is now. I will suggest where.'

'Where's that, Arthur?'

'The United States. The Americans will be dragged into the war, sooner or later. I have no doubt of that, though millions of Americans can't believe it. But our ships will be safe. If necessary, we will stop construction, until a more advantageous time.'

'That's a brilliant idea, Arthur,' Sir William said.

'It's a better idea than mine,' admitted Cuthbert Tilson.

Sir William's secretary bustled into the room. This was highly irregular, because Board meetings of the Red Funnel Line were never interrupted. She whispered at Sir William, who looked up at Arthur.

'Arthur, you and I need to talk for a minute. Gentlemen, I shall be back shortly. We might take a vote on the new proposals when I return.'

In the corridor, with its dimly-lit paintings of early Red Funnel ships under steam and sail, Sir William said, 'Grace has been taken to hospital, Arthur. She's in Crosby General, Lady Crashaw is with her, it was she who telephoned. They were at some meeting. Charity. Steering committee, I don't know what. Grace collapsed. You'll want to leave immediately. My car is at your disposal.'

Arthur skidded out of the lift, ran across the marbled entrance hall with its Corinthian columns and its twelve foot long scale-model of the *English Bay*, presented by the builders. He'd rejected the offer of Sir William's car; he could catch the three thirty-five train from Exchange Station, which would be quicker. He glanced at his watch; it was three twenty-eight. He ran along Dale Street, skipping off the pavement to avoid passers-by, who were surprised to see a not-young man running so fast. The big clock outside the station said three thirty-three; Arthur barrelled across the concourse, waved his season ticket at the astonished ticket collector, who recognised him; made the train. The doors slid shut. The train, at this time of day, was nearly empty, except for a few shoppers with parcels and bags. Arthur stood at the doors, holding on to the steel grab-bars with both hands, recovering his breath. The train accelerated out of the cavernous station; slowing down to stop at Sandhills, then at Bankhall, then at Bootle, then at Seaforth, then at Waterloo, then at Crosby. At Blundellsands Arthur sprang out of it, shoved past two elderly ladies tottering towards the turnstiles. He ran along Blundellsands Avenue, into St Anthony's Road. The streetlights were already on. The Greater Crosby General Hospital stood in a vast park with leafless trees.

Nurses waved him on, pointed at staircases, indicated doors. Lady Crashaw stood in front of him.

'She's asleep. It's not good, Arthur.'

She squeezed his hand, standing aside to let him enter. Grace was on her own, in a small private room. Arthur took off his jacket, dropped it on the floor; his shirt felt glued to his chest with sweat. He sat down on the bed.

Grace opened her eyes. She saw him. Her face broke into the jolliest smile. He'd never seen her look so happy.

'I'm here,' he panted.

'I'm so glad!'

'Don't talk. You were supposed to be asleep.'
'I was afraid you wouldn't make it!'
She still smiled, gazing at him with boundless love.
'I made it, puffin.'
'Bless you.'
'I think I knocked two old ladies over at the station,' Arthur said.
'I always hoped you'd be here... That's why I wouldn't go to Canada. I didn't want to die on my own.'
He leaned forward to kiss her; she slid her arms around him. 'You won't die,' Arthur said, in her ear. 'Not yet. Not for a long time. I promised I wouldn't let you.'
'It's been such fun, darling. It's been tremendous fun.'
'I love you. I love you totally, my puffin.'
'Puffin. Yes. Do puffins dance?'
'I'm sure they do.'
'I loved to dance with you. You were so hopeless!'
She laughed. He was sure of it.
'I'll always love you,' he said, but the tears were streaming down his face and he choked.
'Always turned out to be long enough,' she whispered.
'Never is long enough.'
'Don't cry, darling. I don't want you to cry, when I'm so happy.'
As best he could, he began talking, stroking her neck behind her ears. 'When we get you out of here,' he said, 'we'll go to Canada. Both of us. I'll resign from the Red Funnel Line. We'll sail to Canada. We'll spend the whole time together. We'll dress up in big fur coats. We'll go tobogganing. We'll make snowmen; you're very good at making snowmen, but next time I'll help you. We'll make a

snowman for me, with spectacles, and a snowlady for you, with curls. We'll take long trains across the snow. We'll see the Rocky Mountains. We'll watch green lakes go by. Jagged peaks. We'll dance in lovely hotels. We'll dance, my Grace. We'll dance... indefinitely.'

But she didn't hear him anymore. Grace was dead.

Chapter Seven

So, what does an infernal optimist do when his wife dies?

First, he strode to the door, he must find somebody, grab a doctor: who ran this place? 'Bring her back!' he needed to order. Such incompetence would not be tolerated in the Red Funnel Line!

Then he stopped and turned. She looked so comfortable, curled up there like a sleeping kitten, that he relented. No, best not to disturb her. But for the first time in his life he could see no obvious way ahead. What happened next? Well, he couldn't face what happened next, but he knew that nothing would happen as long as he was there, so he sat down on the little wooden chair beside the bed.

'I let you down, puffin,' he said. 'I never let anyone down before. And you, of all people.'

He didn't want to look at her again so he sat there staring straight ahead. It had been a long day and he was angry with Cuthbert Tilson. Fancy proposing the Red Funnel Line invite Nazi yards to tender! And now Grace was dead. Arthur shut his eyes and dozed for a while; he was woken up by a tapping, scratching, scuffling at the door, as if mice were trying to get in. He knew he had to leave now.

'Good night, my puffin,' he whispered in the dark. 'Sleep tight.'

He stood up, found his jacket on the floor, straightened his tie. He opened the door, two nurses were there.

'Mr Carruth, we—' one of them began.

'It's all right,' he told her. 'You can go in now.'

He walked out of the hospital. It was a quiet night, cold. He strode along St Anthony's Road, and turned up his collar, which must have made him look peculiar, but it didn't matter, there was no one to see him. He couldn't think where to go. Not to the flat, there was no point. He might have gone to see George, but George was in London; perhaps he should telephone George; but George would be asleep; he'd telephone tomorrow. He might have gone to see Enid, but she was in Cheshire, and it was too late to telephone her too. Tomorrow he would have to do some telephoning, but now what?

He stood for some time under the railway bridge, with his collar turned up and his hands in his pockets to try and keep them warm. A train rumbled slowly overhead, stopped at Blundellsands station. Probably the last train out of Liverpool Exchange, the eleven thirty-five. The last time he'd got off a train here, Grace had still been alive.

He set off to walk, swinging his arms to get the blood circulating. Now he was marching, as he'd marched to war, in 1914. He'd worn a kilt then, the black and green tartan of the Black Watch. And he hadn't even known Grace. Not till he came home on leave, and George took him to the tennis club, and he'd danced with her. Yes, and fallen in love. Private Arthur Carruth, Deputy Chairman of the Red Funnel Line, marched through the deserted streets of

Crosby; left, left, left right left, left, left, left right left. Some say, Good old Sergeant-Major. Others...! Chin in, chest out! Left. Left. Left right left. He crossed the Southport Road: Southport, yes. Grace had been particularly fond of Southport, she liked shopping there, on Lord Street, she liked to walk with him to the end of the pier. It would be difficult to go there again. Left. Left. Left, right, left, right, left. Private Carruth! Swing those arms! Left. Left.

He found himself at the river. Halted smartly, and stood there. Breathed in, filled his lungs with the salt air. Exhaled. Breathed in again, slowly. The lights of the city glowed in the sky; behind him, a million people who didn't give a damn. He trotted down a flight of stone steps on to the sand. This was where he'd taken Enid for walks when she was small, and she'd gone scampering through tidal pools, chasing shore-birds. Private Arthur Carruth, Deputy Chairman of the Red Funnel Line, kicked off his shoes and rolled up his trouser legs. It was low tide. Out to sea he could make out the low black line of the revetment. The buoys along the Crosby Channel winked red, winked green. Their gongs tolled. Their gongs tolled for Grace, for Grace Carruth. Godspeed, Grace Carruth. Godspeed, and good fortune.

He splashed through the mud. The tide was on the turn now; and Arthur a long way from the sea wall: black water sparkled all around him. He kicked at the low ripples, in his stockinged feet. There would be quicksands. He should go back. But go back where?

He tried to remember where he'd taken off his shoes. At the top of steps, but steps led down on to the sand every fifty yards. In the end he sat on the sea wall to wait until it was light enough to find his shoes. He looked at his watch. It was two thirty-five. The last time he'd looked at his watch, she'd still been alive. The last time it was two thirty-five, she'd still been alive. He took the watch off his wrist, and threw it as far out into the darkness as he could.

It began to rain at some point, but Arthur didn't move. His elbows on his knees, his face in his hands, he waited. The rain, streaming down his face, between his fingers, joined with his tears. He wept for his Grace. He wept all night, and it rained. The buoys winked, out there in the darkness, and the gongs tolled.

In the morning he walked to the yellow-brick house in Crosby. His mother opened the door.

'I thought you should know,' Arthur said, in his usual, slightly husky, precise way, 'that Grace died last night, at about half past six, in the Greater Crosby hospital.'

'Lady What's-her-name came round. She told us.'

Arthur's father appeared, distraught for him, in his dressing gown. 'My boy,' he said. 'My boy, my boy.'

'Wherever have you been, Arthur?' said his mother. 'You're soaked to the skin. Get out of those wet clothes, you'll catch your death.'

'I need to do some telephoning,' Arthur said.

'Your father spoke to George. He's coming up by train. He'll be here this afternoon. He spoke to Enid too.'

'I must telephone Sir William, and tell him I'll be in late.'

'He left a message. Just to let him know when the funeral will be.'

'I need to know how the vote went.'

'What vote?'

'It doesn't matter. I proposed we asked American yards to tender.'

Grace was buried at St Stephen's, Crosby, where she'd been married fifteen years before. The church was packed for the memorial service. Sir William and Lady Crashaw, Poindexter, Tilson, every member of the Red Funnel Line Board. The Lord Mayor of Liverpool and his wife, the Mayor of Birkenhead, the Chairman of Cammell Laird's and his wife. The Chairman of the Mersey Docks and Harbour Board. The Members of Parliament for Crosby and for Birkenhead. The Chairman of the Liverpool Chamber of Commerce. The Vice Consuls of the United States, France, Argentina, Brazil, and Chile. The Chairmen of all Grace's charities. The Headmaster of the Merchant Taylors' School, Crosby, where she'd taught.

Lady Crashaw herself had arranged for the church to be gloriously decorated with flowers; which hadn't been easy because it was November, and there was no time to ship blooms in by Red Funnel Line steamer, so Lady Crashaw had emptied nearly every florist's shop in Liverpool of all the cut flowers they had.

The minister, in awe of his huge and famous congregation, the largest St Stephen's would ever see, began the service. 'Let us give thanks for the life of Grace Carruth,' he said. 'We will start with the hymn, *The King of Love my Shepherd is*, hymn number four hundred and sixty-four in your hymn books.'

Neither Grace nor anyone in the family had ever been a churchgoer, but her brother Claud had agreed with the minister that the words seemed right. After the hymn, some prayers; then the choir of St Stephen's sang psalm number forty-six, 'God is my refuge and strength, a very present help in trouble', again at the minister's suggestion.

Sir William had offered to speak the eulogy, but Arthur had asked George to; so after the last verse of the psalm George made his way to the front of the church. He wore a grey suit because he didn't have a darker one, and it didn't fit; but he'd found a black tie; and he spoke with hardly a trace of a stammer.

'I think we were all of us in love with Grace Carruth,' George said. 'All of us here. I don't mind admitting that I was in love with her. And perhaps always w-w-will be. When Arthur married Grace, I thought he was the luckiest m-m-man alive. I still do. I would change places with Arthur now, if I could. Because of the memories of her he must have. Private memories which the rest of us can only guess at. Memories of Grace happy. Memories of Grace sad. Memories of places she loved. Memories of the Isle of Man. Memories of Grace throwing snowballs... And other memories, less private, that we can share with him. Memories of Grace laughing. Memories of Grace dancing. Memories of Grace at the tennis club. Memories of Grace on the court. Of her serve. Of her volley. It was d-d-difficult to return that volley, as I'm sure quite a few of us here will remember.'

A stir went through the congregation; there were some nods and smiles.

'Who will forget Grace dancing the Charleston? She always loved dancing, but it was especially the Charleston that she l-l-loved. She used to wear a short white skirt and brown beads that seemed to fly all about her when she danced. The only pity is that Arthur was always such a rotten d-d-dancer.'

More smiles. A few handkerchiefs.

'I could never believe that she'd m-m-marry the worst dancer in the club. I actually thought that Arthur was the only man who didn't have a chance. But obviously, he thought d-d-differently. And apparently, so did Grace.

'Grace knew how to make everyone happy. Even the men she didn't marry. So we can imagine how happy she made Arthur. What a lucky fellow you are, Arthur. Don't expect us to feel sorry for you today. Don't expect anyone. When Grace came into the room, you suddenly realised that life was all right. In fact it was lovely. You wanted to jump up – and shout Hurray! Even if you were feeling b-b-bloody miserable! It was because of Grace.

'She loved flowers. Remember how lovely the flat looked, with flowers everywhere. She would have loved to see this church decked out like it is, thanks to Lady Crashaw. Well, perhaps she sees it.

'Grace loved people. As everybody here knows. She hated people to be sad. She hated it when they suffered. All through the Depression, she worked at the soup kitchens. Ever since, she's devoted all the time she could to helping with charities. I don't know how many charities she was involved with. I think they're probably all represented here today, which is only right. I wonder if there were any charities Grace was not involved with, one way or another. I somehow doubt it.

'Above all, of course, and above everything, and above everyone, Grace loved Arthur. She loved Arthur very much. You lucky dog, Arthur. You l-l-l-lucky d-d-d-dog.

'I think that's all I c-c-c-can s-s-s-say.'

George went back to his place. For a few minutes nobody moved, then the organ started playing. It was Walter, who'd never sat down at an organ until four days ago. He played Rachmaninoff's *Prelude in C Sharp Minor*, Grace's favourite piece.

After the service, Arthur stood outside, shook everyone by the hand; he was very composed, wore an immaculately cut dark suit. He'd never gone back to the flat on Laburnum Road, in Blundellsands: his mother had had the place cleaned out. The furniture he and Grace had bought, and been so excited about, at Waring and Gillow's, on Lord Street, was sold.

On the day of the funeral the four Red Funnel Line ships in port at Liverpool wore their flags at half mast. So did the *English Bay*, which was loading bales of cotton, at Savannah.

Arthur moved in permanently with his mother and father. He did not entertain.

On a lovely September afternoon in 1940 Enid Miller walked the pushchair, with two-year-old Alan in it, through leafy lanes to Prestbury, Cheshire. It was a walk she liked to take, when the weather was fine. She followed the road that ran past the house as far as Potts' farm, then turned right: the fields smelled of grass and manure. After two hundred yards there was an ancient barn, black and white, and then the road went through woods for half a mile. There'd been no autumn gales so the leaves were still on the trees, crisp and golden: after strong winds there'd be seagulls in the fields, and gulls would follow tractors as they ploughed, but today was soft and balmy; in fact Enid hadn't even bothered with a coat; she wore a white cotton dress, open at the neck, the top buttons undone; she had no stockings, but good walking shoes.

As she came out of the trees and into the sunshine a jay flew along the edge of the wood, and in the fields there were rabbits. Enid stopped and lifted Alan out of the pushchair so that he could walk for a while. She was mindful of traffic but traffic was rare these days, because of petrol rationing. Alan toddled along the hedgerow, picking up leaves, twigs, stones, and examining them; and a lark sang, rising high into the clear blue Cheshire sky, rising and singing, rising and singing, then falling a hundred feet before rising and singing out of sight. Enid heard a tractor coming, so she held young Alan's hand as it passed, an old man in a flat cap perched up on it.

'Skylark,' she told Alan. 'Tractor.'

'Tractor,' the child agreed.

'Shall I push you again?'

'Walk.'

Flat meadows with hawthorn hedges, and then a brick bridge over a small brook; a stile, with a footpath across the fields. Enid climbed the stile, lifted the pushchair over it, helped Alan clamber over. He stood on the bank of the stream, watching the burbling water. Cress grew there, pressed flat by the current; there was clover, and vetch. In the shade of a weeping willow, gnats skipped on the surface of the water, and two ducks snoozed.

'Brook,' said Enid. 'Water. Ducks.'

'Quack, quack,' Alan said, but the ducks didn't quack.

Walter had joined up in January. The old Vauxhall had been put up on chocks of wood in the garage; wouldn't be using it again for a while. Walter was in the Air Force; he wanted to fly. He was afraid of the sea but thought he might like the sky; and he was shocked when they told him he was too old, because with his mop of red hair he looked younger than he was, and felt it. But aircrew were nineteen, twenty, twenty-one. Twenty-five was old. The pilots who flew Halifax bombers over the Ruhr each night were boys hardly out of school. Notwithstanding his disappointment, Walter at once made friends with everybody, with lads from the slums of Manchester as well as the sons of Hampshire viscounts who talked about hunt balls and polo. The Royal Air Force found out he was a photographer, so they offered him a commission as an intelligence officer and sent him off to a rambling redbrick mansion in the Thames Valley. The house had been requisitioned by the Royal Air Force; it had spectacular views of the river, but was otherwise surrounded by the gloomiest trees in the world, and massive rhododendrons that never flowered because the sun never penetrated those miserable woods. Walter hated the place, but he learned to interpret aerial photographs of cities, distinguish railway yards and road junctions, airfields, military installations, the smoke from chimneys that betrayed camouflaged factories, so that he could brief aircrews on what to bomb. When he took the King's commission Flight Lieutenant Miller came home on leave. He had forty-eight hours. He made the best of them: Enid found herself pregnant again. Walter's first posting was to a Bomber Command base in Lincolnshire called Linton-on-Ouse, where he lived in prefabricated officers' quarters and ate poached eggs in the mess.

His brother Greg had also joined the Royal Air Force, but was not considered officer material: Greg didn't mind at all, he became an LAC2 with Fighter Command, working on aircraft maintenance in hangars that were constantly under attack by the Luftwaffe. He learned to run quickly and throw himself into foxholes piled high with sandbags as the bombs detonated. Once he was working with three other men on a Spitfire when the air-raid sirens wailed. He'd already had to run for cover twice that day, and Greg had had enough. The others ran, but Greg went on tightening nuts. He was flung into the air by a bomb exploding fifty yards away, but when he sat up he was still holding his spanner, and he went back to work. He might have got a medal; instead he was severely reprimanded and cashiered, but he didn't mind.

At Liverpool, the docks burned, incendiary bombs turned warehouses into infernos, cargoes blazed; each night the sirens howled, firefighters rolled out miles of hose, and the sky glowed red. But tiny Mrs Miller refused to budge. Half the houses on the other side of her street were demolished, reduced to smoky rubble, splintered furniture, scraps of wallpaper. Exhausted men, their faces black with smoke, lit cigarettes; women in shawls pushed prams loaded with pots and pans, pillows, whatever they'd been able to save. A pall of smoke hung over the river.

The inbound Blue Star Line vessel, *Auckland Star*, was bombed in the Crosby Channel. As the fires spread, her captain ordered the helmsman to put her on to the revetment. Trailing smoke and flame, she went aground in twenty feet of water; survivors were taken off by lifeboats. She burned there for three days, clear of the channel; years later, after the war, their Uncle Arthur would point out to his nephews her rusting boilers, still visible at low tide.

Arthur Carruth had stayed in the house at Crosby, on his own; his parents moved to Cheshire, took up what would later be the boys' room, where Walter had stood at the open window smoking all night when Alan was born, and seen owls.

Enid showed Alan the cows. The cows came to the barbed wire fence, which they liked to scrape their sides against lazily; flies buzzed about their eyes.

'Cows,' said Alan.

It was a very still afternoon, with a few high white clouds. Enid liked to get out of the house. Her mother fried onions all the time. The old lady was bored: for the first time in her life, she had nothing to do, except help Enid cook, and look after the baby. Each day, whatever the weather, she'd get into her huge black coat and walk up to the village, queue in every shop, fumble with ration books to buy bread, margarine, dried eggs, potatoes, some meat or fish; sometimes Mr Partington, the butcher, or Mr Ellis, the fishmonger, would sneak her something extra in a package, produced with a friendly wink from under the counter.

'Now we're going to pick blackberries,' Enid told Alan. 'You can help your Mum, only be careful, because of the briars. And only pick the nice black ones, which are ripe. The red ones aren't ripe yet, but they will be if we come back here next week.'

Along the side of the lane the two of them collected the ripe berries, filling two basins Enid had brought, their fingers stained purple.

'Granny will make us a blackberry pie. We'll have blackberry pie and custard. Before the war, we used to have blackberry pie and cream, but we can't get cream now. Sometimes, we had blackberry pie and ice cream. What a shame you don't know what ice cream is. Well, after the war, when it's over, I'll buy you ice cream.'

Not having any idea what she was talking about, Alan felt in no way deprived of ice cream. He liked blackberries, and he liked the blackberry pie his grandmother made; most of all though he liked blackberrying with his mother. She enjoyed it too: Liverpool children did not get to pick blackberries, and she was glad that Alan would grow up here in Cheshire, deep in Walter's territory, and be able to wander down pleasant lanes with green hedges and brambles.

She trundled him in his pushchair the last mile and a half, into Prestbury village, where there were black and white houses, including a fifteenth century mansion, once the home of a glover, or a furrier, or a hosier, now the branch of a bank. There was a village green where in summer men played cricket as the shadows of enormous trees lengthened across the field, and as the low sun coloured the stubby tower of the sandstone church a faded rose. Cheshire rose! Walter had loved Prestbury; before Alan was born the two of them had driven here sometimes on a Sunday, to have tea at the Bridge Hotel, with its low black beams and shiny horse brasses and tiny diamond window panes. She folded the pushchair, took Alan's hand, and the two of them went in. She had an hour before catching the bus home – it was too far to walk both ways, with the pram – so she'd have some tea, and perhaps a piece of cake. She put their two basins of blackberries on the little table, and propped Alan up in a real chair; the table had a little net tablecloth. The radio was on.

It was here that Enid learned about the fall of France.

The waitress, an elderly soul in a black skirt and white apron, did not seem unduly upset, but to Enid the fall of France was terrible news. Her brother Arthur has assured her the Allies would win, but with the fall of France Britain didn't seem to have any Allies. It was late summer in Prestbury, Cheshire, and Britain was on her own.

Enid had been to France. Apart from Private Arthur Carruth of the Black Watch, in 1915, Enid was the only Carruth to have visited the continent of Europe. She'd been fourteen at the time, and one of a party of gawky maidens from Merchant Taylors' who'd stayed in a convent for ten days, at St Germain-en-Laye, just outside Paris. Nuns escorted them through the streets of Paris, where their neat school uniforms, and perhaps especially their short pleated skirts and bare legs, caused a stir. Enid in particular, with her lithe figure and dancer's features, was singled out for praise, and had a notion of it; she blushed when they were taken into cafés. She fell in love with Paris, the first place where she'd suddenly felt grown-up; she sipped her bowls of café au lait thoughtfully, occasionally risked a glance, over the rim, at the moustachioed but friendly men who stood at the bar with glasses of red wine and watched her.

'*Elle est belle, la petite, là,*' she heard them say.

'*Celle-là, oui; un de ces jours elle sera vraiment belle.*'

The waitress in Prestbury brought two little plates, each with a slice of cake. Enid dipped hers in her tea, as she'd learned, in France, to dip croissants in coffee.

And now her beautiful Paris would have horrible Nazis tramping about it in jack-boots. She couldn't believe it. Today, Paris; tomorrow, Prestbury. Would German soldiers be sitting in this little hotel, drinking tea, in a few weeks' time? It seemed likely. Would Nazis march through the sunny lanes where she and her little boy had just been picking blackberries, singing their hateful songs?

That evening she telephoned her brother Arthur, in Crosby.

'What's going to happen?' she said. 'Should we have gone to Canada, like you wanted us to? We should have, shouldn't we? But it's too late now. And with Walter in the Air Force I wouldn't want to leave.'

'America will enter the war,' Arthur told her. 'I think quite soon. Certainly our backs are against the wall, right now; but as a nation we seem to do better that way. We behaved disgracefully for ten years; I believe we shall now start behaving well.'

Enid felt better. She went into the kitchen feeling quite cheerful. Her mother was frying onions.

Shortly after ten o'clock, on the morning of 15th January, 1941, Oberleutnant Karl Georg Schaufuss of the U-boat U729 fired a single shot across the bows of the Red Funnel vessel *Chesapeake Bay*. The submarine rose and fell, low and grey, with the greasy blue swells of the South Atlantic, one hundred and eighty-four miles east-north-east of Cape Pernambuco. It was a magnificent day, with the faintest line of cloud on the western horizon, towards Brazil. The British ship – her wartime camouflage spoiled, somewhat, her otherwise graceful lines, her fine bow, her old-fashioned counter-stern, her single, slightly over-sized funnel – lost way. The young German lieutenant nodded his approval.

'I was concerned she might try to outrun us,' he told his First Officer.

'I would have been tempted to try, if I was her captain,' agreed Leutnant Kaspar Ernst.

'Gun detail! Action stations!' the U-boat captain ordered, over the intercom, pressing himself against the sides of the conning tower as the men came scrambling eagerly up the steel ladder. They clattered down on to the narrow deck, grabbed the single lifeline, gulped welcome draughts of fresh sea air: they'd been underwater for seventeen days and the ship stank. They manned the gun; from the tower, Oberleutnant Schaufuss watched it swivel towards the British cargo ship. He could hear bells ringing on board her. His First Officer had a message from below, where the radio officer had been leafing hurriedly through his silhouettes to identify the target. He'd scrawled on a message pad, '*James Bay* or *Chesapeake Bay*, out of Liverpool, owners, Red Funnel Line, Liverpool.'

Oberleutnant Karl Georg Schaufuss grinned at his First Officer as he raised the loudspeaker to his mouth and hailed the other ship, which now lay beam on to the long roll of the Atlantic; a thin column of black smoke rose vertically from her funnel.

'Good morning!' he shouted, in excellent English. 'I will give you ten minutes to lower your boats. I forbid you to radio your position. If you try, I will open fire.'

He lowered the loudspeaker, waiting for acknowledgement. A figure on the bridge of the British ship held a loudspeaker to his lips, but it was difficult to catch the words over the slapping of the waves against the steel hull of the submarine.

'What does he say?' asked the German First Officer.

'He says he has three women passengers and requests we take them on board.'

'Ask if they are pretty!'

'I very much regret we cannot take your passengers!' shouted the captain. 'You must all get into the boats. In one hour's time I will put out a distress call on all frequencies. With any luck you will be rescued quite soon.'

'He is taking a long time,' observed the First Officer; but the first of the ship's boats was being swung out.

'A handsome ship,' said the captain. 'It is almost a shame to send her to the bottom. The Red Funnel Line. Yes, they have four new ships under construction at Newport News, in America. There is someone in that company who thinks ahead. I wish we had some people in Germany like that. Starting with our idiot Führer.'

His young captain's reckless talk always shocked the First Officer.

'We'll sink this ship, then when they launch the four new ones we'll sink them too,' said Leutnant Ernst.

'Ah yes. If we're still around.'

The First Officer was watching through his binoculars. He chuckled. 'I see the three women,' he said. 'They wear white dresses. Perhaps nurses. They do not look very pretty.'

'She must have come out of Buenos Aires, was homeward bound for Liverpool,' said his captain, thinking of the ship. When the boats were clear he'd put a torpedo into her engine room; it would be quicker than trying to sink her by gunfire. 'I once met a man from Liverpool. It was when I was very young. This man came to see my mother, in Cologne, after the First War. He gave her a photograph which my father had entrusted to him before he died, in some foxhole near Armentières. Isn't that a good story? A good man, to go to that trouble. A good man.'

Two stupendous columns of water obscured the captain's view of the British ship, followed by the thump-thump-thump of gunfire. The *Chesapeake Bay's* second salvo hit the submarine just above her waterline; the first shell exploded below the gun, the second and third forward of her conning tower.

'Dive! Dive! Dive!' screamed her captain, but his mouth was full of blood. Leutnant Ernst tried to hold him upright, but small arms fire from the *Chesapeake Bay* raked the U-boat's conning tower. A third salvo blew off most of her bow; her torpedoes, which were armed, detonated one after the other.

Captain Ditchfield of the *Chesapeake Bay* lowered his binoculars. 'That's one for you, Mr Carruth,' he said to himself, as his second mate, purser, and radio operator struggled out of the white dresses they'd put on over their shirts and rolled-up pants. Sir William Crashaw was notified a few days later by the Admiralty, in a coded telegram. He passed on Their Lordships' congratulations to Mr Carruth.

Chapter Eight

Years later, Alan Miller remembered that all the curtains had been drawn, so that it was dark in the house, except for bright stripes of stray sunlight that would fall across a carpet. He remembered that his mother was upstairs in bed, and that he wasn't allowed in there; and that his grandmother seemed to be going upstairs and downstairs all the time, her arms full of sheets. He remembered that once she was carrying a basin and the basin was full of blood. He remembered his Uncle Arthur arriving and telling him rather solemnly 'Your mother is very poorly.' He remembered there being another lady in the bedroom with his mother, a fussy lady with her hair done up in a bun; and if this lady wasn't in the bedroom she was in the bathroom whenever he wanted to go there himself. But he never had any idea what was happening.

His brother, Toby Walker Miller, was born in April, 1941. One day his grandmother went about pulling back the curtains and flinging open the windows: and the house lost its smell of dried blood and disinfectant; and the fussy lady with the bun stopped coming. Now Alan was allowed in to see his mother again, and there she was, sitting up in bed. Her eyes glittered but she looked pale and tired.

Enid never recovered her dancer's figure, though Alan thought her, and rightly, 'really smashing.' She liked flowing white dresses, gathered loosely about her waist, and she grew her hair much longer, so that the lovely black curls floated about her white shoulders. She sat in the garden a lot, in a deckchair; and took to gardening, but she had no patience with it, she'd potter about with a trowel, or pruning shears, but only for a little while, then she'd flop in her deckchair again, and she could never find her garden tools afterwards. Walter had never shown any interest in gardening, though before the war he'd enjoyed wandering up and down with a cigarette, admiring the unkempt glory of his lupins and his peonies. Until Uncle Arthur took matters in hand, the grass grew very long; daisies and dandelions flourished, there were tiny brown mushrooms and a fairy ring.

'Why don't you mow the lawn, at least?' Grandmother badgered Grandfather. 'The garden is a disgrace. I feel ashamed when people look over the gate.'

'I haven't got time,' he'd say.

It had been many years now since the old man had attempted a painting. Yes, he'd made a few sketches of the *English Bay* in her fitting-out basin at Cammell Laird's, and it was the kind of thing he could have done well, with his eye for detail; he'd have captured, wouldn't he, the liquid quality of the light, the short chop on the water; but then he'd left his sketches on the train to Crosby, in a black canvas bag; perhaps on purpose because he never even telephoned the left luggage office at Liverpool Exchange, and by the time Arthur found out, and personally turned the left luggage office inside out, there was no trace of the bag.

He got up very late, did idle Arthur Simon Carruth, never before ten o'clock, and he spent the morning wearing his pyjama jacket as a shirt, tucked into his trousers. His beard had grown white and wiry, and his breath smelled, so Alan absolutely hated being kissed by him; but luckily this happened only rarely. The old man became very absent-minded and sometimes appeared in the village still wearing his pyjama top. He was short-tempered with the children, who learned to avoid him.

Annie Sadie Carruth was incontinent and her skirts smelled of pee; she could never wash the smell out. She busied herself about the house as best she could, because she was incapable of sitting still, never had done all her life; she did the washing and ironing; she also did nearly all the cooking, because Enid didn't have the patience any more: some afternoons Enid would set out to bake a cake, but by the time she'd measured out the flour, and the margarine, and the water, and found a mixing bowl, she was tired of it all and just left everything for her mother to put away, grumbling. The boys were brought up on their grandmother's Lancashire hotpots, her cottage pies, her breast of lamb stews, all of which reappeared at least twice, first as leftovers, then as rissoles, because the old lady despised waste. The smell of cooking, as well as the smell of pee, clung to her, even when she put on her enormous black coat and went out: it followed her to the village; it followed her into shops; into the butcher's and the fishmonger's where she queued up with her ration cards; into the haberdasher's where she bought elastic to mend Enid's suspenders.

Unlike Alan, who had been a wonderfully good-tempered baby, Toby bawled all the time. His howls drowned most other noise in the house.

'He's a howling Harab!' his grandmother complained, frying onions for a hotpot. 'A shrieking Alec!'

'Stop crying, baby,' Enid would say, but she didn't seem to mind the baby yelling, and would sometimes try to carry on a normal conversation although nobody could hear a word because of Toby.

'How can you put up with that child screaming its head off like that, all the time?' Grandfather would fuss.

'Would you like to take him, then?' Enid would smile.

'It's your job to make him shut up, not mine.'

'Why? He's your grandson.' The dancer's eyes flashed; her mother recognised her own temper. Yet Enid, post-Toby, and without Walter, had become a stranger – she didn't even recognise herself, she didn't notice things, she didn't seem to care, nothing mattered very much.

In September, Uncle Arthur stayed for a week. He insisted Enid get out of the house, which she'd hardly done since Toby's birth, except to sit in the garden, in her deckchair, and stare around. The garden was a riot of goldenrod and Michaelmas daisies by now; all yellow and purple, the leaves on the great weeping wych elm crinkled at the edges, turning red and brown. Arthur took Enid blackberrying; Alan came scampering along, Enid pushed Toby in his pram.

'You shouldn't go out, it'll rain,' grumbled Annie Sadie.

'We will shelter,' said Arthur.

And in fact a few drops of rain did fall. They'd left the village behind, taking the road to Prestbury; stood under a tree till the rain left off. After the shower, the Cheshire countryside smelled of apples and hay, astonishingly fresh and sweet. Arthur climbed over a fence and pulled Alan through the bars; the two of them ransacked a small wood for mushrooms as Enid, standing in the lane, rocked baby Toby, and sang to him.

'Look!' said Uncle Arthur to Alan. 'We're in luck. These are morels. Morels are very good to eat, and the nice thing is, you can't confuse them with any other kind of mushroom. Some mushrooms are poisonous, though not very many. Look. This is fly agaric. It's a pretty-looking mushroom, but quite poisonous. Now, can you smell something really disgusting?'

Alan sniffed. 'Ugh!' he said. 'Whatever is it?'

Pulling aside the bracken Arthur found a white stinkhorn, its top covered with the green slime that smelled so bad. 'That's a stinkhorn,' he said. 'You certainly wouldn't want to eat that. I don't imagine you'd be much tempted.'

'No, I certainly wouldn't be tempted!' agreed Alan.

'However, these fiddleheads are very good to eat. They are called fiddleheads because they are shaped like the top of a fiddle, or violin. Granny can fry them up with margarine for our supper. Shall we pick some?'

'Yes, please!'

Arthur told his young nephew the names of every tree on the way to Prestbury. And he had more luck with Alan than he ever had with Grace, or his sister, neither of whom could ever remember the things he told them. Alan learned that trees were not simply trees, a tree was an oak, or an ash, or a beech. He learned that the cows that came to rub themselves against the barbed wire fence were not just cows, they were Guernsey cows, black and white, or if they were brown and white they were probably Jerseys, or if they were a nice red all over, they'd be Herefords. When they got to Prestbury his uncle explained to Alan that the pretty, crooked, black and white cottages were Elizabethan, and the tidy little doors with neat pillars were Georgian. They went into the Bridge Hotel for tea.

'I don't suppose you have Earl Grey tea?' Uncle Arthur asked the waitress.

'Oh no, sir, we only have tea I'm afraid.'

'There's no such thing as just tea!' Alan said.

The baby woke up, Granny's Howling Harab, and started howling, before tea could arrive, so Arthur scooped up the child, and took it outside. He indicated the fifteenth century bank that had once belonged to the glover, or hosier; Toby stopped crying, and gazed with interest.

Arthur took to visiting most weekends. He would catch a train from Liverpool Central to Manchester, of a Friday evening after work, then walk up Moseley Street, past the handsome Central Library and the City Art Gallery, with its sooty black Corinthian columns, and take the number 52 bus at Piccadilly. Big grey barrage balloons floated over the city, as in Liverpool, and the red double-decker buses had been painted utility grey. On one of his visits Arthur found that all one side of Piccadilly had been destroyed by German bombs; the ruins still smouldered behind quickly thrown-up barricades; the air smelled of ashes. Two hundred and forty-five people had been killed in that raid, most of them in the slums of Ancoats and Hulme, Greenheys and Moss Side.

Grandmother used to sit in the bay window of the dining room, watching for Arthur to come striding down the lane when the bus arrived, and Alan would sit on her knee, or sometimes on the window sill, to watch with her. She was getting old; she felt mortal. Her bilious attacks happened more often. They incapacitated her; she would crouch for hours over the toilet bowl, retching green bile. She'd never been a patient woman; now she was losing patience with herself, and especially with her own body, that great, sick, shapeless sack wrapped up in black skirts. She didn't understand what was happening to Enid. She was disgusted with George, who seemed to have been defeated by life, and to have accepted defeat. She looked forward almost childishly to Arthur's visits; Arthur, still a handsome man, a distinguished-looking personage with his rimless glasses and streaks of thin black hair, Deputy Chairman, wasn't he, of the Red Funnel Line, of Liverpool; such a patient fellow; so kind, yet quietly so; such a dignified manner. And not pompous, no, not at all pompous, though once she'd thought him that.

Each time he came, his Uncle Arthur brought Alan a Puffin picture book and read it with him; or a painting book which they'd colour together. On wet Saturday mornings the two of them sat at the kitchen table, for hours, bent over their books, Alan with his tongue hanging out from concentration, his uncle patiently experimenting with water colours. Inside each book, at first, Arthur'd always written, in his clear, upright, hand, 'To Alan, from his Uncle Arthur and Auntie Grace.' But in time he brought himself to leave Grace out. 'To Alan, from his Uncle Arthur.'

When he was a few years older Alan found, in a cardboard box, all the books his Uncle Arthur had brought him on these wartime weekends.

'I must have known Auntie Grace, Uncle Arthur,' he said, showing these treasures to his uncle.

'You knew her only a little, Alan. But she was very fond of you.'

'I wish I'd known her better.'

Arthur used to sleep on the couch in the living room, where his mother would make up a bed for him. Alan especially loved Saturday mornings. He'd creep in to the living room and suddenly jump on to Uncle Arthur's bed, whooping. Uncle Arthur would pretend to be the Big Bad Tiddlypod, clutch hold of the boy and not let him go, roar horribly. When Toby was old enough Alan would lead him in by the hand and the two of them would fling themselves on to their uncle, yelling and giggling.

It occurred to Enid that she should be sorry the boys couldn't see more of their father; but she didn't believe them deprived: their Uncle Arthur filled the role more than adequately; Walter would never have spent so much time with them, even if it had still been peacetime. And the boys worshipped their Uncle Arthur. When Walter came home on leave, from time to time, the boys were rather shy of him, and treated him politely, they watched him with a certain respect and became self-conscious when he picked them up to hug.

Walter, for his part, seemed to be enjoying the war, and on leave he talked endlessly about the friends he'd made.

'There is the Colonel. "My dear Walter," he calls me. When I play the piano, the Colonel sings. And not badly.

We do some Irving Berlin and some Jerome Kern. Some Ivor Novello. Then there's Freddie Penn. And Frankie Cook. Really good blokes. Freddie has a rare sense of humour. The stories he tells. Not for your ears, believe me. Frankie is a stamp collector. Asked me if I had anything to swap; I had to tell him I stopped collecting years ago, when I got a job. We have some Polish officers on the base. Poor fellows. They talk about Warsaw. "All the time there was bomffs," they say. "All the time there was bomffs."'

What Walter did not talk about to Enid were the raids he went on himself. Night after night, in the ops room, he'd brief the bomber crews, who sat in wicker chairs in their heavy flying gear, nursing mugs of scalding tea, with three or four spoonfuls of sugar. The walls were covered with maps; Walter projected slides: blown-up aerial photos of the night's target. He gave them the routes they must take to reach it, flying high over the North Sea to the Dutch coast, where there would be no lights until anti-aircraft shells began bursting around them. He updated them on the positions of known German ack-ack batteries. The courses and coordinates Walter read out, and which the navigators jotted down, would turn out to be way-stations on the road to hell.

They were boys of nineteen, some of them. Flight-Lieutenant Miller sent children to unload four-hundred-pound bombs over the Ruhr, over Bremen, over Hamburg, over Berlin. He wasn't supposed to fly himself, but it made him feel better when he could; the Colonel turned a blind eye, so did the Wing Commander: both flew themselves, when they had a chance. Walter had a standing arrangement with some of the flight crews that if anyone couldn't fly for any reason, he'd take the fellow's place. This happened quite often; Walter finished up flying more raids than he should have survived, statistically.

This didn't worry him because he knew he was lucky and he didn't believe in statistics. One night over Caen, in Normandy, the Halifax bomber he was flying was hit by German anti-aircraft fire: caught in the searchlights, the boy pilot put his plane into an almost vertical dive, which was the only way they could escape. None of the crew knew if they'd ever come out of that dive, because they had no means of knowing how badly the plane had been hit. But Walter knew. 'Don't worry, chaps!' he sang out. 'Our problems don't begin till we hit the ground!'

But of course they didn't hit the ground. The pilot pulled the plane out of its dive, at eight hundred feet. They could actually see the fields and hedgerows of northern France. Then, thankfully, they were over the Channel, a ripple of silver.

'We've made it so far, chaps,' the pilot said. 'Trouble is, I've no idea what shape the old kite is in. If I apply full throttle she might break up. So we'll take a scenic route home at low altitude, if that's all right with you blokes. Good job the sea's not too rough, or we might get wet.'

They limped home across all of southern England. A jigsaw puzzle of small fields in the grey morning light; smoke from chimneys. A train. Birds, too, they could see; early sunshine on white wings. The steady drone of the Halifax's four engines.

'Had a spot of bother,' the pilot radioed the control tower at Linton. 'When we get over the base I'm going to make one pass quite low and I'd be much obliged if someone could lean out of the window and see if the old kite still has wheels on. My indicator lights suggest not.'

It was broad daylight by now. Wing-Commander Blakeley had fire engines drawn up along the runway. The Halifax thundered overhead at a hundred feet.

'Your undercarriage looks okay, old chap,' the pilot was told. 'Bloody great hole in the fuselage, though. Might as well bring her in, you can't stay up there all day. We've put the kettle on for you. I suppose you'd better be ready to get out fast in case she goes up.'

The tyres touched down with a puff of smoke and a smell of scorched rubber; the plane trundled down the runway between the fire trucks; came to a halt.

'Told you we'd be okay,' said Walter, as the crew jumped down.

They found they'd been leaking fuel all the way. If they'd had to abort the landing for any reason, they wouldn't have been able to make another circuit of the aerodrome.

On another occasion Walter was booked to go on a raid over Essen: the navigator had jaundice. After he'd briefed the night's crews and was pulling on his flying gear the Colonel walked into the ops room.

'I say, Walter old chap, you're not flying tonight, are you?'

'Well, yes, Colonel.'

'I've rather volunteered the two of us to do some songs, at Manston Hall nearby. You know, provide the entertainment. It's a bit of a party, for the daughter, who is quite a smashing girl. Wouldn't want to disappoint them, and all that.'

A third navigator was procured. The plane was shot down over the Dutch coast. The men were never heard of.

On weekends when he didn't visit his sister and the family, Arthur Carruth would take a train to the Lake District to go walking, which he'd always loved. Instead of the suburban electric with its sliding doors, he'd board an old LMS train with faded maroon carriages, chuffing slowly north out of Liverpool Exchange, across the industrial wasteland of Lancashire, past proud Preston with its tidal dock, to Windermere where varnished wooden motor launches furrowed the still waters of the lake. From here, he could tramp the high fells of the Lakes, where the air was thin and clear; a far cry from the bleak sands that stretched north from Crosby, with the gloomy toll of the bell buoys out along the Channel, and the shifting mists that gave all Liverpudlians catarrh. He had to manage without maps, though, because no maps were available during the war; there was no point making things too easy for invading Germans. The local Home Guard had also changed all the signposts so that they pointed in wrong directions. But Arthur had an instinctive sense of direction, amazing for a boy brought up in the city; would take off for a fifteen mile trudge over mountain ranges wreathed in cloud, across high moorland where lonely sheep loomed out of the mist, scramble at the end of the day down the sides of a heather-skirted hill into a valley where the sun broke through, just where the small hotel happened to be which he'd fixed on for the night.

Arthur, being Arthur, was always well-prepared; wore good walking boots, stout corduroy trousers, woollen sweaters, oilskins. In the summer, sometimes, he'd strip off, bathe in the numbing green waters of a mountain tarn; in winter, when snow lay over the fells, he wore fur-lined boots and a fur-lined, weatherproof jacket with a hood, carried a stout wooden stick. He explored, thus equipped, shadowy Borrowdale, towering Great Gable; climbed Sca Fell, Skiddaw, and Helvellyn, the highest peaks in England; roamed the moors of Blencathra; he knew wild Wastwater, deeper and bluer than anyone could tell, smooth Buttermere, calm Crummock Water, long Coniston, rolling Windermere, Rydal Water with its daffodils, gentle Grasmere, endless Ullswater; he walked over cold Hardknott Pass; made his way from cairn to cairn along the tall line of the Langdale Pikes.

He would exchange a friendly word with the occasional shepherd, contribute opinions when the locals discussed war matters in the snugs and public bars of small hotels in Keswick or Ambleside. But his long walks were solitary; he sought no company; avoided it, if he could. Sometimes he'd fall in with another determined tramper, stride along together a few miles until their paths diverged. A cheery wave, and Arthur was alone again. Well, perhaps not. He remembered so much of what Grace had said, recalled her voice so well, her laughing, that he didn't often feel alone, and certainly never lonely. To be sure, a shepherd would see a solitary figure; but for Arthur, another pair of feet, well shod, too, in good hiking boots, trod beside him; and an arm took his when he lingered to take in vistas of cloud-veiled peaks, or watch the wind scurry across the black surface of a deep tarn; and a voice said, 'I didn't realise how romantic you'd turn out to be,' or ask, 'Do puffins dance?' or sigh, 'It's been such fun, darling; such tremendous fun.'

'Where do you go, Uncle Arthur, when you don't come here?' his nephew Alan asked. The boy had a very clear, rather beautiful voice; like his uncle, enunciated each syllable very clearly; took after him in other ways too: his grandmother said he was the living spit of Arthur when he was a boy.

'I go tramping, in the Lakes.'

'Can I come, when I'm bigger?'

'Certainly you can.'

'Are you very lonely, without Auntie Grace?'

'No, Alan. I'm not lonely,' Uncle Arthur smiled.

He began taking Alan for walks in the wooded hills on the edge of the Cheshire Plain. On Sundays, after breakfast, they'd leave the house and take the cinder path that led past the Regal Cinema to Mottram Road. Desiring to please his meticulous uncle, Alan wore good walking shoes and carried a stick; he had a long stride and kept up with Uncle Arthur very well. 'Good morning, good morning,' they'd call to the men digging vegetables in the allotment gardens that bordered the woods. Then they'd strike up into the hills along a footpath that became a mud-slide whenever it rained, a mud-slide of red clay. Alan liked to swish at fallen leaves with his stick.

'These are beechwoods,' his Uncle Arthur explained. 'Not much grows beneath beech trees. When we get to the top and the path levels out, the trees are mostly birch, and there's plenty of fern and bracken. Look! Do you see the squirrel? A red squirrel. Red squirrels are becoming quite rare. Grey squirrels are replacing them. Now, do you see these tracks, in the mud? That's a pine marten. He's a nice little creature but we'd be lucky to see one. Look at the moss on this rock. That's called velvet sandstone moss. Feel it, you'll see why.'

'It's terrific that you know the names of everything,' Alan said. 'Nobody else knows the names of everything, like you do. I try not to forget a single thing you tell me.'

'Try not to. Poor Auntie Grace never could remember.'

'You told Auntie Grace the names of everything?'

'Oh yes.'

'You must have loved her so much.'

'Mummy tells me you're really enjoying school,' his uncle said.

'Yes, I do. Did you enjoy school, Uncle Arthur?'

'Oh, yes. I daresay. I left school when I was fourteen. I was only an average student, though. The brain's-trust was your Uncle George. I've been trying to catch up ever since.'

'We don't see much of Uncle George. But I think he's coming to spend Christmas with us.'

'Uncle George is a brilliant fellow. The tragedy is, he should have stayed on at university. He could be Professor of Chemistry at Cambridge by now. Instead, he works for a firm that makes shoe polish.'

'I find it difficult to talk to Uncle George, because he stammers so badly. Don't you find it difficult to talk to Uncle George?'

'No. Because what Uncle George says is always very interesting.'

'Did you and Uncle George get on well together, when you were boys? Or did you fight, like Toby and I do?'

'I think we got on pretty well together.'

'Toby and I aren't very like each other.'

After the birch coppice the trees thinned out. Scotch pines grew in crevices between great slabs of rock. There were distant views of the Cheshire Plain. Sounds carried: the bark of a dog, the whistle of a train. Up here in the hills the Romans had mined copper; and the workings hadn't been abandoned until the First War broke out. Lads from Manchester with ropes and flashlights would lower themselves down the old mine shafts to explore: some were killed, so the entrances had been bricked up.

'I've always wanted to go down the old copper mines,' Alan said. 'But Mummy says they're very dangerous and people fall down shafts.'

'Well, I've never fancied spelunking.'

'You've never fancied what?'

'Spelunking. It's what exploring underground caves is called.' Arthur picked up small pieces of crumbly, greenish rock. 'This is copper ore.' He showed Alan. 'You can see the veins of it in the sandstone. But they can't have found enough copper here to make it worthwhile continuing.'

'That's amazing, Uncle Arthur. Green rock. I'm going to take some home and keep it in my drawer. I'm going to show it to Uncle George when he comes at Christmas and see if he knows what it is. I bet he won't know.'

'Oh, your Uncle George will know. He'll also be able to tell you the chemical formula for copper. And what happens when you mix it with potassium.'

'What does happen?'

'I have no idea, Alan. You'll have to ask Uncle George.'

Arthur got back to Liverpool that night during an air raid. Streets had been closed so that fire engines and ambulances could get through; there was a lot of smoke, and the dull roar of flames. Lord Street was ablaze. Together with some two hundred other travellers, Arthur was herded down to the Mersey Railway underground station beneath Liverpool Central, where he lined up for hot, sweet tea from huge urns. He took off his coat to use as a pillow and stretched out on the station platform; it was cold and the tunnels smelled of smoke and urine. The 'all clear' wasn't sounded until five o'clock in the morning, when Arthur walked to the Adelphi Hotel, where before the war he and Grace had hosted glittering dinner parties. The hotel was full, the staff apologetic. Arthur made himself as comfortable as he could on a sofa in the foyer, to wait for daylight. He caught himself whistling under his breath. It was perhaps the first time he'd whistled since Grace died.

At the office, though, dreadful news. The hospital ship *English Bay* had struck a mine in the eastern Mediterranean, and sunk with the loss of seven hundred lives.

In the summer of 1944 Enid took the boys for a two-week holiday in the little village of Borth-y-gest, in North Wales. Alan was very excited to be going on a train for the first time. He watched the telephone wires rise and fall like waves and distant trees move slowly across the horizon. At Crewe they had to change. The station was full of men in uniform, the khaki of the army, the blue-grey of the air force, sailors in white caps and bell-bottoms. Troop trains moved slowly through the station, men stood in the corridors, hung out of the windows. After a three-hour wait the train to Llandudno drew slowly out of platform five, picking its way through a maze of tracks; it picked up speed; smoke flew past the windows. It stopped at Chester for a long time, then was off again; soon, there was the sea, a leaden grey. The train stopped at places with Welsh names: Prestatyn, Abergele, Rhyl. Enid took out a metal box which she'd packed sandwiches in; she and her mother had made the sandwiches the night before, there were tomato sandwiches and jam sandwiches. The bread was sliced very thin and the sandwiches were soggy; Alan thought he'd never tasted anything so delicious.

They had to change trains again, at Llandudno Junction, and it was four o'clock by the time the taxi drew up outside a little boarding house where Enid had rented a room. The house stood on a road that led down to the estuary; the air smelled of flowers and the sea. Two Welsh ladies, who both wore aprons, ran the boarding house; one of them had a son, a boy called Tom, who was nine. Tom lay on his stomach in the kitchen, throwing darts at a dartboard propped up against the wall; he showed Alan how to play, but always beat him. Enid wondered if she should worry about Toby getting a dart in his eye, but said nothing.

Walter joined his little family for a weekend. He always wore uniform, seemed to have said goodbye forever to civilian clothes in 1940. It rained the whole Saturday; Alan and Tom played darts on the kitchen floor. Enid knew that if Arthur were there he would either stop them or join in, but Walter did neither, stood at the window smoking. In the afternoon they went to have tea at a small café called The Bobbing Boats; it overlooked the muddy estuary, with the dark mountains beyond; rain clouds came down to the sea. On Sunday the weather cleared up and they rented a rowing boat; Walter rowed, the oars creaked in the rowlocks and the water gurgled under the bow, where Alan sat, entranced: one day, he would own a boat. Because of the dangerous currents they'd been warned not to go too far. A fine schooner, loaded with slate from Porthmadoc, had gone aground years ago and burned to the waterline: her huge, blackened, stem-post reared out of the sand like a sea-monster.

On the last day of their holiday, Alan's friend Tom was drowned in the river. The fishermen brought his dead body in by boat.

In February of 1945, Uncle George married Moira Turner; he'd met her at the tennis club in Muswell Hill. The Carruths travelled down to London for the wedding: Uncle Arthur, Grandmother and Grandfather, Enid, the boys. Flight Lieutenant Walter Miller had wangled some leave and met everyone at Euston Station; a Piccadilly Line tube train hurtled them to Wood Green.

Auntie Moira had short brown hair which she wore in tight little curls. She had unusual green eyes and a slightly turned-up nose, and her cheeks looked like she was sucking boiled sweets all the time. She embarrassed the boys terribly by bending down and kissing them both; her lips felt sticky. By lying on his back on the floor, Toby discovered that she wore purple bloomers. She had a unique way of pronouncing certain words; she said mountain as if it was two words, the tain rhyming with train, and the same for curtain and certain.

'Oh dear,' Enid said to Walter. 'Poor Moira. She has a face like the back of a bus. Whatever does George see in her?'

They were married in the registry office at Wood Green. Moira's older sister, Jessie, was there, with her nine year old daughter, Janet. Moira wore a bright blue suit with a very tight skirt, which her suspenders showed through; she carried a small posy of white roses and green ferns. Her sister Jessie was in black and wore a pearl necklace; Janet, who had very straight, short hair, had on a purple velvet frock. She and seven year old Alan managed to avoid each other.

After the short ceremony everybody went for lunch in a room over the saloon bar of a pub called The Dick Turpin. The room had a thick blue-and-red carpet; the tables had white linen tablecloths and plastic flower arrangements. The place smelled of stale beer and cigarettes. Arthur explained to his nephews that Dick Turpin had been a famous highwayman who once rode from London to York in four hours. They had roast beef and Yorkshire pudding for lunch; Walter asked if he could have a poached egg instead, but he couldn't. After the dessert, which was trifle, Arthur stood up to make a speech.

'It gives me great pleasure to be here today for the wedding of Moira and George,' he said. 'To begin with, of course, we are all delighted that George has finally married. We were beginning to think he'd remain a bachelor all his life. But now, not only is George married, he's married to a most charming lady, Moira, whom I am delighted to welcome into our family. I am sure George has warned Moira about the Carruths; but as a matter of fact, Moira, the Carruths aren't too bad, with the possible exception of Mother, whom I'm sure you've been warned about. You will find us a fairly close family; I don't mean geographically, of course: you and George will be in London, I live in Liverpool, Grandfather and Grandmother live with Enid and the boys in Cheshire. But we tend to look out for each other; and we will certainly make sure that George behaves himself.'

There was some polite laughter. Toby was bored and fell off his chair; he howled; his mother picked him up and sat him on her knee.

'I suspect that Moira is a fairly useful tennis player. I can't imagine my brother George marrying a dud. I understand also that she plays a good hand of bridge. This is not surprising either. My – my wife Grace was a good tennis player too, and a fair hand at bridge. I suppose I am the odd man out. Can't hit a ball with a racket to save my life. Or at least, not in the desired direction. And at bridge even Grace refused to play with me as her partner.'

Enid laughed.

'I'm sure you'll both be very happy, Moira and George. The war, of course, will soon be over. It's hard for us to imagine a life without black-outs, without rationing, without queues. We have grown accustomed to all that. We have grown accustomed to taking the train to town and finding our office not there anymore. We have hardened ourselves against bad news. The company I work for has lost eight ships, including our flagship, the *English Bay*, whilst serving as a hospital ship in the Mediterranean, and two brand new vessels which were sunk off the eastern seaboard of the United States within days of being launched. We have also, of course, lost hundreds of men, including some of our best. A young man named Cuthbert Tilson, who would probably have succeeded Sir William Crashaw one day as Chairman of the company, was killed when the destroyer he was serving on was torpedoed. The company, all the same, will survive. This country, will survive. As we rebuild, we can look forward, I have to believe, to a long period of prosperity. May you, my dear George, and may you, Moira, share in it.'

George felt called upon to reply. He'd had a few glasses of sherry. He rose to his feet, and clutched at the tablecloth.

'Thank you, Arthur, for the k-k-k-kind words,' he said. 'I don't know about the p-p-p-prosperity you wax so eloquent about. But I d-d-d-do know how l-l-l-lucky I am to have f-f-f-found Moira. You are right, Arthur, she is a f-f-f-fine tennis player, with a serve as g-g-g-good as Grace's. And yes, she also p-p-p-plays a g-g-g-good hand of b-b-b-bridge. But m-m-m-more importantly than that, she is a g-g-g-good sport and a really d-d-d-decent sort.'

Later in the afternoon, when the bars opened at The Dick Turpin, George and Arthur bought each other pints of bitter.

'I'm n-n-n-not really sure that Moira's serve is as good as Grace's was,' George said.

'It's not important,' Arthur smiled, apparently unaffected by all the liquor he'd ingested.

'You know, I c-c-c-could never have married while she was alive.'

'I think I know that, old chap.'

George changed the subject. 'I p-p-p-plan to do something about this ridiculous j-j-j-job of mine, you know, when the war's over,' he said.

'That's good news. There will be enormous opportunities.'

'They weren't very enormous after the First War.'

'The same mistakes will not be made again. America will lend a hand.'

'The t-t-t-trouble is that I d-d-d-don't know anything anymore. Chemistry has advanced quite a l-l-l-lot since 1920.'

'Then you must go back to school, George. You must get another degree.'

'I p-p-p-plan to d-d-d-do something like that.'

'I will tide you through.'

'I know you will.'

During the last weeks of the war Walter Miller flew on several low-level sorties over Germany. Instead of bombs, the RAF dropped thousands of copies of leaflets telling the population what to do as the Allies advanced. He never forgot the sight of one old man, in the middle of a vast field, shaking his fist at the British plane.

Chapter Nine

She thought the end of the war might have been more – significant. She was staying with the children at Criccieth, in North Wales: stone houses with slate roofs, afternoon tea with scones but no cream, fish and chips drowned in vinegar, the fishermen's rowing boats hauled up on the shingle, ruined castle on a grassy promontory. A bonfire lit on the stony beach and a Guy made of canvas stuffed with straw set fire to: not Guy Fawkes of Gunpowder Plot fame, but the Japanese General Tojo, complete with pipe and spectacles, for the bonfire celebrated VJ Day – Victory in Japan. She let the boys stay up until after dark to watch the fire, but when the fireworks flared and popped she escorted them to their little room at the boarding house called Sea Cliff, on a sedate but wind-blown little street, to watch from the window. Some rockets were shot off from the walls of the ruined castle; but it was not a spectacular display; a few yellow flashes and bangs, a red starburst, courtesy of the lifeboatmen. She put Toby to bed in the cot she'd begged, then she and Alan climbed solemnly into the big double bed. Stray whizzes and bangs continued long after the children had gone to sleep, and some men reeling home from the pub sang *Men of Harlech*.

She wondered what things would have been like if it hadn't turned out this way, if the Germans had invaded, which in the days following the fall of France she'd been sure they'd do, not believing, really, in her wise brother Arthur's confident promises. And she'd often wondered what it would have been like to have German soldiers around, perhaps even billeted in her house. Would they have been respectful, or would she have been raped? On the whole she thought they would have been respectful; she would have treated them politely, and made them tea; they would probably have bounced her little boys on their knees.

Now that the war was over she assumed that Walter would come home immediately, but he told her in his letters that he didn't expect to be demobbed until early the next year; nor did he show, it must be said, much regret. Arthur explained to her that they couldn't just send everybody home at once; because Germany was occupied by Allied forces and German airfields had been taken over by the Royal Air Force; so Halifax and Lancaster bombers still thundered down the runways at Linton-upon-Ouse, ferrying men and military supplies; and the Wing Commander and the Colonel still tippled gin and tonic in the mess; and Walter sang at the piano.

Arthur Simon Carruth, painter of Welsh castles and cosy farmhouses, caught pneumonia in November. The boys were taken up to see him, in bed; ushered in with solemn looks: their unloved grandfather lay propped up on pillows, his little round velvet smoking cap perched on his skull, clutching his fine gold watch in a bony hand; he looked yellow and cadaverous; his eyes pink and watery, as if he'd been crying. The boys had no idea what to say to him; and he watched them for a few minutes, as if he was trying to remember who they were.

'Hello, boys,' he said eventually.

'Hello, Grandfather,' Alan said.

Toby said nothing, but stood on one leg.

'Are you poorly?' Alan asked politely.

'I caught pneumonia. It must have been when I went to the shops to buy a newspaper. I left the house at a quarter past four, I don't remember which day. Why would I want to buy a newspaper? Listen and I'll tell you the truth: it was to find out if the war was really over, and that peace had been signed. You can't necessarily believe what they tell you, you know. Your grandmother tried to stop me going out. "You'll catch your death of cold," she said. But I was going. They will try to stop you, but you mustn't ever let them, boys. Believe me – they'll try.'

'Give your grandfather a kiss,' Enid said.

They obediently did so; Alan backed away, rubbing his cheeks where the old man's beard had prickled him.

This was the last time they saw him alive. Enid asked him if he wanted to see the boys again, but he said he didn't have time, and for once he was probably right, because he died three days later; the boys' mother gave them the news. She didn't seem to them very upset, but in fact she'd sobbed all night, in her big lonely bed. Sobbed for the painter who never painted; sobbed for the dancer who never danced. She hung her favourite painting of her father's, Conway Castle, on the wall in her bedroom, where she could see it as she lay awake; beneath it, on her dressing table, was a faded photograph of herself aged eight, in ballet shoes and dimples.

Annie Sadie Carruth had run out of patience with her husband many years ago. She didn't miss him; she had more room in bed; and the bigger she became, the more room she needed. She was a restless sleeper, too, would need to get up several times a night to wander, sit on the lavatory, boil the kettle and sip a glass of hot water for her indigestion, stand at the dining room window where she used to watch for Arthur on Friday evenings. What an unquiet spirit she'd make when she died, Annie Sadie Carruth, wouldn't lie still, surely, even in the grave. For now, she was better on her own.

Arthur said, 'Enid, Walter will soon be home. I don't think the old lady should go on living here. Mother is not the easiest of people to get along with, and anyway, you and Walter need to be on your own, with the boys. What I propose is that we sell the house in Crosby, which is much too big. I will move into a small house, or perhaps a flat, with Mother. I will be able to keep an eye on her.'

Enid stood there, looking at her brother. She stepped forward and wept in his arms.

'What's happening to me, Arthur? What do you think's happening to me?'

'I think, when Walter's back, the two of you will be fine,' Arthur said.

'It's been such a long war.'

'Yes. It has been a long war.'

'Will you come back, though, at weekends, and take the boys for walks? They'll miss you terribly if you don't.'

'Certainly I will. And you and Walter will bring them to Liverpool, to stay with us. I'll take them on the Overhead Railway. And the ferry boats. And we can tour Red Funnel Line boats, when they're in dock. I think the boys would like that.'

'Don't let them go to sea, though! I don't want them to go to sea.'

'I don't expect they'll want to go to sea.'

'Don't encourage them!'

'I encouraged you to dance,' he reminded her, after a moment.

'That's different!'

'Is it really so different?'

'I don't know! I don't know!' Enid wept, and it was a long time before he could console her.

Walter came home in April, 1946. He arrived at Victoria Station, in Manchester, which didn't look as if it had seen a lick of paint in a hundred years. Trains stood there panting steam. They came from some of the smokiest places in the world, from Bury, Bolton, Rochdale, Oldham, Blackburn, from Huddersfield and Leeds, towns of tall chimney stacks, creaking pit-heads, vast slag heaps, rows of tiny brick houses caked in grime. It was impossible not to arrive at such a place, after such a journey, without feeling dirty, with grit in your eyes and ashes in your hair, as if you'd rolled in the embers of a dead fire. Walter was in uniform, but he carried an old brown leather suitcase which contained the clothes he'd joined up in.

He came out of the huge grey station, its soaring concourse thronged with blank-faced, tired-eyed workers, men in cloth caps, women with their hair in curlers, scarves knotted over their heads. He walked with them, he felt like one of them, he wanted to talk with them, swap stories – but he was in uniform, he was an officer, he was Flight Lieutenant Miller, RAF, and no one would believe that he'd nearly starved as a boy.

He'd been meaning to change out of his uniform on the train, but had not. He caught a bus to Piccadilly, and rode on the top, past the sooty cathedral and the fire-blackened Royal Exchange; how lucky both cathedral and Exchange had survived the war, but they were badly damaged: brave firefighters had tossed German incendiary bombs off the cathedral roof, and been terribly burned. The bus lumbered up busy Market Street, the pavements crowded with shoppers, just as it had been before the war: Market Street was always crowded, and it had fared better than ruined Lord Street in Liverpool. At Piccadilly, though, desolation. A vast empty space, boarded off, where great cotton houses had once stood, and plush cinemas, and tripe restaurants, and turf accountants, and cheap cafés. The barricading, smashed in by louts, revealed gaping basements, twisted girders blackened by fire.

'Christ,' said Walter, aloud, standing there in his Royal Air Force uniform. 'Remember Manchester,' he'd sometimes said to the bomber crews in the ops room, in case of qualms as they shuffled out to destroy the Ruhr. 'Remember Liverpool. Remember Coventry.' And here he stood, the war done. And this was Manchester, happened to be. And this was Cologne. This was Hamburg. This was Berlin.

He went in to Lewis's, thinking to buy a suit: he had his demob pay, he felt flush. Crowds of shoppers jostled him. The smell of people and food, of sweat and hard work. He swallowed a cup of sweet, thick tea in the cafeteria, then left his suitcase under the table. He took the number 52 bus home, still in uniform. The bus picked its way between burned-out factories, shattered warehouses, along streets that had once been the proud addresses of a thousand small businesses and brave enterprises: greengrocers and ironmongers, pork-pie makers and florists, drapers and milliners, hosiers and haberdashers, dressmakers and corsetieres, tailors and booksellers, newsagents and tobacconists, publicans and locksmiths and hobby shops and a man who sold violins – all reduced to ashes, rubble, broken glass, pink fireweed blooming in the ruins.

God! Remember Manchester! Remember Cologne!

And then came Cheshire.

You didn't really have to go very far. Spent shell cases from anti-aircraft barrages had killed people here. So had jittery German pilots, unloading sticks of bombs into the dark night, rather than brave the searchlights and ack-ack fire over the city.

Open fields. Grazing cows. Trees. Neat villages with small pink churches.

Flight Lieutenant Walter Miller got off the bus. Listened to the silence. Breathed air heavy with country smells in spring; fresh-ploughed earth, hawthorn hedges in blossom.

He walked home. Pressed the front door bell.

Alan came to the door, in his little school blazer, black with thin yellow stripes, grey shorts.

'Hello, Daddy.'

'I'm back,' said his father. He picked the boy up, was surprised how heavy he was. 'You're heavy. You've grown, son. You weigh a ton.'

He stood on the doorstep with the child in his arms. He didn't want to put him down.

'You're not going away again?' Alan said.

'Not till the next war.'

'There's going to be a next war?'
'No. Where's Mummy?'
'She's in the garden. Toby and I were playing.'
Walter put Alan down. 'Let's go and find Mummy.'
'All right.'

Toby appeared. Taciturn as usual, he didn't say anything, but he put his arms around his father's leg. Then the three of them walked through the house and into the garden at the back.

'Can we get a pussy cat?' Toby said.

Enid rose from her deckchair, under the weeping elm tree, where his Auntie Grace, years ago, had talked with baby Alan. It was a mild day; the garden crowded with daffodils.

'This is Mummy,' said Alan.
'Yes. Isn't she lovely?'
'Of course. Mummy, this is Daddy.'

Having effected these introductions, Alan took Toby by the hand.

'We're going back to play,' he said.

The boys ran indoors. Enid laid her hands on Walter's shoulders. She seemed thin to him, and frail, like a flower; he could feel her spine. She smiled. Her eyes shone. He didn't want to hurt her with his brass buttons.

'Where's the old lady?'

'Arthur took her away on Sunday. He's bought a car. Moved into a little house in Childwall. It's just us, Walt. Just you and me, and the boys. The way it was supposed to be.'

'Well, I hope you won't be lonely, with me.'

'I won't be lonely with you. Dennis got you a fillet steak.'

'Who's Dennis?'

'Who's Dennis? Dennis Partington, the butcher. He knew you were coming home.'

The boys took their father to inspect the car, which still stood on its chocks in the garage. They'd enjoyed playing in the car, with Alan at the steering wheel, pretending to drive, they'd wound the windows up and down, and pressed the clutch and the throttle and the brake.

'Uncle Arthur has a smashing new car,' Alan said. 'It's a Standard. It's very black and shiny. He was here on Sunday, to take Granny away.'

'Are you going to miss your Granny?'

'No. She was too bad-tempered,' Toby said.

'I think I'll miss her a little,' said Alan.

'Well, I should think I'm about due for a new car, myself,' said Walter. 'The old grey Vaux is older than you, Alan. And gathering cobwebs here in the garage for five years won't have done it much good. I wonder what kind of car I'll have next.'

'Can't we choose?'

'Well, no, the firm does the choosing.'

'Can we come with you when you go to work?' Alan wondered.

'Yes. You'll probably be bored, sitting in the car all day, while I go and chat with customers. But it'd be nice if you came sometimes, and we could share our lunch. A currant bun, a flask of tea.'

A currant bun, a flask of tea. Just like the old days. That's why Walter had gone to war, his aims more modest than those of the dead dictators.

'Are you going to change out of your uniform?' Toby said.

'Of course I am. We'll have to ask Mummy where my old clothes are.'

'I think they're still in the wardrobe in your bedroom. And your socks and handkerchiefs and things are in the left hand drawer of the dressing table. Mummy's underwear is in the right hand drawer.'

'We used to look at your clothes,' said Toby.

'We have a drawer full of special stuff, in my bedroom. Now that Granny's gone, we both have our own rooms, but we used to share. Do you want to see our special stuff?'

They showed him their treasures. A piece of green rock, copper ore from the old mines. Three tiny bird's eggs, each cracked. A small, long dead, mummified mole. A tin box with dried ladybirds in it. A pretty moth with three out of four wings. Some pages from an old exercise book in which once, when he was on leave, their father had drawn, at Alan's request, an express train approaching a tunnel, a battleship firing its fifteen-inch guns, and a Halifax bomber taking off on an air raid; for Toby he'd drawn a tree, a chair, and a chamber pot.

'Why did you ask me to draw a chamber pot, Toby? Do you remember?'

Toby didn't. He shrugged.

Walter enjoyed the fillet steak the butcher had given Enid. 'This is as good as any we ate in the officers' mess,' he told her.

'It's difficult to get fillet steak.'

The boys ate baked beans on toast.

'Mummy forgot how to cook,' Alan said. 'Granny always used to cook for us, when she was here.'

'Before the war, Mummy was a very good cook,' Walter said.

'She's awful now,' said Toby.

Walter was still in his uniform.

Three weeks later the Millers drove to Liverpool to spend the weekend at Uncle Arthur's new house in Childwall, where he'd moved with his mother: it was to be the first of many such trips. They left on Saturday morning, after breakfast, in the old grey Vauxhall; the firm had told Walter it would be at least a year before they could give him a new car: the factories were still converting from wartime production, geared to turn out tanks and aircraft, and he could hardly drive around Cheshire in a tank, could he? The boys sat in the back, with the kitten; the kitten in a cardboard box with lots of crunched-up newspaper, though he spent most of the time in the arms of the boys. Alan and Toby were excited to be going to Liverpool, but they'd only had the kitten four days, so there was no question of leaving him behind. And of course they'd never been on a long car journey, though Walter had taken them on a few short outings as soon as the old grey Vaux was recommissioned, and they'd never been to Liverpool, which was all of thirty-five miles away, and that was a fair distance in those days, by way of country byways and busy towns.

They drove in sunlight through the jolly lanes of Cheshire. Walter felt so happy that he sang. He sang some verses of Jerome Kern. Enid felt happy, too. She remembered the first time she and Walter had driven through this fairyland, when they were exploring his territory, and how lovely everything had seemed; she'd imagined young animals in clothes picnicking by little brooks, hadn't she? And my goodness, how long ago that had been. The war made everything seem so long ago, as if it belonged to another century. But now was nice too. She put her hand on her husband's knee and squeezed it; she looked at her children, in the driving mirror; she was happy. She couldn't remember why she'd felt sad for so long.

Walter didn't think she'd changed. He still thought himself the luckiest man in the world to have married this beautiful woman, with the dancer's features and exciting eyes. During the war, he'd snatched every leave he could, twenty-four hours, forty-eight hours, to be with her; he'd caught rides in trucks, taken troop-trains, stood on buses; had sometimes spent only hours with her and left before dawn. Even so, it hadn't amounted to much, only days over five long years. But unlike her, he'd enjoyed the time in between: good chums, the mess, the piano. The job, too: he'd enjoyed winning the war; the fact he was killing civilians troubled him, but he saw no alternative: and besides, as everyone said, 'they' started it. But he wouldn't forget the old German farmer in his field, shaking his fist at the sky.

Enid, though, saw the changes in Walter, because the man who came back from the war was not the cheerful, happy-go-lucky, carrot-haired young salesman who'd jumped on to a number 52 bus one afternoon in 1940, with his old brown leather suitcase, waving at her from the platform till the bus was out of sight. No. Walter had always known his own limitations, but they'd never worried him; and he'd got what he wanted early in life. The difference was that now he was worried. He was happy to be home, happy enough to sing as he drove his family towards Liverpool, but Walter had begun to worry, and about the one thing he'd never worried about: his luck. He'd had a good run. A wonderful wife. A nice house. A comfortable job. Two fine boys. Flown on forty-two raids over the Ruhr and three to Berlin; over Caen, in northern France, he should have been killed; getting home had been a miracle. Walter began to worry, now, that one of these days his luck would run out.

And because he was worried, he found it difficult to decide anything. He'd take no chances. He'd weigh the pros and cons till he gave himself a migraine headache. He'd had those headaches when he was a boy, but had grown out of them; now they were back.

And he drove so slowly. The drive to Liverpool took ages; the boys got crotchety, and fought; the kitten clawed the upholstery, then went to sleep. Things looked up when they were held up at the Manchester Ship Canal bridge by a ship. Alan leapt out of the car, followed by Toby, and ran past the line of waiting cars for a good view. The ship was the Shell tanker *Drupa*, inward bound for Manchester; she moved slowly out of the Latchford locks, a floating forest of masts and derricks; she seemed enormous here in the country, dwarfing little trees and little houses, tiny cars and tiny people. She was the biggest thing Alan had ever seen; he was prodigiously impressed; the sea, he knew, was in his blood; always had been. How he'd loved going out in rowing boats, when they were on holiday in North Wales; loved especially to crouch in the bow, where he could hear the slap and gurgle of waves, and by closing his eyes imagine himself on a real ship, on a real voyage. And here, right in front of him, was a real ship; so close he could almost jump down on to her decks. He knew that his Uncle Arthur worked for a shipping company; had a notion he was quite high up in it, though not much notion what that meant; he would talk to his uncle about ships and perhaps his uncle would take him aboard one.

They arrived at number 118 Taggart Avenue, in Childwall, before lunchtime. Alan noticed that the trams and buses in Liverpool were green, unlike the ones in Manchester, which were red. He liked the wide avenues with the tram tracks laid down the middle, on grass, between green hedges, and he admired the speed with which the green trams pitched and rattled along; they had curved roofs, were streamlined, and made the flat-roofed trams in Manchester look positively antiquated.

Enid was surprised that Uncle Arthur should have moved with his mother into such a very modest house as number 118 Taggart Avenue turned out to be.

'When you think of the house in Crosby,' she said, 'or the lovely apartment he had with Grace, in Blundellsands, why on earth would he want to come here?'

The house, like all the others, had walls of grey pebbledash, a small bay window, and a front porch with stained glass flowers over the door. Their grandmother was very pleased to see the boys, and pressed them close to her; the strong smell of stale pee made them both feel sick.

'Hello, boys,' said Uncle Arthur.

They shook hands with him. Arthur was such an imposing man, in his dark grey suit and well-polished shoes, that hugs seemed out of the question. Oddly enough they had never hugged Uncle Arthur, though they adored him more than anyone else in the world; they'd jumped on him in bed, sat on his face and tried to stifle him, but that was different. When Uncle Arthur got dressed, he was a grown-up, and the terrific thing was, that he treated you as if you were a grown-up too.

Alan held up the precious cardboard box with the kitten.

'Who's this?' Uncle Arthur said, lifting the little animal out and holding it in his arms.

'He's our new kitten. His name is Wilson.'

'Why Wilson?'

'We wanted to call him a sensible name, not a silly name like Fluff or Tibbles. The head of my house at school is called Wilson, and he's a splendid batsman, so we decided to call him Wilson. Mummy used to have a cat called The Woo, and she wanted to call him that, but we won.'

The boys were ravenously hungry. Their grandmother opened cans of soup, and poached an egg for Walter.

'Why can't you cook like this, Mum?' Toby said.

'I can open a can of soup,' Enid protested.

'We never have soup at home,' Alan explained.

'What would you like to do this afternoon, boys?' asked Uncle Arthur. 'I expect your grandmother would like to lie down, but we could ride down to Pier Head on the number 73 bus and perhaps take the ferry.'

'Why don't you take the boys,' Enid said. 'I'll stay here with Mum.'

'Daddy, will you come with us?'

'I think I'll stay here and smoke a cigarette.'

'Uncle Arthur, can't we take a tram?' Alan asked eagerly, as the three of them, Uncle Arthur and the two boys, walked along Taggart Avenue. 'They're green! They're streamlined! They must go frightfully fast!'

'We'd have to walk to Childwall Five Ways to take the tram,' Uncle Arthur explained. 'We'll take the bus today, because it's quicker. We'll take the tram when we have more time.'

'We want to see boats, not trams,' said Toby.

They sat on the top deck of the bus, at the front, and their uncle told them the names of the streets: Penny Lane, Ullett Avenue, Croxteth Road. Then they were in the city. Philharmonic Hall, where the Phil played; huge, sooty St George's Hall, the Mersey Tunnel. Devastated Lord Street. The Alfred Holt Building, the Cunard Building, the Red Funnel Line Building, the Liver Building. And Pier Head, where the bus turned round. They clattered down the stairs, jumped off. Seagulls and pigeons; the ancient, intoxicating, sad, salty, smell of the river. The tide was low and the covered passageways down to the Landing Stage sloped steeply; the boys ran down, whooping with glee, they hadn't realised that the Landing Stage floated, which was a thrill in itself. The Wallasey ferry was in; so they hurled themselves aboard, raced all over the boat, ran up the stairs to the upper deck, stood at the rail as the gangways were raised with a clang and a clatter. The ferry moved away from the Landing Stage; brown water churned. Her siren blared; the boys jumped, burst out laughing. Their uncle pointed out the Manx boat, *King Orry*, which would sail at midnight, and the Irish boats, and the Cunard liner *Ascania*, alongside the Landing Stage. In the distance, in the Gladstone Dry Dock, was the beautiful *Mauritania*, being reconverted from troop-ship to luxury liner. The ferry forged across the river, and passed close astern of the Red Funnel ship *Bantry Bay*, fully-laden, riding at anchor, yellow quarantine flag flying off her mast; sailors staring down from her rails.

'Why is she anchored in the middle of the river, Uncle Arthur?' Alan asked.

'She has to wait for the tide before she can go into dock. She arrived this morning from Argentina.'

'What is her cargo?'

'Roast beef and Yorkshire pudding! The *Bantry Bay* is one of our refrigerated cargo carriers. She and her sister ship, the *Jamaica Bay*, sail between Liverpool and Buenos Aires. Did you know that a lot of our beef comes from Argentina?'

'Our Yorkshire pudding doesn't come from Argentina,' Toby said.

'Wow! Oh wow!' gasped Alan. 'If only I could – one of these days I – when I grow up, Uncle Arthur, I'm going to sea!'

'I don't think your mother will like that, Alan.'

'She won't stop me, if it's what I want to do more than anything else in the world. Her father, my grandfather that is, stopped her being a ballet dancer, and she won't stop me going to sea.'

'I don't want to go to sea,' said Toby.

'What do you want to do, Toby?' Uncle Arthur smiled.

'I want to be a doctor.'

'A doctor?' said Alan. 'You never said you wanted to be a doctor!'

'Boys, boys!' laughed their uncle.

'Don't worry, Uncle Arthur,' said Alan. 'We always fight.'

'Well, you don't fight when you're with your Uncle Arthur. You behave like gentlemen. If not, you will be punished.'

'How will we be punished?' they both wanted to know.

'Severely.'

Alan the romantic; practical, focused, Toby. For all his enthusiasm for it, and sure as he was that the sea was in his blood, that his father's failure to go to sea was an aberration that another generation would correct, Alan did not fulfil that ambition, either, in the end, not even by cheating like his Uncle Arthur. Nor did Toby become a doctor; though he came closer to reading a pulse than Alan did towards striding the bridge of a ship: Toby went up to university to read medicine, but fainted at the first sight of a cadaver.

The ferry docked at Wallasey, the decks shuddering as the engine telegraph rang slow astern; her mooring lines, thrown by deck-hands over giant bollards, groaned like men on the rack as they took the strain.

'Do we get off here?' said Alan.

'No. We stay on the ferry for a round trip. There isn't much to see at Wallasey. Except for your Uncle Fred, I suppose.'

'I didn't know we had an Uncle Fred,' Alan said.

'He's a great-uncle. We should go to see him one day, because he builds model ships. There are model ships in every room of the house, each one perfectly to scale; they are works of art.'

'Can we play with them?'

'Absolutely not. They live in glass cases. They are not toys, they are scale models. The least you can hope for, boys, is that if Uncle Fred takes a liking to you, he'll give you one.'

Oh dear, thought Alan. Another relative who failed to go to sea.

'I'd love to meet Uncle Fred,' he said.

'When we have more time we'll take the ferry to New Brighton,' Uncle Arthur promised. 'That's a bit further. We can get off at New Brighton. There is a pier with amusements on it.'

'Amusements? What kind of amusements?'

'Machines you put pennies in. There are machines where you pull a knob and send a little steel ball whizzing about. If it goes in the right hole you get your penny back. And there are machines which show scenes like the Spanish Inquisition.'

'What's the Spanish Inquisition?'

'That was when the Spanish used to torture people for not being Catholics. Did you know that you are now in Cheshire?'

'Cheshire?' said Alan, incredulously. 'This doesn't look like Cheshire. This looks more like Liverpool.'

'It does, but on this side of the river, you are in Cheshire. It's called the Wirral. A lot of people live here and take the ferry to work in Liverpool, every day. And some take the underground train, the Mersey Railway.'

Alan found it difficult to concentrate on being in Cheshire because he wanted to know more about the Spanish Inquisition, and people being tortured for not being Catholic, but he didn't feel he should ask his uncle in case his uncle thought him morbid. As the ferry ploughed its way back towards the Liverpool Landing Stage Uncle Arthur pointed out the cranes at Cammell Laird's. 'That's where they build large ships,' he explained. 'That's where the *English Bay* was built. Before the war, she was the flagship of the Red Funnel Line. Your Auntie Grace launched her.'

'Auntie Grace launched her? I thought only the Queen launched ships. Or Princess Elizabeth. Auntie Grace wasn't a princess, was she?'

'No. But she was as lovely as one.'

After supper that evening – their grandmother made a shepherds' pie, and the boys wolfed their helpings down as if they hadn't eaten for weeks – Mrs McMahon and her daughter Pat came round to visit. They lived close by, in Gateacre, a twenty minutes walk. Alan was curious about the McMahons, because he knew they were Catholics, but he didn't feel he should ask them about the Spanish Inquisition.

Mrs McMahon had grown old gracefully. She'd kept her figure; she wore her silvery hair in a neat bun; favoured tweed skirts, comfortable cardigans, sensible walking shoes. She still spoke softly and at speed. She would take no nonsense from cantankerous Mrs Annie Sadie Carruth; but the two had renewed an old friendship. On Monday nights she and Pat came to play bridge with Mrs Carruth and Arthur.

Pat was now thirty-two. She had soft, wavy, brown hair and rather heavy eyebrows, and deep-set eyes, very deep brown, almost black; but they were very kind and patient eyes. She had a thin nose, and her throat was as white as her teeth. In spite of her ill health she was extremely even-tempered; nothing upset her. Nor was she, though she'd never known much company apart from her mother, at all old-maidish; and, though the two women didn't go out, she was very well-informed. The boys both thought she was beautiful; and were surprised to find that neither their mother nor their father liked her. Enid had no patience at all with sickness: the boys were never allowed to be ill, and when they caught colds they were packed off to school in all weathers, just the same.

'I think ill-health is just an excuse, for some people,' Enid said.

Arthur came to Pat's defence. This was later that night, when the McMahons had gone, and the boys were in bed.

'I don't think you're being very fair, Enid,' he said. 'Pat has suffered from ill-health all her life. Not everyone can be as robustly healthy as you.'

'It's just that I don't see why I should have to feel sorry for her,' Enid said, tossing her head.

'Who asked you to feel sorry for her?' Arthur reasoned. 'Not Pat herself. I don't think I've ever known anyone who was less of a complainer.'

'Oh, she has that long-suffering look.'

'I think that's because she has to play bridge with me as her partner,' smiled Arthur.

Enid laughed. 'I should know better than to quarrel with you. No wonder you're Deputy Chairman of the Red Funnel Line.'

'If I was a better quarreller maybe I'd be Chairman,' said Arthur. 'On the other hand, my record might count against me.'

'What record?' Walter said.

'My record is one of unmitigated disaster. In my efforts to minimise the Line's exposure, as I saw it, I sold off half our fleet for scrap. I put guns on our fastest ships: six out of eight of them were sunk.'

'Maybe the guns weren't big enough,' said Walter.

'Maybe. I converted our flagship, the *English Bay*, into a hospital ship, because I was convinced that would make her proof against attack. She hit a mine. I had our four new motor vessels built in the United States so they'd be out of harm's way: two of them were torpedoed on their maiden voyages, within sight of the coast of New Jersey. And now I've recommended to the Board that we buy the Anchor Line. So far, what's happened? The Anchor Line's shares have more than doubled, on the stock market, and ours have gone down by twenty-five pence.'

'Why the Anchor Line, Arthur?' Walter said.

Arthur smiled, and shrugged. 'Handsome ships,' he said. 'I never could resist a handsome ship.'

'Or a sick woman,' flashed Enid.

After a moment Arthur said, 'I hardly think that's fair, Enid.'

'I'm sorry, Arthur. It slipped out. I shouldn't have said it. I'm sorry,' Enid apologised. 'None of us had any idea that Grace had a weak heart. None of us.'

'She tricked him,' Mrs Carruth said.

'Mother, please,' Arthur said.

'Don't "Mother, please" me, Arthur. You know darned well she tricked you. She could have told you she had a bad heart. She chose not to, till after you were married.'

'What Grace chose or chose not to tell me, and when, is none of your business, Mother.'

'I have to agree with Arthur,' Walter said; he stood up, lit a cigarette. 'And unless I missed something, I don't know that Arthur plans to marry Pat McMahon. He plans to buy the Anchor Line. I fail to see the connection.'

'Thank you, Walter,' said Arthur.

'That's enough,' laughed Enid, picking up the kitten. 'What will Wilson think of our family? We like each other really, Wilson. He looks like he understands, doesn't he? He's taking it all in. He's taking it all in, and one day he'll write it all down. Won't you, Wilson?'

The cat purred happily.

Arthur was too much of a gentleman to deny having any plans to marry Pat McMahon – even if he did. As for all that amusing talk of failure, well, yes, it was true that the Line's available tonnage had dropped from a high of 270,000 tons in 1938, a total of eighteen ships, to 150,000 tons at the end of the war – a total of nine ships. However, the late Cuthbert Tilson, before attacking him all those years ago, would have done well to remember that Arthur's early experience of management was in insurance. The company was more than satisfactorily compensated for the loss of its ships during the war, and as a result, the Line's working capital was now estimated at well in excess of sixty million pounds, about three and a half times what it had been in 1938. The company may have been running out of ships, but it was not exactly insolvent, and Arthur's solution, to buy the Anchor Line, would remedy the tonnage problem overnight. What's more, the Anchor Line competed on some of the Red Funnel's most profitable routes, between Liverpool and Montevideo, Buenos Aires, and Valparaiso, Chile. Oh, it was a brilliant solution in every way, and Sir William Crashaw was tickled pink: he even suggested they make an offer for Cunard, and no one was quite sure whether he was joking or not.

On Sunday, to the boys' dismay – before breakfast they had nearly stifled the Big Bad Tiddlypod with pillows, and wanted to go on playing – the Millers drove to Waterloo, to see Little Gran, as they called Walter's diminutive mother, and Aunt Beatrice.

The little house on Oakdale Road was one of the few to survive the Blitz undamaged; every house on the other side of the street was destroyed. Nor had Little Gran once left it, even with fires raging across the street. She'd made cups of tea for the firefighters, night after night. These men realised the old lady was starving and brought food round from the fire station every day. In fact, Walter had been sending her money for years, but his mother had never spent a penny of it on herself: instead she'd put a shawl around her head and walked to the savings bank on Southport Road. This was the first time she'd dealt with any kind of financial institution. She opened an account for her grandchildren. She might have actually starved if it hadn't been for the firefighters, because the neighbours who'd promised to keep an eye on her were all bombed out and gone. It was Greg who went to see her on one of his leaves and sized up the situation. As a result it was agreed that cousin Beatrice should move in.

For Beatrice, this was simply further proof that life was not going to work out for her the way she'd hoped. She moved in, with a sigh and a sniff, taking over the front bedroom, over the parlour, and filling the house with a heavy perfume that balanced the old lady's rotten breath.

The boys found the house a dismal one; very cramped and dark, with heavy curtains, thick carpets, and curious combinations of smells. Aunt Beatrice did not approve of their kitten, who had to stay in the car, in his cardboard box; at least this gave them the excuse to duck out every so often to check up on the cat. Beatrice made the boys cups of Bovril for their lunch, which they didn't like very much, but drank politely.

What was particularly depressing was that Aunt Beatrice always insisted on speaking about dead people, which was something their own mother and father never did, and nor did their Uncle Arthur, unless you asked them questions. Uncle Arthur, of course, would tell them about Auntie Grace when they asked, but not otherwise, and their father would tell them about his own father, engineer with the Cunard Line, when they asked about his photograph in the dark-room. But everybody Aunt Beatrice knew seemed to be dead, and she was always talking about them, and making herself unhappy.

'It was tragic, Kathleen dying like that,' she sniffed. 'I don't suppose poor Greg will ever get over it.'

'Greg will get over it,' Walter said.

'I can't see him marrying again.'

'It would be the best thing, for the girls,' said Enid.

The boys' Aunt Kathleen, whom they had never known because she lived in West Bromwich, had died of obscure complications following childbirth, a few months ago. The baby, her second, who would be their cousin Anita and who would grow up to be a ravishing beauty, was of an incredibly cheerful disposition.

'I don't agree at all,' said Aunt Beatrice. 'I don't trust step-mothers. The girls are better off with their father. I go down there and see them whenever I can.'

Having become surrogate mother to Greg's children, Beatrice strongly resented any suggestion she be replaced. And in fairness the two girls – sensible, straight-haired, strait-laced Sally, the older, and irresponsible, winsome Anita – had fun with her. It was impossible for the boys to imagine anyone having fun with Aunt Beatrice, but the girls did; they made a jolly threesome. Aunt Beatrice didn't sniff so much when she was with them, in fact at times she was almost skittish: they didn't horse around, like Uncle Arthur and his nephews did, but they listened to the radio together, laughed at Tommy Handley in *Itma* and Richard Murdoch in *Much Binding in the Marsh*; they went shopping together in Birmingham and the girls made Aunt Beatrice try on dresses she'd never consider buying. She was sharp with them, which must sometimes have been necessary, because their father adored them and would never get angry with them, even when he should have, it just wasn't Greg's nature. But they never seemed to resent her admonitions, always behaved themselves, in her company, rarely got on her nerves, and took care of her in her old age, taking turns to visit.

Greg, who in view of his cheerful disregard for his own safety and his low opinion of the Luftwaffe had survived the war miraculously, had been demobbed early, with the same rank as he went in, LAC2, so that he could be with his wife when the baby was born. He'd hitchhiked happily from Kent to West Bromwich, amusing the lorry-drivers who stopped for him with cheerful tales of harrowing escapes. He was distraught over Kathleen's unexpected death. He'd got a job but he kept crying at the office where he worked. He was allowed to leave early to pick the two girls up from the nursery where they spent the day; he was shown how to change nappies and boil them. Walter and Enid told him he should hire a help to come in and look after the house, but Greg said he couldn't afford to, so he managed as best he could, which turned out to be not badly; by the time Aunt Beatrice realised how much the girls meant to her, and started coming down to West Bromwich regularly, small Anita was already singing little songs.

Before they set off for home Walter produced an old leather-bound stamp album, the cover red and faded, polished smooth by much boyish handling. He held it as if it was a thing of enormous value, and liable to come apart, sitting in an armchair in the dark front room, which had impenetrable curtains, never opened, so the room was airless, it was hard to breathe; the boys perched on each arm.

'This is the stamp album your Uncle Greg and I shared when we were boys,' he told them. 'It's yours now; and we want you to share it too. I'd really appreciate it if you don't take out the stamps. As you'll see, none of them are valuable, because we couldn't afford to buy stamps, we only swapped with other boys. If you want, I'll buy you new stamp albums of your own, loose-leaf ones, for you to collect your own stamps.'

The boys watched, very interested, as their father carefully turned over the pages. He and Greg had added many pages of their own, painstakingly cut to shape and glued in, with spaces neatly ruled for stamps they'd never acquired, but learned of from the Stanley Gibbons Catalogue. What a thrill it must have been when one of them, during break or after school, managed to swap one of their duplicates for a missing denomination, a fifteen-cent black-and-magenta or a twenty-rupee red. Alan felt a sudden awe and pity for his father and his uncle; their stamp collection had been their poor boys' passport to all the marvellous places the stamps came from. They had voyaged in their imagination. But why, oh why, had they not become sailors?

'Daddy, why did you never do to sea?' Alan said.

'The sea's all right to look at,' his father told him. 'But it's a dangerous place, and it will drown you.'

'Not if you can swim! I don't want to just look at things. I want to do them.'

'I won't stand in your way if you want to go to sea. Though your mother might. But you'll probably change your mind by the time you're old enough.'

'I'll never change my mind!'

The album also had pages for stamps from all kinds of countries which no longer existed, for which forgotten capital cities and populations were given, like the Middle Congo, and Santander (capital, Bucaramanga). There was a page for something called the New South African Republic. There was a page for a place called Germany, but Walter and Greg's collection had ended with Kaiser Bill.

'So many changes,' Alan said. 'Do you think, now the war's over, the world will settle down?'

'Your Uncle Arthur believes so,' their father told him.

Chapter Ten

When the Crashaws retired to await old age in the South of France, where they had a villa nestling in expensive hills and reached through wrought iron gates – when you swam in the blue pool you looked over Cannes as you breast-stroked – Arthur Carruth was elected Chairman of the Red Funnel Line of Liverpool. Champagne was brought into the Boardroom on a silver tray inscribed with the coat of arms of the Line, magnums of Moet et Chandon, and Sir William raised his glass to say:

'We used to suspect that all Arthur's best ideas came from Grace. Now we know that's not so. Arthur has deftly steered this company through the war, successfully "minimising our exposure" with, it is true, some help from the German Navy – so that we emerged from the war years in such good shape that we were able to acquire the Anchor Line. Which was also Arthur's idea. And now, as you know, we are about to turn a new page in the long history of Red Funnel. We are entering the luxury cruise market. Thanks, again, to the vision and initiative of Arthur. But Arthur, of course, is not only a visionary. He is also a deuced charming fellow – and a friend of mine. My dear Arthur, I know I speak for all of us when I wish you a long and successful term as Chairman of this great Line. And for God's sake – marry again!'

Alfred Poindexter, who had now been Company Treasurer for nineteen years, in a short speech said 'I have always made a point of challenging every proposal Arthur has made – as you've probably noticed. I have done this, I must confess, more out of curiosity, than with any real confidence my view would carry. I wanted to see what would happen. Well, nothing happened. I have never, not once, not ever, won any support at all for my opinion. My hearty congratulations, Arthur.'

The *Liverpool Echo* published a photograph of the new Chairman that made him look much younger, and the lofty *Manchester Guardian* carried the news, even *The Times* and the *Daily Telegraph* mentioned it, and shipping journals said it was the right thing for Red Funnel to do.

Cunard weren't pleased, and thought Red Funnel was getting too big for its boots, when young Princess Elizabeth in a clear voice like a dainty bell launched the Line's new flagship, named *English Bay* in honour of her gallant predecessor, and designed for the luxury cruise trade. At forty thousand tons, the new liner was nearly twice the size of any other ship in the company's fleet, and she was indeed a passenger liner: instead of Argentine beef or Chilean nitrates she would carry fox-trotting holidaymakers on glamorous fourteen-day cruises from New York to the Caribbean.

She was reckoned a handsome ship. She still had the fine bow and long counter-stern of a Red Funnel boat, and the single, oversized, raked funnel, but instead of the expected thickets of derricks and samson posts, her squarish, Jersey-cream superstructure ran from her bridge to her stern; with long promenade decks, forty outside cabins with views, depending on the latitude, of rolling waves or pleasant islands, a first-class dining saloon that had new menus printed every day and fresh flowers on each table, and a second-class dining room with a buffet that included lobster, a first-class lounge with a grand piano and a second-class lounge with wicker furniture and magazines, a billiards room, and a swimming pool. On her trials she reached twenty-five knots, and she would have made a fine sight, steaming at full speed down the Gairloch, smoke pouring from her huge funnel; shepherds watching from the bare hills must have scratched their heads and wondered what the Red Funnel Line was coming to.

It hadn't been easy for Arthur to convince the Board to build her though, even if he spoke as Sir William's obvious successor, because what did Red Funnel know about the American cruise business, which was unknown, uncharted territory, and owned by the Americans? And Arthur was frank about the risks.

'I don't think any of us question Arthur's enthusiasm,' Poindexter said. 'Obviously, there is money to be made. We have seen the figures. Arthur's projections make sense. As I see it, there are two problems. One is that, as Arthur admits, we know absolutely nothing about the American cruise market. But there are ways we could learn. One way would be to lease a vessel for, say, a year. This would be much less costly than building a ship of our own. It would enable us to get a feel for the business.'

'That's not a bad idea, Alfred,' said Sir William, slumped in his chair at the head of the Boardroom table, his blue-eyed gaze fixed on the magnificent chandelier, only recently removed from wartime storage deep in the vaults and painstakingly restored. 'What's the other problem, as you see it?'

'The other problem's a more serious one, and I don't really have a solution. I'm talking about the risk of retaliation. We're setting up stumps in our neighbour's back garden, uninvited. We can hardly expect him to put out the red carpet for us. He won't like it. And I don't have to remind you that between thirty and forty per cent of our business is between the United States and Europe. I believe that business will be at risk.'

'I agree with you,' grunted Sir William. 'Well, Arthur? What say you?'

'I think we have to look to the future,' Arthur said. He took off his spectacles to dab his eyes; and waited a few moments before replacing them. 'The cruise business is one of the very few sectors of our industry that is certain to grow. As world recovery continues, people will enjoy more and more discretionary income. The whole travel market will change. We will see tour operators packaging holidays to destinations most people haven't even heard of – yet. Ten years from now, gentlemen, no one will conceive of crossing the Atlantic by ship, except for the pleasure of the crossing itself. But leisure travel will grow by leaps and bounds. I believe we should be in that business. I believe that to succeed in that business we need to realise that the name of the business is not shipping; it is leisure travel. The ship is incidental. The ship is just the beginning. But I believe we should begin by building the ship; a ship dedicated to the leisure travel business. Why delay? Shall I tell you what's going to happen? With declining passenger revenues, our competitors – Cunard, P&O, the French

Line, Holland America – will be forced to take ships off their present routes and convert them into cruise liners. If we get into the business now, we'll have a few years' start on them. I believe that the financial rewards of this start will be considerable.'

Arthur took a glass of water. Sir William stared at the chandelier. Poindexter smiled to himself.

'Cunard, P&O, the French Line, Holland America?' grunted Sir William. 'Are they our competition? I thought our competitors were Alfred Holt, the Blue Star Line, Elder Dempster, Booth—'

'Raise your sights, Sir William,' said Arthur.

Sir William caught his breath, then chuckled. 'If we're going to get into the cruise business,' he eventually said, 'why don't we start over here? Mediterranean cruises, out of London, or Southampton?'

'Because the US cruise business is where the money is, Sir William. People over here haven't begun to think about Mediterranean cruises yet. They will, but so far they haven't. The real money, for the foreseeable future, will be in the United States. That's where our competitors will go. The competitors I just mentioned.'

'What about reprisals?' said Sir William.

'If by that you mean that we could lose some of our US cargo business, as Alfred suggested, I would remind you that we have a number of very long-term contracts with our American friends. Uncancellable, without heavy penalty. As you know I was in Savannah last month; we have a ten-year contract with Fouquet. I was able to obtain Jefferson's signature after we had both consumed a rather excessive amount of his excellent Bourbon. The Red Funnel Line will be in cotton for the foreseeable future. But the whole nature of our cargo business will change too, over the next two decades. We will be operating eighty-thousand ton container carriers. And I suspect that most of our transatlantic business will be into Antwerp or Rotterdam. Not Liverpool. The Mersey isn't deep enough. But that will be the subject of another proposal, another day.'

A long silence. Sir William Crashaw pushed his chair back from the table. He poked his fingers into the corners of his eyes and rubbed them. He looked around at his Board.

'Do you chaps really want a bloody visionary as your next Chairman?' he said.

'I don't know about a visionary. We certainly need someone who can drink Jefferson Fouquet's Bourbon.' The speaker was Geoffrey Cumberland, a new Board member with a reputation as a wag.

'Arthur's vision has stood us in good stead so far,' sighed Poindexter.

'Shall we take a vote?'

'I don't think it's necessary,' Poindexter said.

'All right. Gentlemen, we are now in the – what did you call it, Arthur? – the leisure travel business.'

The day before the new *English Bay* sailed from the Liverpool Landing Stage on her maiden voyage, Arthur found time to take his nephews on a conducted tour of the ship. They gasped with admiration at first sight of her, she towered over the yellow passenger buildings like a magnificent wedding cake, there were tiers and tiers of her, mountains of Jersey cream, with coloured bunting a-flutter; she dwarfed the two puny Irish boats berthed ahead of her, and the Seacombe ferries sidled past her to give their passengers a close view.

On the bridge, Alan felt like he was in church, spoke in a hushed whisper, laid his hands reverently on the great, varnished wheel, peered into the binnacle, handled the brass levers of the engine-room telegraph: imagined what it must feel like to ring Full Speed Ahead! Tomorrow Captain Burleigh, Commodore of the Line, archbishop of this floating cathedral, would strut here, with his officers and high priests, in stiff white shirts, black ties, black uniform with gold braid. Captain Burleigh would take up his position on the port side of the bridge; raising his megaphone, he'd order the lines dropped, one by one. 'Single up!' he'd boom, and stationed alongside, to starboard, the tugs would churn the greasy brown waters of the Mersey into white froth, their screws racing, dense black smoke billowing from their tall yellow funnels. The captain would pull the chain that operated the siren; a single, long, deep blast would echo across the river: 'I am turning to starboard.' If only he were six years older, Alan thought, he could be up here, a Junior Officer of the Red Funnel Line! He cursed his youth. He couldn't wait to go to sea.

The boys gaped at the enormous first-class lounge, three decks tall, bathed in soft afternoon light from skylights as high up as clouds. A grand piano waited to be played: what a pity their father wasn't here; he'd have pulled up the stool immediately and launched into Jerome Kern for invisible dancers. An oil painting of the ship's gallant predecessor, outfitted as a hospital ship, faced the grand staircase that led to the first-class dining saloon, and Alan clip-clopped across the dance floor to examine it: the painting was cleverly illuminated so that the beautiful white ship, the Red Cross painted on her sides, seemed to shimmer in eternal sunlight. A plaque beneath the painting, which was by the famous marine artist Norman Wilkinson, read: *English Bay*. Launched by Mrs Grace Carruth, May 28th 1932. Destroyed by enemy action off Alexandria, Egypt, September 9th 1943.

They descended endless stairs to visit the engine-room, where instead of the old, intoxicating smell of oil and steam under high pressure, there was the pungent reek of diesel fuel from the huge Thorneycroft twin engines, each one rated at thirty-four thousand horsepower. Men stood on the catwalks wiping their hands on scraps of cotton waste; they wore orange ear muffs against the tremendous hum of the engines. Then the boys went clattering up steel ladders, to emerge finally on to the breezy promenade deck, where neat rows of chaise longues stood ready for tomorrow's passengers and guests, each one with a carefully folded tartan rug bearing the initials 'RFL': it was the tartan of the Black Watch, and their uncle Arthur, the former Private Carruth, A., had obtained special permission from the colonel of the regiment to use it. Moving aft, they came to the swimming pool, where Alan gaped at the turquoise-blue water, illuminated from underneath by powerful lights. A ship with a swimming pool! He shook his head in wonder.

'Thank you so much for taking us on the tour, Uncle Arthur,' Alan said, as they climbed into their uncle's shiny, silent car afterwards. 'She's a beautiful ship! Absolutely beautiful! But I think it's a tragedy she won't be coming back to Liverpool, if she's going to sail out of New York all the time.'

'She'll come back here for refits,' Uncle Arthur said. 'What do you think of her, Toby? Would you like to sail on the *English Bay*.'

Toby thought for a minute, then he said, 'I'd be bored.'

'Bored?' screeched his brother. 'How could you be bored, on a ship like that? You could do anything you possibly wanted to do! If you wanted to play the piano, for instance, you could play the piano. If you wanted to go for a swim, you could go for a swim. Daddy's teaching Toby to play the piano,' he added, for his uncle's benefit.

'Is he teaching him to swim?' smiled Uncle Arthur.

'No! Daddy can't swim! Didn't you know that? That's why he didn't go to sea, unfortunately. But Toby knows how to swim; he learned at school. We both know how to swim.'

'I'd be bored,' Toby said again.

'Where are we going now?' asked Alan.

'Would you like to see where Auntie Grace is buried?'

The boys looked at each other. They had never seen the grave, in fact they'd never seen any grave, had never been to their grandfather's grave and weren't even sure where it was; and weren't graves in cemeteries? And if so did they really want to visit a cemetery, especially as it would be getting dark soon? They didn't know why their Uncle Arthur should suddenly have suggested this, but Alan thought it was perhaps because of the ship.

'Well – yes, please,' he said, because although he wasn't particularly keen he didn't see how they could refuse. He was the spokesman, anyway, and Toby would leave such decisions to him.

They drove out of town by the Southport Road. It was late afternoon, and the lights were coming on, necklaces of orange. They drove through Bootle and Seaforth as shops were shutting up and people were beginning to queue for the first showings at cinemas, all pink and lit up, and music and laughter came out of the open doors of pubs. Then Uncle Arthur turned off the bright road and they were in gloomy trees; and when he stopped the car, and they all got out, a bat swooped. But it was still light enough to see as he led them through the lychgate with its little tiled gable and wooden seats, and the red gravel of neat pathways crunched under three pairs of feet. Alan tried not to look at the rows of dark tombstones with names carved on them, till their uncle stopped before a simple slab with a white orchid in a vase, like a solitary snowflake. The stone said: Grace Carruth. 1895–1938. Always won't be long enough. A.

'The flower is lovely,' Alan said, not really knowing what else to say. 'Where does it come from?'

'It comes from Costa Rica,' their uncle said. 'Auntie Grace loved flowers. The flat in Blundellsands, where we lived, was always filled with flowers. The Red Funnel Line used to ship them to us. When she died I arranged for the flowers to go on being delivered. Improbably enough, they went on being delivered all through the war, in spite of attacks by German U-boats.'

'Who is "A"?' said Toby.

Alan turned on him. 'That's Uncle Arthur, you ninny!' he hissed.

'Do you know where Costa Rica is?' smiled Uncle Arthur.

'I think it's in Central America,' Alan said. In fact, he knew perfectly well.

'That's right. That's very good, Alan.'

After a few moments Alan said, 'Uncle Arthur, would you like Toby and me to wait for you at the church gate? Maybe you want to be alone with Auntie Grace for a while.'

Their uncle said, 'No. Thank you, Alan. But that was very thoughtful of you.'

So Alan, who was curious, and wanted to get out of the cemetery, said 'One day, will you take us to see where you and Auntie Grace lived?'

'Certainly, Alan. We can pass by on the way home.'

Alan had not been sure that Uncle Arthur would show them the house, because although he'd always answered all their questions about Auntie Grace, and didn't seem to mind, the boy knew how sad he'd been when she died and that there was a part of his uncle he would never know, because it belonged to her. But he drove them, now, along Laburnum Avenue, and there was the house, and he slowed down, and pointed it out to the boys.

'We didn't have the whole house, of course. There were only the two of us. We had the top two floors. You can see, the windows are open, and the lights are on. Whoever lives there now must like fresh air and lots of light, just as your Auntie Grace did.'

He had never been back to Laburnum Avenue since the day Grace died. The last time he'd walked out through that front door, to stride off to Crosby Station, she had been alive. She was to attend a fund-raising meeting with Lady Crashaw, and give a speech.

'It's a beautiful house,' said Alan.

'Look, that's where she made a snowman once,' Uncle Arthur said. 'He was a very fine snowman and she put a pair of my spectacles on his face, so that he looked like me... And that's where the two of us played at snowballs. She caught me a beauty, right on the back of the neck. Snow fell down inside my shirt, but I didn't have time to change because I was on my way to work.'

It began to rain. Raindrops on their hair, and on Uncle Arthur's suit. They drove back to Childwall.

The boys would remember this year as a rather peculiar one. Walter Miller was suddenly asked to move to Head office. Grant Leighton, the enterprising new Sales Manager of the company, with a wide jaw and a dark green jowl, a man not much liked, in fact distrusted, had taken rather a fancy to Walter when he spent a day with him doing his rounds; admired Walter's obvious rapport with his customers, who treated him like an old friend; and decided the man was wasted in Cheshire.

'Come to Liverpool,' he said. 'I need a right-hand man. Someone to show me the ropes.'

Walter went. He lived with his small mother and the fierce Aunt Beatrice, sleeping on a couch in the dark front room with stifling curtains; drove home to Cheshire on Friday nights. He really didn't want to commit himself to a permanent move. Though he liked Grant Leighton, he was unhappy at Head Office; he missed the freedom of the road; he missed his customers; missed the invitations into little dark storerooms to sip tea and smoke a cigarette and talk about a beloved daughter's wedding, the wife's worrying illness, look at snapshots of a holiday in Scarborough; missed driving into lay-bys at lunchtime, to uncork his thermos flask of hot, sweet tea, and munch the currant bun or Eccles cake Enid had wrapped up in greaseproof paper for him, and then to walk up and down with a cigarette, shaking the crumbs from his trousers and enjoying the sun, before dozing for twenty minutes behind the steering wheel, and waking up to find curious cows gazing over a fence.

But Leighton seemed to appreciate his advice. He called Walter his Executive Assistant, but Walter wasn't very happy with that title.

'If they'd name me Assistant Sales Manager, that would be different,' he told Enid one Friday night, as they sipped their evening cup of tea in front of the electric fire, the cat stretched out on the sheepskin rug between them. 'But Executive Assistant – what the heck is an Executive Assistant? I don't know whether I've been promoted or demoted. Nobody else does, either. I know it would probably upset a lot of people if they made me Assistant Sales Manager. That would be seen as promoting me over the heads of all the Area Sales Managers. But I just feel I'm in limbo.'

'Walt, you'll have to talk to Mr Leighton and explain,' Enid said.

'I've talked to him. He knows the position. What he says is, 'Do a good job for me, and I'll look after you, Walter.' Fair enough. But what if Grant Leighton goes? He's a queer fish. He's not even a salesman. He's an accountant. No one knows why he got the job. He's not popular. The blokes in the field don't like him.'

'But you like him.'

'Yes. I do. I like Leighton. He's smart. He wants to change things. But I'm not sure the company wants to be changed.'

'They must do, or they wouldn't have given Leighton the job.'

Walter lit himself another cigarette. 'It's one thing to give someone the job. It's another thing to change.'

'Maybe if he goes, you'll get his job,' Enid suggested, throwing her head back.

'Oh. That's very unlikely. There are so many blokes in line. I'm a nobody.'

'Well. You'll have to decide, Walt. If you want to come back to your old job, I'm sure they'll understand. You've been at it rather a long time to suddenly have to sit in an office all day.'

'He wants me to look for a house.'

'A house in Liverpool?'

'Yes.'

'Well, that shows he's serious. He couldn't uproot you like that and then dump you.'

The next weekend Walter and Enid, with the boys in the back of the car, drove up and down avenues planted with sycamores and horse chestnuts, staring at houses with 'For Rent' signs nailed to trees, in places Enid had always dreamed of one day living: Formby, and Freshfield, and Ainsdale, on the electric train line to Liverpool Exchange, but further out of town and quieter, with wide sandy beaches and dunes where it was fun to hide. They found a beautiful house, in Ainsdale, on a quiet road leading down to the sea. There was a round rose bed, with a brick pathway, and a sundial; the roses needed pruning; Virginia creeper grew up the walls of the house, which had low grey roofs and pretty casement windows, and lots of them; it was like a bunch of country cottages somehow thrown together; climbing roses grew on either side of the porch. Inside, it was darker than the house in Cheshire, because of its smaller windows and the way the Virginia creeper crowded in on them, but the rooms smelled fresh and empty; and their footsteps sounded hollow on the wooden floors, like a ballroom. Outside the kitchen window birds gathered, twittering, used to being fed.

'The bloke was promoted, and moved to London,' Walter said.

'Well, we've been promoted, and could move here,' said Alan.

'Would you two like to live here?' his father asked.

'Oh yes, rather! I'd move in a jiffy!'

'What about you, Toby?'

'I wouldn't mind.'

'You wouldn't miss all your friends, at school?'

'Not really,' Toby said.

'I'm going off to Repton in September anyway,' said Alan.

On Monday morning Walter told Grant Leighton he wanted his old job back. Leighton was shocked, pursed his lips. Walter agreed to give himself another month.

'I'm disappointed, Walter,' Leighton said. 'Just when I was beginning to know my way around here. What'll happen to me if you go?'

'What will happen to me when you know your way around?' Walter said.

'My Executive Assistant,' shrugged Leighton.

'Your husband's a fool,' Mrs Carruth told her daughter, at Childwall. 'Fancy throwing up a chance like this! The only chance he'll ever get, and he throws it in their faces!'

'He hasn't quite thrown it in yet,' Enid said, drinking tea in the little kitchen.

'But he will. I know Walter. He is a little man, Enid. A little man. You should have married Harry, like we all hoped you would.'

'I think you mean Jeffrey, who's now on the Board of the Royal Insurance Company. We've been through all this, mother.'

'Jeffrey, then. Why didn't you take that house in Freshfield you liked so much?'

'It was in Ainsdale. We decided it was too expensive, and with Alan going to public school, it was just too much.'

'You're sending Alan to boarding school, and you're going back to teaching, because your precious Walter can't make his mind up.'

'We'd already decided to send the boys to boarding school, Mother. You know that. That was before this Head Office job ever came up.'

'Yes, but if Walter took the job, you wouldn't have to go back to teaching.'

'I don't mind going back to teaching.'

'And I don't know why you'd want the boys to go to boarding school, anyway. The world is changing, Enid. Listen to Arthur talk. He knows the world is changing.'

'We want to give the boys the best chance we can.'

'And why do you think sending them to boarding school's going to do that? You're wasting your money. Well, it is your money.'

'Yes, it is our money!' Enid suddenly shouted. 'Why can't everybody mind their own business? Why can't everybody leave us alone?' Her eyes flashed.

'Because they hate to see you make fools of yourselves,' her mother said.

But in fact Enid really was expressing all that Walter actually wanted; and she too, by now: they wanted to be left alone. Walter didn't want Head Office to come after him, lure him to Liverpool, give him an office with a map of Britain on the wall, and a big grey steel desk, and a bunch of memo pads, and a secretary, Miss Clark. He wanted to potter about the leafy lanes of Cheshire and the green hills of North Staffordshire, calling on small-town newsagents and tobacconists, drinking tea with them, taking their orders for cigarettes and pipe tobacco, chatting about their sons and daughters, their families, friends, and little worlds. He knew those little worlds; he understood them; he was happy in them.

And Enid, too. She had no particular desire, anymore, to move to a nice house in Ainsdale, though she would like to have walked along the beach and watch seagulls, and it would have been nice to be nearer to Arthur, and her mother. She was happy where she was. And she didn't at all mind going back to teaching kindergarten, especially now that Alan would be away at boarding school, and Toby going too, all being well, in another couple of years. She was content that Walter had no further ambition. She wished that this Grant Leighton, or whatever his name was, at the office, would realise that, and let him be.

In June they'd learned that Alan had won a scholarship to Repton School. Well, he'd seemed to be quite bright, he was always top of his form at the prep school he and Toby went to, down the lane; and the headmaster, Oglethorpe, a pompous fellow with the complexion of a ripe peach, who spent most of his evenings in the snug at the Queen's Hotel, near the railway station, had told Walter and Enid that he thought the boy was 'scholarship material'; recommended the lad try for Repton, the school he himself had gone to. For Alan to win a Repton scholarship would be greatly to the credit of the little prep school; it had been years since any pupil had achieved as much, and the honours board in the school dining hall, stone-flagged and smelling of generations of gravy, looked empty. So Alan was coached, at no charge, by each of his teachers, in maths, in French, in Latin, all year, including the holidays, when he had to ride, in all weather, on buses, to their small homes and flats, where their wives gave him tea. But he put up with all this attention cheerfully, he really had set his heart on this scholarship, and he was furious with himself for all the stupid mistakes he kept on making in French and Latin grammar, when he knew what the right tense was perfectly well. On the other hand he so much enjoyed solving simultaneous and quadratic equations that he'd make up his own problems and work on them in bed.

Oglethorpe drove him to Repton one warm summer evening, to sit the exam; left him in the care of Mr Wilmot, the housemaster, and made for The King's Arms. Alan was at Repton for four days, and loved everything about it. He loved the loud talk at table, in the dining room of his house, and the echoes in the corridors, where everybody was always in a rush, and the hush in the evening, during prep. The place was busy and exciting and alive. It made him very proud to walk with four hundred young men from Chapel, every morning, to the thirteenth century Old Priory, where the thirty-seven scholarship candidates sat at plain wooden tables in what seven centuries before had been the monks' refectory, scratching away with steel nibs on yellow foolscap paper. And each day when the exams were over he'd watch Reptonians at cricket: there were cricket fields everywhere, below the Old Priory, behind the Chapel, beyond the squash courts, between the boarding houses.

'Want to bowl?' a cheery youth shouted, as Alan watched practice in the nets, the sun low, making everyone squint.

'I'm afraid I'm not much of a bowler, but I'd love to bat,' Alan blushed. He took off his prep school blazer, was tossed a bat. He played forward defensively at the first few balls, then timed a nice cover drive which would have gone for four runs.

'Nice shot, old chap!'

'Thanks!' Alan was in heaven. If only he could win this stupid scholarship and play cricket here!

One warm evening, back home, a couple of weeks later, he'd been watching trains from the bridge at Davey Lane, where they roared through a deep cutting and filled the trees with smoke. On his way home Toby met him, running, with the tremendous news.

'The headmaster just telephoned. You've won a scholarship to Repton.'

It was Enid's idea to thank the masters who'd coached Alan so devotedly, giving up their free time during school holidays, so they had a queer, stiff little cocktail party, and the masters stood around with their wives, sipping gin and French: as far as Alan remembered, it was the only time his parents ever entertained anyone outside the family. The boys were prevailed upon to take a break from their eternal cricket in the garden, and Walter was prevailed upon to play the piano. Alan was asked to sing, but drew the line at that.

In fact he had a beautiful voice; and he sang in the choir at St Philip's, the local church; perhaps he'd join the choir at Repton, which was a fine one. Play cricket and sing in the choir! How exciting the future looked! Alan was ambitious, much more so than his father; and in fact Walter, if he'd achieved everything he personally wanted, had plenty of ambition for his older son.

Alan was a nice boy, and he more than made up for his deficiencies with sheer enthusiasm. He was intelligent, rather than smart; certainly not brilliant, like his Uncle George; and if he'd been top of his form at prep school it was largely due to lack of competition. But he'd swotted hard for that scholarship, and at Repton he worked hard; had to, to keep up. Alan was passionately interested in all kinds of things, from ships and the sea to natural history; and he got that from his Uncle Arthur; in fact he was always compared to his Uncle Arthur, though Arthur was not only intelligent, he was also extraordinarily wise, which Alan really wasn't, and never would be.

Toby was wiser. He found that very often he didn't have an opinion, and when that was so he kept his mouth shut. He liked watching things; he was a great observer. He loved to watch work on building sites; on trips to Manchester, shopping with his mother, he'd have stood for hours, if she'd let him, watching them build eleven-storey office towers where the Germans had done the work of demolition. He liked going to plays, and concerts; and he became, in later life, a great lover of music, and especially of chamber music. But his father had given up on teaching him the piano. Toby wouldn't practise; at the first opportunity he'd escape into the garden to play cricket with Alan. In the summer holidays they spent hours playing cricket, those boys, taking turns to bat and bowl; the neighbourhood rang to their howls of triumph, and cries of despair and appeals to God, resounded to the crack of bat on ball; and the occasional crash of broken glass. Lofted balls sailed through bedroom windows, but their mother didn't seem to care; the boys cleaned up the mess. It was worse when Alan hit a ball high over the hedge into Mrs Beale's garden next door, smashing the cucumber frame where Mrs Beale puttered about most days: luckily she was indoors when it was smashed.

Mrs Beale was a widow; a disagreeable woman of fifty, and uncommunicative. She wore rimless spectacles and shapeless cotton frocks with polka dots. She also wore black bloomers, as Toby could see as she crouched over her cucumber frame. Toby was very interested in women's underwear and would watch hopefully when Mrs Beale went into her garden. When a cricket ball was hit into a neighbouring garden the boys just climbed through the hedge to get it back; but if it went into Mrs Beale's garden they had to walk round to her front door, and ring the bell, and ask Mrs Beale if she minded. She obviously did, though she told them they could get their ball; how the boys hated those expeditions. When the cucumber frame was demolished it was with particular dread that they rang her front door bell.

She was always a long time answering, though she was invariably in. The boys had no idea whereabouts in the house she spent her time: why did take her so long to get to the front door? Toby thought she was probably on the lavatory all the time. This would explain her pained expression when she opened the door.

'We're terribly sorry, Mrs Beale,' Alan said; he was crimson with shame and embarrassment. 'We seem to have broken your cucumber frame.'

'It was an accident,' Toby added. 'I was bowling. Alan lofted the ball. He'd have been caught in the deep field if we'd been playing real cricket.'

'I'm surprised your mother allows you to play cricket in the garden,' Mrs Beale said, after a moment.

'Yes, it er – it is surprising,' grovelled Alan.

Enid told the boys not to worry about Mrs Beale. She laughed when she came back from the shops and heard what had happened.

'She is very upset about her cucumber frame,' Alan said. 'She'll probably complain to Dad.'

'Let her complain,' said Enid, and her eyes flashed.

'She wears black bloomers,' said Toby. 'Is that because she's in mourning?'

'I don't think so,' laughed Enid.

'You don't wear black bloomers.'

'I don't wear bloomers.'

'I know.'

If Annie Sadie Carruth was disgusted with Walter for failing to make the most of what she saw as his terrific opportunity, she was even more disgusted with her son, George, who had borrowed two hundred and fifty pounds from Arthur and quit his job inventing new kinds of shoe polish to enrol in a London University extra-mural course in molecular chemistry. But after a year he quit the course, without even a diploma, and got a new job as a research chemist with a company that made feminine hygiene products, at a slightly higher salary than he'd earned before, but also without much prospect of advancement. And he didn't see how he could repay Arthur the loan.

The family was together at Christmas, in Cheshire. It was a mild winter; the boys had always hoped for a white Christmas, but had never seen one; this year Christmas Day was sunny.

At Repton, Alan had been the solo treble chosen to sing the first verse of *Once in Royal David's City*, at the beginning of the Festival of Nine Lessons and Carols in the school chapel. Walter and Enid, with young Toby, had listened in the north transept, where visitors were put, and Walter thought he'd never heard anything so pure and so beautiful as his son's soaring voice. Apart from this triumph, Alan had struggled in his first term; competing with boys who were cleverer than he was was a novel experience for him, and he didn't much enjoy it. He had particular difficulty in maths and science, which was surprising, because he'd loved quadratic equations so much. He finished up about halfway down his class; and his school report was disappointing.

Uncle Arthur had arrived on the twenty-third, bringing the old lady, and on Christmas Eve, seeing the day was mild and pleasant, Uncle Arthur and the boys took a long walk in the woods; it was like old times. Arthur wore a grey windcheater, perfectly-creased flannel trousers, and good brown shoes; the boys both armed themselves with sticks which they swished at dead leaves in the beech woods. They reached the old copper mines; the bricked-in main entrance to the abandoned workings had been smashed open by determined spelunkers from Manchester armed with coils of rope, torches, and – presumably – a pickaxe.

'We could go in,' said Alan,

'We could if we had a torch,' Uncle Arthur said. 'In the dark we'd risk falling down a shaft and getting ourselves killed.'

Retracing their steps they came to an extraordinary cleft in the rock known locally as the Devil's Grave. Here they could lower themselves, one by one, into a wide natural cavern, which smelled of wet rock, leaf-mould, human pee, and long-dead fires.

'We could make a fire,' Alan said.

'We could if we had a match,' laughed Uncle Arthur. 'We don't seem particularly well-equipped today, do we?'

'It's really spooky in here, don't you think?'

'Alan, you don't believe in spooks, do you?' Uncle Arthur remonstrated.

They hoisted themselves out of the Devil's Grave. A breeze had come up and the Scotch pines sighed. They crossed great slabs of sandstone; stood looking down over the Cheshire Plain. It was good to be with Uncle Arthur again. Alan was somewhat in awe of him now, because he realised what an important man he was, but Arthur treated the boys with exactly the same uncondescending courtesy. But Alan realised that he himself was changing; he felt he didn't quite belong here anymore; here in these woods of his childhood, here in Cheshire; he already moved in a different, more complicated and more enticing world. He was no longer even quite sure if he should go to sea. A distant train crawled across the Plain; they watched its smoke.

Walter had been given his old job back: Grant Leighton was very decent about it in the end. Leighton had a son who was the light of his eye; a fighter pilot in the Royal Air Force. The boy was killed in a crash, and Walter was the only man Leighton telephoned: they talked for hours, far into the night, and Leighton seemed comforted.

'I wish I had you here with me in Liverpool,' he told Walter.

The old lady was in top form on Christmas Eve.

'What do you think Alan's learning at that school?' she began. 'He's learning to sing! What good is that supposed to do him? Do you want him to be a singer? Do you want him to go on the stage and sing Madame Butterfly, is that what you want him to do? I'm surprised at you. He's not doing well at his lessons. He was always top of the class; he isn't anymore. And why? Too many distractions. All that singing. All that time in church.'

'Oh, I think old Alan's doing all right,' Walter said.

'I don't. Have you talked to him?'

'Well of course we've talked to him—'

'I've talked to him. He's worried. He doesn't understand things anymore. He'll get left behind. That's what'll happen to him. He'll do worse and worse; you mark my words. I'll have a mince pie.'

She'd spent the afternoon baking pies, and getting the Christmas Pudding all ready for boiling in the morning; she'd drawn the turkey and made sage and onion stuffing. The kitchen smelled like it used to, when she lived there, during the war; smelled of pots boiling on the stove, chopped onions, and heavy skirts saturated with pee; you'd expect her mince pies to taste of pee, it was a miracle they didn't.

Walter lit a cigarette. He hated argument. 'I don't want Alan to be brilliant,' he said. 'He doesn't have to get a scholarship to Oxford. I just want him to mix with the right sort of fellows. I want him to learn how to get on with the people who'll be able to help him one day.'

'Help him do what? Go on the stage? Sing Madame Butterfly?' scoffed Annie Sadie.

'No, nothing like that. My dearest wish would be for Alan to join the Foreign Office. The diplomatic corps.'

'They only take lords,' said the old lady. 'Alan's not a lord, never will be. You can't teach anyone to be a lord.'

'That's no longer true,' Arthur said. 'Britain has a socialist government. I think we'll see a new breed of people running things, in the future. Smart people. Clever people. I don't see why Alan couldn't make it. It's rather early to say.'

Enid reached for the cat, Wilson, who was dozing in front of the electric fire; she hauled him on to her knee.

'What do you think, Wilson?' she said, stroking the cat's smooth black fur. 'Do you think they're all talking rubbish?

Tell us, Wilson. Go on, please. Tell us. Talk. You hear everything. Talk. Make all our fortunes.'

'Well, Arthur, if Alan was your son, would you have sent him to a public school?' the old lady challenged.

'If Alan was my son he'd have probably been a duffer,' Arthur said, ducking the issue.

'There's no way any son of yours would be a duffer, Arthur. And you should have sons of your own. When are you going to get married again? Since Grace died you've lived like a hermit. You never go out, you don't see anyone. When I think of the high times you used to have, you and Grace. Entertaining all the time. Parties, receptions, concerts, I don't know what. It's sad to see you now, living with your old mother, playing bridge once a week with Mrs McMahon and that goose of a daughter of hers. It's sad. And you, George. When are you and Moira going to have children? I wouldn't wait much longer if I were you. You're neither of you so young as you used to be.'

'Moira and I d-d-d-don't really w-w-w-want children,' George said.

'That's ridiculous. That's unnatural. Moira, you can't sit there and tell me you don't want to have children. Only very selfish people don't want children.'

'Then I suppose that m-m-m-makes us very s-s-s-selfish,' said George.

'We don't want children,' Moira confirmed, splitting the word in two in that odd way of hers.

'And I don't understand why you never finished that course. You could have got another degree if you'd completed it.'

'And what would I have d-d-d-done with another d-d-d-degree?'

'Got yourself a real job for a change.'

'I have a r-r-r-real job.'

'He has a real job,' said Arthur. 'He has a very interesting job in a category that is bound to develop.'

'You s-s-s-say that because you're an infernal optimist, Arthur, and you're interested in everything,' George said.

'I say that because it's true,' smiled his brother.

'Why didn't you see it through, anyway, that course?' Annie Sadie wanted to know.

'I couldn't be b-b-b-bothered. I'm too old. I m-m-m-made a mistake, I shouldn't have enrolled.'

'You're not yet fifty. That's not too old.'

'It's too old f-f-f-for me.'

'I can understand George's getting fed up,' his brother said loyally. 'I couldn't go back to school. I wouldn't have the patience.'

'You have the patience of a saint!'

'Saints don't go to school.'

In the summer term Enid wrote to Alan at Repton to tell him his Uncle Arthur was going to marry Pat McMahon. She didn't write to him very often, maybe three or four times a term, though Alan dutifully wrote a long letter home every Sunday, during prep. His father wrote occasionally, but he wrote long, slushy letters full of advice, letters that made Alan blush and which he read in private; but he'd received one only a few days ago. Most of his friends received letters more frequently. So he was surprised when at breakfast he was handed an envelope with his mother's handwriting.

'My cat must have been run over, or something,' he told the boys around him, as they ate their bacon and mashed potatoes.

He slit open the envelope with his butter knife. 'I say!' he exclaimed, pleased. 'My Uncle Arthur's getting married again! That's super news! He's a terrific sort. He was married before, but his wife died of a heart attack. I hardly knew her, but it seems she was a cracker.'

'So who's he getting married to now? Do you know her?'

'Yes. Quite well, as a matter of fact. It seems the family doesn't approve. How incredibly stupid of them.'

Enid did not say, in her letter, that it was unlikely Alan would see his uncle again for a very long time.

Annie Sadie Carruth had convoked a family meeting, which took place in the living room of the house in Cheshire, one Saturday afternoon late in May, during a heatwave. George came up from London, and for once Arthur did not pay for his ticket; and although the purpose of the meeting was to try and talk him out of marrying Pat, Arthur had agreed to attend. Toby was packed off to spend the afternoon at a friend's, and not even told that his Uncle Arthur was visiting.

Because of the heat all the windows were open, and sometimes bees buzzed in, and wasps, and if it hadn't been for the stink of cigarette smoke, which over the years had permeated the upholstery, and the curtains, and the carpets, the house would have smelled of garden flowers.

'I have nothing against Pat,' Enid said, though this was not quite true; for some reason she had never liked her.

'But she can't give you children, Arthur. And you could still have children.'

Arthur, in his impeccable dark suit, remained unruffled under attack; well practised in overcoming opposition, he stood in front of the empty fireplace, drinking tea.

'Pat has seen her doctor,' he said. 'He says there is no reason why she shouldn't have children.'

'Arthur, that's nonsense,' said his sister. 'She's a very delicate woman. She wears a steel corset to hold her stomach together. How can she possibly have children?'

'I can only tell you what the doctor said.'

'I blame myself,' the old lady said. 'I should never have had Pat and her mother to our house all the time for bridge. Enid was right all along. She did warn me, but I took no notice. I couldn't imagine what would happen. That woman set her cap at you, Arthur.'

'That's unfair, Mother.'

'Oh, it's n-n-n-not unfair at all, Arthur,' George said, 'and you know it. She is a very c-c-c-clever, c-c-c-conniving woman. She knew exactly what she was d-d-d-doing. And Mum's r-r-r-right, she ought to have r-r-r-realised the danger.'

'Danger?' smiled the Chairman of the Red Funnel Line. 'I fail to see what danger is involved. Danger is when bombs are coming down. Danger is when ships get torpedoed. I have decided to marry Pat McMahon. That is not dangerous.'

'No, you haven't decided to marry Pat McMahon,' said his mother. 'Pat McMahon has decided to marry you. I don't know how long she's been plotting this – probably for years.'

'It's not as if you'd suddenly met,' Enid argued. 'So what's the big attraction, all of a sudden? She used to come round with her mother when we were all little – but you weren't exactly childhood sweethearts. You can't have fallen in love with her, Arthur, after all this time. You're sorry for her, that's the trouble! And being sorry for the woman isn't a reason to marry her! If only you weren't such a darned – gentleman!'

'Her mother was in on the plot too,' said the old lady. 'I can just see her plotting it with her daughter. 'Be patient, my dear,' she must have said. 'Never raise your voice, and look at the ground, and sooner or later he'll ask you to marry him."

'Mum's right,' said Enid. 'Can't you see that, Arthur? Can't you see through it all? I can't believe that you, with all your experience of – people, at work, the office – could be so – hoodwinked!'

George leapt to his feet. 'The only thing that woman's after is your m-m-m-money, Arthur!'

Arthur shook his head. 'That is a terrible thing to say, George,' he objected.

But George had only begun. 'Well, in my opinion, she is a t-t-t-terrible woman. It's an – insult to G-g-g-grace!'

'An insult to Grace? What on earth do you mean?'

'I mean, it's an insult! You l-l-l-let Grace die. For all I know you – I don't know what you did, but when she died she made you rich! I only hope you can afford the insurance p-p-p-premiums on this one!'

'George!' gasped Arthur.

Enid jumped in. 'George, what are you saying!' she cried.

George glared around, then sat down. 'Well, I – I apologise!'

'I – what gets me is – well, she's a Roman Catholic!' said Enid, who knew she had to change the subject before George talked more nonsense; so often lackadaisical about things, she looked beautiful now she was worked up into a passion; she seemed five years younger; her lovely eyes gleamed. 'The McMahons are Irish Catholics. You'll have to become a Catholic, Arthur. Do you realise that? Don't you mind?'

'Why should I mind?'

'Oh, because it's all nonsense, Arthur!' exclaimed Enid. 'You can't possibly swallow all that – that mumbo-jumbo! You'll have to go to mass, and everything! I just can't imagine my own brother Arthur – sweet, patient, wise, practical Arthur – becoming a Roman Catholic! And at his age!'

'Pat and I have discussed the matter,' he said. 'We have talked to a priest. Yes, I will become a Catholic.'

His old mother gave a contemptuous snort. 'I'm sure Father Mahoganybottom was in on the plot too!' she said. It's what she called all Catholic priests. 'He'll talk you into leaving all your money to the Pope!'

'Arthur,' begged George, 'please r-r-r-re-consider. It's not too late. I'm sorry – I know I went t-t-t-too far. But obviously, we are all against your marrying Pat. I believe that should c-c-c-count for s-s-s-something. You'll make M-m-m-mother very unhappy. You'll make your s-s-s-sister very unhappy. You'll make me very unhappy, but that doesn't m-m-m-matter. Marry again by all means. We'd all be d-d-d-delighted to see you marry again. But f-f-f-find yourself someone more suitable.'

There was a miserable silence.

'What do you s-s-s-see in her, Arthur? She's not exactly a b-b-b-beauty.'

'Oh, come on, George,' protested Walter, which was the first thing he'd said all afternoon; the poor fellow found the whole affair horrid; he didn't understand why the Carruths took such exception to Pat McMahon, because he'd always thought her a nice enough person. He understood their point about her not being able to have children, and he actually understood George's sense of outrage, seeing that he'd been so fond of Grace, but as for those terrible allegations – well! And he'd no idea why they objected so strongly to Pat's being a Roman Catholic, or to Arthur's becoming one: the family was not remotely religious; the only time they'd ever been near a church was when someone got married or had to be buried. And that remark of George's about her 'being no beauty', especially coming from a man who'd married Moira, described by Enid as having a face like the back of a bus! Walter thought Pat quite attractive in a melancholy sort of way. But he'd decided the best thing he could do was stay out of all this, as best he could: Enid was his wife; Arthur her brother; this really wasn't Walter's business.

'I think I should point out,' Arthur said quietly, 'that I am not asking any of you to marry Pat; nor am I asking any of you to become a Catholic. I should have thought that what I do is my affair. I see no point in continuing this discussion. I shall drive back to Liverpool.'

Enid said, 'Arthur, why did you agree to come here if you're not going to listen to us?'

'I have listened to you insulting the woman I have decided to marry. I don't think I need to listen any longer.'

George gave up. 'Then marry the stupid woman,' he said. 'But don't expect any of us to c-c-c-come to the w-w-w-wedding.'

Arthur smiled at him. 'Why would you expect an invitation?'

'Pat McMahon will not be welcome in this house,' Enid said.

That offended Walter too. 'Well, that's something I'm sure we can discuss,' he said, waving his cigarette at a wasp that winged across the room.

'No. I don't want her here,' insisted Enid.

'I don't think I'd want to bring her,' said Arthur.

'You're a fool, Arthur,' the old lady said.

'One day, we'll all turn against you,' George had told his brother. But Arthur could have had no idea how the family would react to his engagement, and must even now have assumed they'd come round; sooner or later, that's what happened: other people came round to his way of thinking: he'd built his career on it, hadn't he. He shook hands with everybody; dignified to the last.

'Goodbye, Enid. Goodbye, Walter. Goodbye, George. Goodbye, Mother.'

The cat followed them outside, where it rubbed itself affectionately against Arthur's beautifully pressed trousers, as if to cheer him up. That cat, Walter thought, has more sense than anyone else here. Arthur slid behind the driving wheel of his car, a new one, expensive, with not a speck of dust; backed down the curved driveway; waved once; and drove away. They heard him brake for the halt sign at the main road, then the squeal of tyres as he accelerated. Late afternoon sunshine made the garden golden. Enid asked if anyone wanted more tea.

Afterwards, Walter stood in the garden smoking; he was appalled by the sad implications of this rift, and wondered whether he should have spoken up. What about the boys, for instance? They'd had no part in any of this nonsense, but it looked as if they wouldn't be seeing their Uncle Arthur again; or not for a long while; and Walter knew how much he meant to them. And Arthur, it was clear, wasn't about to change his mind, could hardly have been expected to. Did they really expect they could talk him out of marrying Pat, once he'd proposed to her? Arthur? Go back on his word? Not in a month of Sundays! So would the others apologise, in the end? Walter didn't see it happening. The Carruths had dug themselves into a deep hole, and would find it awfully difficult to climb back out.

Chapter Eleven

He was hopping mad, was Alan.

He was beginning, as his mother said, to shoot up, seemed to be growing inches every few months; so his pants never fitted him, they ended six inches above his ankles; also his hair had got wavy, and he had no eyebrows. He still sang treble in the school choir. He hadn't done so well at cricket as he'd hoped; true, he could hit the fast bowlers, just as he'd hit his younger brother Toby's fast bowling into the neighbours' gardens at home, but the spin bowlers foxed him, they drove him into a passion: he'd play forward defensively, and either miss the ball completely or snick it dangerously, then lose his temper, and dance down the wicket like a dervish, and swipe viciously at space, and get easily stumped by the wicketkeeper.

At Manchester Central Station, when his mother met him off the train from Derby at the end of July, he immediately took her to task for her part in what he and Toby called the Great Family Rift.

'I can't understand why you'd behave like that!' he shrilled. 'That you and Uncle George and Grandmother, that old battle-axe, should gang up on poor Uncle Arthur and try and talk him out of marrying Pat is bad enough! But that you should say such horrible, vindictive, wounding things about her that Uncle Arthur won't talk to anyone again – is absolutely unpardonable! Whatever got in to you?'

The two of them stood there in the crowded station concourse, while passengers streamed past them off the Derby train, and Alan's protests were half-drowned by the placid, masculine announcement of departures to London and to Liverpool; the place was full of smoke and sunlight. Alan was now an inch taller than Enid. Her eyes flashed; she might have shouted back; instead she laughed at him.

'Welcome home,' she said, tossing her head so that the black curls rippled.

It stopped him; he was a bit ashamed; he thought of giving her a kiss; but after three terms at Repton had become too much of a stranger. He picked up the brown overnight bag which he'd dropped to the ground.

'The one thing I will say,' he said, in a more normal tone, 'is that Toby and I dissociate ourselves from what happened, and as soon as we can we'll go to Liverpool to see Uncle Arthur and Aunt Pat.'

'We made a mistake,' his mother confessed, as they walked up Moseley Street, past the Central Library, past the noble, sooty portico of the art gallery. 'I suppose we thought we could talk him out of it. That was silly of us, as your father keeps reminding me. But I do believe it's an unfortunate marriage. I admit I don't like Pat. I admit we all said things we shouldn't have said, including me. But I'm not going to apologise to your Uncle Arthur.'

'Why not? That would seem to me an admirable first step.'

'No. I'm not apologising. We may have made a mistake in opposing the idea as strongly as we did, but he's made a bigger mistake in marrying a woman who can't give him children. And, do you know, he's become a Roman Catholic; of course, he had to. He goes to mass; did you ever hear of anything so stupid?'

'What's wrong with going to mass?'

'Oh, Alan, don't tell me you're thinking of becoming a Roman Catholic!'

'No. I don't think so. But I don't understand why it's such a big issue. I mean, it's not as if you and George were Orangemen, you don't exactly march in Orange Parades. You're hardly even Protestants. The only time you've been to church, that I know of, is when I sang *Once in Royal David's City* in chapel, at Christmas.'

There were lots of Irish Catholics in Liverpool, no wonder it was called the capital of Ireland. And the Protestants did march in Orange parades, which commemorated King William of Orange's victory at the Battle of the Boyne, in Northern Ireland, and the Catholics paraded in green on St Patrick's Day; and yes, on Saturdays, at soccer, the Catholics supported Everton, on the whole, and the Protestants supported Liverpool; and in Manchester, United was the Catholic team, and City the Protestant: what a mess. The Carruths called themselves Protestants because they weren't Irish, which did not make them churchgoers, or even believers, but they came from Liverpool, and Enid had been brought up there, and gone to school there, so she was prejudiced – which she admitted was stupid, but she couldn't help it, and that was that.

Walter talked the boys out of paying a visit to Uncle Arthur and their new Aunt Pat.

'I happen to agree with both of you, one hundred per cent,' he told them, strolling about the garden, smoking. 'What everybody said that day was very unfortunate. But I think if you went to see Arthur and Pat right now it would only make things worse. Your mother would be more upset than she'd ever tell you. I love your mother, and you do too. I think your first duty is to her. My advice is to lie low for a while. Perhaps next year, when tempers have cooled down a bit, you could go and stay with Arthur and Pat.'

'Sure, Dad,' Alan flashed. 'Perhaps next year. Perhaps never.'

'Well, now,' their father said, inhaling deeply, 'never is a long time. I don't think it'll come to that. But just now, it would really not be a good idea. You can write, of course; in fact, you should write.'

'If you agree one hundred per cent with us,' Alan said, 'why didn't you speak up?'

'How do you know he didn't speak up?' Toby said.

'I didn't speak up,' Walter admitted. 'If you'd been there, you'd have realised how useless that would have been. The Carruths are a funny lot. I don't belong.'

'Dad's probably right,' said Toby. 'We can go and see them next year.'

'Hey, Toby!' Alan said, noticing the cricket stumps that his younger brother had planted at the end of the garden. 'Let's play cricket! Want to play, Dad?'

Walter dropped his cigarette end, trod it into the grass. 'All right.'

He didn't often play with them, because he was generally preoccupied with his photography, and he bowled slow leg breaks, which Alan hated. Toby came running back with bat and ball.

'Bowl me some fast ones!' Alan cried, as he grabbed the much-used bat and strode to the wicket.

'No, I'll bowl you some slow ones,' said Walter, taking the ball off Toby. He took off his jacket and placed it on the ground to mark a crease; polished the ball on his trousers. With a run of only two steps, he pitched a spinning ball at Alan, which bounced, and turned; and Alan, changing his mind at the last moment, played a back defensive stroke, and missed.

'I can't hit slow bowling!' he called to his father, tossing the ball back to him.

'So I see.' Again Walter polished the ball, took two steps to the crease, and bowled. This time Alan played forward, caught an edge; and snicked the ball into the rose bed, where it decapitated a Mary Harkness, planted by Uncle Arthur.

'How's that?' Walter appealed. 'Caught at first slip!'

Alan laughed, but he was furious. He chucked the ball back at his father. This time Walter bowled a googly, and Alan came well out of his crease, aiming a straight drive which would have carried for a six if he'd hit the ball, but he didn't.

'Let Toby bowl, for God's sake!' he called.

'You really need to work on the slow stuff,' said Walter, as he picked up his jacket, threw the ball to Toby, and lit another cigarette.

Toby, who was a good fast bowler, took as long a run as he could, and delivered a very fast ball, with just a slight amount of spin. Alan read it perfectly, and timed his shot marvellously, he met the pitch with a beautiful late cut. There was the ringing thwack of bat on hard leather ball. And a dreadful crash of broken glass, as the ball went through the bedroom window of the house next door.

'Oh, cripes,' said Alan. 'Mrs Beale's bedroom! She'll go spare. I'll have to go round. What rotten luck, my first day home from school! I say, Dad, could you lend me a pound note? I'll have to offer to pay.'

'You can relax,' Walter said, putting on his jacket. 'Mrs Beale has left. Didn't your mother tell you in a letter? We have new neighbours.'

'She didn't tell me. The last letter I had was when she wrote about Uncle Arthur marrying Aunt Pat.'

'Well, Mrs Beale sold the house and moved to Bournemouth. Our new neighbours are a vast improvement. Very friendly. Major Roberts is a retired army officer, his wife is Dorothy. Nice people. The Major is a pipe smoker. They have a little dog called Topsy, who's friendly too. Topsy and our cat Wilson are good friends. You should see them together.'

'That's a relief. All the same, the Major won't be very pleased about his bedroom window.'

'He's a good sport. Let's all go round, and you can meet him.'

Years later, as he lay dying of lung cancer upstairs, Walter remembered how Alan had missed his bowling three balls in a row, then smitten Toby's fast spinner high through the Major's window; and a smile flickered across his face; and they thought he wanted to tell them something, and leaned forward; but Walter was in the back garden, polishing a cricket ball on his pants, and the boys were home from school, and laughing.

Arthur and Pat had been married at the end of June.

They might both have preferred a quiet ceremony, but Arthur was too prominent a figure in Liverpool, so the wedding was an event; everybody was there, even a bunch of Carruths: including Uncle Fred from Wallasey, who built the astonishing scale model ships which Uncle Arthur had told the boys about, and which made his house look like a maritime museum, with the *Lusitania*, four feet long, on the sideboard in the dining room, and the Mersey ferry *Royal Daffodil* on top of a medicine cabinet in the bathroom; there was also Auntie Gladys, Auntie Edie, who'd always threatened to play with the boys ('We'll have such fun!') and Auntie Freda. But Annie Sadie was not there, though she had received an invitation, and nor was any of the immediate family.

A nice photograph of the couple appeared on the front page of the *Liverpool Echo*. Pat did not wear white, though technically, God knows, she was entitled to: instead, a dark suit, with a calf length skirt, and a hat with a small black veil; she looked very strained, but smiled a lot; and in the photographs she and Arthur made a handsome pair; he tall, imposing, with his rimless glasses and nicely-cut grey suit; and she very self-possessed, surely happy. She wore no make-up; her soft brown eyes being well set off by her strong dark eyebrows; and her lovely hair, only faintly streaked with grey, fell almost to her narrow shoulders, where it ended in curls, and framed her thin nose perfectly, and made her white cheeks snow-like.

After a reception at the Adelphi, Arthur and Pat took The Merseyside Express to London, where they spent the night at the Dorchester Hotel; and in the morning it was the Golden Arrow to Paris, from Victoria Station. Arthur's first idea had been a quiet honeymoon in the Lake District, maybe at The Swan at Grasmere, where he had often stayed on his lonely walking weekends, eating at a table for one, and fussed over by a head waiter in tails; but Sir William Crashaw had offered them his villa in the hills above Cannes; while he and Lady Crashaw stayed for a while in Liverpool, where they had grandchildren to spoil; so Cannes it would be.

On the ferry across the Channel Pat sat in a deckchair under blankets, watching the black smoke from the ship's two tall funnels hurry astern, and the cartwheeling, diving gulls that hung over the wake; and Arthur smiled at her with quiet satisfaction. There was a slight mist on the Channel, and ships' sirens boomed everywhere; at one point the ferry slowed down and altered course to starboard; and Arthur strained his eyes to see the vessel they must have given way to, but never saw her. At Calais, French porters in blue pants and jackets, their faces weathered by Channel gales, carried Pat and Arthur's luggage to a first-class compartment; and Pat read the destination boards hung on the sides of each coach; she wanted to go everywhere, climb into every car; would very much like to see Basel, and Lyon, and Dijon, and Marseille, and Genova, and Roma, and wondered if there were any trains fast enough for her to see them all while she was alive. The Rome train had the big blue sleeping cars of the Wagons Lits company, and beautiful tasselled lampshades on the neat white tables in the dining car; and every train was full; people stood in the corridors, or sat doggedly on their suitcases.

With a snort of steam, the Paris train, first to leave, moved slowly through the docks, holding up traffic. After a stop at Calais Ville it settled into the clickety, clickety, clickety so different from English trains; white smoke from the locomotive's twin exhausts rolled across a flat landscape of endless fields. Pat and her new husband blasted up the chalk hills to Boulogne, and looked down on the grey Channel; they careered down to the Somme at Abbeville; stopped for a few minutes at Amiens; then thundered through the summer dusk past Creil, rattling over the junction that Brussels and Amsterdam trains took; they woke every dove in the forest of Chantilly; clattered through the northern suburbs of Paris; and glided to an imperceptible stop in the vast Gare du Nord.

They were in Paris three days; they stayed at the Georges V. Arthur had travelled several times to the United States, and once to South America, but he hadn't set foot in France since he was invalided out of it in 1916, blinded by mustard gas. He sat with his wife at cafés on the Champs Elysées, where they sipped coffee and dipped croissants into it the way young Enid had learned to do, many years ago, under the watchful eyes of nuns. They strolled arm in arm down the great avenue towards the Louvre; and watched the fountains play, and boys sailing toy yachts on the stone pools in the gardens.

'What are you singing?' Pat smiled.

'I can't sing, but I know the words, or at least some of them,' Arthur said. And he sang them to her, quietly and out of tune:

> 'Mademoiselle from Armentières, parlez-vous?
> Mademoiselle from Armentières, parlez-vous?
> Mademoiselle from Armentières,
> Mademoiselle from Armentières,
> Inky-pinky, parlez-vous?'

She laughed and clapped her gloved hands. 'That's pretty!' she told him.
'Old First World War song.'
'Do you remember others?'
'I don't think so.'
'Did you meet any mademoiselle from Armentières?' she smiled.
'No, but I met a number of German soldiers.'
'You can pretend I'm your mademoiselle from Armentières.'
She didn't speak French, but she pronounced it perfectly; he was enchanted by the quiet, low, slightly hurried way she articulated things. The truth is, he found everything about her most becoming. He marvelled at her: she'd spent all thirty-eight years of her life with her mother, in very modest circumstances; she'd hardly ever been out; the only restaurant she'd ever been to was probably the Kardomah, in Liverpool, with its famous potato croquettes; she'd never mixed with people; and certainly never with men; she'd never travelled. Yet she carried herself with astonishing poise. She had, in her quiet way, quite charmed Sir William and Lady Crashaw. ('My God, Arthur, you've

done it again. You have the most remarkable taste in women. Where did you find this treasure?') Arthur had the idea that Alfred Poindexter, an incorrigible bachelor, had fallen instantly in love with her; she had moved among the aldermen, the company directors, the politicians at her wedding with modest assurance; acted, in expensive hotels and restaurants, in first-class accommodations on grand trains and ships, as if she'd frequented them all her life.

Outside every café and restaurant in Paris were great wooden barrels of oysters, in mouth-watering variety. They worked their way through Belons and Fines Claires, which had been trucked through the night from chilly Brittany and breezy Arcachon, served on plates of crushed ice and shredded seaweed, with thin slices of lemon. They rode the funicular railway up to the Sacré Coeur church in Montmartre; ate pheasant braised in cabbage at Mère Catherine's. In the little streets off the Boulevarde Clichy prostitutes wearing fishnet tights stood in doorways; and Pat commented on them approvingly.

'She's nice… She's beautiful… She's a lovely girl… or is she a man? That one has beautiful eyes.'

Arthur raised her thin hand to his lips. She really did amaze him. You'd have thought she'd be prim and narrow-minded and old maidish, but not a bit.

'None of them is more beautiful than you,' he told her, and he meant it.

'None of them is nearly as old,' she smiled.

They visited Versailles, taking the bumpy electric train from the Gare d'Orsay; and walked through the brilliant galleries of the palace; she found the grounds rather gloomy, with their endless vistas, their haughty statues, and their silent trees; but she loved the Grand Trianon, and even more the Petit Trianon, all pink and white marble like a delicious cake, and she adored Marie Antoinette's little farm, where the silly Queen and her lady's maids had played at being shepherdesses. When they came out of the grounds they ate roasted chestnuts, red hot; they burned their fingers and laughed.

She was so knowledgable; knew a great deal about all kinds of places she'd never been to: surprised Arthur all the time. It was because she'd read so much: in thirty-eight years, she'd had plenty of time to read. But unlike Arthur, who night after night at the Crosby Public Library, after long days at the office, had studied encyclopaedias, memorising facts and figures, Pat had read novels, and travel journals, and learned how exciting life could be, and how people sometimes behaved, and the things they might do.

They took the Blue Train south to Cannes, after dinner at the sumptuous restaurant at the Gare de Lyon, with its luminous murals of destinations served by the old PLM railway company – Lyons, Grenoble, Orange (home of King William), Avignon, Marseilles – all awash in Edwardian sunshine. They ate oysters, Fines Claires; and Arthur ordered a bottle of Moet et Chandon champagne.

It was a clear night, with a brilliant half moon; Pat, who never slept well, watched the dark hills of Burgundy slip past the windows of the train; she was awake at Dijon; awake at Lyons. As the moon faded, she watched, fascinated, the olive and umber landscape of the south as a great orange sun rose above cypresses and brown villages perched on hills. The Blue Train moved too fast for her to identify the towns they swept through, the still sleeping stations with a wakeful station master holding up his furled flag. Then the brakes came on and the train slowed down, and Arthur woke up, and they pushed up the window blinds in time to see the early morning sun dye the long stone walls of fabled Avignon carmine and gold.

'Did you sleep?' smiled Arthur.

'No,' she smiled back. 'It doesn't matter. It's been wonderful.'

They reached Cannes in the late morning. Pat had slept a little as the train wound along the coast, whistling through tunnels in the red rock of the Esterel mountains; between the tunnels, tantalising glimpses of tiny coves with yellow sand and clear blue water, and children splashing in the waves. He helped her down from the train; pressed her hand gently as she winced. They were met at the station by Sir William's chauffeur; and sat in the back of an open Rolls Royce as he drove them up steep, narrow lanes that twisted between huge gardens; crimson bougainvillaea cascaded from tall white walls. The driver got out to open double wrought-iron gates, painted dark green; beyond them, a pink gravel drive. The house was of pink cement; bougainvillaea again, petals the colour of apricots, and white oleanders; a purple jacaranda tree in full bloom. They walked through the house to a terrace with a blue swimming pool overlooking, way below, the red tiles and white hotels of Cannes, the soft, very pale Mediterranean.

'Do you mind if I sleep for an hour?' Pat said.

'I'll watch you.'

She closed her eyes on the pillow, but he wasn't sure if she slept. He wondered at her tolerance of pain. A light breeze stirred the white curtains; and apricot-coloured petals from the bougainvillaea danced skittishly across the floor. After a while he saw that she was looking at him with her patient smile that was never quite a smile.

'You're thinking of Grace, aren't you,' she whispered.

He sighed and put the palms of his hands together; smiled at her fondly. 'How did you know?'

'I don't mind at all, Arthur,' she said. 'It was jolly sporting of you to marry me. I'll try my best to make you glad you did.'

'I am very glad I married you, dear Pat.'

'They all hate me so.'

'But I love you.'

She closed her eyes for a moment. But she would not dwell on it. 'Shall we go and find some lunch? I think I'm ready for more oysters.'

They lunched at the beach restaurant of the Carlton Hotel, at a table shaded by palm trees in tubs: where they demolished more Fines Claires, and hearts of palm, and cold lobster with a garlic mayonnaise, and a bottle of light rosé de Provence, which sat in an ice bucket tucked in with a white napkin. Afterwards they walked along the promenade with its scintillating white hotels that caught the sun in ten thousand windows, and its four rows of palm trees, towards the old town, stopping now and then to rest in blue iron chairs. There was a small park with an old-fashioned carousel; prettily-carved wooden horses rose up and down on brass poles; children shouted and nannies scolded. They studied boats in the fishing port, painted blue and green and red with enormous lanterns hung over the stern, and eventually stood at the foot of the hill leading up to the castle.

'I'm not sure I can make it to the top, but – perhaps halfway,' Pat smiled gamely.

They paused at a café on the Rue St Antoine, where they drank peppermint syrup with water and ice, and men in berets who'd dropped in for a glass of red wine stood at the bar and noticed Pat, and Arthur sang to her again, half under his breath and still out of tune.

> 'Oh, the noble Duke of York,
> He had ten thousand men;
> He marched them up to the top of the hill,
> And he marched them down again.
> When they were up they were up,
> And when they were down they were down,
> But when they were only halfway up
> They were neither up nor down.'

'And here we are,' Pat laughed. 'Neither up nor down. But I think we can go on now. If you're going to make me walk up hills, though, we'll have to buy me proper shoes.'

She'd always dressed well, soberly; she preferred dark colours; but very femininely: and though all the indications were that she would never marry, she had never looked like a spinster; on the contrary, although she had excellent taste and did not dress at all coquettishly, she liked nets and gauzes that showed her thin, bare arms, and the whiteness of her throat. Now that she could suddenly afford almost anything she liked, she didn't change her style, though her skirts were more expensive, and Arthur had bought her pearls, and a diamond necklace, and a fur stole; and she'd bought more shoes, and fine stockings. She'd always looked carefully after her clothes, washing and folding and ironing, to make them last as long as possible; she'd kept her few pairs of shoes well polished, and always in lasts so that they'd keep their shape; she used shoe horns so as not to wear down the heels; she was extremely careful with her stockings, not to ladder them. Out of long habit she continued to do the same, with everything she had, though she told herself she didn't have to. She was a credit to Arthur; or that's how Arthur saw it; she'd turned heads in Paris; and she turned heads now, here in Cannes, at the Carlton Beach, and along the Croisette. Well, Arthur's brother George may have described her as 'not exactly a beauty'; but most people, it seemed, thought differently; and the French, less inhibited about showing how they felt, eyed her approvingly. There was an ephemeral quality about her looks that men remembered, long after she'd passed by on her husband's arm; she left you sad; she wouldn't be here again; life was short.

They reached the top of the hill, and looked down over the old town and the fishing port from the parapet of the square stone castle. She drew a deep breath.

'I told you I could make it!' she smiled.

'You told me you could make it halfway,' Arthur corrected her.

'Poor Arthur. I wish I was a better walking companion for you.'

On the terrace of Sir William Crashaw's villa, that night, with the half moon hanging over the Esterel mountains to the west, she said, 'I am a very poor substitute for Grace. I can't do any of the things she was so good at. I can't walk, and I can't dance, and I can't play tennis. I'm not fun, like she was.'

'Grace hated oysters,' said Arthur, and they laughed together.

'I can't believe I'm married to you,' she said later.

'Well you are, Mrs Carruth.'

'Mrs Carruth! Who ever thought, one day I'd be Mrs Carruth! But you were always kind to me. You gave me books, when I was a gawky girl. You read to me. But I was such a poor thing – and you were so handsome!'

After their honeymoon Arthur and Pat moved into a flat in Aigburth Vale: the ground floor of an elaborate Victorian house, with high roofs and delicate gables, completely hidden from the road by massive trees, cedar and laurel and rhododendron, and standing in its own secret, shady park, with well-kept lawns and enormous fir trees. From a stone terrace with a wrought-iron bench Pat and Arthur could sit looking down towards the river, where oil tankers bound for the refineries at Ellesmere Port moved slowly on the brown tide. They bought antique furniture and beautiful, heavy, French curtains; and yes, they hosted small but elegant dinner parties, which were catered so as not to tire Pat, though – unlike Grace – she did cook, when the two of them were alone, and very well: she had books; she flambéed escalopes, poached fish in white wine, and baked soufflés.

Walter Miller's hopes that the passing of time would see a rapprochement between Arthur and the family did not look as if they'd be realised. Arthur wrote to his mother every week, but she never wrote back; when he telephoned, to make sure she was well, she assured him, crossly, that of course she was.

But in time Enid began to worry about the old lady being on her own. And Annie Sadie really didn't know anyone who could help because she refused to speak to her old friend, Pat's mother, who she was sure had plotted this ridiculous marriage for years, maybe ever since Grace died, maybe even before; and she wouldn't make up with Arthur. She had three sisters who toddled by sometimes, for a cup of tea, but two of them, Auntie Edie, playtime over, and Auntie Glad, died the following year, leaving only Auntie Freda. Her bilious attacks were becoming more frequent; they laid her low for days. But she was, you'd have to admit, a game old soul; as devoid of self-pity as her unwelcome daughter-in-law. She watched television for hours, and would have known everything there was to know if she'd only listened, but she kept shouting at her set.

After two years Enid broached with Walter the subject of having her back to live with the family, in Cheshire. It was late in the evening; Major Roberts, next door, had tapped out his pipe on the grate: which had become the signal for bedtime.

'The alternative,' Enid suggested, 'is to put her into a home. But I don't think I have the heart to do that. She still won't talk to Arthur, and I can't imagine Madam Pat putting up with her anyway. Of course, there's George, but he hasn't offered and they always seem to be so tight for money. Also, I can't see the old lady agreeing to go to London. I think we're stuck with her, Walt.'

Walter Miller shut his eyes, and inhaled the smoke of his cigarette.

'All right,' he sighed. 'Let's have her live with us.'

'It won't be easy. I know. She'll drive us nuts. Of course, you can go off to your darkroom and ignore her, but I won't be able to. She'll get on the boys' nerves. But they're both away at school most of the time. This is not a good idea. But she is eighty-three. What if she had a fall, or something? She could be lying there for days before anybody found her. At least if she's here we can keep an eye on her. Thank goodness your old Mum has Aunt Beatrice to look after her.'

Walter's tiny mother still lived in the dark little house in Waterloo where Walter had spent his impecunious boyhood: she was now eighty-five, and she hardly ate a thing, she lived on mugs of hot Bovril; she was like a little shadow, but her heart pumped away and she was never ill. Aunt Beatrice, the year before, had finally married: her husband was an officer with the Pacific Steam Navigation Company, sailing out of Liverpool through the Panama Canal on the old *Reina del Pacifico*, a fine but elderly vessel built long before the war, so obviously the pair did not spend a lot of time together. Uncle Jack, as the boys briefly remembered him, was a quiet, pleasant man in his late fifties, nearing retirement; he'd never married until he met Beatrice. Between voyages the two of them lived in the upstairs front room of the house on Oakdale Road: but Jack died of cancer within six months of his marriage.

Annie Sadie moved back to Cheshire at the end of September, 1953. She took over what had been Toby's bedroom, across from the bathroom, which she had to be very close to; so Toby and Alan now shared the other front bedroom. Enid was always down in the dumps when the boys went back to school. It wasn't as if they talked together much, she and the boys, or went out together; and she realised now that she'd never been particularly close to them; but it was good having them around, and without them she was lonely; perhaps she'd always been lonely. But she'd kept her trim figure, and her slightly exotic dancer's looks, with the beautiful, difficult eyes, and her thick black curls.

Annie Sadie Carruth spent her first week at her daughter's house in bed, with a severe bilious attack. She would stumble out of her room into the bathroom and occupy it for hours. On her worst days she was unable to make even this short journey, and would call out for a basin. 'Fetch me the joey, Enid!' she'd cry. 'Quick, fetch me the joey!'

When she first wobbled downstairs she was a frightening sight. She'd taken to wearing a hairnet all the time, and her mouth hung open because she'd lost control of the muscles in her jaw; so her upper set of false teeth kept falling out. She wore heavy black cardigans, at least two of them, and the ankle-length black skirts that no amount of boiling and hanging out to air in soft Cheshire breezes could ever get the stink of pee out of; and she proceeded to make everyone's life a misery, as Enid had known she would. She had a number of pet issues which were never laid to rest: Enid's marrying Walter, a man of limited ambition; their sending the boys to an expensive public school; Walter's smoking. Enid handled her as best she could; but she didn't have Arthur's endless patience; so often she ended up in tears.

'You're low because the boys have gone back to school,' the old lady would say. 'You're wasting your money sending them.'

'Walt and I don't consider it a waste of money, Mum.'

'Of course it's a waste of money. Arthur left school when he was fourteen, and look where he's got.'

'Arthur's a brilliant man.'

'Not brilliant, just smart. And a fool. It's not as if you had money to waste, with Walter's job.'

'We manage all right.'

'Managing isn't living, Enid. You could be enjoying yourselves. When was the last time you two went on holiday?'

'We decided not to go away on holidays while the boys are at school.'

'You've never even been out of England.'

'Nor have you,' Enid pointed out; and laughed. Sometimes she would laugh, like that, out loud, when a moment before she'd been about to cry.

'It was different in my young day. You and Walter could go for a nice holiday on the Costa Brava if you didn't spend all your money on the boys.'

'The Costa Brava can wait. We go for nice picnics in the hills. The boys love going for picnics.'

'Those are just day trips!' snorted the old lady. 'Day trips aren't holidays! Where are you going?'

'I'm going to hang out the washing!'

'It's raining, you'll catch your death of cold!'

'I don't care!'

Inevitably the two women finished up shouting at each other.

'I don't understand why you let that man smoke the way he does,' Annie Sadie said, a few days later.

Enid faced her, smouldering, shook her black curls angrily, forced herself to stay calm.

'I don't see what business that is of yours.'

'Of course it's my business. You're my daughter, he's the man you married, against my better judgement. You could be the wife of a director of the Royal Insurance Company by now, if you'd played your cards right. How much does he smoke, anyway? The whole house stinks. It must be three packets a day, easily.'

'I don't count.'

'You should. What kind of example do you think he sets the boys?'

Enid drew in her breath. 'If the boys begin to smoke, it'll be because their friends do,' she said. 'That's something they'll have to make up their own minds about. If they want to smoke, I won't be able to stop them. I can tell them smoking is bad for them, which I do.'

'You can stop them very easily. You tell them that if they smoke, they get no pocket money.'

'I don't want them to have no pocket money, and have to beg off their friends.'

'You're giving them permission to go ahead and kill themselves.'

'Walt smokes three packets a day. He's still alive.'

'He won't be much longer, at this rate. When was the last time he had a check-up?'

'I don't know.'

'Enid, at least insist he has a check-up. If they catch these things in time they can sometimes operate.'

'Walt has no reason to suspect there's anything wrong with him.'

'Of course he has! He smokes three packets of cigarettes a day! Have you ever even tried to get him to cut down?'

'Yes, I have, as a matter of fact. He tried to give up last year. But he couldn't. I'd find cigarette ends in the garden.'

'Where are you going?'

'I'm going outside!'

The black cat, Wilson, followed Enid out of the house and wrapped itself around her ankles. She picked it up and walked around the garden with the cat in her arms.

'You understand everything that goes on, don't you, Wilson. Of course you do. And you don't smoke, do you. Of course you don't. You have more sense. Your master coughed up blood the other night. But I know he can't stop.'

When the boys came home for the Christmas holidays the old lady lost no time starting in on them.

'When he was your age, your Uncle Arthur was working for a living. But you have no idea what you want to be.'

'On the contrary,' Alan said. 'I am going to Calcutta to work with Mother Teresa, helping the poor.'

'Pooh! What kind of a job is that? How much does Mother Mahoganybottom pay? Nothing!'

'I had thought of being a doctor,' Toby told his grandmother. 'But I'm probably too squeamish. So I may be a lawyer. But I'm probably too honest. So I may be a chartered accountant. But I can't count. Or an architect. But I can't draw. So I'll probably be a gardener.'

Unlike his mother, or Alan, Toby was impervious to the old lady's attacks. He just didn't care. She amused him.

'A gardener! You never do any gardening here!'

'No. That's absolutely true, Grandmother. The trouble is, I don't much like plants.'

She upset the cat too, the old lady did. It hated being picked up by her, always struggled to get free.

Clutching the cat tight, she said, with no one else in the room, 'I don't like it here. I wish I had my own place.'

Chapter Twelve

She had a fourth operation in the spring of 1954, did Pat Carruth; and it was the devoted Alfred Poindexter who insisted that Arthur take six months' leave of absence, to nurse her.

The Red Funnel Line had continued to prosper, under its new Chairman. The second *English Bay*, which young Alan and Toby had galloped over so excitedly as she lay at the Liverpool Landing Stage before her maiden voyage, was a huge success; it was impossible to get a cabin for love nor money; so now she'd been joined in the Caribbean by a second Red Funnel cruise liner, the *Admiralty Bay*, which sailed out of Miami. The *Admiralty Bay* was built by John Brown's of Clydebank, and she didn't even look like a Red Funnel ship, she had a cruiser stern like a Cunarder, like the new *Medea* or *Parthia*; with a single, raked mast, and a large, peculiar-looking funnel, right aft of her streamlined bridge; and she caused quite a furore in Liverpool, the one time she visited; in fact people couldn't understand how Mr Carruth could have condoned such a departure. The truth was she looked pretty well like the American cruise liners she competed with; and if they didn't like her on Merseyside she was a popular ship where it counted, in the balmy anchorages of the West Indies.

And Red Funnel had also opened a luxury hotel in the Cayman Islands! The Hydro, it was called; it had battlements, and a tower. 'We are in the leisure travel business,' Arthur insisted, at every Board meeting, and the Line was investing heavily; at the same time, though, it had not abandoned its position as a cargo carrier; in fact the keels of two sixty-thousand ton container ships had been laid side by side at John Brown's; and two eighty-thousand ton bulk carriers were on the drawing boards: odd-looking things they'd be, too. The Red Funnel Line was surging ahead of its traditional rivals, and its stock soared; there was even some speculation in the shipping press that the Cunard White Star Line might be interesting in acquiring Red Funnel; but Cunard had put out no feelers, and the Red Funnel Board would have resisted to the last man if they had; indeed some boasted that Mr Carruth would make a counter-offer to buy Cunard.

As for Arthur's leave of absence, well of course he made the perfect nurse. He'd sit at Pat's bedside for hours, and read to her, and sometimes sing his tuneless little songs, *Mademoiselle from Armentières*, or *The noble Duke of York*. He made her laugh; that was what he did. He brought her the few things she could eat, like puréed vegetables and fruit – babyfood, really – and porridge, scrambled eggs, and such, which he cooked himself in the vast Victorian kitchen of their flat in Aigburth Vale, where for a short time Pat had turned out her flambéed escalopes and her soufflés, and where in bygone days serving maids had squealed and scurried. He carried her to her chair at the heavy sash window so that she could look out and see the flowering cherries in blossom, and smell the grass when it was cut, and on warm enough days he'd carry her outdoors and sit with her on the wrought iron bench, she propped up with pillows, watching the shipping on the river: the tankers on their way to Ellesmere Port, or outward bound for the Gulf, riding high, unladen; and the handsome Manchester Liners, floating thickets of yellow derricks, their red funnels black-topped, with two thick black bands, heading for the Ship Canal locks; and Arthur would tell Pat all their names. And he bathed her too, lowering her into the long white tub, sponging her thin shoulder blades. He carried her to the toilet. And all she could do was turn an exhausted smile at him, and sometimes touch his cheek.

One day she said, 'Do you remember the oysters we used to eat in France? The Fines Claires? Outside every restaurant in Paris there were great wooden casks of them. Do you think we can get Fines Claires in Liverpool?'

'We can certainly try,' Arthur smiled.

He couldn't find Fines Claires but he tracked down Colchester Natives, which had been good enough for the Romans; and he sat with Pat at the bedroom window, shucking oysters, and they laughed together.

It wasn't until July that she could make her way about the flat; she walked painfully with her cane, the one she'd had so long, with the duck's head, grasping the Louis Quinze buffet with a scrawny wrist, bumping into the enormous vases of cut flowers that Arthur liked everywhere, so the place looked like the Winter Garden of a Tsar's palace.

'Don't help me!' she told him. 'I have to make it on my own. I can't be an invalid for the rest of my life.'

She became a little stronger. Her eyes were hollow with the hurt of it all, but she was always cheerful. Arthur wrapped her up in blankets, like an Egyptian mummy, and took her for slow drives in the car; at first around Liverpool, not straying too far from the flat, then one day through the roaring Mersey Tunnel to Chester, where Enid and Walter had spent their wedding night many years ago, and where Arthur now bought his Pat a necklace of Columbian emeralds; then on into Wales, up over the hills to the Vale of Clwydd. Stopping the car and winding down the windows, they sat and filled their lungs with the sweet, thin air that smelled of clover and vetch; the hills green and blue; two sparrow-hawks hung motionless under slow clouds drifting towards England, like the ghosts of old ships.

'Oh, Arthur, I'm such a burden to you,' she smiled. 'Why don't you just prop me up against a stone wall and leave me here? Drive away and don't think about me, I'll be all right. The view is so beautiful.'

'The view includes you.'

'You're so gallant! You must regret, though, marrying me.'

'I regret not marrying you sooner.'

She reached out a hand, and stroked his face. 'I believe you,' she said, and for the first time ever he saw a tear in her eye; Pat did not cry, had never, as far as he knew. The tear rolled slowly down her white cheek until he stopped it with the end of his finger.

The boys wrote sometimes, but they had not been to visit. Now that Pat and Arthur had been married for nearly three years, Walter thought Enid might not object to the lads' going to stay with them, but when Alan suggested it in a letter Arthur had to write that Pat was too ill.

'We would love for you and Toby to come,' he wrote back. 'Pat is looking forward to seeing you again. She is feeling a little stronger every day. Perhaps next year.'

Pat added a postscript. 'Sorry to be such a mope. I really am looking forward to next year. I hope you like oysters. Love, Pat.'

Her recovery, all the same, was dreadfully slow, and she had a fifth operation, a minor one, in November. But what tremendous courage she had. In the spring Arthur wrote to the boys at Repton, proposing that he and Pat visit them there. Repton was neutral territory, and he felt that his sister would mind it less if this encounter took place at the boys' school. And how could Enid refuse – he contributed two hundred pounds a year to their fees, having promised to help years ago, before the rift, and he'd continued to send her cheques, which she'd acknowledged, each time, with a short thank you note. What a rare event a letter was for the boys, these days; their mother hardly ever wrote anymore; and Alan read this letter from his uncle as he wolfed down fried bread and sausages.

'Is that from your father?' he was asked.

'No, actually. This is from my uncle. It's terrific to hear from Uncle Arthur.'

'Chairman of the Red Funnel Line, is that the one?'

'That's the one.'

He sought out Toby after breakfast, and gave him the letter to read. As Toby was two years his junior, and still a fag, the brothers could hardly talk to each other at school, because such things weren't done, seniors did not talk to juniors except to order them about. But they agreed that the idea of Uncle Arthur and Aunt Pat visiting them at school was a splendid one, so Alan posted an enthusiastic reply. And then when they emerged from Chapel one grey March Sunday they headed eagerly for the small bunch of visiting relatives, who parked their cars under beech trees: boys were shaking hands with their fathers as if they'd never met them before, and giving their mothers reluctant kisses. Arthur and Pat stood slightly apart, Arthur in a dark suit and tie, Pat in a black dress, with a half-length fur coat and a hat with a small black veil. She was very pale but she laughed happily.

'We weren't sure we'd recognise you,' she said.

'We weren't sure either,' said Alan. 'It's been a terribly long time since we saw you.'

'It has been a long time,' smiled their uncle.

They shook hands all round; somehow kisses didn't seem right. Alan was now tall and gangly, Toby chunky. Toby, unlike his brother, fitted his suits, but hated them, and couldn't wait to tear off his jacket and tie as soon as they were officially off school premises.

'Shall we drive into Derby for lunch?' their Uncle Arthur suggested. 'Or do you know some other place? Where do you go when your mother and father visit?'

'Well – they don't come very much,' Alan said.

'They came last term,' said loyal Toby.

The boys climbed into the back of Uncle Arthur's beautiful black Jaguar, which other boys were inspecting enviously, boys whose parents were driving them off in Vauxhall Veloxes and Standard Triumphs. Arthur helped Pat into the front. She took off her hat with the veil and turned round to talk to the boys as Arthur drove out of the village with its spires and long stone walls, its classrooms where ivy scratched at the windows, and playing fields that stretched as far as you could see, across the green flood plain of the River Trent, where swans floated in fields.

The boys were impressed. They remembered Pat imperfectly from their trips to Childwall, when she'd visited with her garrulous mother yet somehow struck up a kind of rapport with the boys; almost a conspiracy; she understood they were bored and embarrassed. And as Arthur drove into Derby under low spring skies, they were, now, not surprisingly in awe of this woman who had split their family in two, and who'd been ill for so long, and who wore a very faint perfume which neither of them would ever forget.

'I'm sorry you haven't been able to come and see us,' she told them. 'But if you'd seen me last year, you'd have run a mile. I looked like a witch, hobbling about with a stick.'

'I bet you didn't really look like a witch,' Toby said, affronted at the thought, because he'd have punched anyone else for suggesting it.

'Oh yes, I did. I frightened cats when I went out into the garden.'

The boys laughed. Alan couldn't see his Aunt Pat as a witch, but there was something supernatural about her; maybe it was because she was a Roman Catholic, which for him meant incense and heretics burned at the stake, the Spanish Inquisition. And her voice was one of the most delightful he'd ever heard; she spoke so softly and quickly, never stressed anything. She always sounded as if she was about to laugh, or say something funny, and quite often she did.

'So, we have to deliver you back to Chapel at half past six?' she said. 'What if we don't? What if we abduct you and drive all the way to Dover and take the boat and we all live together in Paris?'

'Oh, wow!' Alan cried. 'Please abduct us!'

'Good, it's settled then,' said Pat. 'I always wanted to live in Paris, even before I ever went there. But Aigburth Vale is the closest I've got. We'll probably get tired of Paris after a few years, of course, so then we'll take the Blue Train and go down to the Riviera, descend to it as the French say, and live in Cannes. We'll make friends with millionaires and get ourselves invited aboard their yachts.'

'We'll get into awful trouble if we're late for Chapel,' Toby pointed out; ah, he had no imagination.

'You two could stay for Chapel if you want to,' said Alan. 'I mean, for Evensong. Parents and relatives sit in the north transept. Oh, but – I suppose, being Roman Catholic, you couldn't.'

'Why on earth not?' laughed Pat.

'Well, I – I don't know. Would you like to come to Chapel?'

'It sounds fun.'

'Fun?' said Toby. 'I wouldn't call Chapel fun. I'd call it purgatory. It's where they make you go for being wicked.'

'We'll come,' said Uncle Arthur. 'Though I don't suppose you're in the choir now, Alan.'

'Not since my voice broke. It's funny, I can't sing anymore.'

'I can't sing either,' Pat said. 'Nor can your Uncle Arthur, though it doesn't stop him singing to me.'

'He sings to you?'

'Sometimes. When we're on our own.'

'What does he sing?'

'Oh, he sings marching songs from the First World War: *Mademoiselle from Armentières*. That's what he calls me.'

'He calls you Mademoiselle from Armentières?'

'Sometimes. When we're on our own.'

'That's really nice.'

'I think so too.'

By the time they walked into the Midland Hotel at Derby, for lunch, the boys were in love. The four of them seemed to be the only people in the grand dining room who talked; because everyone else ate in a Victorian silence imposed by whispering waiters in black ties and dinner jackets, whereas Uncle Arthur and Aunt Pat and the boys chatted and laughed gaily, and Alan felt that everyone must be looking at them, and wondering who they were. Grey light filtered through high white curtains, and they ate vichyssoise soup and roast lamb with mint sauce, and Uncle Arthur ordered a bottle of Chateauneuf du Pape and insisted Alan have a sip, but Toby wouldn't. In the afternoon they drove to Swarkestone Bridge, where Bonny Prince Charlie had turned back in 1745. They stood watching the brown waters of the Trent swirl past, making dangerous eddies and whirlpools, the river in spate from the spring rains.

'Aunt Pat, you'll get your shoes all muddy,' Alan said, as they walked along the bank, watched by suspicious heifers.

'Oh, it doesn't matter,' she laughed.

Little things didn't matter to Pat; never had done. She was unfussy about the minor inconveniences that annoy other people. And Alan couldn't help noticing her legs, and the seams of her black stockings. Later that evening, in Chapel, as four hundred boys stood singing lustily, and knelt praying, and snoozed through the visiting archdeacon's sermon, Alan couldn't stop thinking about his aunt's stockings, and the whiteness of her face under the little veil, and the elusiveness of her perfume. He decided that his Uncle Arthur was a lucky chap: so what if the rest of the family never spoke to him again? That was a small price to pay; in fact it could even be viewed as an added bonus. He, Alan, would take Pat over the rest of the family, any day. He couldn't wait to see her again, and his Uncle Arthur of course, but he wondered if there was any chance of spending some time with her alone, so that they could talk together, and laugh, and when she laughed she'd be laughing just for him, and he could let her know how well he was doing at cricket, how he was bound to be in the school first team next year; and they could plan jolly trips to France together. Then he thought how ridiculous it was that for three years he'd been forbidden to see her, or his uncle, and how stupid the rest of the family was, and how awful his Aunt Pat must have felt, and how angry his Uncle Arthur must have been, not that he'd ever show it.

'Miller!' the boy next to him hissed. 'Stand up!'

He blushed scarlet and leapt to his feet. The visiting archdeacon had finished his sermon and was mumbling a short prayer.

The instigator of all that upset, Mrs Annie Sadie Carruth, no longer lived with the Millers in Cheshire. After an autumn, a winter, and a spring, Enid and Walter decided they couldn't face a summer; the old lady had unforgivably complicated their simple life. They found her a place in an old peoples' home nearby, in Wilmslow, where Enid could go and see her every afternoon; it was a quiet old house, much too quiet for Annie Sadie, who thrived on conflict, upset, and hurt feelings. She and her daughter played cards, and watched television; and each visit ended in bitter argument. After six weeks Mrs Carruth was asked to leave, because she made the other inhabitants so miserable they wouldn't come out of their rooms; so Enid had to find her another home, where the same thing happened. Finally, upon appeal to surviving Carruths in Liverpool, a room was found for her with a pleasant, and thankfully deaf, widow, a distant relative, in West Kirby, on the Cheshire side of the river.

These two ladies got on better than Enid had dared hope; Aunt Beth's deafness must have been a help. Her guest's room was on the ground floor, and it looked out on to a cemetery, not that this would at all disturb Annie Sadie, she'd have welcomed any kind of company. The ladies took their meals together; and went for short walks as far as the Promenade, from which there was a view of Hilbre Island, a rock in the estuary of the River Dee said to be the haunt of puffins. At low tide, miles of sand stretched, you might think, as far as Ireland; and when the water came in it lapped at the Promenade itself, and smelled of kelp.

During their school holidays Enid took the boys to visit their grandmother. Walter wouldn't come; so they went on a weekday and took the train to Liverpool Central, then the Mersey Railway, which gave Alan tantalising glimpses of the Great Float, the big dock in Birkenhead, where interesting ships berthed: he was still passionate about ships, and the sea; it's true he no longer considered the sea as a career, but he had a vague idea about shipping to Calcutta as a deck hand, because he was serious about working for Mother Teresa.

How the boys hated their West Kirby afternoons, except for the walk along the Promenade, which wasn't too bad, and the view of Hilbre Island, and the endless sands. But there were no ships to be seen from West Kirby, because the Crosby Channel followed the Lancashire coast, which was too far away; only the gallant Welsh boats used the shallow Rock Channel, heading out past the long pier at New Brighton and along the Wirral coast, their decks packed on fine days with day-trippers in rolled-up sleeves, bound for an afternoon ashore at Llandudno, where they'd eat sticks of rock and candy floss, and ride the electric tramway up the Great Orme. So the nearest you got to seeing a ship, from the Promenade at West Kirby, was the long line of smoke behind the *St Seriol* or the *St Tudno*; and there were no young people at all at West Kirby; it was as if the place had a minimum qualifying age, for residency, of about seventy.

In their grandmother's dark little back room there was only one chair, so the old lady sat in that and Enid squatted with the two boys on the bed, which was against the window. The old lady must have been grateful for these visits, and the truth is she was pleased to see them, but her sharp tongue always got the better of her.

'Well, I'm sure you had a good time with Arthur and that woman he married, when they went to see you at school,' she said; it seemed she couldn't bring herself to pronounce that woman's name.

'Yes, we did,' Alan said. 'They took us to lunch at the Midland Hotel, in Derby, and we had roast lamb. You used to make good roast lamb, Granny, when you lived with us. In the afternoon we went to Swarkestone Bridge, which is where Bonny Prince Charlie turned back in 1745.'

'What did you talk about all the time? Bonnie Prince Charlie?'

'No, of course not. I don't know what we talked about. We talked about living in Paris. We talked about everything.'

'I bet you didn't talk about your poor old gran.'

'No, Granny. Everything but you,' cheeky Toby said.

'She had an infernal nerve, making him take her to that school so she could butter up you two.'

'What do you mean?'

'I mean what I say. It was her idea. She'll have set out to charm the pants off you, the same way she charmed the pants off your Uncle Arthur. I can see through her game. She wants you on her side, against the rest of us.'

Alan was confused and embarrassed, as well as outraged.

'I'm not on anyone's side!' he said; but he knew it was a lie.

'She knows how fond of you both Arthur is. She knew he'd agree to take her.'

'What makes you think it was Aunt Pat's idea to come and see us? Why are you so sure? It wasn't she who wrote, it was Uncle Arthur who wrote.'

'Well, of course he'd write. She probably dictated the letter.'

Enid interrupted. 'Mum, I don't have any objection to Arthur and Pat taking the boys out at Repton.'

'You should have. The next thing you know, she'll talk Arthur into inviting the boys to stay with them in Aigburth Vale.'

'I don't really mind if they do.'

'Pat's too poorly,' said Toby.

'It's a good thing!'

'Granny, what a cruel thing to say!' cried Alan.

'I think it's time for us to leave,' said Enid, standing up from the bed. 'We don't want to miss the train.'

'There hasn't been any more talk of children, since they got married.'

'Well, of course not, Mum—'

'He goes to mass every Sunday! Can you imagine it? My boy Arthur going to mass! Hobnobbing with Father Mahoganybottom! It makes me sick!'

The journey by train back from West Kirby was always a gloomy one, because Enid felt guilty about her mother's living in such a small dark place, and on her own except for deaf Aunt Beth; but she was convinced it was the best solution. She didn't know that Arthur paid Aunt Beth twenty-five pounds a month, which she spent on Friday night bingo. Aunt Beth faithfully nursed Annie Sadie through her frequent and debilitating bilious attacks, and helped her to the bathroom, and fetched her the joey on request; and the rest of the time she ignored her.

Alan stole a packet of Richmond Gems from his father; he took Toby for a walk in the woods, because he felt they needed to talk. They stood on the edge of the curious cleft called the Devil's Grave and smoked cigarette after cigarette; and when it began to rain they lowered themselves into the cavern. It was evening and nearly dark except for their two glowing cigarette ends.

'Do you think it was really Aunt Pat's idea, to come to Repton?' Alan said. 'I know Granny has it in for her, but what if she's right? What if Aunt Pat is manipulating Uncle Arthur?'

'I wish she'd manipulate me,' Toby said.

'But seriously, Toby. I mean, I think Aunt Pat's terrific, but she certainly doesn't have many admirers in our family. Maybe she really is an awful woman. Maybe it's true she's only interested in Uncle Arthur's money.'

'Maybe, but I don't think so,' said Toby, as he lit another cigarette with the butt of the previous one.

'Why don't you think so?'

'Because I think she's in love with him. And Uncle Arthur dotes on her. I mean, it's pretty obvious, isn't it. But that's something Granny can't admit, and won't allow. So she puts the worst possible construction on everything. Has done from the start. I think it's because all she herself has ever cared about is money; or, should I say, not having it. Because Grandfather never did a stroke of work in his life, and Granny had to run that laundry, and there were three kids to bring up. And Uncle Arthur had to leave school early to help pay for the others to finish school. So she's obsessed with the thought of money. And that's why she criticises Dad for only being a salesman, and for not taking that office job in Liverpool, whenever it was; and that's why she attacks Mum for not having married some richer bloke she met years ago at the tennis club. And that's why she attacks us for not knowing what we want to do. It's all because of money.'

Alan puffed at his cigarette. He thought hard. It was damp and chilly in the Devil's Grave.

'Christ,' he said, eventually. 'You're right, Toby. I actually think you're right. It makes you feel sorry for the old battle-axe, doesn't it.'

Toby shrugged. 'In a way.'

'It's just that she has such an evil tongue.'

'It's just that she's always been so worried about money, and she hates it when other people don't understand.'

When the old lady turned eighty-five the boys' Uncle Arthur telephoned his sister and proposed they bury the hatchet for long enough to celebrate so significant a birthday. He would make all the arrangements, he said. Enid discussed it with Walter before telephoning back. Yes, she agreed, good idea. Perhaps a lunch, at a nice hotel. She thought it likely George and Moira would come up from London for the occasion.

'I was thinking more of a small, catered reception at our flat in Aigburth Vale,' Arthur said.

'I don't think that's a good idea, Arthur,' Enid told him. 'For myself, I don't mind. I would gladly come, and so would Walt. But I don't think George would agree; and more importantly, I can't see Mum agreeing either. Lunch at a hotel is a better idea.'

So Uncle Arthur hosted a birthday lunch for Annie Sadie Carruth at the Blossoms Hotel in Chester. The birthday girl refused to drive with Pat and Arthur, so Walter and Enid picked her up at the small house near the sea at

West Kirby, and she sat in the back of the car, between the two boys; Aunt Beth was not invited.

'This is where your dad and I came on honeymoon,' their mother told the boys, as they marched up the steps from the street, into the hotel, with its rose and gold foyer and the enormous vase of flowers.

'You spent your whole honeymoon here?'

'No, no. Just the first night. Then we went to Wales.'

'The place must have romantic memories for you,' Toby said, without smiling, because he knew his father had never seen his mother with no clothes on, and couldn't imagine how they'd spent their honeymoon.

Arthur had reserved a small private room for the function, and was already there, with Pat, and Pat's mother, Mrs McMahon, by the time the Millers arrived with the guest of honour. Arthur, his remaining, well combed hair now quite silvery, stood erect and gracious as ever, dabbing his eyes with a handkerchief; and Pat wore an ankle-length, off the shoulder, midnight-blue gown, with sequins. The boys clutched hold of each other and gawked at her; Alan thought he was going to faint. He was ashamed of the extremely shiny old blue suit he wore; he'd bought it to take an office job in Manchester during the summer holidays, and he wore it every day; he should have thought to put on something smarter, but he didn't have anything. Toby wore an old black anorak, with an open-necked shirt, but was quite happy that way. Pat's soft brown hair fell to her white shoulders, which the boys saw for the first time were covered in freckles; and as usual, she wore no make-up but the faint, unforgettable fragrance they'd fallen for on her visit to Repton.

She shook hands with Walter and Enid, with a charming smile; they in their turn perfectly correct, not quite frigid. The old lady did not take Pat's hand, but busied herself removing her heavy black coat, which a waiter, at a nod from Arthur, whisked away. Alan glanced at Toby, who gave him a half-nod; and thus prompted, Alan, the palms of his sweating hands on his aunt's thin elbows, kissed her on the cheek; and Toby did the same.

'Who does she think she is, the Queen of England?' grumbled the old lady, at Enid.

Out of the side of her mouth Enid said, 'Now, Mum, just for once, try and be nice. This is your birthday.'

George and Moira arrived, half an hour late; they'd taken the train up from London. George shook hands with his brother and sister-in-law stiffly, kissed Enid, shook hands with Walter and the boys. His suit didn't fit; never had; and he'd developed a slight twitch in one eye. Moira wore a blue suit, heavily rumpled from the long train journey, and a lot of lipstick; Alan and Toby exchanged looks and might have been overcome with the giggles if they hadn't been mesmerised by their Aunt Pat.

'Christ,' Toby had muttered. 'I have to go the bathroom.'

'What's the matter?'

'I need a woman. Any woman will do.'

'How about Aunt Moira?'

'Any woman but Aunt Moira will do.'

The party took their seats for lunch, the old lady between Arthur and Enid, with George opposite her, and Pat on Arthur's right, more or less out of sight of her reluctant mother-in-law, and across from Alan. After eating his mock turtle soup in silence, by the time Alan put down his spoon he'd worked up the courage to say, 'Aunt Pat, do you mind if I say something?'

'That depends on what it is,' smiled Pat.

'You look absolutely stunning!'

'I thought you were going to say something awful!'

'Like what?'

'Well, like, 'You look dreadful' or 'You look old'.'

'But you don't, you look – well, like I said, you look stunning. That sounds awfully corny, Aunt Pat. If it does, I'm sorry.'

'It doesn't sound corny. There's not a woman in the world who wouldn't be delighted to be told that, even if it's not true, as in my case.'

'But it is true, in your case,' blushed Alan.

'Then why don't we run away to Paris?' smiled Pat.

'That's the second time you've suggested it,' Alan said, by now red as a beetroot.

'Shall we invite Toby and your Uncle Arthur along?'

'I suppose we should.'

Uncle Arthur was tapping on his champagne glass with a small spoon, for silence. He rose to his feet.

'I'm not going to make a speech,' he said. 'Except to say thanks to all, for coming; especially to George and Moira, who've come such a long way; and to Mother, a very happy birthday.'

As Uncle Arthur sat down, young Toby stood up. He looked solid and broad-shouldered, in his awful old black anorak.

'Well, I am going to make a speech,' Toby said. He looked at his brother, who shut his eyes. 'A short one. I just wish that everyone here would grow up and stop behaving like jackasses.'

'Nice speech, Toby,' hissed Alan.

Uncle Arthur, ever the diplomat, said, 'I think we all know what you mean, Toby, and how you feel about things. I'm sorry if you're ashamed of your family. But the fact is, we are all here, in spite of our differences, and I don't think that's all bad.'

After lunch, Uncle Arthur proposed a walk along the city walls. It was a fine August day, with lots of tourists; and because the walkway along the walls was narrow, the family soon split into small groups; Arthur, holding his mother's arm, bringing up the rear. The boys of course walked with their Aunt Pat, whom no one else would talk to anyway.

'You don't really have the right shoes for walking, Aunt Pat,' Alan said, because he'd inherited his Uncle Arthur's preference for suitable attire.

'I didn't realise I was holding you up,' Pat smiled.

'No. No, not at all,' Alan protested. He felt encouraged enough to take her arm. Toby walked behind them. Alan was immensely proud to be seen walking with this beautiful, obviously rich, and sensationally dressed woman. He felt her weight on his arm.

'You are very gallant,' Pat said. 'Do they teach you gallantry at Repton?'

'Well, not really. They teach you to eat everything with a fork, if that counts. Aunt Pat, there's something I really want you to know.'

'Can I make a suggestion? Why don't you just call me Pat. Aunts are old.'

'All right. It'll be funny not calling you Aunt Pat, though, because that's how Toby and I have always talked about you.'

'Do you talk about me a lot?' she smiled.

'No. Well, yes. I suppose we do.'

'What did you want to tell me?'

'I wanted to tell you that I've always thought – that is, Toby and I have always thought – that marrying you was the best thing Uncle Arthur ever did. And we don't understand why the rest of them feel the way they do, but we feel quite differently.'

'I know you do.'

'So – please don't worry about what the rest of them think; Granny, I mean, and Mum, and Uncle George. They're all just stupid. It must be awful for you, the fact they won't talk to you, or have anything to do with you and Uncle Arthur; and I'm really sorry. But Toby and I – that's not how we feel.'

'I know you don't.'

'And we really would like to come and stay with you. That is, when you're feeling all right.'

'I'd love you to come and stay. So would your Uncle Arthur. He's very fond of you both. Perhaps at Christmas, or Easter. As long as it won't upset your Mum and Dad.'

'No, it won't. They've agreed.'

'I'm very glad. But do you know what I think you should do now? That's walk with your Aunt Moira. She's lonely, and no one seems to want to talk to her, either.'

'She's so stupid, that's the reason,' Toby said.

'All the same, I think it would be nice. Make the effort. You made the effort to talk to me.'

'That requires no effort!' blushed Alan. 'But I think you're right; it's a good suggestion.'

The boys pushed on ahead; they excused themselves as they overtook strolling sightseers; and left their Aunt Pat standing on the parapet, looking down at the excursion boats on the River Dee, swinging her bag.

'She's not only smashing, she's also a very nice, considerate person,' Alan said to Toby, 'which is more than can be said for most of our family.'

Pat's prompting them to talk with Aunt Moira was to have quite unexpected consequences.

When they caught up with Aunt Moira and their Uncle George Alan said, 'I understand you two are going back to London this evening. That's too bad. Er – it would have been nice to spend a bit more time together.'

'We have day excursion tickets,' Aunt Moira explained.

'Why don't you c-c-c-come down and stay with us in London some time?' said Uncle George.

This had never been suggested before; and the boys were caught off guard. They couldn't very well refuse the invitation, but they were anxious to remain available for a trip to Aigburth Vale.

'We'd love to,' Alan said. 'I'm not quite sure when, though. I have this job in Manchester during the summer holidays, to earn some money, and at Christmas – well, I'm not sure what's happening at Christmas. Generally you two come up to stay with us in Cheshire.'

'How about Easter?'

'Well – yes. Why not? Easter would be terrific.'

'We can go into London and see the sights,' Aunt Moira said.

The prospect had some appeal, but they would probably have found some way of not going to London if they'd been invited to Aigburth Vale. No such invitation arrived, though, all through the spring term.

Alan was now writing poetry, inspired by his Aunt Pat; not, of course, addressed to her – that would have been highly indecent – but to an unnamed, woebegone maiden who languished, in straitened circumstances, awaiting rescue. Toby thought it was drivel, but the school magazine published an excerpt from a very lengthy poem which made frequent, but not very clear, reference to female body parts; not surprisingly, the appearance of this piece made Alan the target of a lot of coarse humour and nearly cost him the friendship of his best friend, an upright boy named Day, who was disgusted that Alan could have imagined such things, let alone write about them. Alan decided it was very important his parents didn't see his poem, but Toby, the scoundrel, produced the offending publication one night when they were home for the Easter holidays and insisted on reading it aloud. Alan squirmed with embarrassment, but Walter said the poem was brilliant; his mother was more ambivalent, but told him she liked the descriptions of nature. Alan's revenge was to savagely punish Toby's fast bowling, next day, in the back garden, lofting one ball right over the roof.

'You'd make the school eleven if you could only hit the spinners,' Toby told him.

This was probably true, though Alan had played for the second eleven a few times and expected to play regularly this coming summer term. Toby was the opening bowler for the house first team.

'You'd make the school team if you could turn the ball in the air more,' Alan said.

'I can on a wet wicket.'

'Well I'm not going to pray for a wet summer.'

'I wonder if Uncle George's garden is big enough to play cricket in,' Alan said. 'God, I wish we didn't have to go. It's next week.'

'I'm not going,' Toby told him.

'Toby! You've got to! You promised! We can't let them down like that!'

'You can't, but I can. I've got a job. I start on Saturday.'

'Doing what?'

'Driving Mr Castle's delivery truck.'

'You'll miss the sights!'

'The hell with the sights.'

Alan took the train on Sunday. They were working on the track so his train was very late arriving at Euston, where his Uncle George had come to meet him.

The house was a fifteen minute walk from the tube station, and it was exactly like number 118 Taggart Avenue, in Childwall, clad in grey pebbledash, with a small front garden surrounded by a boxwood hedge. Inside, there was a strong smell of Airwick, as if to mask awful smells. Aunt Moira turned out to be quite a good cook and she'd roasted a chicken, which Alan thought would have tasted better if he'd been able to get the smell of disinfectant out of his nose, but he was hungry after his long, slow, Sunday train journey and gobbled his food.

'We heard about your poem,' Aunt Moira said.

Alan was horrified. 'Oh – er – yes,' he got out; but nearly choked on a mouthful of Paxo stuffing. 'I should have brought a copy of the magazine,' he lied, blushing terribly, 'but I didn't think to.'

'Your brother Toby promised to send us a copy, but it hasn't arrived.'

The bastard! Alan thought, wondering if he'd have a chance to sift through the mail in the morning and remove any copy of *The Reptonian* which might arrive. He didn't know how early he'd have to get up in order to do this.

It was his Aunt Moira who rode with him on the tube next day, to see the sights; Uncle George had left the house at half past seven in his tight grey suit and a bowler hat, for his job at the research laboratory, while Alan was still fast asleep in bed, but fortunately there was no copy of *The Reptonian* in the mail, just a harmless catalogue for Dutch bulbs. They started at Trafalgar Square; where Alan gazed up at the statue of Admiral Lord Nelson on his column; it had never occurred to Alan to join the navy, as a career, because Royal Navy ships rarely put in at Liverpool, or hadn't since the war, when they escorted convoys; and as they walked under Admiralty Arch and along The Mall he briefly considered this new idea. It was a fine spring morning, sticky green buds were opening on the grand chestnut trees, and by the time they reached Buckingham Palace Alan had shelved the Navy plan, because it didn't seem right for a writer, which is what he now aspired to be. Yes, he would write, and he'd write exactly what he wanted; he'd shock the bourgeoisie, people like his mother, and his Aunt Moira, who were irredeemably bourgeois – the only difference between them was that his mother probably knew what it meant – and everyone else in his family, except obviously Aunt Pat, who was not bourgeois, and maybe Uncle Arthur. The important thing was to write not to please other people, but from his own heart, and his own gut, and his own head, fearlessly; and if that meant his books were banned, or maybe even burned, so much the better, it would prove they were really good, and worried people; and if that also meant he starved, so what, starvation was no big deal, lots of people starved, ask Mother Teresa. Maybe he would still go and work for Mother Teresa.

In the course of the day, Alan decided that he'd been a bit unfair on Aunt Moira; she was a friendly soul, if bourgeois, and if plain, and she seemed concerned that Alan have a good time and not get bored; which was jolly decent of her, because he certainly hadn't done much to deserve it, except talk to her on the walls, at Chester, and even that had been Aunt Pat's idea. She bought him lunch at Lyon's Corner House at Piccadilly Circus; where they ate braised lamb chops with piles of onions and mashed potatoes; and Alan was excited to be in London, because one day, as a writer, he'd have to live here. Writers didn't live in Cheshire, he knew that much, or even in Liverpool.

'It's extremely nice of you to have me,' he told Aunt Moira. 'And to take me around like this. I'm really sorry Toby couldn't come, but it's his first job and he needs to earn some money.'

'We quite understand,' said Aunt Moira, who really didn't seem much offended. She was wearing a brown two-piece suit with large buttons down the front and Alan couldn't tell if she wore anything underneath, because there was no sign of a blouse or slip. He tried not to wish it was his Aunt Pat sitting across from him, with her thick brown eyebrows and thin white throat; and he imagined how wonderful it would be to spend a whole day with Aunt Pat, just the two of them, in London; perhaps they'd tour the National Gallery, which Aunt Moira had not proposed, or the British Museum, or some other quiet place where they could talk; and afterwards they'd sip cappuccino in a dark coffee bar, certainly not chomp lamb chops in a Lyon's Corner House.

'Aunt Moira,' he said suddenly, 'what do think of my Aunt Pat?'

'Oh, your Uncle George isn't very fond of her.' Unlike Aunt Pat's low, breathless, enchanting chatter, Aunt Moira spoke slowly and deliberately, as if she didn't quite trust herself to pronounce words rightly; maybe this was what led her to split up words of more than one syllable and pronounce each syllable as if it were a separate word.

'I know. That's obvious. But what about you?'

'I don't really know your Aunt Pat.'

Alan realised that Aunt Moira wasn't going to commit herself, but he persisted.

'The reason I ask, is that Aunt Pat seems to me – seems to Toby and me – to be a rather nice person, and we've never been able to understand why everyone else in the family hates her so much.'

'I really couldn't say,' said Aunt Moira.

In the afternoon they took the boat down the river to Tower Bridge and the Tower of London. To Alan the Thames did not seem like a real river: it was too narrow, its muddy banks smelled of sewage, it was crossed by low bridges with countless arches; only the passage of tugs with squat funnels and low masts, hauling long barges laden with coal, gave it any respectability. Real rivers were too wide to see properly across; they had ferries and freighters from Montevideo and Montreal lying at anchor, waiting for the tide. Also this glass-roofed boat that he sat in with his Aunt Moira was not a real ship; it was more suited to an amusement park than a navigable waterway; and he didn't like the running commentary provided by a cheerful Cockney in white shirtsleeves and a greasy captain's hat, as if he was an actual officer in the merchant marine, describing the features on either bank: splendid, grimy Somerset House; the bombed-out towers of Cannon Street Station; the great dome of St Paul's Cathedral. Alan especially didn't like the fellow's whining plea at the end: 'This commentary is entirely voluntary, ladies and gentlemen, so we hope you will be able to show your appreciation as you leave the boat.' He told his Aunt Moira she shouldn't give him anything, but she dropped sixpence into the greasy white hat.

He was not much impressed by the Tower of London, except for its lurid history; but he loved Tower Bridge, and insisted on walking across it and standing with his feet on either side of each draw. And beyond the bridge were real ships, genuine vessels unloading bacon and butter from Denmark; real cranes, real warehouses; and further down the river there were real docks. Alan sniffed the oily, watery smell of tidal mud, and felt homesick for Liverpool.

He was surprised when his aunt and uncle took him to a local pub that night, after dinner. Alan was below drinking age, though sometimes, at home in Cheshire, he'd been to The Red Lion with Toby, who looked older than he was, and the two of them had rolled home drunk on a couple of pints of cider and made fried egg sandwiches in the kitchen.

He asked for a lager; Uncle George nursed a pint of Courage and Aunt Moira sipped a gin and lime. It was she who told Alan that his uncle was writing a book.

'You're writing a book? Uncle George, that's terrific!' Alan enthused. Uncle George didn't seem to him at all like a man who'd write books.

'I'm having a lot of d-d-d-difficulty with it,' Uncle George said. 'In f-f-f-fact I w-w-w-wondered if you'd c-c-c-care to read it. You might have some s-s-s-suggestions. I know you're a writer.'

'Uncle George, I'd love to read it!' cried Alan, enormously flattered to be called a writer. 'What's it about? Do you have a title yet?'

'It's about myself. I thought I'd c-c-c-call it *Incommunicado*.'

'Your uncle thought that as you wrote poems and things you might be able to help him,' Aunt Moira said.

'Do you plan to publish it, Uncle George?'

'I'd l-l-l-like to. I thought it might h-h-h-help others who have my p-p-p-problem.'

'More importantly,' said Aunt Moira, putting down her gin and lime with a fond look at her husband, 'I think that writing it has helped George.'

'Yes. Yes, I can understand that,' Alan said. He was very touched as well as flattered they'd ask him to read the book, which his Uncle George had laboriously typed on foolscap paper; he'd bought himself an old Royal typewriter and taught himself to use it. His typing had improved as the book progressed; and when they got home from the pub Alan read the whole manuscript, which was over a hundred pages long and had taken his uncle a year to type.

Like his brother Toby, Alan had always treated Uncle George's stammer as a bit of a joke. They had never been particularly close to Uncle George, in view of his rare trips; compared to Uncle Arthur, George didn't stand a chance with the boys; they'd been told he was brilliant, but knew he had only a humdrum job; nor had they much taken to Aunt Moira, who said so little, and pronounced words so queerly; and of course they didn't understand Uncle George's extreme aversion to their Aunt Pat, which did not endear him.

But the man who'd written *Incommunicado* turned out to be a witty, gifted, unquestionably brilliant and tragic figure; a chap who might indeed have become Professor of Chemistry at the University of Cambridge; might indeed have split the atom; might also have played tennis at Wimbledon. But for one ridiculous disqualification, the stammer he hadn't even been born with. It was clear to Alan too, reading the manuscript, that this stupid stammer was much more of a disqualification in George's own mind than for anyone else. But for him it was indeed, in the fairy tale sense, a curse.

Alan spent his week in London retyping his uncle's sad manuscript; editing it with all the enthusiasm of a precocious sixteen year old. He never saw the Changing of the Guard, or Westminster Abbey, or Hampton Court Palace; the hell with the sights, as Toby had said.

Incommunicado was published a year later; and it was quite a hit, it was almost immediately reprinted. Some talk of turning it into a film came to nothing; but Uncle George found himself written about, and interviewed on television, and he became, for a few months, a minor celebrity. He was also, because of his negative comments on business, fired from his job designing tampons.

Chapter Thirteen

Annie Sadie Carruth choked on her own bile one night when her cries for the joey went unanswered. She was eighty-seven. She would be buried at St Stephen's, in Crosby.

'That's blasphemy!' Alan told Toby, when he read the letter from his mother. 'They should bury her in unhallowed ground!'

Alan was wearing his school first team cricket blazer, dark blue with broad yellow piping: because he'd finally mastered the most devious of slow bowling, and he'd wear the spinners down with patient defence until he saw a loose ball that he could hit over the pavilion. He was in his last term. The boys decided they should probably show up at the funeral – as long as Alan could be back at Repton in time for the key match against Uppingham.

'There's a chance we'll see Aunt Pat,' Alan said.

'Why would Aunt Pat go to Grandmother's funeral? The old battle-axe hated her.'

'Uncle Arthur will want her with him. Appearances are important,' Alan assured him.

Toby smoked his way through a whole packet of Senior Service cigarettes on the train from Derby to Manchester; a spectacular trip in those days, through deep tunnels blasted through the High Peak, and over viaducts spanning the leafy dales where trout twinkled in rivers that sometimes disappeared underground. Alan had given up smoking, because he believed that any day he might meet some beautiful, miserable maiden he could fall in love with and rescue, but who mightn't want to be rescued by someone who reeked of smoke. He also didn't think his Aunt Pat would approve of him smoking. Uncle Arthur had never smoked.

Uncle Arthur had made the funeral arrangements, of course; and the short service was well attended; surviving Carruths turned up, as they always did, from all over Liverpool. The boys dutifully flanked their mother and father in the second pew, bawling out the hymn *Abide With Me* with gusto, but at the grave they stood at the back of the small crowd, along with Pat Carruth; who wore a long black coat, tucked in at the waist, with a black hat and veil; a little fox hung over her thin shoulders. Even the boys could see how pale she was. They stuck as close to her as they decently could, breathing in the remembered perfume, and the faint smell of talcum powder on her little fox; and hoped they'd have a chance to talk with her once their grandmother had been committed to the earth.

Their Uncle George wore a dark suit which looked expensive but still didn't fit, with a maroon waistcoat underneath, which made him look like the university professor he'd never been; and Aunt Moira was in a black two-piece suit, which also didn't fit, with a black taffeta rose. She also sported a pearl necklace and earrings; and she'd certainly never worn jewellery before. This was the first time the rest of the family had seen the pair since George became a celebrity and could afford to splash out on earrings for Moira; of course they'd all seen him on television. *Incommunicado* was now in its third reprint and had been translated into French, German and Spanish, and with the royalties, George had finally paid back the two hundred and fifty pound loan his brother Arthur had advanced him for his second degree. However, he was out of work, and at his age didn't seem to have much prospect of landing another job.

George had not lost his distaste for Pat; he could hardly bring himself to be civil to her. The boys had seen this when he shook hands, the way he avoided her look and talked to someone else; and it was the first time they really questioned their Uncle Arthur's judgement in insisting that his wife, for the sake of appearances, go through with this. Pat, though, if she was made to feel uncomfortable, was not one to betray it; and who knows, maybe she really was thick-skinned enough not to feel uncomfortable at all. And if it pained Arthur to see how the rest of the family continued to treat her, it must have pleased him enormously to see how well she got on with her nephews; and it comforted him, too, to think of the boys as Pat's young relatives, because in marrying her, he feared, he'd made her the loneliest person in the world.

He pressed the boys' hands, as the party stood about under the brooding green trees. He spoke very softly now, as it hurt him, but still as if he treasured every husky word. He thanked them for coming all the way from school, and walked with them, holding Pat's arm, as far as the lychgate.

'I'm not sure if you ever met Uncle Fred,' he said suddenly, introducing them to a wizened little man with bushy grey eyebrows and twinkling eyes, wearing a brown raincoat and a flat cap, and who seemed to be on his own.

Alan was thrilled. So this was the master-modeller!

'Uncle Arthur often spoke to us about you, Uncle Fred,' Alan said. 'We always dreamed of coming to see your ships. Do you still make them?'

'Ah, no,' said the old man. 'Not since Minnie died. That would be your Aunt Minnie. I made them for her. Then last year they got me a place at the seniors' home. There was no room for my boats.'

'What happened to them?' Alan gasped.

'I have them,' said Uncle Arthur.

'At Aigburth Vale?'

'They're all over the place,' Pat smiled. 'They are wonderful.'

'Then we'll see them when – when we come to visit!' said Alan.

'You certainly will.'

'They let me keep one,' said Uncle Fred.

'Which did you keep?'

'It's the *Royal Daffodil*. I took the big *Royal Daffodil* to work every day for forty-four years. Crossed the Mersey in every weather.'

'Did you ever think of going to sea, Uncle Fred?'

The old man seemed to think for a moment, then he said, 'Oh, the sea is no life for a married man,' and turned away, and Alan suddenly felt like crying, because Uncle Fred must have loved Minnie so much.

No one seemed to know what to do next, so Arthur suggested lunch; and everyone talked about whether they should come or not, until a gang of the more distantly related Carruths said they would, foreseeing that generous Uncle Arthur would almost certainly foot the bill; and in the end everybody came. And the presence of great uncles, great aunts, second and third cousins, half brothers and sisters they didn't really know, made it possible for the boys to monopolise their Aunt Pat, and even sit next to her at table without anyone noticing; and lunch, as it happened, turned out to be a noisy affair. Somebody ordered beer; and other male Carruths did likewise; which had a predictable effect, so before long the room was filled with loud voices and peals of laughter. Walter and Enid did not join in this general merriment, they just sat there looking glum and preoccupied, in Enid's case guilty of course: the old lady might still be alive if she'd been living with them, and they'd heard her cry out, again and again, whereas deaf Aunt Beth, who was at the funeral of course, took no notice. In fairness to Aunt Beth, she seemed to have taken her feisty relative's death very badly, and she was the only one at the funeral to cry. George and Moira, in fact, seemed out to have a good time, and George had taken off his jacket, and rolled up his shirt sleeves; and when the waiters were trying to serve a Baked Alaska dessert George climbed on to his chair to make a speech.

'I don't want to steal Arthur's thunder,' he said, holding on to a glass of beer and swaying. 'I'm sure he has a fine speech p-p-prepared for the occasion. All I wanted to s-s-say is that I p-p-personally am glad that everyone's here today. My m-m-mother was a d-d-difficult woman to get along with, as we all know; but I think she'd be glad to know we're all here; and that we seem to be enjoying ourselves. As for me, I know I've been a d-d-dull d-d-dog and n-n-not an awful lot of fun either. But things have changed for me of late, as I think you all know; thanks in large p-p-part to my nephew Alan here, whom I would like to thank.'

This did not seem quite the right speech for the occasion, but George sat down to generous applause; poor Alan had no idea how to react; he blushed and half stood up, then sat down again.

'That was nice of your Uncle George,' Pat told him. 'Did you notice he hardly stammered at all?'

'That's because he's drunk,' Toby said.

Arthur now stood up, as anticipated. He took off his glasses and dabbed his eyes with a handkerchief, and for some reason everyone shut up.

'I have not prepared the fine speech my brother George has promised you,' Arthur began. 'He's wrong there. But he's right, of course, in describing Mother as not an easy person to get along with. That being so, the first thing I want to do is thank my sister, Enid, and her husband, Walter, for having had Mother live with them, in their home, for most of the war, and again, more recently. We can all understand what a strain on Enid and Walt that must have been. Not only that, but Enid continued to spend time with Mother, right up to the end. It is only unfortunate that my wife, Pat, and I were unable to help shoulder the burden.

'Thank you, dear Enid. Thank you, Walter. And thank you, boys, Alan, Toby, for your patience; for all the time you, too, spent with your grandmother when you could have been playing cricket. Apropos of which, in case there's anyone here who doesn't know it, Alan now plays cricket for Repton School. He scored eighty-four runs in the match against Malvern a fortnight ago. Clearly, his talents are not only literary.'

Alan received his second round of applause, but this time he didn't try to stand up.

'Congratulations,' Pat whispered.

'What I think we should all remember about Mother,' Arthur went on, after a brief pause, 'is Father.'

There was some tittering from cousins and uncles who thought this was a joke.

'Father, to be charitable, was not without good qualities. He believed in what he believed, and would have been seen by many to have high principles. He was also the laziest man I have ever known. He was an artist. I am not an authority on art, so I cannot really judge. Enid has a few of his paintings. To me, they are most remarkable for their detail. He would paint every stone on a beach, every leaf on a tree. I don't know what this says of him, either as an artist, or as a man. That he had an obsessive interest in detail, one would think; but at the same time he had no interest at all in the detail of earning money, or the detail of raising the family. All this, as you know, Mother had to do. She had to do it from an early age, too; she was only seventeen when she married Father. Father held down a job for longer than a week. Never earned decent money. Mother took in laundry. Mother washed and ironed other people's sheets, tablecloths, shirts, underclothes. Mother made sure there was food on the table. Mother took us to school. Mother – Mother put clothes on our backs. She mended our shirts, she knitted us socks, she sewed skirts for Enid, she darned and stitched. She made sure we brushed our teeth. She kissed us goodnight.'

Arthur paused. Some of his listeners stared into space, and others studied the dessert they didn't feel it right they should eat yet, though honest Toby had quietly eaten his as his uncle spoke. Enid's lovely dark eyes glistened.

George cleared his throat. 'That was nice, Arthur,' he said.

But Arthur wasn't quite finished. 'She was also a vicious and vindictive old battle-axe,' he added, and beamed around at the company, taking off his glasses. Then he sat down.

He had spoken of the mother only he and his younger brother and sister remembered; and his final words more or less summed up everyone else's opinion of Annie Sadie Carruth, so after a moment's shocked hush, there was a roar of laughter, then applause; and distant cousins even banged on the table with their spoons, before attacking their desserts with pent-up gusto.

'Will you both come and stay with us in Aigburth Vale?' Pat suddenly asked her nephews.

'Absolutely!' spluttered Alan, putting down his spoon. 'We'd love to come and stay with you! When would be a good time? Term ends on 29th July, and I have my summer job in Manchester before I do National Service – but I'll take time off. What about you, Toby?'

'I'll come any time,' Toby shrugged.

'Then perhaps September – will that be all right?'

'It should be terrific.'

'Do you like oysters?'

'I've never eaten oysters,' Alan said.

'A treat in store,' said Aunt Pat. 'We'll eat oysters in the garden, and watch ships on the Mersey.'

'Can we visit the Walker Art Gallery? I mean, perhaps while Uncle Arthur is at work.'

'Well, certainly. I didn't know you were interested in art.'

'Not terribly, but – I thought it would be fun to go there with you.'

'Then go we will. And I'm sure your Uncle Arthur will take us for rides in the car; perhaps at the weekend we can drive into Wales; and take the road to Bettws-y-Coed, where there's a wonderful waterfall we once saw salmon jumping up, and a nice hotel; and you three can scramble up a mountain.'

'No, no, we'll stay at the bottom with you,' Alan insisted.

'That's silly!' Pat laughed. 'You must have fun!'

'It's fun just being with you!'

'That's very sweet of you, Alan, but I'll feel bad if you don't climb the mountain. When you come down, you can tell me about it. You forget, I've never been to the top of a mountain; well, only a very little one, in France, with your uncle; and when I got to the top of that one, I thought I was going to die.'

In the car on the way home, Enid said, 'Pat looked dreadful, didn't she. Worse than ever. Poor thing. She's had one foot in the grave for years.'

Alan was shocked. 'She's invited us to go and stay with her and Uncle Arthur in September,' he said.

'What about your job?'

'The hell with my job. I'll take a week off. I'll quit, if I have to.'

'You're supposed to be putting money by for Cambridge,' Enid said, with that disapproving toss of her head.

'The hell with Cambridge.'

'You don't mean that.'

'No, Mum, I don't mean that,' said Alan, after a moment. 'But Uncle George sent me some money, for helping with his book. And you know we've been wanting to go and stay with Uncle Arthur and Aunt Pat for ages. You don't still object, do you?'

'No,' said his mother, with a slight sniff.

'I can tell you do. But you admitted yourself you all made a bad mistake talking to Uncle Arthur like you did.'

They were held up at the Manchester Ship Canal bridge while the Manchester Liners vessel *Manchester Progress* moved through the Latchford locks; but the boys didn't even get out of the car. They weren't interested any more.

'Well, it was George who really went too far,' Walter said, peeling the cellophane wrapping off another packet of Richmond Gems. 'He just about accused Uncle Arthur of poisoning his first wife for the sake of the insurance; and he said he hoped Arthur'd be able to afford the premiums on Pat.'

Alan caught his breath. There was an astonished silence in the car. Up ahead, the masts and ochre-painted derricks of the *Manchester Progress* passed slowly by.

'You're joking,' said Alan, eventually.

'Well, I don't think Uncle George really meant it,' Enid said. 'Your father shouldn't have told you that.'

Walter said nothing. Alan reached forward and took a cigarette off his father. Toby took one too. Their mother wound down the window.

'Maybe it's true,' said Toby.

'Oh Toby, don't be ridiculous,' snorted Alan.

'Do you think it's true?' Toby asked his mother.

'No, of course not. George got carried away, that's all. He did apologise.'

'It's an interesting theory,' Toby persisted. 'I wonder if Aunt Pat knows what Uncle George said.'

'I expect so,' said his mother. 'Arthur tells her everything.'

'If it was true, though, he wouldn't tell her,' argued Toby. 'And if Uncle George is right, the reason she's so sick is because he's poisoning her.'

'That's nonsense!' cried Enid. 'She's always been sick! She's been sick since she was a child.'

'But she might have got better, if Uncle Arthur wasn't poisoning her.'

'I want to get out of the car,' said Alan. 'This family is crazy. I'll walk.'

But the long line of cars was starting to move. Alan flung his half-smoked cigarette viciously out of the window.

'Maybe we should rescue Aunt Pat,' said Toby.

'Toby,' said his mother, 'what Uncle George said was nonsense. He admitted it. The trouble is that George adored Grace. He was in love with her. You should have heard the speech he gave at Grace's funeral. It was obvious he'd always been in love with Grace. When she died, I think he was more upset than Uncle Arthur was. I think in a way he half-blamed Arthur for her death; I don't mean that he really thought he'd poisoned her. He was just terribly, terribly upset. Then when Uncle Arthur said he was going to marry Pat McMahon George thought that was an insult to Grace's memory. That's why he hates her.'

'Uncle George is crazy,' Alan muttered.

'When we visit in September,' Toby said, 'I'll taste all Pat's food before she does, just in case.'

'What on earth will she think?' Enid laughed.

'I won't do it in an obvious way. Nobody will notice.'

Alan scored one hundred and eighteen runs in the Uppingham match before he was caught on the boundary. His innings included two sixes and twelve fours; he'd hit fast and slow bowlers with equal relish. It was only the second century ever scored by Repton against Uppingham, who were ancient adversaries. He sweated over his School Certificate A levels, but reckoned he'd probably done well enough to get his place at Cambridge, though before that he'd have to spend two years in the army, which he was quite looking forward to: the first few weeks, by all accounts, were tough, but then you passed your Wosby – War Office Selection Board – and trained as an officer at Eaton Hall, which as luck would have it was near Chester. He'd probably be able to sneak up to Liverpool on leave, and see Pat and Arthur at Aigburth Vale without either of his parents knowing, though he might tell his father later. In due course Alan would be commissioned as a Second Lieutenant, probably in the Sherwood Foresters, like most Reptonians; the Sherwood Foresters seemed a gentlemanly sort of regiment, unlike the Manchesters, a rough bunch, or the King's Regiment Liverpool, rougher still. He would probably be able to play cricket for the Sherwood Foresters, perhaps in Germany, where a battalion of the regiment was stationed.

Both the boys had interesting summers: they fell in love; which took their minds off other family foolishness; Alan with a fifteen year old filing clerk at the office he worked in, in Manchester; Toby with a thirty-seven year old divorcée, met when he delivered her groceries. They both felt they were somehow betraying their Aunt Pat, and prayed she wouldn't find out, because they were enormously looking forward to their trip to Aigburth Vale in the autumn, a trip when anything might happen.

Alan, it's true, was shocked when he discovered how very young Lyn was, because she was tall and wore her dark hair in a very grown-up, rather old-fashioned way, the curls in pretty coils about her neck; but for him it had been love at first sight. She was not the distraught maiden he'd been dreaming of, in fact she was a happy soul, who often seemed to be smiling at some recollection, maybe some family jollity, or television show she'd seen; but her skin was very white and she had delicate features, with slightly downcast eyes. And unlike her friends at the office, who prattled incessantly about their boyfriends, and who were soon able to flash their engagement rings – you were an old maid if you weren't engaged at seventeen and married at eighteen, and at nineteen you brought your first baby into the office to show off to all your former pals – Lyn's life seemed to revolve around the Girl Guides. Alan found out she was a Grey Owl; he had no idea what that entailed, but it gave him something to talk to her about, and he desperately needed topics of conversation; it wasn't enough just to ask her for a file and hang around while she searched for it, though when she bent down he sometimes had a glimpse of her bare skin between the top of her skirt and her cardigan, and thought he was about to pass out.

Mr Castle, who ran the grocer's shop across from the railway station, had again offered Toby a summer job driving his nice white station wagon, delivering his customers' orders and, if possible, collecting money from them. Mr Castle was taking a risk, because Toby had no driving licence. Toby was also hopeless at simple mental arithmetic, and because he could never figure out the right change he'd just hand anyone who asked for it a fistful of coins and drive off.

Toby looked older than his age. The second time he delivered groceries to Mrs Empson, an attractive redhead, she invited him into the house. It was mid-afternoon; she was wearing a loose gown and within minutes she and Toby were locked in a passionate embrace on her living room sofa. Toby had never handled female flesh before. He made up quickly for lost time. Two hours later he came reeling out of Mrs Empson's house, climbed into Mr Castle's white station wagon, and drove it into a tree.

Claire Empson was a demanding lover; she exhausted Toby every afternoon for weeks. In order to complete his deliveries he drove at breakneck speed around the neighbourhood; it was a wonder he didn't have more crashes. His elder brother made absolutely no progress with his beautiful filing clerk, who was too young to understand his stuttering attempts to ask her out with him, though he did find out more about Girl Guide activities than most young men of eighteen cared to. His frustration led to a rash of new poetry, full of lurid and unlikely sexual adventure, which considering the tender age of the beloved was in rotten taste. Fortunately there was no school magazine to print it in anymore, but Toby found his brother's manuscripts and sent them to the local newspaper in Alan's name. The editor had the good sense to throw them into the wastepaper basket.

A week before the boys were due to go to Aigburth Vale their Uncle Arthur telephoned. Aunt Pat, he said, was too ill.

'We understand, of course,' Alan told him. 'We're terribly sorry. We were really looking forward to coming to stay.'

'I know, old chap. I'm sorry.'

'Perhaps at Christmas.'

'Yes. Perhaps at Christmas.'

'I'll be in the army but I'll probably get some leave. I'll be at Eaton Hall. It's not very far from Liverpool.'

'I know your Aunt Pat would like that. She is very fond of you boys.'

'Can we talk to her on the phone?'

'She's sleeping just now, Alan. I don't think we should wake her.'

'Well, no, absolutely not. Then tell Aunt Pat we're really sorry not to be coming, and we hope she feels better soon.'

'I will be sure to tell her.'

'And that we love her.'

'I know. I'll tell her.'

'I know Toby would like to talk to you, but ah – he's out just now. Could he telephone later?'

'Of course. It would be good to talk to Toby.'

Toby came home very late, and drunk. He'd finally broken up with Claire Empson, at his father's suggestion. When Alan told him they wouldn't be going to stay with Uncle Arthur and Aunt Pat, he was mad.

'I have to telephone,' he insisted.

'You can't telephone now, it's after midnight,' Alan said.

But Toby grabbed the phone.

'What's all this, Uncle Arthur?' he shouted. 'We're not coming?'

'Not just now, Toby.'

'Isn't there anything we could do? Couldn't we help in some way, if we were there? I mean, Aunt Pat doesn't have to – look after us in any way, we can look after ourselves, we – we'd like to help look after her. We could put her to bed and bring her things. I'm sorry, I'm not sure if I'm making any sense because I've had a few drinks and I'm feeling rather emotional tonight.'

'She's very weak, Toby. I don't think it would be a good idea for you to come.'

'Is she asleep now?'

'Yes. She is asleep.'

When Toby put the telephone down the boys stared at each other.

'Do you think he's really poisoning her?' Toby said; he was on the verge of tears.

'No. No,' said Alan, who was much calmer. 'She is just – very ill. Very ill.'

Their mother seemed quite pleased the boys wouldn't be going to Liverpool, which didn't surprise the boys.

'I didn't think that trip would come off, somehow,' she said.

'It would have done,' Alan said. 'But Pat is ill.'
'She's an invalid. Always has been.'

Their father was more sympathetic. He stood in his darkroom, developing photographs in the dim red light of a coated light bulb, lifting the prints with tweezers, the boys either side of him; all three of them smoking, because Alan had given up trying to impress Lyn and his call-up papers had arrived. Walter had started doing wedding photographs, to make extra money; and he was in some demand, too; so he spent many of his Saturdays at Cheshire churches and country hotel receptions.

'I really wish I'd been at Uncle Arthur and Aunt Pat's wedding,' Alan said, as another happy couple emerged from the developer. 'I don't suppose anyone from the family was there. Not even Granny.'

'I'm afraid that's true. But I think a lot of Liverpool bigwigs were there.'

'Are all families as crazy as ours?'

'Probably.'

On their last drive together Arthur took Pat to Southport; she was very weak. They cruised the length of Lord Street in the black Jaguar, then parked the car on the Promenade, windows open.

'I'd love to – take a walk – on the pier!' Pat said. Arthur looked at her; he didn't think he'd ever seen such a flush in her cheeks; was it fever, or the late afternoon light?

'We could take the little tram,' he suggested.

'No – I want to walk!'

It was the first time he'd walked along that interminable pier since Grace was alive. Pat held on to his arm; they walked very slowly. She wore a heavy veil, and pulled her little fox tight around her thin neck.

'Perhaps we can make it to the end,' Arthur said. 'They have machines. They have the Spanish Inquisition.'

'I'm sure we can make it halfway,' she tried to smile.

She walked with such obvious pain; but she was determined. He assured her they were halfway there long before they actually were. They stopped; below them stretched endless sand. No: they had much further to go before they reached the sea.

When she'd got her breath back she sang, in a very low voice:

> 'Oh, the noble Duke of York,
> He had ten thousand men,
> He marched them up to the top of the hill,
> And he marched them down again.'

Arthur joined in, though only Pat sang in tune:

> 'When they were up they were up,
> And when they were down they were down,
> And when they were only halfway up,
> They were neither up nor down.'

'Just like the hill, at Cannes, and the castle,' she smiled. 'And the Rue St Antoine.'

'You made it to the top,' Arthur reminded her. 'I didn't think you would.'

'How far is it to the sea?'

Her voice was very low, very quiet; as if she was talking in her sleep.

'We're halfway there,' smiled Arthur.

'We can make it,' Pat said. 'We can make it, as far as the sea.'

'It's a long way to the sea.'

'I always thought, it would be fun to go to sea. To have nothing else around, but waves, and blueness. To toss up and down in a boat.'

'I would like to have gone to sea, too,' Arthur said. 'My nephews could never understand why I didn't. Alan. And dear old Toby. But, I couldn't afford to. I was the breadwinner when I was fourteen.'

'I know.'

'I did the next best thing. I worked for a shipping company.'

'Not the same.' The ghost of a smile.

'Not quite the same.'

'Not so much fun.'

'No. Not quite so much fun.'

'This is the nearest I'll get,' Pat smiled. 'Southport Pier.'

Walking oh so slowly, she hanging on his arm, they actually did make it to the very end of the pier. And they looked down at the brown waves breaking on the sand. Children played among the steel pilings of the pier, with little buckets and spades, making sand-pies; an older boy had built an elaborate castle, with towers and turrets, and a moat for the tide to fill, as it came in; their shouts echoed, and seemed much closer than the shouters. On the horizon, two faint smudges of smoke drifted across the low sun.

'*The Empress of Canada*, I think,' Arthur said. 'Outward bound, for Montreal. Handsome ship.'

'Oh, my poor Arthur. You should have gone to sea.'

'Should have? I don't know about 'should'. Might have. Yes, I might have gone to sea... I might have... and George might have been Professor of Chemistry at Cambridge, but Mother wanted him to get a job... and Enid might have been a dancer... but they wouldn't let her.'

After a long time Pat said, 'Let's hope the young ones – let's hope the boys get to do what we never did.'

'Let's hope so!' Arthur sighed. 'Ah, let's hope so!'

They sat together on a bench, as the *Empress of Canada's* smoke became imperceptible; the day was unusually warm for so late in October; but they had the pier to themselves. When she spoke, Arthur had to lean forward to hear her.

'You never brought me here,' Pat said, after a while. 'I know Grace liked Southport, very much. Thank you for coming. Thank you for taking me to sea.'

'It is my pleasure, mademoiselle.'

It was, perhaps, the wind that raised her veil for a second or two; he saw that she was smiling.

'Mademoiselle from Armentières,' she whispered.

He nodded. 'Armentières is a long way from the sea,' he told her.

The smile had not left her face, and the sun touched it. He carefully took off her veil; she shut her eyes.

'So is Southport,' she smiled.

The electric tramway that ran along the pier had long since made its last run of the day.

Pat drew a deep breath; felt the warmth of the late afternoon sun on her face still.

'Once, in Wales, I asked you to leave me,' she said. 'Leave me now. It's so nice here. I can't make it back.'

He reached for her knee, so thin under her black coat.

'Mortal sin,' he said.

Beneath them, the tide had washed away the boy's brave castle, and lapped against the pier.

'No. Not mortal sin. Physical impossibility.'

'Well, we don't have to go back... we are at sea.'

He made her very comfortable, nestling against him. As the sun went down it grew cold, and he stayed there with her; and when it was dark, there were stars, stars enough to navigate, navigate and discover all the world's marvellous places.

'We are at sea, Mrs Carruth,' he whispered.

'Yes. We are at sea. We are all at sea. You and I. Your brother, George. Your sister, Enid. Poor Walter. The boys... Our whole family. We are all together at last. I think we finally made it.'

Very late at night, Arthur telephoned Enid.

'I am terribly sorry,' she said. 'Arthur... I am terribly sorry. Do you want – I would like to come to the funeral. Would you let me come?'

He stood in the dark hallway of the fine house in Aigburth Vale, where for so many months he'd carried his beloved Pat from room to room, propped her up on cushions, covered her with warm blankets, read stories to her, and sung his tuneless little songs.

'Thank you, Enid. But I don't think so. I don't want anyone to be there. Only Pat. And I.'

'Are you sure?'

'I am sure. But thank you.'

The boys went, though. Didn't tell anyone. They just turned up, at the chapel. Alan was in uniform. Toby wore his awful old black anorak, with the hood pulled up. They walked in, stood on either side of their Uncle Arthur. In spite of his terrible grief, it's difficult to think he wasn't glad. At the end, they each reached out a hand, and took his; and the three of them stood there, holding hands, for a long time.

Afterword

by Alan Miller

This story of not going to sea having acquired some of the attributes of a 'family saga', I have been persuaded to add the few words of conclusion that readers of family sagas might expect.

My Uncle Arthur, who began life as a jaunty optimist, possessed of rare judgement, astonishing patience and, as far as I could see, bottomless compassion, ended it as Arthur Carruth, CBE, Chairman of the Red Funnel Line for twenty years, Chairman, for a while, of the Mersey Docks and Harbour Board and, for three years, on his retirement from business, Liberal Member of Parliament for Crosby. He refused the knighthood which was offered to him 'for services to British shipping'.

He did not marry again.

Uncle George, at Arthur's prodding, sued the company which had fired him for wrongful dismissal, and won. He was awarded sufficient damages to afford a small annuity. He and Moira sold their house in London, and moved to Torquay, where they lived in modest comfort for the rest of their lives. Although there had been some hopeful signs, following the publication of *Incommunicado* and the temporary limelight this brought him, of an improvement in his speaking, his stammer got worse as he grew older.

He and Arthur were never reconciled, though they exchanged occasional letters.

My father, who'd been scared of the sea, scared too of an executive job at the office, died of lung cancer at the age of seventy, at home: after all, he'd smoked three packets of Richmond Gems each day for forty-five years. My mother survived him; she moved in with Uncle Arthur; they spent their last years in a little house in North Wales, not far from where she, and we boys, in our case with no understanding at all of what it meant, once watched an effigy of General Tojo burned on the beach.

As for me, I failed only partly: instead of becoming a famous writer, I ended up in advertising; Toby – incredibly, given his hopelessness at counting – a chartered accountant. His job bored him, but he survived it. The two of us visited Mother and Uncle Arthur in their Welsh home. A lovely climbing rose clung to the stone walls, and there were distant views of the sea.